Praise for
The Widow Rules

A DUKE IN TIME

"Janna MacGregor dazzles her readers with sexy stories that are also endearingly tender. Her characters tug at your heartstrings and make you sad to turn the last page."
—*New York Times* bestseller Eloisa James

"Mesmerizing! Janna MacGregor pens enchanting characters and passionate romance that offers the perfect escape."
—*New York Times* bestseller Lorraine Heath

"Janna MacGregor's stories positively sparkle. Filled with heart, humor, and passion, she is an absolute must read!"
—*USA Today* bestselling author Christi Caldwell

"If . . . looking for something new with Austen's spirit, humor, and dashing heroes, they can't do better than MacGregor." —*Entertainment Weekly*

"[A] saucy Regency-era romp . . . [that] will melt readers' hearts." —*Publishers Weekly* (starred review)

"Superbly conceived and smartly executed . . . with a brilliantly rendered cast of characters, including a resourceful, resilient heroine and a heart-of-gold hero, as well as a captivating story line that splendidly celebrates female friendship." —*Booklist*

The Cavensham Heiresses
WILD, WILD RAKE

"Passionate, tumultuous." —*Publishers Weekly*

"Incandescent." *—Booklist*

"Will delight those looking to warm their hearts with a tender read." *—Library Journal*

ROGUE MOST WANTED

"A decadently delightful love story that refuses to conform." *—Publishers Weekly*

"An unforgettable love story." *—Booklist* (starred review)

"Deliciously romantic and poetic." *—Fresh Fiction*

THE GOOD, THE BAD, AND THE DUKE

"Sparkling . . . a richly engaging romance with a heroine we should all resolve to be more like." *—Entertainment Weekly*

"Utterly delightful in every possible way." *—Book Riot*

"Effervesces with lighthearted romance . . . sweet and sultry in equal measures." *—Publishers Weekly*

"[An] emotionally rich, exquisitely wrought tale that superbly celebrates the redemptive power of love." *—Booklist*

THE LUCK OF THE BRIDE

"Sparkling dialogue, a dash of deliciously tart humor, and just enough soul-searing sensuality to keep romance fans sighing happily in satisfaction." *—Booklist*

"Brimming with family, hope, and tender sensuality, this shrewdly plotted, gently paced romance is especially satisfying."
—*Library Journal*

THE BRIDE WHO GOT LUCKY

"Rising star MacGregor once again demonstrates her remarkable gift for effortlessly elegant writing, richly nuanced characterization, and lushly sensual love scenes."
—*Booklist* (starred review)

"A heady mix of action, wit, and sexual tension. Readers will eagerly turn the pages to see how this intense story concludes."
—*Publishers Weekly*

THE BAD LUCK BRIDE

"With its beautifully defined, exceptionally appealing protagonists, intriguing secondary characters, and graceful writing deftly leavened with wry wit, this classic romantic story line becomes something marvelously fresh and new, thus making MacGregor's stellar debut a must-read for any fan of Regency historicals."
—*Booklist* (starred review)

"Delightful! Janna MacGregor bewitched me with her captivating characters and a romance that sizzles off the page. I'm already a huge fan!"
—*New York Times* bestselling author Eloisa James

Also by
Janna MacGregor

WILD, WILD RAKE
ROGUE MOST WANTED
THE GOOD, THE BAD, AND THE DUKE
THE LUCK OF THE BRIDE
THE BRIDE WHO GOT LUCKY
THE BAD LUCK BRIDE
A DUKE IN TIME

RULES FOR ENGAGING THE EARL

JANNA MacGREGOR

St. Martin's Paperbacks

With love to Priyanka,
you've always been a part of our family.

First published in the United States by St. Martin's Paperbacks, an imprint of St. Martin's Publishing Group

RULES FOR ENGAGING THE EARL

Copyright © 2022 by Janna MacGregor.

Excerpt from *How to Best a Marquess* copyright © 2022 by Janna MacGregor.

All rights reserved.

For information, address St. Martin's Publishing Group, 120 Broadway, New York, NY 10271.

www.stmartins.com

ISBN: 978-1-250-76161-3

Our books may be purchased in bulk for promotional, educational, or business use. Please contact your local bookseller or the Macmillan Corporate and Premium Sales Department at 1-800-221-7945, ext. 5442, or by email at MacmillanSpecialMarkets@macmillan.com.

Printed in the United States of America

St. Martin's Paperbacks edition / May 2022

10 9 8 7 6 5 4 3 2 1

Acknowledgments

Sometimes in my author life, a character won't leave me be. This is the case with Jonathan Eaton, the Earl of Sykeston, who first appeared in *The Bride Who Got Lucky*. Over the years, I've received countless inquiries from dear readers asking if he'd get his own story.

Here it is. He's such a special character, and I had a tremendous amount of help in bringing him and Constance to life.

Kayla Bashe has my eternal gratitude. Her sensitive insights on *Rules for Engaging the Earl* and specifically, Jonathan, were priceless as his character took shape on the pages.

Finally, I'm in awe of Dr. Lauren Neuman. Her medical specialty is physical medicine and rehabilitation. She was so generous in giving me her time to discuss how Jonathan's life would have been impacted by the wounds he suffered during the war without the help of modern medicine. Dr. Neuman patiently answered all my questions and offered suggestions regarding Jonathan's mobility and the lingering physical symptoms he might have encountered from the gunshot wounds to his lower extremity. I'm forever in the good doctor's debt.

   Finally, a huge thank you to my darling husband, the author of my romantic life.

Prologue

Only one person in the entire world had the power to make Jonathan Eaton, the Earl of Sykeston, push everything aside and ride like the devil over the fields at breakneck speeds to reach her.

Constance Lysander.

With each gallop of the horse's hooves, his eagerness grew. Finally, he'd come upon the stately home that sat on a hill overlooking the English Channel. He slid off his horse, then with a natural ease vaulted the stone wall that surrounded their meeting place.

Most saw Constance as a serious-minded fifteen-year-old, but not Jonathan. If you looked long enough at her steady gaze, you could see an extraordinary world open before you. Her intelligence, spirit, and kindness never ceased to amaze him. Her insights on what mattered most in life helped keep him on a steady course. After their respective parents had died from an influenza that had swept through Portsmouth years ago, he'd discovered how much they had in common. When he told her of his hopes for his future and his ambition for life, she'd listen and offer her advice without censure.

She was his best friend, and he couldn't wait to share his unexpected news with her.

Jonathan removed the dust from his ride with a few well-placed slaps of his bicorne hat against his thighs, folded it under his arm, then entered her house. It was her late parents' vacant home and their secret meeting place. Constance lived next door with her widowed aunt, Mrs. Venetia Hopkins, whom everyone called Aunt Vee.

Jonathan headed toward the conservatory. It was the room where they always met. As he was about to call her name, a muffled conversation drifted toward him.

"Come lie next to me."

Jonathan's quick strides came to a halt. There was no mistaking it was Constance's voice.

"What a handsome fellow you are? Give me a kiss," she crooned.

A kiss?

Jonathan hurried on his way. There was only one creature to whom she'd murmur such sweet nothings.

Reggie.

Damnation. He'd always wanted to kiss her but foolishly thought it might change their friendship. Now he might never have the chance.

"Don't, Reggie." Her tone changed from playful to warning. "*Reggie, no.*"

Jonathan entered the room where there was only one piece of furniture. A sofa sat in the center facing the endless banks of windows that overlooked the sea. A massive animal slowly rose and peered over the sofa back, then emitted an ungodly sound.

A belch.

"Don't move, Constance." Jonathan took a running leap and jumped over the sofa with the beast watching his every step. He landed on his feet and faced her nemesis. "What have you done, you cretin?"

With deliberate ease, Constance sat up. "It's too late. He ate my sandwich." She released a woeful sigh. "Thank you for your valiant try." She turned her attention to the beast. "Reggie," she scolded. "You're a naughty pup." Her voice melted into a cooing sound like a mother to a child. "That sandwich wasn't yours."

Jonathan closed the distance between them. When he reached her, he took her hands in his then pulled her off the sofa. Without another thought he hugged her close.

She stiffened slightly, then melted into his embrace.

Her body fit perfectly against his. He inhaled her clean scent. It reminded him of the wind that skipped across the sea right before a rainstorm—wild and beautiful at the same time.

"What's that for?" she said softly.

"I couldn't remember the last time we hugged." Jonathan didn't want to think that it might be their last. He pulled away and looked into the deep blues of her eyes. Midnight blue, sapphire, and indigo all melded into a unique color that was hers alone.

"That's sweet." She playfully swatted his chest, then grabbed his hand and brought him to the sofa. "Come and sit with me but give Reggie enough room."

"You care for that mastiff more than me, I think." Jonathan slid his gaze up and down the gigantic animal while the animal did the same to him, licking its chops. "If I didn't know better, I'd think you were trying to make me jealous."

She slid him a side-eyed glance, then smiled. "Perhaps."

Jonathan felt an instant sense of relief. With his leaving, Reggie offered protection and companionship for Constance and her aunt Vee. "You're home early from the shipyard today."

Her face grew animated. "After I finished my morning studies, I helped Mr. Bridges. He's teaching me the business.

Soon, I'll be the 'Sons' in Lysander & Sons Refitting Company." She waggled her eyebrows.

Jonathan waggled his own. "I'd say there's not much resemblance between you and sons."

"You think so?" She waved a hand down the front of her muslin dress. "I can still wear my breeches, but they don't fit as well as they did last year."

He was quite aware of that fact. She was an attractive young woman. Even more so, there was a beauty to her innocence. Jonathan had seen it from the very first time he'd met her. Young men had started to notice her too. They were already vying for her attention. Every Sunday after church, Jonathan would escort Constance and Aunt Vee home. His chest tightened. Which of the young bucks would escort her when he was gone?

"I've started to wear dresses to the dockyard." She exhaled. "I guess all good things must come to an end."

"True." He took her hand in his, and together they sat on the sofa. "How are the knots coming along?"

She smiled sheepishly. "I spent half the night working on them. I may have conquered the figure eight, but the bowline still has me for a loop."

They both laughed.

"You'll master it, I'm certain." Still holding her hand, he clasped it tighter, not wanting to let her go. "I have news."

Her gaze flew to his, and a brilliant smile appeared. "I do too." When the dog tried to nose his way between them, she patted him on the head. "Lie down."

Instantly, the dog obeyed.

"Why didn't you tell him to do that before?" Jonathan asked. "He wouldn't have stolen your sandwich."

She bit her bottom lip as she stared at him. "He doesn't listen if there's food involved." She laughed, then regarded Reggie. "But I still consider him my second best friend."

"Who's your first?" He rubbed his neck as a flush of heat crept up his cheeks.

"You are."

He lifted his gaze to hers. The tenderness on her face held him spellbound.

"You're my best friend and one of a kind, Constance Lysander." One of her dark-brown locks fell forward on her face. He lifted his hand, the tremble in his fingers visible to both of them, then gently pushed it behind her ear. "I'd do anything for you."

She nodded once. The movement so slow that they never broke eye contact. "The same for me. For whatever reason."

Her gaze did strange things to him. His body felt hot and the need to hold her again became nigh unbearable. He swallowed and studied her face. The pink of her cheeks was a tad lighter than her full lips. At first sight, some might consider her eyes too large for her heart-shaped face. Jonathan never thought that. They were perfect. Every spark of light seemed to be reflected in them. The dark waters of the sea below paled to the deep blue of her irises.

Only inches separated them. He leaned forward slightly and lifted his hand again. Only instead of brushing back a fallen lock, he brushed the back of his fingers against the supple softness of her skin.

She leaned against his touch, and his breath stood suspended in his chest. Something magical was happening between them, and he never wanted to forget this moment.

As he would never forget her.

"Have you ever been kissed," she whispered, the hint of berries on her breath.

"No." With any other, he'd be too ashamed to admit that at seventeen he'd never experienced such a simple thing. Yet with her, there were no secrets. "You?"

She shook her head. At the answer, he leaned closer, his lips a mere inch from hers.

Suddenly, an absurd sound erupted, as if the earth split apart and bellowed.

She drew back. "Isn't he lovable? He's snoring."

"Adorable," Jonathan groused.

With a laugh, she put her hand over his and squeezed. "Tell me your news."

"You first," he said quietly, hoping to recapture the magic between them. The joy on her face stopped him cold. Her expression was a rare foretaste of the beautiful woman she'd become. He blinked slowly. He wouldn't be there to see her grow into such a person. Telling her his plans was becoming harder by the minute.

"I'm attending my first country assembly next month. It's my official introduction into Portsmouth society. I have a new dress for the occasion. I'm saving the first and last dance for you."

He did his utmost to keep the smile on his face, but his heart hiccupped that he would miss such an important event in her life. He was leaving on the morrow.

⁓

Constance sat on the edge of the sofa facing him. "My dress is white silk trimmed in dark-blue ribbons with matching ones for my hair. Aunt Vee thinks we should braid blue and white flowers into my hair ribbons."

Jonathan's handsome face had frozen in a half smile.

"What's wrong?" She tilted her head, then her eyes widened. "Don't tell me you're bored." She released their hands before gently pushing him in the chest. "I always listen to your stories. You could do the same for me."

He took her hands again and pulled her closer. "You will always keep me enthralled. It's . . . I'm a little dejected that I won't be there to see you."

"I can't imagine that you'll not be there. It's the biggest

social event of the year outside of Lysander & Sons' annual party." A profound cloud of bewilderment settled around her. "Why won't you come?"

"Because that's my news. I'm leaving for London on the morrow."

"For how long?" The disappointment he wouldn't be there for her first dance stung, but she'd always considered herself an optimist. "If you're not there for the assembly, then we can dance at my company's party . . ." The shake of his head stopped her from finishing. "Tell me," she whispered.

He looked to the sea for a moment. "I'll be gone for years." His resigned gaze locked with hers. "I may never come back."

"What?" She didn't hide the hint of hysteria in her voice.

"Some men from the war secretary's office came to see me today. Seems they discovered I speak French, Spanish, and German fluently and have a keen ability to shoot. Said I'm precisely the man they're looking for. They've asked if I'd be interested in a special assignment. It's quite the honor. As soon as my sister marries, I'll be stationed with the British army on the Continent wherever they need me."

"No, Jonathan." She shook her head as if she had the last word in denial. "Did your guardian agree to this?"

"Yes. My father had discussed it with him before he passed. He'd want me to do this if he were alive today." Emotion flared in his dark chocolate-colored eyes. "I thought you'd be happy for me."

Why couldn't he be the best farmer in all of England instead of the best marksman the country had ever seen?

"How could I be happy with you being sent into danger?" She sucked in a breath after having the proverbial wind knocked out of her. He gently tilted her chin until they could see into each other's eyes.

"Besides Mr. North, you're the only one I've told that I'll be on a special assignment. It has to remain secret." He cupped her cheek with his palm. "You can't save a dance for me." His eyes clouded with some emotion she'd never seen on him. "You can't wait for me either."

"Why not?" she asked softly.

"Because it wouldn't be fair to you if something happened to me."

"For instance?" As soon as she uttered the words, she understood his meaning. "You mean if you're killed? No. I beg of you, do not go." She closed her eyes at the horror of what he was saying. "I won't allow you to go and die over there. Whatever they want you to do is not worth giving up your life. I always thought . . ." For the love of heaven, what was she saying? They'd never discussed their future together. But ever since she'd known him, she thought they'd somehow, some way be a part of each other's lives.

"You mean the world to me." Jonathan pulled her into his arms, and she drank in the familiar evergreen scent. Chest-to-chest, their hearts beat in rhythm. "I'll be helping our country." He pulled away and looked into her eyes. "I've always thought that we'd build something together, but sometimes life has other plans. Listen, I'll do my best to come home, but I can't"—his voice broke with emotion—"I won't ask you to wait for me."

The pounding of her heart urged her to defy him. "You can't tell me what to do. I will wait for you." Tears were streaming down her face as she angrily wiped them away. "I hate those men who came to see you. They have no right to take you away from Portsmouth and me."

"I don't want you pining away for me. I want you happy." He brought her hand to his heart and held it there. "If you care for me, you'll promise me this."

His heart's steady beat encouraged her to look at him, but she held her ground.

Then the kind and handsome fiend threw down the gauntlet. "I need you to support my decision."

She drew her hand away, then wiped her remaining tears.

She nodded, but they both knew that her heart wasn't in the gesture.

He reached into his inner coat pocket and pulled out a piece of paper. "I have some suggestions of what to look for in a man. He has to earn the right to court you."

She wrinkled her nose much like when she smelled something foul. Which was appropriate. The idea that she'd even consider anyone besides him was putrid.

"Don't look at me like that." He stood holding a piece of foolscap in his hands.

She immediately felt the loss of not having him near, and for an instant, she wanted to pull him back. Their moments together dwindled by the second.

"You should settle for nothing less than a man who loves you for who you are. He shouldn't try to change you." He peeked over the paper. "He should love who he becomes when he's with you."

"All right," she said softly. "Is that all?"

"Hardly. I have an entire list." He took a step closer. "He should revel in your accomplishments."

With every word, his deep voice laid claim to her heart.

"His heart should be revealed to you through his kindness and his care. He should love you with every part of his being. He should never, ever say a harsh word or glare at you in anger. And, finally"—Jonathan lifted his eyes to hers—"he should worship all the bountiful gifts you possess that are uniquely yours. Only that man is worthy of you, Constance Lysander."

Though only several feet separated them, it felt like two miles. "Please . . ."

In seconds, he stood before her, his eyes red with unshed tears. He pressed his list into her hand. "Keep this as a reminder of me and what I want for you."

She nodded. "I promise to save a dance for you at every event I attend." Her voice grew softer until it became a whisper, a vow that she'd keep until her dying day. "Whether it's next week, next year, or the next decade, I'll save one for you whether you're there or not." She cupped his cheeks with her hands. "But I beg of you . . . come back to me."

She searched his face, and the tenderness threatened to steal her breath. How could she let him go?

Without another word shared between them, she pressed her lips to his. Her breath caught at the softness of his lips against hers. For a moment they didn't move as this newness between them unfurled, then wrapped them together in its embrace.

With a soulful sigh, he pulled her tighter, never letting his mouth leave hers. It wasn't simply a kiss but a sweet, soulful conversation about the past they'd shared and the future that had been robbed from them.

When they broke, he traced his thumb across her lips, the look of awe clear on his face. "I'll cherish you forever." He reached for his satchel, then pulled out a book. "For you."

She took the book and reverently opened it. Her gaze flew to his. "It's an illustrated copy of *Nautical Knots*."

He clasped his hands behind his back as he rocked back on his heels. "I thought it might be easier to learn the knots if you had a manual of sorts." He bent close and lowered his voice. "I don't want you staying up for nights on end trying to create them from memory."

"It's perfect. Thank you." She turned to the front page where he'd inscribed it. *To my best friend, Constance Lysander. May our lives always be entwined no matter the time or distance that separates us.* "Oh, Jonathan," she murmured. It was all she could manage as her heart tumbled in a free fall. She wanted to pull him to her and never let go. Without hesitating, she rushed to her basket and pulled out her journal. "I want you to take this."

A line formed between his brows. "But it's your book of essays. You always carry that with you."

"I can always start another. I've written about Portsmouth, the sea, and our neighbors. It'll be as if you have a little part of home when you . . ." Her words trailed to nothing as she tamped down the swell of emotion.

With their gazes locked, he cupped her cheek. "More important, I'll have a part of you with me . . . forever."

The bell from the village tolled, reminding them both that evening would soon be upon them.

"I must go," he whispered before pressing his lips to hers again in a brief kiss.

"Jonathan." His name on her lips left her breathless. "Come back to me."

He smiled with a wistfulness she'd never seen before. He reached for Reggie and patted his head. "Take care of our girl, Reginald."

Once more, he pressed his lips to hers, then he was gone. Gone from the room. Gone from her life.

She forced herself to run after him. By the time she reached the drive, he was already galloping across the fields. He turned back once. When Jonathan saw her, he bestowed that heart-swelling, familiar, confident smile and waved his hat in the air as a goodbye. She lifted her hand in answer.

The image of him assured and happy was permanently etched in her mind.

Then and there, she made a vow. If God would bring him home, she would keep Jonathan's silly rules and do her level best to follow them. The simple truth was that she'd never meet a man who would compare to Jonathan.

He already ruled her heart.

Chapter One

London
Ten years later

The coach lumbered so slowly that pedestrians were traveling faster than Jonathan's carriage. Once again, he pulled his timepiece from his waistcoat. Time was of the essence, and he was wasting it. Hell, at this speed, even he could outrun his coach.

After a few minutes, they started to move faster through the streets.

"My lord?" Thomas Winstead, his persistent estate manager, demanded his attention again.

Without warning, the carriage tilted, knocking Jonathan against the side panel. A ragged pain tore through his leg at the sudden jarring from hitting a rut. He sucked in a breath desperate to keep from crying out. "Damnation," he muttered.

"Lord Sykeston?" With his brow creasing into neat lines, Thaddeus North, his butler, leaned forward.

"I'm fine." Jonathan let out the breath he'd been holding.

"Your mind is elsewhere." North's lips turned downward. "It's perfectly understandable."

"The sooner we arrive, the sooner it'll be over," Jonathan grunted in response. He didn't acknowledge or deny the butler's comments.

"As I was saying, I've climbed every tenant's roof," Thomas continued. "Two hundred and thirteen pounds for roofing supplies and labor should cover it."

Jonathan stared at his estate manager. Only a couple of years older than Jonathan, Thomas was the perfect specimen of a man at his best. Jonathan subdued the urge to curl his lip at the thought. There was a time he had relished climbing the ladders with Thomas by his side and inspecting his tenants' roofs.

Now he couldn't look at a ladder without grimacing.

Jonathan couldn't deny that Thomas was a godsend. He completed the tasks that Jonathan could no longer perform. Strong and swift, Thomas had earned the promotion to estate manager.

"Fine," he answered. "I'll prepare the funds when I return to Portsmouth. Start work when it's convenient for the tenants and you."

"Perhaps you'd like to visit when Thomas starts the repairs?" North prodded gently.

It was the same litany Jonathan had heard repeatedly since he'd returned home. North goading him to see his tenants. Encouraging him to call on his neighbors. It was a waste of time.

"I'm certain they'd welcome your interest." North's tone sounded similar to a nursemaid coaxing her charge to take his medicine.

Jonathan carefully swung his gaze to his butler. "I show my interest by paying for whatever repairs are needed. I offer fair rents and don't gouge them at the end of the harvest season. My share of the bounty is quite minimal compared with others. That's how I show my interest."

Thomas's Adam's apple wobbled at his curt tone.

Years ago, Jonathan had found immense pleasure working on the betterment of his estates. Now he was thankful Thomas relished the estate work. It gave Jonathan more time for designing the perfect pistol cartridge and his plan for a training school for army marksmen. Too many of them didn't have the proper training when they were dropped into battle. Even his former commanding officer, the Marquess of Faladen, thought it an excellent idea when Jonathan had presented it to him last month.

The carriage pulled to a stop in front of a modest townhouse in Mayfair.

"We're here," North announced with a hint of excitement in his voice.

"Finally," Jonathan mumbled. "Let's hope I'm not too late."

A footman opened the door, and Jonathan carefully made his way down the steps while holding to the handle inside the carriage. Once on the ground, he took his cane from North, then patted the pocket inside his blue broadcloth morning coat, the crinkle of paper reassuring. A special license was a rare and expensive investment, but this moment called for the extraordinary.

Sometimes for the greater good, a man had to venture into the world and claim his wife. Jonathan doubted if today's events could be considered good for anybody, especially him. Being saddled with a wife would upset his routine, but a promise was a promise. Though he'd left his full-time position in the army years ago, he was still a man of habit. And his habit didn't include entertaining a wife.

A sensible, more balanced man might have turned on his heel and never looked back. Since Jonathan's right leg had been completely mangled by two snipers' bullets, he'd been anything but balanced.

In more ways than one.

Jonathan adjusted his beaver hat with a tug.

"Good luck, my lord," North called from the coach.

Without acknowledging the kind words of his butler, he made his way to the town house door. What was he even doing here?

He smoothed a hand down his waistcoat. Honestly, he wanted to see her. But if she gave him one pitiful look, he would turn on his one good foot and leave—marriage or no marriage. It made little difference that she had asked for *his hand* in marriage. With his fist, he knocked on the door. When no one answered, Jonathan repeated his movement, but this time a little more forcefully.

"Come in," a woman called out, her voice muffled behind the wooden panel.

He entered the modest but elegantly decorated town house not far from the Duke of Randford's Mayfair home. Christian Vareck, the Duke of Randford, was a friend, one might even say his best friend. Which meant Jonathan should have made the effort to call on him, but that would have required even more pretending on his part to be amenable to social calls and gatherings. A visit to Doctors' Commons was enough for one day.

Jonathan's throat narrowed to the size of a small twig, and his grip tightened on his walking stick. It was only natural to be a little queasy. It wasn't every day that a man married, particularly, when his bride-to-be was carrying a baby.

To be precise, she was carrying another man's baby.

But his wife-to-be had asked him to marry her before the baby was born to ensure it was legitimate. Simply put, Jonathan couldn't refuse.

Because it was her.

With a small tea tray in her hands, an older woman looked up and immediately her eyes widened. "Lord Sykeston, is that really you?"

"Indeed, Mrs. Hopkins," Jonathan answered. Frankly, he was amazed that he sounded so amiable. "Pleasure to see you once again."

Still striking with white hair and blue eyes that noticed

everything, Mrs. Hopkins, Constance's aunt Vee, smiled at him. "Shall I escort you to her?"

He nodded once.

"Follow me." Her directions sounded like marching orders.

"I have a clergyman who will be joining me shortly," Jonathan said. "Perhaps we should wait?"

"Let's leave the vicar to his own devices," the woman said cheerfully. "Constance is anxious to see you."

Everything within him stilled. It had been a decade since he'd last laid eyes on Constance Lysander. Memories swept through him faster than a storm-swollen stream. He still remembered that kiss. At the touch of her lips against his, he'd found something special.

She was the sweetest thing he'd ever tasted.

Years ago, when he lay injured in the surgeon's tent, all he wanted to do was die. The surgeon insisted he had to lose his leg, but Jonathan had said no. He was at his breaking point with the unrelenting and excruciating pain. He couldn't bear the additional torment of an amputation. The surgeon's special recipe for laudanum made him sick and did little to provide much comfort. As he lay in the cot praying death would steal him away from the agony so he could be at peace, Constance wouldn't let him go. Her face haunted his dreams, compelling him to fight for survival.

Now Jonathan stood in her home ready to marry and give her his name. He'd never thought to marry, but when she'd asked if he'd wed her, he couldn't turn her away.

Aunt Vee started up the staircase, not waiting for him.

Jonathan took a step forward and exhaled. Bloody stairs. They were punishment for him and his disfigured leg. If there was any god above, he or she or they would make certain there weren't too many for him to maneuver.

With measured steps, he carefully climbed the set of stairs, each one a torture device.

By the time he reached the top, his heart pounded and sweat covered his brow. God, he always felt weak like a newborn colt after ascending a flight.

"You'll find my niece in the second bedroom to the right." Aunt Vee turned her back on him to continue down the hallway.

"Madame, shouldn't you announce me?" Jonathan asked. Though he didn't participate in society, he was raised a gentleman. Thus, he was acquainted with polite society's dictates that it was uncouth to barge into a lady's bedchamber unless invited.

"I can't," Aunt Vee said dismissively. "I have to see about my great-niece."

All sound ceased as he stood stock-still. "Constance had the baby?"

"Yes. Three hours ago. She named her Aurelia. In my humble opinion, the child looks like her father," Aunt Vee said dreamily.

Jonathan smirked slightly. Hopefully, the baby didn't inherit any of her father's other traits. Indeed, the baby's father, the late Lord Meriwether Vareck, was the golden child of the dissolute, no-good men who lost what little morals they possessed to chase their own selfish pleasures. After practically marrying three women at the same time, Meriwether had all but ruined Constance, then disappeared leaving a plethora of gossip in his wake.

It made little difference that the baby was born before they married. Jonathan had paid the vicar enough to say that the child arrived in the world after the "I dos."

"Miss Aurelia Jane Vareck," Aunt Vee sighed. "She's an angel and her name is perfect." Aunt Vee put her tea tray down on the side table in the hallway. "It's a fairy tale, wouldn't you agree?"

"How so?" Jonathan asked, all the while thinking it was a tragedy.

"Constance discovered she was the real Lady Meriwether, and now Aurelia won't suffer the stigma of being illegitimate."

For a moment, Jonathan didn't hear anything but his pulse thrashing through his body. "Pardon me?"

"She doesn't need to marry you." Aunt Vee smiled. "But I'm sure she'll still want to hear your proposal. You'd best make it a good one." The woman continued on her way down the hall humming a merry tune.

With an awkward couple of steps, Jonathan found himself outside the designated door. He lifted his hand to knock, then lowered it slowly.

The news was for the best, but a sudden melancholy that Constance didn't need to marry struck with such force that he almost dropped to his knees. It was illogical.

The truth was Constance didn't deserve someone like him. He'd make a horrible husband, let alone a ghastly father. With a resigned sigh, he knocked twice, then heard the dulcet tone of a woman saying, "Come in."

He stepped into the room the same time that the earth stopped its orbit.

At least, that's what it felt like.

My God, the years have been generously kind to her. She was breathtakingly beautiful. Her dark locks shone and her eyes twinkled as if the sun's rays adorned her. She was one of those rare women, a natural beauty who didn't need any jewels or fancy gowns to be stunning. Her eyes widened. Her unique smile, the one he'd longed to behold for years, proved her delight in seeing him.

He blinked to make certain she was real. He shook his head slightly. He'd best get ahold of his emotions before he made a fool of himself.

"Hello, Jonathan." The softness of her voice calmed his ridiculous impulse to flee.

"Lady Meriwether," he said with a slight bow.

"It's good to see you." Another devastating smile appeared.

It thrilled something deep inside him. But he dismissed it as a fond memory of his youth.

"How long has it been?" She straightened slightly and held his stare, but the constant smoothing of the bedcovers betrayed her anxiety.

"Ten years give or take," he answered. "Your aunt met me at the door. She told me you delivered your baby."

"Yes, a healthy, beautiful girl." That radiant smile appeared again.

His first year back from the war, he'd spent most of his time in London handling his deceased sister's estate. By then, Constance had married Lord Meriwether, and Jonathan didn't bother to call and wish them happiness. It would have been too painful to see them together. Yet he'd heard that Constance's husband had married two other women practically at the same time as he'd married her. The lout disappeared with their dowries before he met his untimely death by drowning in a mud puddle.

"Your aunt said you're the rightful widow of Lord Meriwether. What happened to the other two wives?"

She let out a sigh. "I just found out the truth about my marriage. Randford sent a letter informing you. Didn't you receive it?" she asked.

"No."

Constance glanced downward, then she drew her gaze to his. "My friend Katherine, the new Duchess of Randford, discovered her marriage to Meriwether was void because the vicar who married them had been defrocked. And my friend Miss Blythe Howell was the third woman he'd married." Her gaze strayed to the window.

"You're Lady Meriwether." He shook his head trying to clear the muddle created by these new facts. The story was incredible.

She nodded slightly. "I'm his wife . . . I mean widow.

That changes my circumstances somewhat, doesn't it?" She lightly worried her lower lip by clasping it between her teeth. The action emphasizing the fullness of the tender skin.

He closed his eyes at the sight. Everything within him tightened into a knot that he doubted would ever be untangled. He had to remember that her change in circumstances was the best for him. He could return to his previous existence as a recluse. That's what he was good at.

Yet he'd never considered himself lonely until now. For some odd reason, he tasted a disturbing new flavor on his tongue.

Bitterness.

Chapter Two

Pure madness had possessed Constance.

Maybe it could be explained by the fact that she'd just spent the last eighteen hours in labor. With the final push that had brought her beautiful Aurelia into the world, Constance had also expelled the last piece of common sense she possessed.

Why did she even want to marry again? The last man she'd married had been a consummate liar and had abandoned her without a glance back. There was no other way to describe Lord Meriwether Vareck. He was a trigamist, marrying three women.

But Constance's belief in fairness and justice had been somewhat proven true. Katherine James, formally the first Lady Meriwether Vareck, had been devastated when she'd discovered she wasn't Meriwether's legitimate wife. Yet fate had found a way to heal Katherine's heart when she'd fallen in love with Meriwether's half brother, Christian, the Duke of Randford. They'd recently married, and Constance was confident that their marriage was destined to be a love story for the centuries.

If only she could have experienced the same. Marrying Jonathan might give her the chance.

Standing before her, Jonathan was still as strikingly handsome as he had been in their youth. Only bigger. His broad shoulders seemed to fill her room along with his clean scent. He was still the only man who could filch her breath away. The slight hitch in his gait didn't detract in the least from his aura of sureness and virility. Though his black hair was a trifle too long, it was perfect with his broad forehead and regal aquiline nose. The only faults in his fine face were the current obstinate set of his square jaw and the sharpness in his coffee-colored eyes as he observed her.

During the war, people had compared him to a kestrel, a precise killing machine. He'd become a legend for his war efforts during his years with the British army.

She sighed silently. Best to get on with it. She squared her shoulders ready to explain her circumstances, then grimaced. The movement shot a sharp pain through her lower extremities, reminding her that she'd given birth several hours ago.

"Are you unwell?"

"Simply a little tender," she replied as she smoothed the covers around her.

"Let me help you lean against your pillows." He placed his hand under her elbow and assisted as she adjusted herself to a more comfortable position. "Better?"

She nodded. Her gaze darted to her hands to hide the new pang of hurt that clutched her insides. She'd always imagined their reunion a little differently.

In her dreams, they would laugh and flirt while renewing their acquaintance. They'd touch again as they danced in each other's arms. Such silly musings from a lifetime ago. They'd both changed drastically since the last time they'd seen each other.

"Would you care to sit?" Constance waved to an ornate Georgian hoop backed chair with ball and claw feet next to her bed.

"Thank you," he murmured. He pulled the chair close to her side, then slowly lowered himself to the seat. Though his face remained stoic, the creases around his eyes deepened, betraying the pain the movement caused him.

"I can't believe you're here." Her voice so low, she didn't know if he could hear her. "I heard you were . . ."

"Dead?" He waved a hand down his body. "I'm still alive. Still with the army too. Half-pay."

"I'm sorry about your sister's passing," she said softly.

His brow furrowed. "Thank you for your condolences. She's at peace now."

The silence grew awkward, and Constance struggled for something to say. "What happened to your leg, Jonathan? Randford mentioned you were shot several times."

"You're rather blunt, aren't you?" he murmured under his breath as he straightened his leg out, careful not to bump the bed.

"Just concerned," she answered.

When his gaze shot to hers, a new aloofness resided there. He turned his attention to his fine doeskin breeches. He flicked an imaginary piece of lint from the garment before he straightened the tails of his blue broadcloth coat.

He looked unsettled, and his unexpected gruffness brought forth a need to soothe him. If he smiled, the sight would be brighter than the gaudy gilding that decorated the feminine chair he rested against.

"The day I left my regiment, a couple of French sharpshooters hit our camp and took me down. If it hadn't been for Randford, I wouldn't have survived." Another thick silence settled around them.

"How horrible." A chill skated up her back at the dispassion in his voice. "Jonathan . . . I'm glad you're here."

He grunted in response, a clear indication they were finished with that conversation. An unexpected but tentative smile broke across his lips. "Since you're the real wife to Lord Meriwether, then your baby is legitimate. Do you still want to marry me?"

Of course she did. An unfamiliar sense of absurdity bubbled from within at her situation. She'd asked him to come and wed her though they hadn't seen each other in years. But her heart encouraged her to follow this path wherever it led. She'd always trusted her instincts, and they were telling her to grab ahold of him and not let go.

Which begged the question: Where had her intuition been the day she pledged her troth to Meriwether? Probably completely charmed by her first husband, as she had been. "When I sent the Duke of Randford to ask you to marry me, I was . . ."

"Desperate?"

"Not entirely. Just hopeful." She held his gaze. "Do you have any reservations?"

He leaned closer, giving her a clear view of the twitch in his right jaw. The fingers of his right hand thrummed gently against his doeskin breeches. "A few. Don't you?"

Constance nodded slightly, then took a deep breath. "I must share that I'm heavily burdened with responsibilities. I have a daughter now. Not to mention the unfolding scandal that my husband had three wives. It's too much." What she really wanted to say was that her life felt like a spinning top. At any moment, she was afraid she'd tumble out of control. "I have to protect Aurelia. I need respectability so my business doesn't suffer. I need a husband, a man to be a father to her."

He didn't move an inch. His brown eyes were shuttered, revealing nothing of his thoughts.

Trepidation threatened to choke her, but she swallowed as much of it as she could. "If you'll be patient, I'll explain. When we marry, I want to give you and our marriage everything I have to make the endeavor successful. However, I need a few months before I join you in Portsmouth."

Jonathan blinked slowly, then lifted one brow in a perfect arch. "So, you're not changing your mind about marrying me?" He stopped the discomforting rhythm of thrumming his fingers against his thigh.

She shook her head. Her last marriage had been a farce. Her husband had stayed with her for a month, then scurried off to Cumberland to marry his third wife, Miss Blythe "Beth" Howell. Constance's friendships with Meri's other wives had been a gift, like Aurelia. Funny thing, they'd become family after discovering Meriwether had married all of them.

"I haven't changed my mind." Constance leaned her head back and stared at the ceiling. Anything to keep her mind off his thighs. Heaven help her, but why was she thinking of his legs and how muscular they appeared—even the injured one, which was slightly smaller? It was ridiculous. "The midwife thinks it best for my recovery," she said quietly.

"The midwife." A hint of disbelief in his voice was unmistakable. "Let's be honest with each other. We always have before. Is it because I'm lame?"

"Never." She jerked her gaze to his and stared. He'd not leave this room unless he believed her. "Where would you get that idea? Please, don't call yourself that."

"I saw you glance at my leg. Several times as a matter of fact." His accusation sliced the dense air between them.

Heat bludgeoned her cheeks. She leaned forward as far as she could without hurting herself and reached out her hand to him. He regarded it as if poisonous, but eventually took it in his.

When last she'd seen him, he'd been galloping through the field on his way home, a brilliant specimen of a man who was sure of his place in the world. But now he reminded her of a wounded animal ready to defend himself against all enemies, real or otherwise. She might as well confess to the embarrassing truth. "I was admiring your form." She didn't glance away and held her head high. "That's why I was staring at your leg."

"What?" he said, clearly taken aback and releasing her hand.

"Is it that surprising I find you handsome?" Then she threw out the challenge. "It bodes well for our marriage. Plus, we have a lot in common."

"We used to." His eyes softened, and a sad smile broke across his lips.

"We come from the same place, same society as it were." Her eyes blurred as tears threatened. This was ten times harder than she ever imagined. She could feel the heat of his gaze on her profile. Fatigue blanketed her. All she wanted to do was to take a nap. For God's sake, she'd only delivered her firstborn hours ago. However, she couldn't rest until she convinced him and made him understand.

"Jonathan, I have no dowry. Lord Meriwether spent it."

"All of it?" he asked incredulously.

She nodded. "He spent the other wives' dowries also. The only thing he left each one of us was a small packet with our names on it. Inside, it was filled with individual receipts." She blew out a breath and forced her gaze to his. "Thank heavens, I have the maritime business my father left me."

"Lysander & Sons Refitting Company," he said.

She nodded. "I wouldn't allow it to be part of the marriage settlements to Lord Meriwether. It means a great deal to me. It was my father's pride and joy after my mother and me. But I can promise I'll be a good wife to you."

His eyes sparked with some undefined emotion.

"You told me all those years ago, you'd help me if I asked. You also told me to marry when it felt right. That time is now."

He reached for his cane. "Constance, your lack of money will not be an impediment to me. I won't take your family's business from you either. I know how much you value it. I can't say that about other men." He leaned back in his chair, his rapier gaze never leaving hers. "If you want to marry me, be careful. I beg of you to take an honest measurement of me. You'll thank me later for such sound advice."

Perhaps she'd been wrong in her earlier assessment of him. He sounded almost embittered. "I don't understand what you mean."

For a brief moment, the warmth in his rich brown eyes reassured her everything would be fine. "I'm certain it's not your intention, but the fact remains you married a man who put your and your daughter's reputations at risk. I'm not much better."

Chapter Three

Jonathan didn't say a word as a thousand emotions—none of them complimentary to him—fell across Constance's face.

"That doesn't say much for you then." Her honeyed voice trembled as her blue eyes flashed with pent-up fury.

"Forgive me." For the first time in ages, he felt something, much like a horse kick in the chest. She'd always been a bright star in the darkness of his nights. It was unexpected that after all his years of living alone, she still had that effect on him.

She twisted slightly in bed to have a better look at him and grimaced.

"Careful," he said. "You just gave birth."

"I'll not forget that for quite a while."

"Perhaps you're not well enough to make this decision." He should leave, but something stirred within him. Her face was like a beacon, drawing him nearer to a future he'd once dreamed would be his—marriage, children, and all the trimmings. She reminded him of a happier time in his life when he was noble and had a future with all the wonderful things life had to offer a man.

But that had been his fickle youth when he saw everything as a lark or an opportunity to show off his physical prowess. If he wanted to leave this room with his remaining dignity intact, he had to push the memories and her away.

Yet he couldn't leave her.

She blew a stray lock of hair from her face. "Giving birth is not a disease. If you're suggesting I'm not in my right mind, perhaps you aren't ready for this discussion."

He much preferred this tart version of her to the cautious one. "No. I don't want you weary from the pain." A deep breath escaped. "Coping with it is exhausting. I'm an expert at it."

"Oh." The tension immediately melted from her. "The midwife said I'd be able to move back to Portsmouth in two months. It'll be the summer. However, I'll need to travel frequently to London. I always buy supplies, visit vendors, and the like."

She slipped the hand farther from him to her side. Immediately, she fisted it into the coverlet. Such a small movement indicated she was unsure of herself. The urge to lean over her and place his hand on hers grew near impossible to ignore.

That would be the height of foolishness. People changed and sometimes not for the better, as in his case. It was a hard lesson to learn.

"I'm looking forward to coming home." A forlorn smile graced her lips.

He was too. He wanted nothing more than to welcome her home and leave his lonely existence behind. But that wouldn't be fair to her.

"Perhaps you should stay here." He stood slowly.

She didn't move an inch as she took stock of him. Her gaze skated down his body and back up to rest on his. "Why?"

"You are a social creature, I expect. I'll be honest with you the way you were with me. I don't have many friends." The truth was a little more obscure than that. Besides Randford and Julian Raleah, the Marquess of Grayson, he avoided people. However, nothing productive would come from delving into all the gory details—at least not yet. "You might be more comfortable here. Living with me will be an isolating experience. Is that what you want?"

Her slight gasp pierced a small part of what remained of his heart. But then that mulish expression he'd seen hundreds of times in their youth transformed her face. She normally could convince him with that look. But not this time.

"What I want is a husband who will be a partner to me. Will you open that drawer next to you and retrieve that small book?"

He did as asked and gave it to her.

She pulled a piece of folded foolscap from the book. "This"—she waved the paper in the air toward him—"is the man I want to marry. These are the rules you gave me the last time we met."

He tamped down a ridiculous grin. It sent a thrill through him that she'd saved his list. After he'd left her the last time, he'd always wondered what she'd done with it.

He had the good sense to look chastised, but only for a second. "Constance, that man is no longer here. I'm what's left of that fantasy," he said softly, willing her to understand. "No matter what happens, I will always help you if I can. All you have to do is ask."

"I'd do the same for you. Isn't that the definition of friends?" Her eyes flashed, then narrowed.

He smiled slightly. If her optimism ever met his realism, Jonathan would be hard-pressed to say which was stronger or more virulent. He leaned forward, narrowing the distance to mere inches between them. He took a deep breath to capture her familiar scent. She still used orange blossom water to bathe in. He was certain of it. He'd always had a weakness for such a clean sweet fragrance. He'd always had a weakness for her.

He took her hand in both of his and held it, her warmth a balm to the cold loneliness that was his constant companion. If they married, he'd disappoint her. He had little doubt of that. He disappointed himself. But at home, in his study, he didn't disappoint anyone. "Let me be direct. I don't socialize. I don't invite people into my home. Ergo, I don't want or need friends. Thus, I don't need a wife."

It felt as if he were stabbing himself in the heart. He wanted her—always had—but she'd be miserable married to him. And he never wanted to be the cause of her unhappiness.

"You can't be serious," she protested softly.

"Dead serious."

"Why?" Her word hung in the air between them.

That one word always begged the same answer.

Because the miasma of a future court-martial always loomed in his future, and he wouldn't make her go through it. If only he had more time to clear his name before she needed to marry him.

"You don't need me. Neither does your daughter. Our marriage was designed to protect you and the baby. Besides, how I described my existence? That's my life . . . now." Before she could press him for more, he let go of her hand, then continued in the kindest voice he could muster, "Congratulations on the birth of your daughter. I wish you a happy life."

He drank in the sight of her face, the soft curves of her cheeks, and the familiar blue of her eyes. His Constance. She would always be his whether they were married or not.

Without waiting for her reply, he dipped his head. Then as quickly as his limp allowed, he turned toward the door.

"Wait," she cried. "Why did you come here if you don't want to marry me?"

He slowly turned around to face her.

"I want to marry you. The sooner the better." She lightly worried her lower lip by clasping it between her teeth. "Tell me you want the same. If not, then I release you from any and all obligations." She met his narrowed gaze with a defiant tip of her chin. "I just want you to be honest with me."

He was cornered without an escape. He'd never lie to her. "I have a special license, and a vicar will arrive soon."

"Thank you. It'd be an honor to marry you."

She thought it an honor now, but if he was summoned before a military tribunal, they'd both suffer. He should have pursued the rumors when he'd first become aware of them, but he'd thought nothing of it. Whenever he was in camp, the rest of his fellow soldiers always kept their distance from him. It was understandable. Jonathan always reminded them of death. As a marksman, it was his duty to go after the most elusive of targets, and he always hit his targets.

However, when his supervising officer had mentioned he'd heard a rumor that one of his marksmen had acted in a manner unbecoming of a gentleman, Jonathan had dismissed it. As an officer in His Majesty's army, he knew the rules of conduct and how to act honorably on or off the battlefield. Over the last year, however, the rumors had grown. His commanding officer had said his name had been linked to the disastrous and disreputable event.

But it wasn't true, and after all, this was Constance asking for his hand.

A luminous smile lit her face, and for the first time in months, he felt a peculiar enthusiasm about his future.

But her smile melted into a slight frown. "Would it be too inconvenient if we wait until tomorrow? I've been awake for almost a full day . . . giving birth."

He'd known she was tired by the drawn look on her face when they'd talked. He should have suggested it. It was more proof that he'd been away from polite company for too long. "Of course. Tomorrow."

"Tomorrow, then." Her smile hinted at her joy in his agreement.

He nodded, then departed. Once he was outside her bedroom, he leaned against the oak door and closed his eyes. It was over, and there was no going back.

His chest suddenly felt uncomfortable with a foreign sensation, much like lightness blooming deep in his chest. She didn't care about his leg or his solitude. She wanted to marry him.

"Sykeston?" a voice called out.

Jonathan straightened and opened his eyes to find his old friend Christian Vareck, the Duke of Randford, coming toward him with a grin of welcome on his face. The duke was a war hero. If it hadn't been for the duke's bravery and quick action to save Jonathan, he'd have surely died on the godforsaken day.

"Imagine seeing you here." Randford stopped before him. "Why are you out in the hall? Are you here to marry Constance?"

"She's in there." He pointed to the door.

"That doesn't answer my questions," the duke retorted.

Jonathan delivered his best glare, the one reserved for people who reminded him of gnats.

The duke returned the glare. Then an aggravating half grin tugged at his mouth, proving he was a novice at the art of intimidation.

"Katherine and I came over as soon as we heard she was about to deliver." Randford stuck out his hand for a formal shake. "Congratulations."

"For what?" Jonathan grunted as he took his friend's hand.

"You don't have to do it. Marriage, you know. She's the

legitimate wife of my nefarious half brother, God rest his soul," the duke said quietly.

Jonathan didn't say a word in response. For a moment, the urge to pound his fist through the wall turned fierce. But he forced himself to relax. It wasn't the duke's fault. Randford was aware of the horrid way his cowardly brother had treated the women he married.

"I haven't married her," he answered.

"Really?" the duke asked in astonishment. "Then we're in time to witness the marriage."

"Marriage," he repeated while shaking his head. "We set the date for tomorrow. I tried to change her mind. But she couldn't be convinced otherwise. Mayhap you could talk some sense into her."

"She knows her own mind." Randford studied the floor before raising his gaze to Jonathan. "It was good of you to come and see her. My letter telling you that she was the real Lady Meriwether must have crossed your path as you traveled here." The duke stared at Jonathan's face. "Are you all right? You look like you waltzed with a banshee."

"Of course I'm all right," Jonathan snapped as he stiffened his back. He took a handkerchief from his navy silk waistcoat pocket and wiped his forehead.

He really wasn't all right.

My God, I came to London to marry her. He never thought he'd see the day. Was it too much to ask for a little privacy so he could put his thoughts in order? He should have pressed her until she cried off. Once they married, he'd have Constance and Aurelia's futures to worry about. He didn't have his own future secured.

He rubbed the center of his chest where it ached like never before.

He'd been determined not to care about anything, but Constance had changed all that. In a roundabout way, she'd always possessed that ability.

Randford smiled. "What time is the wedding tomorrow?"

"I'll keep you informed." Jonathan nodded his farewell, pushed away from the door, then made the laborious trip downstairs to the outside. He took a deep breath to control the increasing pain in his leg, then started across the walk to the waiting carriage.

Dashing around a corner and no more than five feet ahead of him, three little hellions with their heads down were chasing a cat at full speed. He couldn't get out of the way fast enough. As they barreled toward him, it became clear a collision was unavoidable. He braced himself for impact.

"Whoa there," he shouted as the cat whizzed by.

Reaching for the cat, the first child rammed into his stomach, knocking him to the ground. Jonathan landed with such force that he lost his breath, stealing his speech.

"We're sorry." A neat and prim little girl scrambled to stand in front of him. "Please don't tell our mother. My brothers and I were trying to catch Oribelle."

Both of her brothers jumped to their feet. One had managed to grapple the scrawny feline under one arm. He handed the creature to his sister, then reached out a hand to assist Jonathan to his feet.

By then his favorite footman, Franklin Arkwright, had knelt by his side. "My lord, are you injured?"

The children gasped in horror at the address.

The boy who had rammed into Jonathan had the wide-eyed look of someone who'd been caught stealing from the biscuit jar. "He's a nob. We're done for."

The girl hugged her cat as if Jonathan would demand it for restitution.

He sat up and with an audible grunt was helped to his feet by Arkwright. Immediately, his leg grew weak and threatened to give out. "My cane," he grumbled.

The children stepped back as Arkwright handed it to him.

"We've broken his leg," the other boy blubbered.

The little girl twisted her mouth and a cry that sounded eerily like a pig squeal erupted. "We're doomed when Father finds out."

"Quiet," Jonathan admonished. "You didn't break my leg. However, it would behoove you to watch where you're going when you run around like ruffians and ill-mannered wildcats." He brushed the grass and crushed leaves from his sleeves.

"Oribelle isn't a wildcat." Tears were running in rivulets down the little girl's face as she held up the cat for Jonathan's perusal. "She's a tabby."

And a mangy one at that.

For the love of mankind, Jonathan hated tears of any kind. To make matters worse, a crowd had started to gather. He hated that worse than tears. It made his skin crawl to be the center of attention after he'd fallen.

"Don't cry," he murmured. If only he could crouch and look her in the face, he could calm her down. "You have your kitty. I won't tell your parents."

She looked up at him with big brown eyes and black lashes soaked with tears.

"I promise," he said softly. He waved a hand. "Now, off with you."

"How'd you hurt your leg?" The little girl sniffed.

For a moment, he wasn't going to answer. "I was injured."

Before he could continue, two men wove their way forward around several spectators.

One of them tipped his hat and bowed. "I'm sorry for my children's behavior, sir."

The children instantly quieted as they hung their heads.

"Father, don't be angry," the little girl said.

"You know better." The scowl he held for his children slowly melted as he turned his attention to Jonathan. "May I offer my humblest apologies . . . Captain Lord Sykeston?"

Jonathan turned his full attention to the father. "Colonel Peterson?" He straightened his shoulders as if preparing to salute. It was an old habit. The colonel had originally re-cruited Jonathan for the military.

"In the flesh, my lord." The colonel nodded briskly, then turned his attention to the hooligans he claimed as children. "Lord Sykeston was under my command. Brave man. You could learn some discipline and manners from him."

"He's a cripple," the first boy said, stating the obvious.

"Don't say that, Edward," the little girl scolded. "He can't help it." She turned toward him. "We'll pray for you, sir."

He needed more than prayer at this point. He needed wit-nesses or divine intervention to clear his name.

"Be on your way. I'll meet you at the corner." The colo-nel's face turned beet red as he made a shooing motion with his hands. "I apologize for their misbehavior." He turned his attention away from Jonathan.

The colonel's unease at Jonathan's appearance was unex-pected. Had information crossed his desk about the court-martial? It couldn't have if he still called him brave. For God's sake, the colonel had known Jonathan's every movement in battle and knew his reputation.

The colonel mumbled an apology. "They'll receive their punishment as soon as we return home."

It was on the tip of Jonathan's tongue to say *no harm done* but he couldn't form the words. There was harm. Every time he had an encounter such as this one, it chipped away a piece of his self-worth, a constant reminder that he was no longer the same man as before. For a moment, he stood fro-zen. Being injured was one thing, but to be constantly under the threat of a court-martial was an entirely different matter altogether. Automatically, he replied, "They apologized."

The colonel nodded. "They take after their mother. Too in-quisitive for their own good." He turned to his companion. "Come and meet Lord Sykeston."

The man stepped forward.

"Lord Sykeston, may I introduce Lieutenant Harold Roth?" the colonel asked.

"Lieutenant Roth," Jonathan acknowledged.

"Roth is a marksman much like you," the colonel offered. "I recruited him to join our regiment two years ago. Lord Faladen selected him for a special project recently implemented in Portsmouth. Quite ingenious."

Jonathan schooled his features so as not to reveal his shock. Faladen hadn't said a word about a new project ready to start in Portsmouth the last time he'd called upon him. "Special project?"

Colonel Peterson nodded vigorously. "School to develop the raw talent that only England can produce. Take the men who are gifted at shooting much like yourself and train them to be the best shots in all of Europe." The colonel rocked back on his heels.

Those were the exact words he'd shared with Faladen. Jonathan squeezed his cane until his hand was throbbing. "Indeed? Was my name mentioned?" He wanted to roar at the injustice of it all. It was inconceivable that Faladen had stolen his idea and claimed the credit for himself. If he wasn't getting married, he'd returned to Portsmouth immediately and confront the marquess.

"It was. We discussed putting you in charge." Clearly uncomfortable, the colonel stared at the ground. "Lord Faladen thought a younger man would be a better fit for the position."

"If only I had half the talent you did, sir." The young lieutenant had the good manners to look embarrassed.

Jonathan narrowed his eyes at how Lieutenant Roth referred to his talent in the past tense. The fact that Jonathan still practiced every day ensured his skills were as sharp as they were when he was seventeen. "It's not only talent, but awareness of your surroundings with the ability to adjust to any new situation accordingly."

"I quite agree," Roth said earnestly. "I couldn't have said it better myself."

"We won't take up any more of your time," the colonel announced.

Hasty goodbyes were exchanged, and the crowd dispersed, leaving Jonathan with the eerie feeling that the colonel pitied him. What he heard next as the men walked away confirmed it.

"Faladen was adamant that Sykeston not receive the command. Said Sykeston can't physically demonstrate the way to approach an enemy without detection. He can't hide in a crowd or climb a tree," the colonel murmured to Lieutenant Roth.

Jonathan straightened his gloves as a way of deflecting the slight he'd overheard.

"Bloody bastards," his footman cursed under his breath.

Jonathan had been proud of his military service. He'd been good at it. He had little doubt he'd have been successful at teaching men how to shoot and survive on the battlefield. This was what he despised: being thought of as less of a man because of his leg.

Immediately, a sneer pulled across his mouth. Even without the innuendo of misconduct, his superiors thought him weak and unable to contribute to the cause even though he'd been the best marksman the military had ever seen. His cheeks burned with a fire straight from hell as his stomach roiled. If he'd had a sword hidden in his cane, he'd very likely have run the colonel through. That would have definitely earned him a court-martial.

"Come, my lord. I'll help you to the carriage." Arkwright wrapped a hand around his arm.

Jonathan immediately shook him off. "I'll do it on my own," he growled.

Chapter Four

With the help of Aunt Vee, Constance had donned her most elegant morning gown, a vibrant turquoise silk that she'd had altered for ease after giving birth. She washed her face, then combed the rat's nest of her hair and twisted it into an acceptable chignon. Such simple actions had exhausted her, and she settled into the chair her bridegroom had occupied only yesterday.

"How do I look?" Constance tucked a couple of loose hairs into her hastily arranged coiffure.

"Marginal." Aunt Vee's critical gaze wandered over her face. "You're flushed." She peered closer. "Fever?"

Constance ducked her head. "Nervous."

Aunt Vee nodded. "Well, I'll say this isn't the most romantic of weddings, but it'll have to do." She picked up a small bouquet of flowers tied together with ribbon from a drum-shaped side table. "Here's a little something for you to hold during the ceremony."

Constance took the bouquet and inhaled deeply. "Roses, my favorite."

"Randford brought them." Aunt Vee pulled something out of her pocket. "I brought this for your left shoe."

"What is it? A sixpence?"

With a look of solemnity, Aunt Vee nodded. "I wore it when I married your uncle Albert. It'll ensure luck and prosperity in your marriage."

Her heart swelled at the kind gesture. Only dear Aunt Vee remembered such details.

Her aunt leaned closer to Constance and winked. "And happiness in the bedroom."

"Aunt Vee . . ." Thankfully, before she could say more, a knock sounded.

Aunt Vee answered the door, then cooed softly. "Look who's here making a grand entrance." She took the baby from Dahlia Fitzgerald, the nursemaid Constance had hired two weeks ago, and kissed the baby's cheek. After a rock or two in her arms, Aunt Vee brought her to Constance.

Dahlia followed. "Begging your pardon, ma'am, but I think Miss Aurelia needs her mum."

Constance carefully held the warm bundle close to her body. The urge to protect and nurture this little human came from a place so deep inside her that she couldn't think about her upcoming marriage to Jonathan at the present. Her beautiful child would be loved and cared for like no other.

It was a welcome addition to the priorities in her life. It went without saying that she was always busy. The house, her company, and sometimes even Aunt Vee needed her to manage their day-to-day affairs, but Constance would do anything for this precious baby. Just as she'd done over the last four weeks when the midwife had commanded Constance stay in bed until she was born.

Aunt Vee peeked over and brushed an arthritic knuckle over the baby girl's cheek. "She's a natural at feeding, like you were."

"She likes me well enough, doesn't she?" A swell of emotion rolled through Constance. Love, hope, tears, and a prayer for her baby's future combined into a flurry of emotion. After a while, Aurelia nestled against Constance signaling her hunger had been satisfied.

"She loves you," Aunt Vee said softly as Constance patted her daughter's back. "I love you too."

"And I you," Constance said, ignoring the joyful tears that fell. She bent her head close and pressed a gentle kiss against her baby's forehead. "I love you, Aurelia. Now and forever." She handed Aurelia to Aunt Vee then put herself to rights before she took her daughter back into her arms.

Another knock sounded, and Dahlia answered the door. "My lady, it's Lord Sykeston."

"Come in," Constance said. When their gazes met, his eyes widened.

"What's happened?" The silkiness of his voice had sharpened in alarm. "Is the baby . . . ?"

"She's fine," Constance reassured him. "I'm a little overwhelmed at the moment." That was putting it mildly. The amount of responsibility she held in her arms was—frankly—more than daunting at the moment.

Not to mention that she'd agreed to marry the man who now stood inside her bedroom with a look that could only be described as panic. Perhaps it was the same trepidation that she felt at the upcoming nuptials.

"Constance, might I talk to you privately?" The earl's voice deepened, signaling to everyone that he'd brook no arguments to the contrary.

"Of course." She turned to Dahlia. "I'll bring Aurelia to you."

"Oh, dear," Aunt Vee whispered for Constance's ears only. "He's a man who takes charge. If he wasn't your bridegroom, I might swoon in his arms." She lowered her voice even more. "A solid choice for a husband this time around, my dear. That man"—she wrinkled her nose and shimmied her shoulders in approval—"means business. Always an attractive and desirable trait in the male species. My Albert had it.

Now, your earl? He'll be a tiger in the bedroom. You are a lucky woman, dearest." With another discreet wink, Aunt Vee escorted Dahlia out of the room before Constance could reply.

As soon as the room was empty, Jonathan walked to her side. "Why are you crying? Did you change your mind about marrying me?"

She squeezed her eyes together, determined to present a semblance of calm. She shook her head once, then forced her gaze to meet his. Everything would be all right. She would ensure it.

"Just a little overcome. It's nothing." She smiled at her daughter, then turned her attention to Jonathan. "Would you like to meet Aurelia?" Constance adjusted the baby's position in her arms so he could see her daughter's face.

He crept a smidge closer.

She pushed the blanket away from Aurelia's cheeks so he could have a better look.

His eyes brightened, then he cleared his throat, making the baby jump slightly in her arms.

Instinctively, she tightened her arms around Aurelia, letting her know all was well.

"Your aunt said she looked like your late husband. I disagree. Aurelia takes after you." His gaze captured hers. "She's beautiful, Constance." The gruffness in his voice betrayed his unease. He carefully took a step back, then reached for the baby's hand.

The tender sight of his large forefinger brushing Aurelia's fingers nearly ripped a hole in Constance's heart.

It was her most fervent wish that Jonathan would be there for Aurelia so she'd know the loving touch of a father's finger brushing away the tears when she skinned her knee. She'd feel the comfort of a father's arms when she lost a beloved pet. He'd be her defender and knight errant when a boy broke her heart.

Jonathan's features softened as he smiled at the baby. "I have no experience, but I'm certain it must be natural to feel such a whirlwind of emotions after giving birth and tending to a newborn." He stared at Aurelia for a moment or two longer before he turned his attention to Constance. "You will never have to face this task alone. I'll make certain you have a cadre of the most loving and qualified servants to help you care for your daughter."

The words were on the tip of her tongue to ask if he would love and care for her daughter and stand by Constance's side as Aurelia grew. She wanted him to promise that he'd never leave them as Meriwether had. Those were her pressing needs. "Thank you. I'll only need a nursemaid. I've hired one to take with me to Portsmouth."

He glanced down at the baby again. "Do they all do that?"

By now, Aurelia was sound asleep.

"I have no idea," Constance confided softly. "But I think it's normal."

Jonathan took a finger and brushed it across the baby's cheek.

"Do you want to hold her?" Constance asked.

A look of horror crossed his face. "I don't know how."

"I could teach you."

"No," he said tersely in a low voice careful not to wake the baby. "Constance, there is unfinished business between us. You should stay here in London until I call for you. It shouldn't be a hardship as you're planning to stay here for several months anyway."

"Why? Are you being called back into service?" She searched his resolute face for some sign of regret. The sunlight slid down his black locks, casting a bluish tint to his hair.

The color reminded her of a crow's feathers, an omen for change.

"No. I have work to complete before you come to Portsmouth."

"What kind of work?" She was careful not to change her expression, but the air stilled at the importance of the moment. She didn't take her gaze away from his. When her first husband, Meri, as he liked to be called, had left, he hadn't taken her with him either. Not only that, but he left her without a word of when he'd come back. She'd not go through that heartache, not to mention embarrassment, again.

"I'm developing a project for the army, and there's been a complication. I have to get things in order before I send for you." He ran his fingers through his hair. "It wouldn't be right otherwise to have you and Aurelia come to Sykeston Gardens. You should stay here where you have friends. I've had my solicitor prepare the arrangements. The house in London is ready for your arrival. All expenses are paid by me. I've provided you a personal allowance. Spend it on what you want. If you need more, just write my solicitor."

She blinked once. It wasn't fair to compare Jonathan to Meri. Her first husband had done nothing to see that she was provided for. Nor did he tell her where he was or what he was doing. She couldn't even tell him she was carrying. She inhaled slowly. Meri had taken all her money while Jonathan was giving her funds and a house to live in.

More important, he promised to send for her. She had to remember this was Jonathan.

Her Jonathan.

Finally, she came out of her stupor. "Is there anything I can do to help with your work?"

He shook his head. "No, thank you. Take your time and concentrate on Aurelia and yourself. I should go see if the vicar is ready. After the ceremony, I'll return to Portsmouth straightaway."

"You've just arrived. Can't you stay for a day or two?" Constance didn't care that she was practically pleading.

"I wish I could . . . but I can't." His gaze held hers. For a moment, he seemed to be reconsidering his decision.

She shouldn't be hurt by his words. What could she expect? Here she stood with another man's baby in her arms, and her husband-to-be, a man she had begged to drop everything and marry her, was offering all the support he could summon under the circumstances. What other man would be by her side offering such a commitment?

No one except for Jonathan. She trusted him.

"All right," she whispered.

"Do you still want to marry?" he asked.

She nodded.

"Who would you like to have as the witnesses?" He rested both hands on the silver handle of his cane as he studied the floor. "Your aunt and who else?"

"Is Mr. North with you?"

"He arrived with the vicar," Jonathan replied.

She rocked Aurelia gently in her arms. "He should be your witness."

"Why?" he asked.

"He's been with you for years . . . it will be like we have our own family here witnessing our troth to each other." She let the words trail away as she considered the ramifications. She refused to look away and held his gaze.

His eyes seemed to lighten and darken much like waves bashing against the shore. "I agree." He pulled away, and she wanted to protest. Then a slight grin tugged at the corner of his lips. The endearing look reminded her of a conquering hero.

For the first time in a long time, she had an inkling of hope that someone would stand beside her, and they'd face all of life's challenges together. At that moment, she'd give him everything and anything including all the vulnerability she'd felt since her first husband had left her pregnant and alone to fend for herself.

Constance searched his face. She wanted to believe he was still the same Jonathan who had promised her in their youth that he'd be her champion when things grew dire. She had to believe, or otherwise all was for naught.

"Let's marry," she said softly.

He nodded once decisively. "I'll see you both downstairs." A wistful smile tugged at one corner of his mouth. "She's beautiful, and lucky to have you as her mother." Without waiting for her reply, Jonathan stoically walked out the door, his gait uneven but strong.

One lone tear cascaded down her cheek as she gazed at her daughter.

"Did I do the right thing?" she whispered. The baby nestled a little closer in answer.

Constance looked at the door and sighed.

"We'll have to wait and see what happens in Portsmouth." Still holding Aurelia, Constance slipped the sixpence into her left shoe and whispered, "For all our sakes, this better work, love."

Chapter Five

Jonathan was actually going to do *it*. He blew out a breath. Next to him stood Constance only an inch away. He slid a sideways glance in her direction. The turquoise silk gown she wore fell in graceful folds. She was extraordinarily beautiful today, and he hadn't said a word. He was the definition of a cad.

"You look . . ." He'd been so out of practice that he couldn't even spit out a compliment.

Constance turned toward him, the ghost of a smile on her lips.

"You look . . . exquisite."

"So do you." She winked.

Before he could respond, the vicar began the ceremony.

"Does anyone have good reason to object to this couple joining together in holy matrimony?" The vicar cleared his throat and made the customary glance around the attendees.

Jonathan did the same. He was expecting pure pandemonium to explode throughout the room. Constance's aunt's stoic features met his, but she nodded her agreement to Jonathan. He bowed his head in answer.

Randford and his duchess wore matching expressions of happiness. It felt unerringly right to have them here.

Jonathan's butler, Mr. Thaddeus North, stood beside him with an expression reminiscent of a bloated puffer fish ready to explode from pure bliss. On the way to London, he'd confided that he'd been waiting for Jonathan's wedding day for years.

So had Jonathan a lifetime ago. Frankly, after returning from the war, he'd thought it'd take a miracle to get him to the altar.

The so-called miracle was currently screaming her little head off.

Aurelia decided it was the perfect opportunity to bawl at such a pitch that everyone shrank at the little one's distress. Constance turned to the sound and nodded. Immediately, the nursemaid carried the baby from the room. After a moment, things quieted down, yet the irony didn't escape Jonathan's notice.

The baby, who was not even two days old and couldn't form a word, had objected in her own way.

Was it any wonder Jonathan considered her to be the most astute person in the room? While Randford and his duchess smiled like fools, the truth unfurled around Jonathan. This was a disaster waiting to unfold.

While the vicar droned on about loving, honoring, and cherishing each other, the tender touch from Constance's hand in his caused Jonathan's heart to pound. It was all he could concentrate on as he repeated their vows. He grasped the top of his cane with his left hand as his own brow grew damp. Constance leaned against him as if fatigued. Though his right leg had throbbed from standing so long, he bore her weight without complaint.

His fingers shook as he placed the ring on her finger.

Soon thereafter, the vicar proclaimed, "I now pronounce you man and wife."

Constance turned to him and squeezed his hand.

As cheers rang out from everyone in attendance, he stood there frozen like a block of freshly cut ice. He couldn't even bring himself to kiss Constance, so she took matters into her own hands. She stood on her tiptoes, and he held her arms to keep her steady. When she pressed her lips against his, everything faded in view except their kiss. The touch reminded him of home, a place from long ago where he'd always been happy and joyfully welcomed.

The moment was destroyed when her aunt came forward to congratulate them. Jonathan took advantage of her enthusiasm and created distance between him and his wife.

Merely thinking the words *his wife* sounded foreign, a language he couldn't understand.

"My lord?" The vicar stood beside him. "You and your bride must sign the register."

He took Constance by the arm and led her to the table where the book lay open ready for their signatures. As the others continued to converse around them, they completed the task.

"I should be leaving," he said softly.

Her brow creased, then she smiled tentatively. "I'll write to you."

"I'd like that." He couldn't take his eyes off her. "Now concentrate on you and Aurelia."

"I will." She faced him. "Take care."

He nodded.

"I'll miss you."

At the words, he paused. Only she could say those words and twist his heart into one of her nautical knots. Without a word, he pressed a kiss to her forehead.

He said his farewells to the others. As soon as he left the room, he found a secluded corner under a staircase at the opposite end of the house. He ducked under the steps and leaned against the wall, his breath heavy as if he'd run across a field to escape the enemy.

At least that's what it felt like. But there was a monumental difference.

When he'd been fighting, he'd never run from anything. If anything, the French ran from him.

That had been the talent and expertise he'd brought with him when he fought the French. He'd been a deadly weapon, one that could infiltrate encampments with a stealth similar to the plague. A known enemy that one couldn't see until it was too late.

For the love of God, he'd done his duty and carried out his superiors' orders all the while praying the days would pass quickly so he could come home. When he arrived in England and limped off the ship, only North waited for him as per Jonathan's request. He didn't want a hero's welcome for fear a court-martial was in his future. How could he be a hero if they thought him a traitor?

Today he felt like the epitome of a weak and scared man, which meant he was destined to be a failure at the only thing that mattered—family.

His wife was a stellar example of how to care for loved ones. The exact opposite of him. He was running away from her within the hour of saying "I do." Today his darkness receded a bit, but the urge to confront Faladen brought it all back, crashing like a rogue wave against a chalk cliff.

If he was found guilty, he had nothing to give Constance and her daughter except a man mentally and physically broken.

As promised within the hour, Jonathan had arrived at his London home, Sykeston House. He gave explicit instructions to his footmen George Riley and Fred Loring to prepare for the return trip. When he was a younger man, he had loved his house in the city. But now, navigating four staircases was a nightmare. At least in Portsmouth, he only had to manage one.

He poured himself a brandy and gingerly sat in his favorite study chair, the one his father had always preferred. Jonathan had loved him, and his father had loved him in return. All Jonathan had wanted in life was to be like him.

He released a slow exhale. It was impossible now as he was unwilling to perform the simplest of duties, like calls on his tenants, neighbors, and acquaintances. What was the use? Faladen had ordered that until he was cleared, he keep a low profile. Even his friends Randford and Julian Raleah, the Marquess of Grayson, didn't know what he was facing.

But if he was honest with himself, the stairs weren't the only reason he didn't tarry in the city. It was Constance. Now that he'd married her, he didn't want to let her go. He swallowed the tightness that lingered in his throat. He had other things he needed to concentrate on, namely the Marquess of Faladen.

"My lord?" George peeked his head inside the ground floor study. "The carriage is prepared. Whenever you're ready, we can depart."

He nodded, then carefully walked to the entry. He said his goodbyes to the few servants on staff and asked them to take care of Constance and her daughter. After taking his leave, he carefully climbed into the forward-facing seat. Thomas Winstead, who'd accompanied them to London, had taken a horse to see his family outside of London. So, it was just Jonathan and North.

"When will Lady Sykeston come home?" North asked while blinking slowly.

"Soon," he answered.

North looked out the window capturing the last views of London. "Her aunt said she'd have to convalesce for several months. That'll give the staff time to get the house in order."

"Hmm," he answered. He didn't want to think about his

wife or her soft, sweet lips. He'd much rather think about pistol cartridges.

Perhaps he should consider silver as a suitable cartridge casing. Though expensive, it was malleable. However, it might tear if too thin. He'd been working on the idea since he'd returned home. The successful design of the cartridge required the proper amount of powder and a ball wrapped in a thin sheet of metal. If he was successful, it'd eliminate the need for a flint strike outside the gun to combust the powder. The French had used paper cartridges, which were highly unstable in humid weather and rain. Just as a flintlock weapon was.

While in London, Jonathan had taken his latest design to Joseph Manton, the famous gunsmith, who'd tested it. It was an epic failure. There wasn't enough powder in the cartridge. His design and everything he'd worked for over the last year had seemed to collapse into nothing. His ideas on how to teach the men survival skills and honing their shooting abilities were completely gone. It was as if he and his ideas had been erased.

He leaned back against the squab as his mind revolted and exhaustion set in.

He rubbed his chest again. A vision of Constance permeated his thoughts. He had a wife now. He'd kept his promise to her when she asked him to marry her. He'd done his duty. She and Aurelia would want for nothing.

"You are going to summon her?" North nudged a white brow upward.

"When it's time." What the hell was he going to do with a wife? He had too many other things that demanded his attention.

Two days later, Jonathan stood outside the manse of Harold Evert, the Marquess of Faladen.

He was determined not to go down without a fight.

Faladen had been his lieutenant colonel, the man who sent him on his assignments and to whom he ultimately reported. A superior he'd once respected. Any advice he'd received from the marquess, he'd accepted without question.

After being ushered in by two footmen, Jonathan carefully sat in front of the marquess's desk. His palms were sweaty. Funny that he never experienced such a sensation when he was holding a pistol.

The marquess made a grand entrance, strolling in as if nothing were amiss. "Sykeston."

Without acknowledging the greeting, Jonathan waited until Faladen was seated behind his desk. "I saw Peterson and Roth in London two days ago."

"How are they?" Faladen feigned a smile.

Jonathan ignored the question. "They intimated that you took my idea for a special class of recruits and claimed it as your own."

The accusation hung in the air. Faladen lifted a brow in challenge. "I wouldn't call it that."

"What would you call it?" Remarkably, he kept his tone civil. "I sat in this very chair and shared everything with you. I spent close to a year developing that project, examining every detail, and reexamining them." He ran a hand over his injured leg. "I even had a special practice area built on my property."

"In all fairness, you sat in that very seat and asked for my advice," Faladen volleyed with a lifted eyebrow. "My ideas are clearly imprinted in the plan."

Jonathan gnashed his teeth so hard that his jaw hurt. "You duplicitous, Janus-faced, snively bastard. I developed the curriculum and even suggested which recruits to mentor, including Roth."

"If I didn't know you better, I'd think you jealous." Faladen thrummed his fingers in an annoying pattern. "I took those under advisement but developed my own criteria. Besides, you have other matters that should concern you."

Jonathan's nostrils flared as he forced himself not to lunge across the desk and grab the man by the lapels. He was tired of the false claims that hung over his head. "You know I'm innocent of any accusations that I behaved dishonorably on the field. Do you really want to spout such nonsensical claims? With my reputation?"

Jonathan waited a moment and let the question stay suspended in the air. Fear could easily be recognized if one had seen it enough. Whether it was from his fellow soldiers or by watching the enemy attack then retreat. A man's face would pale, and sweat would bead on his brow. Faladen was scared. For he knew who would win if honor required that Jonathan call the man out.

"You don't want to do that." Faladen cleared his throat. "You'd be ruined once people found out you challenged me, your superior officer."

"*Former* superior officer."

"That's your interpretation," Faladen said distractedly.

"If people knew the circumstances, they would side with me. Write to Peterson and tell him where you stole the idea, then apologize. Give up all rights to it."

"No." Faladen stared at him.

"You know my reputation. I never miss. I've challenged others to a duel and never flinched." Deliberate and focused, Jonathan leaned back in his chair.

"There's evidence of desertion," Faladen said matter-of-factly.

"I've never run from anything," he growled.

Faladen raised a haughty brow. "You told me that on your last assignment, you turned tail. As soon as you found the target, Jean Davout, you retreated."

His heartbeat stood suspended in his chest at the words. "He wasn't armed." Like the strike of a flint, Jonathan's anger ignited. "You would turn my own words against me?"

Faladen didn't flinch. "If I have to. I have a letter from Davout himself stating as soon as you saw him, you ran."

"That's a lie." Jonathan slowly stood. "I told you everything."

He'd never forget that day. The skies stormed with no relief. As the rain pelted his face and body, Jonathan had wound his way through a copse of trees to find his target. As was his custom, he never shot unless his target had seen him and was armed. A sudden flash of lightning and the pounding of thunder caused Davout to look out his tent in Jonathan's direction. The whites of the French officer's eyes were visible from thirty feet away. He'd been in shock that Jonathan stood before him. In the act of shaving, he dropped his hand still holding the razor, as if waiting for the inevitable. Jonathan had slowly exhaled, then nodded in acknowledgment that the man was unarmed. He had called out "until we meet again" in perfect French. Davout had exclaimed, *"Merci."* Then Jonathan had walked away. His honor as a gentleman dictated such action. As did the English military's code of conduct.

He'd reported back to Faladen that night. Within a week, there were bits and pieces of rumors, rumblings really, that a deserter was in their midst. Terms such as *dereliction of duty* and *traitor* were bandied about. Jonathan had ignored them. After he'd been injured and had healed enough to return home, Faladen had summoned him.

Short and to the point, Faladen had said the rumors were about Jonathan. That was the reason he'd been sent home and placed on half-pay.

As he'd sat there numb, Faladen had stated that there were no formal letters of complaint or charging orders . . .

yet. But since the rumors had grown, he'd been the one to order Jonathan to limit his social interactions as a safety precaution and not tell a soul about the situation.

Now he was threatening Jonathan.

Faladen rested his elbows on his desk and leaned forward. "Sykeston, you were once the best shot in all of England. But we both know that your leg has completely destroyed you. For God's sake, you can't do anything a normal man can. Riding and dancing to name a few." He shook his head and lowered his voice. "You can't walk. I bet you can't even take a woman to bed."

Jonathan didn't move, but the intense scrutiny of Faladen's gaze unnerved him. He hadn't been with a woman in years. He'd told himself it was lack of interest. Truthfully, he'd not subject any woman to his garish scars, nor would he subject himself to the certain humiliation when they discovered the deep wounds on his leg where flesh was missing.

A sickly, totally unsolicitous smile fell across Faladen's face. "I hate to be cruel but you realize your physical limitations. You fell last week getting out of your carriage. All of Portsmouth saw it. You're a broken shell of what you once were."

Jonathan flinched slightly.

"You know that. I know that. The military knows that." On the offensive, the marquess rounded his desk and towered over Jonathan. Faladen was so close that Jonathan could smell the brandy on his breath. "How could you teach evasive moves? How could you demonstrate military exercises? They require stealth and cunning. Unfortunately, people can hear you coming from a mile away." Faladen narrowed his eyes. "Thump, thump. Thump, thump."

Jonathan swallowed the indignity that rose like bile in his throat. What Faladen said was true. He couldn't do any of those things. With each example of his lack of physical prowess, Jonathan's soul shrank inch by inch. His confidence eroded until he refused to take anymore. He might be less of a man, but he'd see this through. Jonathan forced himself to look at the marquess.

"Forget the marksman training. It's mine." The marquess smiled grimly. "In return, once a charging order appears, I'll find a way to 'hide it in my desk.' It'll disappear. If you cause a ruckus, you'll face a court-martial."

"You're blackmailing me?"

"How can it be something that unseemly if my reason for keeping the charging orders quiet is that you've suffered enough." The marquess smiled benevolently. "Just leave well enough alone and forget the new recruits."

"I . . . I . . ." His voice weakened, and the ability to rebut Faladen's words vanished.

The marquess feigned a look of contriteness. "You were masterful all those years when you served. No one could out-think, outmaneuver, or outshoot the enemy like you. Go home and stay there. You don't want all those years of service to be tarnished by a dishonorable court-martial. Imagine never being able to take your seat in the House of Lords. Imagine everyone turning their back with a cut direct when they see you out in society. If you tell Peterson I stole your idea, then I'll bring the charges myself. I have the evidence of Davout's letter and my own testimony. Take my advice. Rest on your laurels. That's all you have now." Faladen nodded in dismissal. "I have work."

A pair of footmen approached to escort him from the room. Too anesthetized to respond, Jonathan stood and began to walk away. The thump of his gait eerily sounded like Faladen's description.

Then the unthinkable happened. His foot caught on the carpet, and he tripped. His bad leg gave out, making it impossible to catch himself. When he crashed to the ground, he clenched his teeth to keep from crying out in pain.

Heat licked his cheeks as the footmen helped him to his feet. Neither would look his way.

"You proved my point," Faladen announced.

Jonathan straightened his coat. With the last scrap of dignity he could summon, he took a step forward. Pure agony shot through his leg, causing his hip to hitch. Nausea came from nowhere, and Jonathan closed his eyes praying that he could make it out the manse without humiliating himself again.

Once he was safely in his carriage, he stole one last glance at Faladen's home. Then and there, he vowed never, ever to subject himself to such shame again—even if it meant he never left his house for the next fifty years.

Chapter Six

One year later
London

Next to Constance, Katherine Vareck, the Duchess of Randford, sat on the azure and crème striped sofa in the formal sitting room of her London home. With the dark pink gown she wore, she looked stunning and ethereally beautiful. She could have easily been mistaken for one of Thomas Gainsborough's famous subjects in his works of art. Kat, as she liked to be called, had been Meriwether's so-called first wife, but more important, she was one of Constance's best friends.

Sitting across from them on the matching sofa was Constance's other best friend, Miss Beth Howell. When they'd walked into the solicitor's office that day for the reading of Meriwether's will, they'd discovered they'd married the same man. They were understandably shocked, mortified, and left wondering why and how this could have happened. Kat took them under her wing and brought them to her house, where they banded together. As they discussed their reasons for marriage, it became clear they had all wanted the illusion that Meri had offered. Kat had wanted respectability. Beth had wanted freedom, and Constance had wanted a partner.

Constance would be forever grateful to the two of them.

After she'd arrived at Kat's house, she'd found herself confined to her bed for a month before Aurelia's birth. She was the only one he'd left pregnant. Thankfully, Kat and Beth had unselfishly taken care of her.

It was a true testament to their friendship that there was no jealousy or animosity. They all realized they were left in an untenable situation. The only way to survive the scandal was to rely on one another.

Calling them her best friends wasn't quite the truth, as Constance considered them her sisters. Besides Aurelia, it was another good thing that came from her marriage to Meriwether. The trio saw one another regularly.

The duchess had propped the new Marquess of Belton over her shoulder and gently patted his back. Two months old, Christian James Arthur Vareck, the Duke of Randford's heir, was a cheerful boy and a big eater.

"Last night, Randford was bringing Arthur to me for a nightly feed. Guess who he found half dressed in the hallway coming out of Willa's room?" A sly smile spread across Kat's face. "My darling Willa is sweet on someone."

"Tell us," Beth encouraged.

"My husband's valet," Kat said with a look like a kitten who'd licked the bottom of a bowl of cream.

"Your *Willa* who practically raised you? Willa and Jacob Morgan?" Constance exclaimed.

Kat nodded.

"What's the age difference between them? Not that it matters," Beth added.

"Willa is less than fifteen years older," Kat said with a satisfied grin.

"I'd say they're perfect for each other," Constance announced.

Kat nodded in agreement. "They've become inseparable. Besides the fact they work well together. I always wanted my Willa happy, and now she is." She turned her attention to Beth, then grew somber. "Share with Constance how your brother is occupying his time," she said softly.

A lady through and through, Beth carefully set aside her embroidery and clasped her hands in her lap. "St. John wants me to marry a seventy-eight-year-old peer. My brother is desperate for cash, and the Marquess of Siddleton needs an heir. A perfect match, wouldn't you say?" Her eyes flashed fire as the ire in her voice made her voice tremble slightly.

Constance's hand flew to her mouth. "Can he make you do that?"

Beth shook her head, upsetting a delicate curl. "No. But he's threatened to cut me off financially if I don't marry as he wants. I need to find my missing dowry. If I had that, then I could wash my hands of my brother and live my life as I want."

Constance looked to Kat, who nodded in agreement.

"Remember the money Randford paid Beth to replace her missing dowry?" Kat took Beth's hand in hers.

"Yes," Constance said.

"I did something foolish. I felt sorry for St. John and told him that we could split the amount. He took it all. I should have never . . . trusted him." Beth let her words trail to silence.

Constance leaned forward. She hated that her friend was in such a muddle. "I can loan you money."

Kat nodded. "I want to help."

Beth shook her head so hard that another curl fell from its pinned moorings. "You both have done enough. I'm going to Cumberland and see if I can find the dowry."

Constance's eyes widened. "How are you going to do that?"

Beth shrugged. "I don't know yet. Maybe I'll ask Grayson to accompany me. I'll split whatever I find with him."

"Do you trust the marquess?" Constance asked.

"I think so," Beth answered, and her face softened. "Plus, he's in much the same financial position as me. No money. We're the perfect pair to find my missing dowry."

"If you're discovered with him, your reputation will be in tatters," Constance pointed out.

"It already is," Beth argued softly.

How well she knew that conundrum. Rumors had circulated throughout London and even Portsmouth about her marriage to Meriwether and now her marriage to the elusive Earl of Sykeston. Some thought she'd created the story to save her reputation. When Jonathan hadn't written after a month of marriage, Constance couldn't help but wonder if he'd left her in the same manner Meri had. It was as if he'd disappeared from the face of the earth.

But then he'd started to correspond, proving his interest in her and their marriage.

"Let me help," Constance offered. "I still have Meri's receipts that he gave us after his death. I want to take another look, then I'll send them to you. If there's a way, we'll find out what happened to your money."

"I'd appreciate it," Beth said.

Kat rubbed a hand up and down the marquess's small back. "I didn't realize how demanding babies were," Kat sighed when the "bwaap" sound softly erupted from her young son. "But you're a good baby, aren't you?" she softly cooed.

Constance sat next to Kat and leaned close to rub her hand down the baby's back. "He's truly a dear. Imagine that he's only getting up once or twice a night. Not like my Aurelia. For the first six months, that child demanded feedings four times a night."

Kat chuckled as her son fell asleep in her arms. "You are a fine specimen of a man who wants nothing more than to sleep and eat all day."

"I'd say he's a typical male." Constance ran a finger across the baby's soft cheek. "Be thankful that he's not able to crawl yet. You'll be exhausted constantly."

"I wished you lived with Kat or me instead of that pile of

stones you call Sykeston House. I'd love to help with Aurelia." Beth's brow furrowed into neat lines. "It's been difficult raising her by yourself."

"Sykeston House is beautiful," Constance said in defense. "It hasn't been *that* difficult with Aurelia."

Beth lifted a brow. "Why don't I believe it?"

"I admit it's been an adjustment. Aunt Vee was a marvelous help that first month. But soon thereafter, she married her old friend Lund Bolen. She spends all her time in Portsmouth. I'm very happy for her." She fiddled with her teacup. "It's lovely when I see her. But don't fret. I have all the staff I need or could ever want at Sykeston House."

Kat hmphed softly. "Has Sykeston written lately?"

Constance's cheeks flamed at her friend's question. It always happened when they discussed Jonathan, a man she hadn't laid eyes on in a year. But in all fairness, he'd thought of her and was interested in her life. Something that Meri had never done. Over the past months, Jonathan had written to her weekly. He'd sent her a beautiful silk scarf and a silver rattle for Aurelia when they couldn't celebrate Christmas together. She'd eagerly answered every single one of his letters. He was ever so kind. He'd even sent her and Aurelia a perambulator. Constance kept the note in her most cherished possessions. *For when you and Aurelia need an escape. Spread your wings from everyday life.*

She couldn't help but smile. Though he wasn't by her side, Jonathan had proven his worth as a good, honorable man.

"Is he back in England?" Beth's gaze bored into hers.

The question knocked Constance out of her clouds. "Yes, and I have news. He's asked me to join him in Portsmouth at Sykeston Gardens."

Kat silently clapped her hands together. "Oh, I'm so happy for you, but sad at the same time. I'll miss having you here."

Her heart faltered in its beat. "You don't know how much

I'm going to miss you both." She reached across and took her friends' hands in hers. "If it hadn't been for both of you, I don't know what I would have done."

Kat waved a dismissive hand at her. "Constance, we don't know what we would have done without you over this last year. Having your guidance during my laying-in and your help with the linen business during the past several months has been a godsend."

"I'm thankful for the opportunity," Constance answered. Kat had started a successful linen business when she'd first moved to London. Recently, she'd been named a royal supplier to the Prince Regent. Constance had been delighted to help her and Beth. It's what family did for one another. "Working kept me busy, so I didn't dwell on Jonathan's covert work for the Crown."

Beth nodded her agreement. "I'm sure you're anxious to resume your presence at the dockyards."

Constance laughed. "Indeed. Mr. and Mrs. Bridges are becoming a little fatigued with coming here every month." She smiled at the thought of the Bridges. Mr. Bridges was her shipwright, and Mrs. Bridges kept the bookkeeping after Constance had left for London. But they'd made the trek every month to keep Constance informed about her business.

"What did your husband's letter say?" Beth scooted closer to Constance. "I hope he made it romantic."

Constance smiled and waggled her eyebrows. "He said that it is his greatest wish that I join him at Sykeston Gardens at my earliest convenience. He wants us to start our life together."

"And Aurelia?" Kat asked.

"He's anxious to welcome her into his home and be her father." She exaggerated that last part, but deep inside, her heart understood Jonathan's. He would love Aurelia as his own.

"I'm thankful he's finally accepting his responsibilities." Beth nodded her agreement.

Beth could be a little dismissive of men, and Constance understood her friend's opinion. Having a brother who tried to sell you to the highest bidder would have made Constance leery as well. But she couldn't allow Beth to make the wrong assumption about Jonathan. "Remember, he was performing important work for the Crown."

"Of course he was." Beth didn't hide her sarcasm.

Once more, the familiar feeling of being deserted rose, demanding attention. Discreetly, she fisted a hand at such nonsense. Jonathan had returned to England and had called for her. "My husband is a vital component of the Crown's efforts to keep us all safe."

Her friends blinked at her stalwart outburst.

She took a deep breath and waited for the inevitable discussion that would follow. Thankfully, it didn't.

Kat smiled in reassurance. "I believe you mentioned he was to interview the guards who watched Napoleon on Elba."

Constance released a shallow breath. "Yes. To ensure that such an escape never happened again."

Beth's head automatically dipped to study the floor.

Kat's kind but sympathetic visage unnerved her.

"What are you not telling me?" Her gaze darted between her two friends.

"Don't be angry with me," Kat pleaded. "I shared your story with Christian. Since Jonathan never answers his letters, Christian asked a friend in the War Office if your husband had returned to service. Christian's friend wouldn't confirm or deny it, but he did share that he couldn't recall anyone doing any type of investigative work about the event."

"Well, naturally," Constance said in defense. "He's not working for the War Office or the army. He's working secretively for the Crown. It wouldn't be confidential if the public knew about his clandestine work."

Kat stared straight at Constance for a moment, then nodded vigorously. "You're absolutely right, dearest." She lowered her voice. "I know that nothing would keep my husband from my side or our son's. I want that for you and Aurelia."

"He's a fine husband and father." Though she hadn't spoken a word to her husband in over a year, she was his biggest supporter. His impassioned rules for love were the ties that would always bind them together.

"Shall Christian and I come with you?" Kat asked. "It might be awkward for the two of you at the beginning."

"Nonsense." Constance squeezed her friend's hands in reassurance. "We'll be fine. Remember, we practically grew up together. As a matter of fact, I plan to send a letter tomorrow or the next day telling Jonathan we're on our way."

"At least, let Randford travel with you," Kat pleaded.

"Take a father away from his wife and newborn child?" Constance asked, then shook her head.

Kat smiled. "I'll worry otherwise."

"Don't, please." She took another sip of tea and sat it down. "My husband may not write to yours, but he writes to me." She smiled, then added, "Faithfully."

"I agree you mustn't tarry in London." Beth stood and walked to Constance's side. She placed her hand on her shoulder. "If you don't want Randford to accompany, I'll go with you."

"Beth," Constance scolded gently. "You're a partner with Kat in the linen business. You work."

This was her journey, and she'd do it herself. Beth was about to speak, but Constance held her hand up and turned to Kat. "Randford has been a blessing through all of this. Your husband could have walked away from all of us including Aurelia, but he didn't. I can't ask for more."

Kat tilted her head, and the dreamiest smile broke across her lips. "I'm so fortunate I married him."

Constance dipped her head and concentrated on the baby's

sleeping face. If anyone deserved such happiness, it was her friend Kat. It was proof that there were such happy things in life. She had little doubt that Beth would find her own peace and satisfaction with her life one day.

Such contentment to Constance meant a husband who loved her and her daughter. She took Arthur's tiny hand in hers. The simple act reminded her of when Jonathan had caressed Aurelia. He would welcome them with open arms.

She would send the letter of her imminent arrival at the same time she left for Portsmouth. She had little doubt he'd be waiting on pins and needles to see her.

Chapter Seven

Jonathan settled into the chair behind his massive Restoration-style desk made of walnut and oak. The walnut had been imported from France, and his great-great-grandfather had commissioned the ornate desk especially for this room. Every earl since had added some unique furniture piece to the room in commemoration of the first earl. The dark wood was softened by the use of marquetry, a way of incorporating colorful veneers into the wood. Normally, they were floral patterns, but on his desk, the images of cupids hugged every corner.

It was too ornate for Jonathan's tastes, but it mattered little. Before he left for the war, he had added a Restoration longcase clock to the décor that matched the furnishings. In hindsight, it had been a mistake. That damnable thing also had cupids frolicking in all their naked glory. When he glanced at the time, the mocking little cherubs smiled directly at him.

Every tick of the clock reminded him that at the age of twenty-eight he wasn't getting any younger. He leaned back and stared at the ceiling hoping for peace, but he'd settle for numbness.

Every now and again, he thought about family, but that would require he call his wife home. He'd been selfish in marrying her in the first place. But who would not want Constance? However, it didn't negate the simple truth that he was too damaged to deserve a family.

His name still wasn't cleared, and he hadn't seen Faladen since that fateful day. However, he'd sent letters to several envoys in France trying to find Jean Davout with no success. Every speck of honor he possessed hung by a thread. How could he prove his innocence if the charges saw the light of day?

With his demons, he'd driven out anything associated with such joy and hope. With his inability to find a way to fight for his honor, a gray shroud enveloped everything that he'd thought important before.

Including Constance.

He'd learned over the last year that life was so much easier if nothing was ever at risk. He'd become an expert at keeping his feelings and memories organized and separated much like the jar of spices in his cook's well-organized kitchen. If such sentimental foolishness was never opened and examined, you never had to taste disappointment. It was easier to keep life bland.

"Well, darling, what shall we do today?" He ran his fingers through the soft fur behind his dog's ears.

Regina, his one-year-old English mastiff, leaned against him in total admiration. Her warm brown eyes regarded him.

He rang for his footman. This time, she wagged her tail a little more forcefully and barked.

"Excellent idea, Reggie-girl. We shall shoot. Must keep our aim and mind sharp." He glanced at the French doors that lined the room's west walls. The stately elm trees in the courtyard outside caught his attention. The boughs blowing to and fro. "The breeze is up. It'll be difficult to hit the target with this wind speed. A much-needed distraction."

Arkwright purposely strode into the room. At this time of day, he was the only servant intrepid enough to answer Jonathan's call. All his other servants magically disappeared. Besides, Arkwright was a hulk of a man with a wide chest and large biceps. He could throw the small handmade disks of clay in the air for hours on end.

"My lord?" Arkwright bowed. "Shall I open the doors and gather the targets?"

"Yes. Thank you." Jonathan reached for his cane and stood.

"You'll be delighted with the targets today. I managed to make them almost blue with a mix of copper and cobalt. It'll be more difficult to see against the sky." The footman rocked back on his heels.

"You know what I like, Arkwright." The man was perfect for the position. He took pride that his duties included making target practice that much more difficult.

"Any progress on your cartridge?" the footman asked.

He sighed silently. "I need to create a new design."

"You'll discover something, sir. A little target practice will help clear your thoughts." Arkwright opened the French doors, then ran down the steps to the small folly that butted against a small pond attached to a stair-stepped fountain in the overgrown courtyard. That's where he kept the targets.

Jonathan picked up a burl-wood box. It contained five of his favorite Manton pistols, gunpowder, and a cleaning set for the firearms. With a surge of energy percolating through him, he carefully walked to the room's west side then sat in a massive chair upholstered in black velvet. It was big enough for both him and Regina to sit in together. He loved to shoot and smell the scent of burning gunpowder. His talent as a marksman made him feel as if he could still control something in his life. Only he decided when and where he'd shoot now.

"Are you ready, Regina?"

His dog sat beside him with a look of longing. A whimper escaped.

"Come on."

At his command, she jumped and sat beside him in the chair.

When he opened the box to retrieve the pistols, North, who had served his family for thirty-five years, came into the room with today's posts on a silver salver. "My lord, the mail has arrived."

"Put it on the desk," Jonathan answered.

"There's one from London." North's voice dropped to a low hum. "Lady Sykeston."

Naturally, North had caught Jonathan reading and rereading Constance's notes that she'd sent throughout the last year. Though he hadn't written her, she'd written him detailing her life in London and sharing news about Aurelia. Because of Jonathan's habit of reading the letters, North had made the mistaken assumption that Jonathan actually cared.

Damn the man for jumping to conclusions. Whenever a post from Constance arrived, North practically skipped in glee to deliver the missive to Jonathan.

Reluctantly, he took the letter and broke the simple wax seal. Her sweet scent wafted his way. She had perfumed the letter as if taunting him.

He scanned the parchment, then let it drop to his lap. Her elegant and beautiful penmanship was a perfect reminder of her person, but the words she'd written made his blood turn to slush. "Damme to Hades," he muttered.

"Sir? Is everything all right?"

"No, it's not all right," Jonathan growled when he wanted to roar. "North, she's bloody coming *here*."

Regina sensed the unease radiating from him and whined softly in empathy. Jonathan ran his hand over her forehead in comfort. He turned back to North. "Write a letter telling her no, and that she's not welcome. I'll sign it, then send Arkwright to intercept her carriage on the road before she arrives in Portsmouth. The sooner she returns to London, the better."

He looked out the window and clenched his fist in a poor effort to control of his emotions. It wasn't her fault per se, it was his for being a sentimental fool. She was beautiful and kind and everything he always thought he'd have in his life. But he'd discovered during all those years at war that he could manage quite sufficiently on his own. The last year had proved it.

North blinked his eyes slowly. "If I might, sir? Perhaps it would be in everyone's interests if she comes home. Besides, as a young girl, Miss Lysander was well known in the area as having a pleasant disposition and a clever mind. She'll provide you with company."

"It's Lady Sykeston now," he corrected as he loaded one pistol. "I don't want her here, and I don't want company."

"Yes, yes. I forgot. Lady Sykeston, then." North smiled. "I'm sure the staff would welcome your wife with pure delight. Mrs. Butler says Mrs. Bridges always speaks so highly of Lady Sykeston when they meet at the market."

"Well, that's wonderful to hear," he said sarcastically. "Need I remind you that the staff doesn't run this house. I do."

"Since when, sir?" North said innocently.

Jonathan delivered his best glare. North was goading him again. They both were aware that Jonathan stayed in his own world, his study. "You know what I mean."

"I have no idea what you mean"—the butler smiled as if wanting back into Jonathan's good graces—"my lord."

"I said no." Then Jonathan's gaze latched onto the movement of the leaves, calculating the wind speed. "Please, see that it's done."

Without another word, North bowed and left the room.

"Ready, sir?" Arkwright called from the courtyard while twirling a clay disk in his hand. A basketful sat at his feet.

Jonathan leaned back in the chair. He might look like an earl at ease, but his pulse pounded in readiness. Now more than ever, he needed to expend some of this reckless energy that came from Constance's audacity in coming here. Hadn't he made it clear by not answering her letters he didn't want to see her?

"On the count of three, if you please, Arkwright."

The footman nodded. "One . . . two . . ." Before reaching three, Arkwright hurled it into the air much like an ancient Greek athlete throwing a discus.

Anticipating when Arkwright would throw was part of the challenge, and Jonathan thrived on it. He took aim and waited for that hundredth of a second when the disk stood suspended motionless in the air, then he pulled the trigger.

It shattered into small pieces then fell to the earth.

"Throw," Jonathan commanded.

Again, Arkwright launched the disk into the air.

For a moment, Jonathan lost it in the shadow of a cloud meandering across the blue sky. Regina whimpered softly as if worried he'd not find it. Most men might suffer from a moment of anxiety at losing their target, but not him. He trained his eyes on the cloud. Swiftly, he located the disk and pulled the trigger.

But all the while, his heart tripped as if caught unbalanced. Why did she want to come here now?

Never again would he allow anyone, including Constance, to upset his perfectly crafted world.

It was his kingdom of void.

"Excellent shot, my lord," Arkwright called out.

The pattern repeated three more times. Arkwright would throw and Jonathan would fire. He only missed once.

"The dye certainly makes the disks hard to see. Excellent job, Arkwright. Let's do it again," Jonathan called out.

Clouds of smoke surrounded him, and the smoldering smell of burnt gunpowder filled the air.

By then Regina had returned to the upholstered black velvet sofa. She didn't mind the sound, but the smoke didn't agree with her. She stretched out where she could see him.

"Ahem," North called from the door. "My lord, I'm delighted to announce that your wife, Lady Sykeston, has arrived."

Chapter Eight

As best as he could manage, Jonathan bolted from the chair using his cane and faced the study door.

Constance glided into the room with her unique, brilliant smile. It reminded him of an unwanted ray of sunshine interrupting a perfect morning sleep. Neither knew when they weren't wanted.

The housekeeper, Mrs. Butler, followed Constance into the room with a smug *Aha! You've been caught* look on her face. Of course she'd be involved in this fiasco.

Though Mrs. Butler was an excellent housekeeper, Jonathan had given strict orders that his study and the gardens that were his private shooting gallery were not to be cleaned, pruned, or maintained. Servants weren't allowed in his private domain. Dawdlers and laggards along with unwanted guests were strictly forbidden. All his correspondence trying to track down Jean Davout was in his desk under lock and key. All of it gave him privacy and a sense of sanctuary.

Jonathan's perfidious gaze sought Constance's, and for an instant, he could have sworn that the cupid clock held time in place. Slowly, he cataloged the gentle sweep of her brows, the brilliant blue of her eyes, and the majestic mahogany color of her hair. Her eyes glistened like a finely cut leaded glass, and a smile graced her naturally pink lips.

He'd always thought her so beautiful, including after she'd given birth. But the woman who stood before him now was startlingly gorgeous. Such a vision almost hurt his eyes. Parts of him that he thought long dead started to stir and swell, namely that organ in his chest.

The damnable thing.

It made him forget his reasons for wanting to keep her away.

Her gaze volleyed between the closed drapes blocking the sun's path through the windows to his desk where her previous correspondence sat in a pile held together by a neatly tied ribbon. Her eyes ricocheted to the open French doors before finally landing on him again. She'd seen enough to know that he was a sentimental dupe who found comfort in her writings. Instantly, he felt naked as the day he was born, completely exposed.

Before he could think of something to say, her smile faltered slightly at the same time her perfect nose wrinkled. She brought a handkerchief to her nose.

"What is that unearthly smell?"

"It's gunpowder." Mrs. Butler's severe disapproval rang through the room.

"Lady Sykeston, his lordship takes target practice in this very room out the west doors," North offered. "They're the only access to the outside he allows open. All windows are shut." The solicitous hum in his voice reminded Jonathan of a teacher's pet currying favor by tattling on another.

"Careful, North," Jonathan murmured.

North didn't bat an eye at his words. "Target practice," he repeated. "Every. Single. Day." He cleared his throat. "Since he's been home."

"The maids are up in arms over the noise." Mrs. Butler nodded in agreement. "I have a hard time keeping a full staff."

"They receive a generous wage for their troubles," Jonathan argued. Why was he even trying to defend himself? He was in charge here—at least in his own study.

North hmphed quietly in revolt, but Constance ignored the sniping of both of them. With a cautious step forward, she kept the cloth over her mouth and nose.

Besides North, Arkwright, Winstead, and the occasional visits by Mrs. Butler, it was the first time anyone had dared breach the sanctity of his study. Everyone knew to stay out.

Except her.

Noticing Constance's movement, Regina regally jumped down off the coach. She was impossible to miss as the dog weighed a good eleven stone.

Constance stilled. Her eyes grew larger than full autumn moons as she watched Regina's every step. In the slowest of movements, she lowered the cloth from her face. "Who is this?"

Her voice full of wonder sent something new that prickled his skin like gunpowder sparks. His shook his head. He must be imagining it. However, he couldn't deny what he'd heard. She didn't ask *what is that?* or even *why is that creature allowed in the house?* Instead, the woman who had introduced him to the breed simply asked, "Who is this?" as if Regina were her equal.

"Regina," he answered.

North's and Mrs. Butler's gazes swiveled in tandem between the two of them.

"She's a beauty," Constance whispered. Her gaze never strayed from the dog.

Knowing they were talking about her, Regina came to her side and sat.

Constance knelt and burrowed her face into the mastiff's soft fur. "Regina," she said softly. "What a beautiful name for a majestic girl. It's lovely to meet you. We'll be fast friends." She stood with a grace that queens would envy. All the while, she continued to pet Regina as her gaze pivoted to Jonathan's. The intensity nailed him in his place. "How did you choose her name?"

"North named her." As soon as Constance turned her attention back to the dog, Jonathan looked to North. With his eyes, Jonathan pleaded with the butler to go along with the story.

The butler lifted an eyebrow in response. When Constance bent to pet the dog again, Jonathan mouthed, *I'll make it worth your while.*

Constance lifted her eyes to him but addressed the butler. "Mr. North, did you know that I had a mastiff named Reginald when I was younger?"

"No, I did not, my lady." The butler clasped his hands in front of him. "Nor did I name the dog."

Constance smiled at Jonathan, completely ignoring the butler's remarks. "Why didn't you make mention you had a dog? When you traveled, you could have sent Regina to me."

Heat assailed his face. First it was the bundle of letters; then, to add insult to injury, she understood the significance of the name. Why had he named his dog after her beloved pet?

His mind skidded to a halt. *Travel?* He stood motionless considering her words. "What did you say about travel?"

Out of the corner of his eye he saw North take a step back to hide behind Mrs. Butler.

Jonathan moved so he had a clear view, then tried to catch his butler's gaze. However, the sly, older gentleman directed his attention to every corner of the room, top to bottom.

"In your letters, you told me about your travels to France, Italy, and Elba." Constance ruffled Regina's ears. "Remember?"

Jonathan shook his head trying to make sense of what Constance was saying. "I didn't—"

"My lady, your luggage will be in your room shortly," North added abruptly.

Mrs. Butler nodded a little too eagerly. "I'll have your bags unpacked."

"Thank you," Constance said. She turned her attention to Regina. "I can't wait for Aurelia to meet you," she cooed, then bent down and pressed a kiss on top of the dog's head. "Darling girl."

Jonathan's heart raced at the honeyed words for his dog's ears. He had to find a way to get his wife out of his study and out of his life. It would help matters much if he would stop staring at the way she was bonding with his dog. Her hands slowly stroked the fur behind Regina's soft ears. In kind, Regina nuzzled against her.

The last few moments exposed the danger he faced. He wanted his wife's hands on him.

Then and there, Jonathan decided he needed her out of the house.

Chapter Nine

❦

Constance continued to stroke Regina's fur as she took her first real gander at Jonathan's person. His morning coat was incredibly wrinkled. She'd wager that he'd slept in it last night. His breeches suffered the same.

She couldn't help but stare at his legs. One was thick with muscles, taut and well defined. The other was slightly smaller, but his breeches hugged both legs in a remarkably appealing manner. To keep her thoughts in order, she breathed deep—only to cough on the stench of gunpowder. His hair was even longer than the last time she'd seen him. It dragged against his shoulders. The black strands hung loose and untended. He even sported a beard. Did the man not have a valet? He looked like a hermit who'd found his way out of the woods after being lost for a year.

He tilted his head in defiance at her close examination. She smiled slightly then glanced around the room. It looked like it hadn't been cleaned in months. Dust covered the majority of the tabletops. What windows were visible had streaks of soot marring a clear view. Pillows were scattered around the floor as if kicked off the sofa. A throw had been tossed to the floor as if he had been sleeping here. The disorder in the room was most disconcerting and frankly, almost as rumpled as her husband.

Constance stood and patted Regina on the head once more, then turned to Mrs. Butler. "After Lord Sykeston and I visit, perhaps we'll have an opportunity to chat?" She smiled at the housekeeper, who was practically beaming.

"Wonderful." Mrs. Butler clasped her hands together as if to give thanks for Constance's arrival. "You must be famished after your travels. I'll prepare a tea tray for you, Lady Sykeston."

"She won't be here that long." Jonathan interjected himself into their conversation. At Mrs. Butler's arched eyebrow, he added, "In my study."

Constance turned her attention to him and smiled. "I must have interrupted your work. I'd hoped to give you more notice of my arrival. But you know how unreliable the post can be." She shrugged but didn't add that she hadn't sent the letter until yesterday morning.

"No inconvenience at all, my lady," Mrs. Butler said triumphantly. "We're all happy you're here." She nodded to the butler. "Mr. North and I will take our leave."

Mr. North grinned and followed the housekeeper out the door, gently closing it behind him. It opened once again, and he peeked inside. "My lady, it's been ages since I've had one of the family to dote upon. I believe I've forgotten my manners. If you need anything or if the smell overcomes you, please don't hesitate to call."

A soft growl came from across the room. Regina perked her ears at Jonathan.

"Thank you, Mr. North. That's very kind, but I'll be fine." Constance waited for the click of the door again, then slowly walked to Jonathan's side.

It was the first time she'd seen him since London. Even disheveled, he was still handsome. However, the year had not been kind to him. He'd lost weight, and there was a sense of fatigue that enveloped him almost as if the weariness and travel were too much for him.

During the time they were apart, she had wanted the days to slow to a crawl. Everything in her life had been measured in Aurelia time. Constance could remember her first smile, her first coo, the first day she crawled, and so many other firsts. Everything seemed to move at the speed of light.

But when evening came and Constance was alone, time halted to a standstill. When she should have been drained from caring for her inexhaustible daughter, loneliness had been her stalwart companion. Her every thought and dream was magically woven around the man in front of her. The hours when she lay in bed had been torture. She would wonder endlessly if he was all right. Did he regret marrying her? Did he think about her as often as she thought about him?

Now that they were alone, it was time to get down to business—starting their lives together. She breathed deep for strength and smiled. "Hello, Jonathan."

He regarded her with suspicion, then his gaze swept from her face down her body, then up again. His nostrils flared as if taking her measure. "Lady Sykeston."

Silence settled between them. She didn't expect him to take her into his embrace, but she'd at least expected more. A declaration of *I'm delighted you're here* wouldn't be asking too much.

Well, her mother hadn't named her Constance for nothing. Calmness and patience were virtues, and she'd honed those skills while caring for her daughter.

"I've been looking forward to our reunion," she offered. Regina leaned against her and looked adoringly as her tail thumped in pleasure. The dog was so tall that her head reached Constance's waist. She reached over and scratched behind her soft ears. "I'm so thankful you're home safe and sound."

Jonathan turned to look out the French doors. A footman stood waiting with something in his hand.

"Arkwright, I have some unexpected business to attend to. We'll finish later."

She flinched slightly at him referring to her as unexpected business. After all, he was the one who'd invited her to join him.

The footman hurried down the walk until he stood at the bottom of the steps. His gaze drifted to Constance briefly and his eyes widened, before he bowed. "Of course, my lord."

Jonathan turned methodically in her direction. "How can I help you?"

The rhetorical question didn't deserve an answer, but she had decided on the trip down that she'd do her best to be pleasant as they started their new life together. "There's really nothing you can help . . ."

He held a hand up, and at first, Constance thought he meant to quiet her. But it was a signal for Regina to come to his side. The dog readily obeyed.

"Are you calling in reinforcements?" She laughed. "She's well trained, I see."

He smirked slightly. It might even have been a smile. All in all, it was hard to tell. His efforts at keeping his emotions close to the vest were remarkable. He was like an impenetrable castle, and she didn't have a clue where to find the rope to scale his walls.

"I didn't want her bothering you." He adjusted his cane to the other hand. "Would you mind if we have this conversation sitting down?" He swept his hand toward the sofa with the smashed pillows.

"Of course." She sat in the middle then proceeded to plump the pillows and put them back into their proper position. As soon as the last pillow was in place, Regina jumped on the sofa and sat on Constance's right. She reached down to fold the throw.

"Don't bother with that." He gripped the sofa arm with his left hand and lowered himself, careful of his leg. Though it took strength to lower one's body weight with one hand, Jonathan made the effort look easy.

"Have you been well?" She turned slightly to face him.

"Yes," he said brusquely. "Now tell me why you're here."

"You told me to come." The flush on his cheeks betrayed his unease. She clasped her hands in front of her.

"Allow me to collect my jaw, the one that has dropped to the floor while I stumble to find a response." The depths of his brown eyes smoldered with an emotion that remarkably resembled amazement with a dash of anger. "I told you to come?" He shook his head for a moment, then stopped suddenly. He stared straight through her. "Help me understand."

Constance opened her reticule and took out his letter. She'd never recalled him suffering from a poor memory. "You don't remember writing this?"

He took the letter from her hands. The furrow of his brow lessened as he scanned the note that he'd written. A wry smile hinted at his lips, then his brows knitted together. "Did you bring your daughter with you?"

"Of course." Her confusion grew by the minute at his responses. "Why wouldn't I?"

"Of course you would." He folded the letter. "Would you mind if I keep this for a while? I promise to give it back."

Before she could ask why, he turned slightly toward her. A blank canvas revealed more than the current expression on his face. "Is your daughter . . . well?"

She relaxed her shoulders at the question. "Very. Every morning Aurelia looks as if she's grown an inch. She's very active. She amazed me at her skill in crawling." Constance couldn't keep her smile contained when she talked about her daughter. "Walking? That came as second nature to her. It takes both me and Dahlia to keep up with her. Dahlia Fitzgerald is the nursemaid I brought with me. You remember meeting her?" She stole a peek in his direction. He stared straight ahead as if not listening to her. "I must be boring you." Heat licked her cheeks. Sometimes she didn't know when to be quiet when it came to her daughter.

The taut line of his mouth tugged upward as Jonathan returned his attention to her. "Not in the least. Aurelia sounds like a child prodigy. You must enjoy her immensely."

Constance studied his face for any sign of mockery. But that ghost of a smile matched a new softness in his eyes. She relaxed a bit but kept her posture as straight as she could. After caring for her daughter by herself over the year, she'd discovered how strong she could be.

"Did you bring anyone else with you? A lady's maid, perhaps?"

"No one else except Dahlia."

"Did you enjoy London?" He leaned back and regarded her with a new seriousness.

"I haven't really thought about it." She bit her lip and concentrated on Regina's soft fur. "I suppose." She faced him ready to confess the truth. "I found it lonely. My friends are busy with their own lives. Kat is married, and since Beth is a partner in Kat's linen business, we don't have the same opportunity to visit now that we don't live together."

Plus, he was never there.

"Outside of my friends and Mr. and Mrs. Bridges who would visit once a month, I concentrated on my work. I mainly visited with my solicitor. He's in charge of the trust my father left me." Constance waited for his reaction, but his face had lost its earlier ease. He regarded her much like a tiger before a pounce.

He stretched his right leg until it was extended straight. A hint of grimace crossed his face before his stoic expression returned. Anyone else wouldn't have noticed his pain, but she did.

"Is there anything I can do to make you more comfortable?" she asked.

"No." The smile on his face didn't reach his eyes.

"I've thought about you often." She answered his feigned smile with a genuine one of her own. "It's good to see you." She reached out to place her hand over his.

As soon as he saw her intent, he pulled it away in a silent rebuke.

"Are you all right?" she asked softly. He was gripping the sofa arm so tightly she could see the whites of his knuckles.

"Yes. This is how I always am. I haven't changed. You saw who I was when we married in London."

"The man I married in London was kind and gentle and wrote me all those beautiful letters," she countered.

Regina's ears perked up at her tone.

Jonathan blinked, then turned to stare at the ceiling. "I'm beginning to understand why North let you in," he mumbled under his breath. He turned from his study of the little angelic cherubs frolicking on the ceiling back to Constance.

For a moment she was lost for words. "What are you talking about?"

"I was thinking aloud. Pardon me for a moment." Jonathan rose carefully from the sofa and crossed the floor to a small side table where a crystal bottle containing brandy sat. He picked up one of the matching glasses and gestured to Constance.

She shook her head at the offer but watched him pour a fingerful. He brought the glass to his mouth and took a sip. His prominent Adam's apple slid slowly as he swallowed. Constance mimicked the swallow as if compelled to do so. The breadth and length of his neck always had the ability to mesmerize her. He was a splendid specimen of a man. She shook her head once to purge such thoughts. To force her mind elsewhere, she took another glance about the room. Though absolutely filthy, it hinted at an elegant, masculine décor. Kat and Beth would approve of the room. A good thorough cleaning would make it magnificent.

He stood with his back to her staring at the courtyard.

She couldn't tell from his stance that he'd been injured. He exuded strength, and the breadth of his shoulders was an invitation to explore. She should not be ogling him like a Gunter's ice flavor of the day. They were still becoming reacquainted.

Jonathan was completely oblivious to her disquiet. He glanced at her over his shoulder. "Are you planning to stay here?"

"In the study?" She looked around. Perhaps he meant for North not to let her into this room until it had been cleaned. "No. After we finished our discussion, I'd hope you could show me the house." Really, he was acting odd.

He poured himself another half fingerful. With the same ease, he came back to her side and slowly sat, the movement halting and cautious. "Constance, I wasn't expecting this."

Constance glanced downward, then she drew her gaze to his. Heat flooded her cheeks. "I know you didn't specify a date. But you were anxious for our arrival." She never imagined this type of reaction from him. "Weren't you?"

"Hard to believe that I was." There was a ridiculous hint of skepticism in his tone.

"You're being crass." This was a hundred times more humiliating than she could ever have imagined. A flight of swallows had taken up residence in her stomach mid-sweep ready to carry her away. She refused to look in any other direction. "This is not the welcome I expected. I'm your wife. I hold you in the highest regard." Her own outrage started to burn through her veins. "*My God, Jonathan*. You and I are married. I don't take our marriage, nor do I take that kiss, lightly."

The memory of that first kiss in her house crowded into her thoughts. Didn't he remember how sweet it had been between them? They were so young but so dedicated to each other.

She silently chided herself. He either didn't remember or didn't care. The marble statue of Mnemosyne at her childhood home exhibited more emotion than the hardened man who stood before her.

"I remember," he answered gently. His brow creased in a perfectly spaced row of lines as he sat in contemplation. Then slowly, much like the morning sun stretches across the horizon to greet a new day, a smile tugged at his lips. "It was your first kiss."

"Yours also," she retorted with a matching smile at the brief glimpse of the carefree man Jonathan had once been. "I thought about the kiss at our marriage ceremony too. It was quite a whirlwind afterward, wasn't it? I've thought about it repeatedly."

"You've thought about the ceremony?"

"No. The kiss that should have been longer," she answered.

He grunted, and slowly his earlier reserve returned.

She crossed her arms over her chest. "We're married. Don't you want me here?" When he didn't answer, she continued, "It makes little difference. Those vows joined our lives together irrevocably. The sooner we accept that, the better our marriage will be. I suggest we start now." She lifted one brow, clearly provoking him. "Unless that would be rushing it too much for you?"

~

Unable to control the roil of emotions that threatened to take him under, Jonathan stood again. The movement quick and painful. He grimaced as he struggled to keep his balance. How many times did that happen in his life? Probably as many times as he'd tried to forget about her.

Which meant too many.

He'd wanted to roar when he read that letter where he supposedly asked Constance to come home to him. The unique penmanship scrawled against the parchment revealed who had written it.

The servant with a penchant to be the ultimate thorn in his side. North, his *loyal* butler, that's who.

Constance stood, then walked to open the French doors. Her mint-green gown shimmered like an aspen tree teased by a summer wind. He fisted his hand to keep from going to her side. When she'd said she suffered from loneliness, he'd wanted to grab her and pull her into his arms. Kiss her blindly and confide he suffered the same malady.

"I almost think you dislike me." The words so soft he didn't think he'd heard her correctly.

"How could I dislike you?" Dislike was too similar to hate, and hate was too similar to love. He wanted to stay as far away from that emotion as he could. He wanted to be indifferent and cold. There was no caring in those emotions. If you didn't care, then there was no disappointment. No betrayal.

But he wasn't achieving that now. Before Constance came back into his life, he could do it.

The truth was that what he felt for her was undefinable and dangerous.

Frankly, this sudden need to hold her was probably because he hadn't seen her for over a year. As long as she stayed away, her appeal would soon wear off. He was certain of it.

Liar. He had thought about her every day and every night since the last time they met. Her smell, her taste, her voice, all of her haunted him as he spent his endless days locked up in here.

Regina hopped down and strolled to Constance's side and nudged her hand. Constance looked down and smiled. "You don't like to be ignored. Do you, darling?"

Her dulcet tone rang like a sweet sonnet through the room. Slowly, she turned around, and an entreating smile crossed her lips. In that moment, he'd give his fortune to walk to her

like the man he once was and kiss her the way he should
have that day they married in London.

Constance wanted him in her life. She had no clue how
damaged he was. As God was his witness, he didn't know if
he could refuse her.

"The truth is . . . I need you, Jonathan." The tenderness in
her voice was like a battering ram against his heart. "My ties
to Portsmouth run deep. The business I inherited from my
father, my community, and my past, they're all here. I want
my daughter to have what I had. You see, my first husband
stole so much from me. I'll not allow another man to do that
to me. Nor will I allow any man, titled or not, to make me
doubt my place in this world. I thought you wanted me, but
if your feelings have changed, perhaps it was a bad idea for
me to come here." She started across the room, and as quick
as he could, he caught her by the arm. Her gaze jumped to his,
the worry clear.

"I'm sorry if you're confused or hurt. So am I. All I can
offer is that you must give me some time to consider how our
marriage will go forward." Since the French doors were still
open, he kept his voice low in case someone might overhear
the conversation. But for whatever unfathomable reason,
he took her hand in his and squeezed. "My good judgment
says . . . we'd have to have a frank discussion on how and
when we'd engage as a married couple. I can't do it otherwise."

Her eyes searched his face seeking answers.

If only he had the answers. Last year, he thought he could
prove his worth by marrying her, providing for her and her
daughter, and creating a new purpose for his endless days,
one that would allow him to be a productive member of society. His plan for helping the military was sound. Still, his
future hung precariously until he could prove otherwise. He
couldn't manage to generate much interest in anything except

his cartridge design, which was proving more difficult than he'd imagined.

Now she was here taunting him with what he desperately wanted but couldn't have. God, this was what it felt like to be truly lost and not able to find your way back into the world.

"Anything else would destroy me," he said softly.

Her eyes glistened with tears, and he wanted to drown in them. She squeezed his hand in return, and he held his breath hoping she'd regain control before he did something stupid like hold her until all her tears had dried.

"I wouldn't hurt you," she said, her gaze pleading with him.

Touching her was not prudent. Thankfully, Regina came and nudged his hand away from Constance's. His intrepid dog proved why the species was known as man's best friend.

He took a deep breath and stepped away. He could no more walk away from Constance than he could run up a hill. He had to find a way to navigate these rough waters around his wife without sinking.

For the love of all that's holy, I'm referring to her as my wife.

"What do you want from me?" His voice deepened, but it still sounded like an appeal.

Her eyes swept across his face deliberately slow, as if weighing how trustworthy he was. He didn't flinch under her examination.

"I want my daughter to have a father." She dropped her voice. "I want a husband, one who will be true and honest with me. The rest of it . . . will have to be examined carefully."

He'd never seen her look so serious. In many ways, Constance was like him. She still suffered from Meriwether's betrayal, just as he suffered from Faladen's and Colonel Peterson's betrayals. Yet there was one difference between the two of them. She was either brave or foolish enough to try again. He, however, had learned his lesson the first time. Once betrayed, twice shy.

"I'm happy to be here with . . . you," she said softly. "If you'll excuse me? I promised Mrs. Butler I'd meet with her."

As she left his study, Regina's eyes followed Constance. When it was the two of them, the dog looked at him with her soulful browns.

Then the deserter made an about-face and followed Constance out the door.

Jonathan rubbed the middle of his chest. Constance didn't understand. It wasn't that he didn't want her here. It was more fundamental. He couldn't risk having her here. He'd promised himself that if he didn't let anyone in, he wouldn't care. Then his wife had waltzed in here and turned his perfectly ordered world of chaos upside down.

Chapter Ten

J onathan waited exactly five tortuous minutes watching those bloody cherubs' arms move. As soon as time was up, he made his move.

"*North*," he roared. "*You prick-eared serpent, get in here.*"

Striding confidently into the room, North bowed . . . briefly. "You called, my lord?" Jonathan's audacious butler clasped his hands in front of him in a dutiful pose.

Leaning heavily on his cane, Jonathan stood from his desk. He motioned to one of the chairs in front of him, then walked slowly to the window overlooking his overgrown courtyard garden. "Do you know why I never allow the garden to be weeded?"

"No, sir, I've never understood it. That garden was designed by your mother, and she was quite proud of it. It was once renowned for its inexhaustible display of English wildflowers."

Jonathan nodded his agreement, then carefully limped to his desk and sat down behind it. He rested his elbows on the desk, then steepled his fingers. "The garden courtyard is overgrown, filled with annoying, clawing weeds, and lacks any real structure. It reminds me of my life, and I like it that way."

"All due respect, but your life is dismal because you're difficult." North smiled slightly. "Opinionated, not to mention judgmental."

"Flattery will get you nowhere." Jonathan thrummed his fingers against the walnut, then threw Constance's letter across the desk where it landed before North. "I recognized your writing as soon as I opened the letter. No one crosses a *t* like you do."

North nodded. "I admit I love to make my signature flourish on the crossbar of the *t*."

"How long?"

The butler didn't even flinch at the abrupt question. "A month after you returned from London, I started writing her on your behalf."

Jonathan lifted a brow. "Where was I traveling?"

A barely contained grin crossed the butler's lips. "You had quite a year, sir. You traveled to France, Italy, and of course Elba. You were in charge of investigating how Napoleon was able to escape."

"Why did she never mention my travels in her letters to me?"

North tilted his nose in the air. "I told her not to." He leaned near and whispered, "*Spies.* She didn't mention it because *you* told her that her letters could be intercepted. You directed her to post her letters here, and that I would forward them."

"Don't look so smug." Thank God Jonathan was a patient man, because the need to reach across the desk and wring his butler's neck made his fingers itch. "You took it upon yourself to write my wife and asked her to move into my home?"

"It's her home too, and besides, it was time for her to take her rightful place here. You were finished with your investigation. You'd arrived home shortly after submitting your report to your superiors. That was the completion of your assignment." North thrust his chest out, his pride evident. "You were marvelous in your thoroughness. I believe the Crown will grant you a commendation for your service. They've never done it before so it'll probably take forever." His butler dramatically sighed. "I had to share that with Lady Sykeston."

"North," he growled. "I never did any of those things. I've been in Portsmouth this last year." If he was charged with desertion or dereliction of duty and this story became public, it'd be another black mark against him. "Did the thought ever occur to you that my wife might have made mention of this idiotic ruse to her friends and others in society?"

His butler nodded vigorously. "I counted on it." His face turned stern. "I'm aware of the rumors Lady Sykeston suffered about her first husband. After the birth of Miss Aurelia, this was a brilliant way for her ladyship to face her critics after you married her, then unceremoniously left her in London. She could say with pride that the reason you weren't living together was because you were providing a necessary service for the Crown." He leaned forward again and lowered his voice. "A hush-hush one at that. Everyone loves to be in on a secret. But there's no need to thank me." He leaned back in his chair with a sly grin. "I must admit that the idea was brilliant."

"You're lucky that my pistols are in the chest across the room."

His elderly butler smirked. "You wouldn't dare."

"Oh, wouldn't I?"

"Of course not." North shook his head. "You'd lose your commendation."

"There is no commendation." He wanted to roar, but Jonathan kept his voice to a rumble.

His butler eyed him as if Jonathan sported a dunce cap. "We both know that, but her ladyship doesn't. I recommend that you not blurt that out."

"What else have I shared with my wife in these letters?"

"The last several were very romantic if I do say so myself. I asked Mrs. Butler's advice on all of them. I needed to have a female's perspective."

"The entire staff is in on this." Jonathan buried his head in his hands.

"Absolutely not. I've been with the Sykeston family for over three decades. Discretion has always been part of my responsibilities as butler." He leaned close to the desk and lowered his voice. "Of course, I had to read them in order to write an appropriate response." He leaned back and smiled. "It's safe to say she is smitten."

His heart slipped in his chest at the word *smitten*. She wouldn't be after she witnessed firsthand what it was like to live with him.

"You went too far," Jonathan grumbled while keeping a certain amount of menace in his voice.

"I disagree." North studied his hands for a second. "If I may be blunt, my lord?"

"You do remember that I'm a skilled marksman able to shoot a target at three hundred yards. A distance of five feet is like child's play."

North ignored him. "As I was saying, you need her here."

"I don't need her here." Jonathan swept his fingers through his hair, trying to make sense of what his butler had done. "I'm not the same lighthearted man she remembers. I don't want her here."

"Yes. You. Do." North's left brow rose again, the habit annoying. It was the expression he used when he was about to give a lecture. Jonathan didn't need to point out that he was the earl and North was the butler. It never made any difference.

He and North had always had a peculiar relationship. They both adored his parents. Yet they could butt heads like two rams determined to best each other.

"Your father would be appalled at your behavior, sir, like he would have been if he'd ever discovered what really happened with his birthday pie," the butler announced.

North had that "gooseberry" look on his face. It was the one that Jonathan had first seen when he was a young lad and had stolen a fresh-baked gooseberry pie from the kitchen sill. North caught him red-handed after he'd devoured half of it.

Jonathan had never forgotten the disappointment on the butler's face that day. Particularly when North had shared that the family cook, Mrs. Walmer, had spent the prior afternoon, her day of rest, to pick them for Jonathan's father as a birthday surprise. But North had covered for him by saying that a pack of wild dogs had stolen it. North had a finesse for doing things in a roundabout way that always taught Jonathan a powerful lesson.

But not this time.

"I can't believe you're bringing up my father." It was the only response that came to mind after Jonathan had remembered that shameful story.

"I'm also bringing up that I'm your loyal servant. If you wouldn't write her, then someone had to." The butler waggled his eyebrows.

"We won't have that type of marriage," Jonathan declared.

"Balderdash." North crossed his arms. "You made your bed by marrying her. Like a good butler, I'm merely helping you lie in it. You should test it out and see how comfortable it is."

"I should give you an early pension," Jonathan countered. He scored a direct hit as his butler was momentarily speechless.

Then a slow smile spread across North's mouth, making

his eyes twinkle. "Maybe I'll be able to travel to France, Italy, then Elba."

"Don't tempt me," Jonathan threw his head back and stared at the ceiling. This was an unmitigated disaster. His wife had the wrong impression of him. He wasn't some military attaché on special assignment for the Crown. Nor was he a romantic who begged her to move into his home. "I'll have to tell her the truth—that it was all a fantasy—then send her away."

"My lord?"

Jonathan returned his gaze to his utterly disloyal butler.

"Let me be frank. You're getting worse. You can barely walk. You sit in this room as if it's your . . ."

"Throne room?" Jonathan offered.

"I was going to say *dungeon*." North hitched his nose in the air. "Your only companion is that dog. You don't even read your correspondence from your friends."

"I don't have friends."

"Yes, you do," North said gently. The kindness on his face almost undid Jonathan. "I promised your father on his deathbed that I'd look after you. I'm not going to be around forever, sir. Your wife"—he pointed upstairs toward the family quarters—"is here now. You should put forth the effort to make your marriage real. She was once your best friend."

"That's my past," he argued.

"And your future," North countered. "Perhaps it would be a good time to introduce your countess to your staff?"

Jonathan exhaled. "You and Mrs. Butler do it. I'm not coming out of my study for the next year or so."

⌒

Constance descended the staircase to the main hall where Mrs. Butler's office was. While her thoughts should be on the staff, all Constance could think of was her husband. His face had turned ashen when she'd entered his study. For a brief moment, she'd thought he would become ill.

He was terrified of having invited her here. Perhaps he was terrified of their marriage.

Well, perhaps they both were. It was only natural.

Mrs. Butler waited outside her office. "My lady, I've seen that your dear daughter is settled." The housekeeper leaned close. "She's a darling baby. I'm not saying that to win favors. She's adorable."

Constance couldn't help but grin at the bubbly housekeeper. Tall in her early fifties with still-dark hair, the woman had an air of authority that oozed personality. Only the gray around her temples hinted at her true age. But Constance immediately had liked her when they first met. "Thank you, Mrs. Butler. I can't help but admit I'm a little partial."

"As you should be," she answered with a firm nod. "Let's go meet the staff."

Constance purposely slowed her stride. "Shouldn't we wait for my husband?"

A sad, sympathetic smile tug tugged at Mrs. Butler's lips. "I'm sorry, my lady, but the earl asked if I would do it."

"Oh . . . thank you." The sting of Jonathan's rejection slapped her in the face. Perhaps the staff would think less of her because of it. She feigned an enthusiastic smile. "Shall we?"

They strolled toward the entry where all the servants were assembled en masse to meet Constance.

Mrs. Butler leaned close. "The earl takes his dinner at seven o'clock. He keeps country hours. But if you have a different preference, I'm sure Cook will be accommodating. You see, my lady, all of us are delighted you're here. The rest of the staff can't wait to welcome you." Without batting an eye, the woman stopped in the entry vestibule. "Are you ready?"

As Constance looked at the expectant faces of the devoted

servants of Sykeston Gardens, she hoped she could accomplish her goal and make this a true home for all of them.

"May I ask a favor before we start?" Constance turned to the housekeeper.

"Of course, my lady," Mrs. Butler answered.

"Will you point out the servants my husband is closest to?" She didn't share why, but Constance decided there and then that she would see what she could discover about her husband and his proclivities for food, entertainment, clothes, routine, and any other activities he deemed essential. A good wife should know what her husband liked, and she wanted to be that for Jonathan. Perhaps it would melt the awkwardness between them. Though it would be easier to ask him outright, she doubted she'd receive much direction from him.

Mrs. Butler's expression didn't change at her unusual request. "His valet Ralph Byerly, and Franklin Arkwright, the footman who encourages his target practice." Her nose tipped in the air in disapproval. "It scares the staff senseless to hear the gunshots echoing through the house."

"I understand. We'll work on that together." Constance patted her arm. "Are there any more?"

Mrs. Butler nodded. "The cook, Mrs. Walmer, has been with the family for over twenty-five years. And of course, Mr. North." She leaned closer and lowered her voice. "The earl may act as if Mr. North isn't a favorite, but he's been with the Sykeston family longer than anyone. He was here for the earl's birth and the death of his parents. Mr. North knows more about his lordship and family than anyone else on the staff." She nodded brusquely. "He's a wealth of information."

"Thank you, Mrs. Butler."

"Another thing you should be aware of." The housekeeper shook her head. "It's unlikely the earl will venture out of his study today . . . or tomorrow."

Constance raised her eyebrows. It was the day of her

homecoming. She'd at least expected to eat with him. "Does he sleep in there?"

Mrs. Butler chuckled and shook her head. "I might have exaggerated a bit. The earl will come out for dinner." She narrowed her eyes, but the censure in her eyes flashed. "Of course, he'll have that mongrel sitting next to him." She leaned a little closer and lowered her voice. "At the table."

"Excellent," Constance said confidently. "Will you make certain to set three place settings this evening? Now let's meet the staff."

Bemused, Mrs. Butler stared for a moment, then with a no-nonsense efficiency, she escorted Constance to the butler's side. "Mr. North, may I introduce the lady of the house, Lady Sykeston?"

Mr. North's eyes glowed with a cheery welcome. He bowed elegantly for such an elderly man. His black morning coat and pants emphasized his perfectly arranged white hair. "My lady, may I say that it's a true honor to have his lordship's wife finally residing here at Sykeston Gardens. If there is anything I can do to help you become familiar with the house, its history, the grounds, or anything else, please don't hesitate to ask."

"Thank you, Mr. North. I'm certain I will become a pest if I ask you all the questions that I have. I'll be relying on you for all sorts of things." Constance took his hand and shook it firmly. "My first question is if you could tell me where the nursery is?" She grinned. "I seem to have lost my daughter."

The rest of the servants laughed.

A young woman piped up. "My lady, the nursery is on the far side of the second floor, but Miss Aurelia's bedroom is right next to the countess's suites. That's where I'm assigned. I saw Miss Aurelia sleeping in her new crib when I introduced myself to Dahlia."

"That's my daughter, Mary. She can fill the role of your lady's maid," Mrs. Butler offered. "For now, I assigned her to help ensure your daughter is comfortable in her new bed-room. Both Mary and Dahlia have unpacked your things." Mrs. Butler leaned close. "I want you settled here as quickly as possible. It'll be good for all of us."

"Thank you." Affection swelled inside of Constance. The staff was truly welcoming and seemed glad that she and Au-relia were here. She turned to the housekeeper's daughter. "Thank you, Mary. Perhaps after I meet everyone, you can accompany Mrs. Butler when she shows me my chambers?"

The young maid nodded. "I'd be happy to, ma'am."

Mrs. Butler efficiently introduced the entire staff. Con-stance tried hard to remember their names. She asked each one a question about where they came from and their family. After meeting everyone, Mrs. Butler took her to the split cir-cular staircase that led to the family's private quarters. About halfway up the steps, the crisp sound of clapping came from below. Constance turned around to find every single servant clapping for her. Soon cheers followed.

Her hand flew to her chest at the welcome, and tears sprang from nowhere. The fine people who served Sykeston Gardens deserved a countess worthy of them. With all her power, she pledged to be that person and restore the previous grandeur to the house.

She bowed her head and said thank you, but her words were lost in the roar of greeting. As her gaze took in the ser-vants' jubilation, a movement caught her interest. In the very same hallway that she'd entered from, her husband now stood with Regina in the shadows.

Her gaze latched onto his before he stepped out of sight.

His exit shouldn't have hurt, but somehow, it tore a piece of her heart, leaving the fragment fluttering suspended in her chest. Did the man feel as if he didn't belong in his own home as she was introduced to the servants?

"Come, my lady," Mrs. Butler said with a wink. "The longer

we stand here, the longer they'll cheer. There's work to be done."

Constance nodded then stole another peek at the hallway.

Regina had maintained her position as sentry, leaving little doubt that her husband stood close by.

His presence gave her another reason to make the house their home.

Whether her husband knew it or not, he needed her.

Hours later, Constance sat on the floor of her richly appointed bedroom next to her daughter. Aurelia was currently engaged in a game of peekaboo with herself in front of a French giltwood dressing mirror. Giggles, smiles, and sputters were freely given in her play. Constance couldn't imagine what life would be like if she didn't have this precious girl in it.

She'd promised herself the day she gave birth that she'd never take Aurelia for granted. Meriwether had, but now with Jonathan, Constance and Aurelia both had a second chance for a family.

A knock sounded in the adjacent sitting room. The sound startled Aurelia, and she looked at Constance with wide eyes.

"It's all right," Constance soothed. "It's just the door."

Her daughter giggled at Constance's reassurance then returned to playing peekaboo with the mirror again.

"Come in," she said, never taking her eyes away from Aurelia.

"My lady?" one of the servants called out.

"By the mirror." Constance made her way to stand. When she turned toward the sitting room, Mary Butler entered.

"Hello, Mary." Constance brushed her dress, but the effort was hopeless. She was wrinkled beyond repair.

"My mum . . . I mean Mrs. Butler sent me up here to see if you needed any help dressing for dinner." The girl pointed to the clock. "It starts in ten minutes."

"I didn't realize how late it is." Constance scooped up Aurelia and kissed her cheek. "I must take you to Dahlia, then dress."

"I can take Miss Aurelia, then come and help you, if you'd like," Mary offered.

"That would be wonderful." With another kiss on her daughter's chubby cheek, Constance gave her to the maid.

Mary cooed to the baby as she strolled toward the door. Aurelia smiled in answer. Thank heavens her daughter had a pleasant temperament. The hustle and the bustle of the day's events didn't seem to have put her in a sour mood.

Mary turned back once again to Constance. "It's lovely to have you and your daughter here. Things are so much brighter now, and I'm sure they'll continue that way." Without waiting for Constance to reply, Mary closed the door.

Constance pulled the scarlet Italian silk gown from the drawer. She'd been saving it for a special occasion. Tonight could definitely be considered such an event. It would be the first meal she'd share with her husband.

As she unbuttoned her gown, she considered her hair. It wasn't the worst for wear. She pinched her cheeks for a little color.

Next, she pulled out the matching shoes and stockings along with her favorite perfume made from orange blossoms. When she walked into that dining room tonight, she wanted her husband to take notice.

If she had her way, he wouldn't be salivating over merely the food tonight.

Chapter Eleven

Jonathan pulled his timepiece from his waistcoat pocket. Fifteen minutes past the routine dinner hour, and the food would be cold. He had his staff trained to serve him at exactly seven o'clock every night. Regina's snout tipped straight in the air as if mesmerized by some succulent smell. Her brown eyes found his, and a soft whine escaped.

"Soon," Jonathan reached down and scratched the soft fur of her head.

Jonathan had poured a glass of sherry for Constance, and a brandy for himself. The glass he'd poured for Constance stood alone, much like him as he waited for her.

"My lord?" Mary Butler stood at the sitting room door. "Lady Sykeston is on her way."

"Thank you." Jonathan took a sip for fortification. He was as nervous as a fox facing a pack of hounds. He hadn't made dinner conversation in ages. Normally, he dismissed the footmen who served him dinner as soon as the dishes were on the table. But tonight, he'd have to find something to talk about with his wife. He looked to Regina for a distraction.

However, his dog had left his side and was waiting by the door when Constance swept into the room. "Pardon me.

I was playing with Aurelia. I'm afraid the time slipped away from me." Dark pink colored her cheeks as if she'd run from the second floor down.

His gaze skated down her gown. Calling it a creation from heaven was not an exaggeration. The lines of the red masterpiece flowed outward, ending in a perfect train. Yet the bodice hugged her curves perfectly and was cut to emphasize her beauty.

As he watched her, she watched him. The intensity of her gaze swept over Jonathan. He cleared his throat slightly. "No need to be concerned. I hope Miss Aurelia is none the worse from her hectic day?"

North stood at the back of the room and gave him a thumbs-up.

Mary smiled slightly, and Jonathan's valet, Ralph Byerly, who had followed after Constance's entrance, beamed at him, then nodded in approval at his answer.

For some strange reason he felt as if he'd been under some sort of evaluation. Apparently, he'd passed muster.

Constance smiled sweetly. "Thank you for asking. She's not tired in the least."

"Perhaps after dinner his lordship could meet her?" Ralph added, "She's charmed Mary and me, and I'm sure she'll have you under her spell in no time, sir."

"I've already met her," Jonathan said more curtly than he had intended. "A year ago."

When his wife's gaze turned to his, a slight scowl suddenly appeared. "Perhaps tomorrow then. I'm certain she'll be abed by the time dinner is finished."

For whatever reason, the idea that he'd see Constance's child again felt a little awkward. What would he say? He had little experience with children, let alone babies. God knows he preferred his seclusion. Simply because his wife had arrived in Portsmouth didn't mean that his perfectly ordered world had to change.

Did it?

"I'd be honored to make Miss Aurelia's acquaintance again," he said, hoping to soothe the ruffled feelings of his wife and the three servants. He turned to Constance. "But as her mother, you should decide."

Constance's face brightened. "Tomorrow then."

In that moment, he could have sworn that the sky had opened and ten thousand stars had fallen into the salon. He'd made her happy. It was a simple thing, yet oh so dangerous. He could not allow her to think that he wanted more.

"Sir?" North prodded from the back. "Doesn't Lady Sykeston look lovely this evening?" The butler turned to Constance. "You remind me of Lord Byron's 'She Walks in Beauty.'"

"Thank you," she said softly.

North turned to Jonathan with a lifted brow and a look that said, *That's how it's done.*

Jonathan shot his butler a death stare. Every single person in the room knew what the old man was up to.

A butler impersonating a busybody matchmaker.

It made little difference that the house seemed to have changed its personality since his wife had crossed its threshold. To crave her attention was out of the question. He had to remember that his current life was too demanding as it was. With all his target practice, cartridge design work, and Regina, he didn't have time for a wife or a child to intrude.

He didn't need anyone and certainly couldn't take the risk of allowing his wife to break through the fortress he'd so carefully constructed around his life.

And his heart.

"Shall we go to dinner?" he asked.

A door off the side of the sitting room led to the dining room. As soon as they entered the room, the footmen stood at attention, but everyone's gaze turned to the dog.

Then like a billiard break that sent the balls careening into one another, the first footman's gaze flew to the second footman next to him. The second footman's gaze flew to Constance's. Her gaze flew from the table to Jonathan's, then back to the table.

Everything was in order in Jonathan's opinion. Regina sat at her normal place waiting for him. The chair immediately to Jonathan's right.

The chair normally reserved for the Countess of Sykeston.

It was the one his mother had always sat in next to his father. His grandmother had sat in that chair right beside his grandfather. By all rights, it should be Constance's chair. But it was Regina's chair and had been ever since she could jump up to the table.

Jonathan tightened his stomach for the soon-to-be fit of ill temper that would surely erupt when Constance saw that her seat was currently occupied.

The staff who would serve them tonight stood in place stone-faced. Jonathan had little doubt they were waiting with bated breath for Constance's reaction.

She didn't waste a glance his way. Instead, she smiled at the staff and walked to the table. She bestowed a quick pet to Regina's head, then walked to the seat opposite the mastiff, the one normally reserved for distinguished guests.

Following her lead, Jonathan assisted Constance as she scooted the chair closer to the table before taking his customary seat at the head of the table.

"I think it's safe to say that the world has literally gone to the dogs," one footman whispered to the other.

"Perhaps it's better to say if you lie with the dogs, don't be surprised if you wake up with fleas," the other answered.

Though they had their backs turned, the utterances were loud enough Constance had to have heard them.

Jonathan threw his serviette to the table. "I'll not have such disloy—"

Constance put her hand over his. "Ronald, would you mind finding another serviette for me?" she asked.

"Of course, my lady," the footman replied.

"Oh, and Jasper, could I impose upon you to bring me my glass of sherry?" She chuckled slightly. "I believe I left it in the other room on the windowsill."

"Yes, ma'am," he answered, leaving the room and Jonathan and Constance alone.

"You didn't leave your sherry by a window," Jonathan said.

"I wanted us to be alone for a moment." Constance's gaze fell on the dog. "Don't be offended with what the footmen said."

"I'm used to such treatment because of the housekeeper's dislike for Regina. I know the staff thinks it's odd." Jonathan shook his head. "I don't want you to be disconcerted with their regard of me."

"I'm not." The light from the chandelier cascaded over her hair and shoulders like little fairies paying homage to their queen. "They're adjusting as we all are to the new circumstances."

No matter how many years had separated them, the fundamentals never changed. His lips twitched with a grin. She'd always had a kind heart.

"She's asking me to call off the dogs," Jonathan whispered to Regina.

At that, a smile tugged at his wife's lips followed by a stifled laugh. She ducked her head and arranged her plate as if it needed straightening. "I think it best to let sleeping dogs lie," she whispered. Suddenly, she laughed.

He became fixated on her deep, rich alto voice. It was a heady sound, rippling with joy and humor. One he hadn't heard in ages that subtlety reminded him of his life before the war.

Like a magnet attracted to another, he leaned nearer and

his own laugh joined hers. "Does this mean you're not angry?"

Constance's eyes met his. In that moment between the two of them, it was if they'd never left that room where they first kissed and were still best friends. Such an intimate moment made him feel human. God, he'd give anything and everything to return to that time and place.

"How could I be angry at Regina?" she said softly. "But I will say every dog has its day."

Her eyes sparkled with mirth, making him want something he shouldn't have. The urge to lean close and steal a kiss drew nigh impossible to resist.

But somehow he pulled away. The magic and smiles between them slowly evaporated. "Shall we eat?" he asked.

She nodded.

By then, the footmen had returned with the items Constance had requested.

With a secret smile shared between the two of them, Jonathan motioned the servants forward, and dinner was served. Clear consommé, mushroom tarts, and perch in a delicate hollandaise sauce were quickly devoured. The exchange between them was pleasant and cheerful. It'd been ages since he'd enjoyed such a dinner. As much as Jonathan thought he'd hate having to entertain asinine conversation at his dinner table, the opposite was true. The evening passed by much too quickly. Regina sat at her chair without nary a complaint. Constance didn't seem to mind a whit that his dog sat in her rightful place.

But the next course caused a major uproar. Earlier he'd asked that medallions of beef with horseradish, ham, topped with a Madeira sauce be served. As soon as a footman brought the dish into the room, Regina started to drool. Not a tad, but like a running stream.

The footmen's eyes widened to saucers.

Constance daintily pressed the serviette to her mouth. "It's a trait of the breed," she announced. "English mastiffs drool. You do become accustomed to it. Their good nature and protective instincts more than make up for the little inconvenience. But one can't fail to notice how exceptionally well mannered she's been throughout dinner."

An awkward silence descended. The footmen stood like statues waiting for the next summons.

"Well, there's only one thing left to do." Without breaking stride, she forked two slices of beef, then gracefully reached across the table and deposited them on Regina's plate.

The dog watched Constance's every move with intense curiosity, then her soulful gaze skated between Constance and Jonathan asking for approval to dive in.

"You may eat," Jonathan said.

In response, his dog devoured the two pieces of meat in one gulp. Noisily, she licked the plate clean, almost knocking it off the table with her big, thick tongue. Afterward, she jumped down and sauntered out of the room with a satisfied look on her face as she licked her chops.

Constance's gaze drifted to his. "Well, her leaving the party means only one thing."

"What's that?

"More vanilla soufflé for us." She smiled sheepishly. "I hope I didn't overstep bounds by feeding your dog."

"No," he answered, then lowered his voice so the footmen couldn't hear. "You have a friend for life now, I'm afraid. She'll never leave you alone."

Just as I won't, now that you're here.

Thankfully, he didn't say it aloud.

He could not wish for a real marriage. It was impossible.

While he struggled with those feelings that made his heart thump louder than a battle drum, Constance played with her dessert spoon. Her hand was inches from his. The sight was unbearably erotic to him. Long fingers and smooth skin. Though she still seemed as innocent and playful as he'd always remembered, she'd faced Meriwether's betrayal, motherhood, and raising a daughter alone. She wasn't the same person he'd kissed those eleven years ago.

Neither was he.

To hell with not touching her.

It wouldn't change the earth's orbit to place his hand over hers. He nodded once to the footmen, who understood the command to leave the room.

When they were alone, barely above a whisper, he said, "Constance?"

When her face turned, he slowly moved his hand to touch her. It gave her enough time to pull her hand away if she didn't welcome his touch.

One part of him wished she would place it in her lap.

Chances were relatively high he'd come to regret this.

Not realizing his torment, she didn't move a muscle except for her eyes. They tracked the progression of his hand across the table until his fingers covered hers. They were softer than he remembered. The finest silk would feel like raw linen next to her skin.

Slowly, she raised her gaze to his.

"I'm not going to apologize for Regina." He swallowed. It would have been easy to spout off that it was his house and he would do what he pleased. But he'd sound like a spoiled brat, and she deserved more from him. "She keeps me company and reminds me of . . ."

He let out a breath. This was too intimate to be sharing with her. For God's sake, they were practically strangers. How to admit to all the pain and failures he had experienced in life and the solace he felt in touching an animal completely devoted to him?

"Of a simpler time?" she answered. She dipped her head and entwined their fingers together. "That's what she reminds me of." Then she did the unthinkable. She squeezed his hand and smiled.

Good God. What had he opened himself up to? He'd be crucified if she looked at him with anything like concern or, God help him, pity.

So he did what any man would do in his position. He averted a catastrophe by deflecting the conversation.

"Shall we have that vanilla soufflé now?"

Chapter Twelve

❦

Constance patted the sleeping Aurelia one last time before she returned to her own bedroom. The Countess of Sykeston's suites were scrumptious and uniquely well designed. Off the bedroom was a small room perfect for Aurelia's nursery. Dahlia slept on the other side of the house where the rest of the servants had their rooms. It had been Constance's preference since the baby had been born that she would care for her daughter if Aurelia woke in the night.

She glanced around the bedroom. No expense had been spared in outfitting the luxurious suite. The bedroom itself was huge. Topped with an intricate dome decorated with a floral fabric, a massive Chippendale gilded four-poster bed stood against one wall. It was furnished with a blue-green damask bedcovering that reminded Constance of sea glass she'd find when exploring the Portsmouth shores. Fringed damask curtains were tied at each post in the same shade.

The white marble fireplace commanded the middle of the room separating the bed from a small sitting room. A toasty fire blazed, casting a soft light around the rooms. Next to the sitting room was Aurelia's room. Every room had been papered in a damask wall covering slightly lighter in hue than the bed linens.

Constance twirled in a circle as she took in the magnificence of the suite. It was slightly musty from little use, but a thorough cleaning would set it to rights. Mrs. Butler had told her that the staff had changed the bedding and had unpacked her belongings. Tomorrow Constance would have the room thoroughly aired and cleaned. The finishing touch would be several massive bouquets from the house gardens. She longed to fill the four exquisite Sèvres vases that sat on the various green lacquered tables in the room.

A door separated her bedroom from a dressing room. On the other side were Jonathan's rooms. The dressing room contained a tub and shower that the earl and his wife shared. According to Mrs. Butler when she showed Constance her suite, Jonathan had them installed after he returned from war. Constance couldn't see it, as the door had been locked from the other side.

No matter how much she tried to distract herself, her stomach twisted into knots whether Jonathan would visit her tonight . . . their first night together under one roof. She walked to a wall-mounted Chippendale mirror and evaluated her appearance. She wore a feminine ivory cotton dressing gown. The neckline dipped in front. Lace decorated the sleeve cuffs with a matching panel on the midriff area. Underneath was a matching sleeveless nightgown. The entire ensemble was simple but elegant. With her hair down and her cheeks pink, she looked like a blushing bride.

She pulled the sixpence from her pocket and squeezed it in her hand. Of course, she couldn't expect him to come in and make wild, passionate love to her. But at dinner, he seemed to enjoy her company. That simple fact laid the foundation for a strong marriage. They could build upon that.

Two sharp knocks sounded. She took one last look in the mirror then raced to the connecting door, her bare feet practically soundless on the wooden floor. She drew to a standstill and smoothed her hair and gown. He was finally here.

She couldn't keep from smiling. Funny, but she'd never felt this excited with Meriwether. With a deep breath, she found the door unlocked and opened it to nothing.

Darkness shrouded the dressing room. For a moment, she thought no one was there and she'd imagined the whole episode. Then like an emissary sent ahead to discover information, Regina walked into the room with her tail wagging. A few seconds passed before Jonathan followed, his uneven gait punctuated with the tap of his cane.

"Good evening," he said.

"Hello." She blinked twice.

His gaze was trained on her face as if hesitant to look elsewhere. "I see you're ready for bed." Finally, he let his gaze skim across her shoulders and follow the length of her hair. He blinked, then took a step back much like she was a poisonous plant.

"And you're not." He was still in the same clothes he'd worn to dinner including his Hessian boots. Bitter disappointment stung with the sharpness of a bee, but she shouldn't have gotten her hopes up that he was here for their wedding night. "Would you care to come in?"

"No. No." He shook his head with such vehemence it was a wonder it didn't fly off into the next room. "I wanted to see if you are settled and comfortable."

"Everything is lovely." She turned and pointed to the room where her daughter slept. "Aurelia is sound asleep. It's a beautiful room, perfect for her." When her gaze returned to his, a hint of sweat glistened across his brow. His right hand was clenched so hard on the silver knob of his cane that his knuckles were white. He was actually tense—more so than her—proving that brides weren't the only ones struck with the case of nerves.

"Jonathan," she said softly. "I won't bite. I'd enjoy your company if you're so inclined. Mrs. Butler sent up a lovely bottle of wine and a tray filled with meats and cheeses." She smiled in reassurance. "I think she thought we would spend . . . some time together."

"I can't." He dipped his head and studied his boots. "I wanted to let you know that I plan to take a shower this evening so the dressing room might be loud." He finally lifted his head, and his aloofness had returned. "I didn't want to interrupt your evening."

"Kind of you to inform me." Desperate to think of something else to say, she chewed on her bottom lip.

Instead of leaving or sharing more, he stared at her lip as if he wanted to bite it. His stare cut straight through her, but she wasn't intimidated. She'd dealt with men practically all her life because of her business. However, this was Jonathan, a man she'd once considered her best friend. Now he'd had a lifetime of experiences that had changed him. But so had she.

"You shower in the evenings?" It was silly, but it was the only thing she could think of to ask.

"Yes." He shuffled his weight to his good leg. "Sometimes the pain . . . I can't sleep. A shower helps."

"I've never seen one." She pointed behind him. "Perhaps you'd show me how it works?"

He tilted his head and examined her. "Another time." He nodded instead of bowing. "I wish you a good night."

"Wait." She placed her hand on his arm to keep him there a little longer. "If you ever find you can't sleep or if you just want to chat, knock on my door. I'll hear it. But just in case, you don't need to knock. I won't keep it locked." Thoughts and feelings were tumbling from her in a free fall. "We're married now. Husband and wife. That's what they do. Help each other. Comfort each other. Be there for each other."

He moved back slightly, increasing the distance between them.

"I would do that for you. And I know you would do that for me." She smiled slightly, then allowed her teeth to graze her lower lip. "We should have an easy intimacy between us." She took a step in his direction. "Don't you agree?"

Never in his life had he felt this on edge—even when the sharpshooters were reloading preparing for the final shots that would put him out of his misery. Yet this woman threatened his space. Why in God's teeth was she in her night clothing?

Then he remembered. It was late in the evening. Time had no relevance in his life anymore. The minutes, hours, and days pushed against one another as if vying for space. His gaze swept across the soft cotton ensemble she wore, a white confection for him to unwrap. If he tilted his head and squinted a particular way, he might see the outline of a perfect breast pushing against her nightgown. Her dressing gown was untied.

Then the truth hit him with the force of a broadax against his chest. God, she had dressed for him. For their wedding night. She'd dressed to seduce him.

The soft scent of orange blossom water wafted in the air between them, making every sense sharpen. He breathed deep, his lungs starving for her fragrance. His chest tightened as if holding back his heart from breaking through his ribs to reach her. His hands itched to take her into his arms and kiss her—taste those lips she'd teased him with.

To have this vision of her imprinted on his mind? With the knowledge she was next door? He didn't know the exact meaning of torture until he saw her. He didn't know if he'd be able to sleep for a year.

She was not beautiful.

She was exquisite. All he had to do was to close the distance and take her in his embrace. It would be the first time he'd ever experienced anything close to ecstasy since he'd lain in that godforsaken tent fighting for his life while drowning in opium dreams.

Yet she'd haunted him there too, giving him the will to push through the physical and emotional pain until he was well enough to limp onto that ship and sail for home.

But there was a huge difference between then and now. She was here next to him in all her glory.

The repeated thump, thump-thump of Regina's tail brought him out of his wayward frenzy. Instinctively, he reached down and stroked her soft fur. Anything to keep his mind off his wife.

Wife.

What had he been thinking? He should have known she'd have this effect on him, the power to steal his resolve. He should have sent her packing when he'd first laid eyes on her. Instead, he'd allowed himself to be tangled once again in her life.

"Jonathan?" Constance murmured.

The sweet sound drilled straight to his heart. He closed his eyes determined not to succumb, but his legs had a will of their own. That had to be the reason he stood so close to her now.

"Yes?" He nodded in a cool, efficient manner.

She smiled that incandescent smile again. Her brows winged upward in a plea. "So you'll stay?"

"No," he said. The abruptness in his tone was a measured device designed to stop them and especially him from making a mistake. "Allow me to invite you to my study tomorrow after breakfast. I think we need to establish some rules between the two of us."

She exhaled and seemed to shrink before his eyes. "Rules? What kind of rules?"

For that flash of a moment, he wanted to be the man worthy enough to clear the worry that marred the brilliance in her eyes. He released a ragged breath, knowing that he might never be that man. "Constance . . . there have to be rules about when and how we engage as a married couple." He ran one hand through his hair and turned toward the dressing room desperate for an escape. "I can't do this otherwise."

He cleared his throat as his stomach twisted in revolt at the thought that he was actually living with her. For God's sake, he hardly ever allowed anyone, friend or foe, to cross the threshold of his home.

Only the woman before him had the fortitude to break through his barriers and fight for what she wanted.

But even he had a line in the sand that could not be crossed. Merely sharing a name didn't mean that he would acquiesce to her or anyone else. He didn't want company and certainly didn't socialize.

The tilt of her chin meant defiance, but the concern in her eyes gave him hope she'd agree.

"If that's what you want." She nodded once. "But I come with my own rules for you."

"Fair enough."

Her eyes reflected a vibrancy that bordered on effervescence. She was actually happy. He had little doubt she wouldn't be at all overjoyed if she knew his intentions. Clear and defined roles between them were all he could offer.

The word *beloved* charged into his thoughts demanding attention, but he quickly dismissed it.

There was no love between the two of them.

And he meant to keep it that way.

⁓

The next morning, Constance stood outside the sitting room where Mr. North had directed her to meet with her husband. She'd worn her best gown, a royal blue striped confection that her friend Kat had embroidered flowers on the bodice and hem. It was a riot of color and beautiful. Constance always felt her best and most confident in this gown. It was so different from her standard navy dresses for the dockyard.

She stood beside North, who knocked on the sitting room door once, then entered. He swept the door open for her, and she followed.

The intrepid butler smiled encouragingly at her, then announced, "Lord Sykeston, Lady Sykeston is here."

Her gaze immediately found Jonathan, and she gasped quietly. He was immaculately dressed today. Much different from the crumpled morning coat and breeches he'd worn the day before. His hair had been cut, his face shaved, and he wore a formal suit.

"Thank you, North," he said, never taking his eyes off her. After the butler closed the door, his gaze slowly drifted down her dress, then rose to meet her face once again.

She was the first one to speak. "Good morning. I missed you at breakfast."

"I eat in my study," he said.

She stood immobile and waited for the invitation to sit. He still examined her until the silence grew uncomfortable. "Shall we begin?"

He shook his head as if coming out of a trance. "Excellent idea." He waved her forward to an intimate sitting area close to a large window overlooking the overgrown courtyard that appeared not to have been touched in years. His study overlooked the same view. "Your dress . . . you're very . . ."

"Colorful?" she suggested.

"No." His baritone voice lowered to a pleasant thrum that vibrated in her chest. "Beautiful in an unexpected way."

This time she was the one lost for words. Eventually, she found her voice. "If that's a compliment, then thank you."

"I meant it as one."

Heat bludgeoned her cheeks. It was difficult to predict his mood, but the change in his appearance was simply remarkable. "You look handsome this morning."

The muscles in his jaws clenched, before he opened his mouth to say something. Then he closed it and motioned to a chair. As she would expect from a gentleman, he waited until she'd taken her seat before he claimed his. Seeking a moment to compose her thoughts, she glanced around the formal sitting room. It possessed a sparkling quality, indicating it had been recently cleaned. A large bouquet of thrift and lilacs filled a vase on a table in the center of the room. The subtle fragrance drifted her way. She took a deep breath, filling her lungs with the scent.

But another layer drew her attention—evergreen. Perhaps cedar, his signature scent. Did she dare think he'd worn it for her? It was her favorite ever since they'd first kissed. Everything about him seemed different today, almost as if he was making an effort to appeal to her.

A table sat between them where a single paper lay. No doubt, it was his list of rules. She exhaled silently to combat her irritation. It was a simple accommodation, and she'd do her part to help their marriage along. A side pocket sewn inside her gown contained a paper with her own rules, the ones she'd prepared. She reached inside and pulled it out.

His eyes narrowed on the piece of paper.

Her pulse raced, attempting to outrun her discomfort.

He leaned against the chairback and straightened his leg.

"We need agreement on how we'll engage with each other," Jonathan said.

She smoothed the paper in front of her. "First, let me say something. Thank you for agreeing to marry me. With your service to the Crown, your absence allowed me to concentrate on Aurelia. But you should know that I want to be a wife to you in every way." She pointed to his paper. "Rules sound so . . . so stringent, don't they?"

"Rules help maintain order." He leaned an elbow on the arm of the chair completely at ease. "Who should go first?"

"It makes little difference to me." She leaned across the table and lowered her voice. "Do we really need these rules?"

He matched her movement as if ready to divulge a secret. "I insist upon it. My life was well defined before you entered into it. I'm trying to keep as much of that intact as I can." He exhaled. "I've given quite a bit of consideration to these rules of . . . shall we say, 'engagement between us.'" With a sureness, he continued, "They're designed to protect both of us."

"Protect us from what?"

He glanced away. "Misunderstanding. Misinformation. Mishap."

"All right." She straightened in her seat. "To help me better understand, tell me how you see our life together."

Without picking up his parchment, Jonathan nodded. "We shall be supportive of each other's goals and dreams. We shall keep clean boundaries between the two of us." He waved a hand between the them. "King of the castle and all that. Same goes for queen of the castle."

"I accept." She nodded once. "Here are a few of mine." She cleared her throat and glanced down at the paper. "We make our marriage a priority. I'm not a mind reader. If something is bothering you, tell me. We have weekly meetings to share these things."

"Miss Efficient, are we? Weekly meetings?" He laughed.

Prickles of awareness spread across her arms. His eyes practically sparkled, and the tiny lines that framed his eyes made him appear more like the Jonathan of old. "Every time I hear you laugh, it makes me smile." For a moment, he looked embarrassed, but she continued, "Your voice is so smooth and rich. It reminds me of . . ." She didn't finish with *a perfectly aged whisky* as a sudden grin appeared, and the gleam in his eyes was pure mischief.

"Coffee?" he offered. "Tea?"

"I was thinking whisky." Butterflies took flight in her stomach. *He's flirting with me.*

"Ah, I like that comparison better. Thank you." His slight grin lingered. "You were saying weekly meetings?"

She cleared her throat trying to distract herself from the sudden warmth that bloomed inside her chest. "My parents did this, and their marriage was an example of how to be a happy couple."

"Fair point." He nodded once. "As I did last year, I'll continue to share my wealth with you."

"Thank you." An excellent start to this marriage if she did say so herself. She always suspected he'd be a wonderfully kind and thoughtful husband.

He stared at his parchment and played with a corner of his paper. "We don't discuss our respective pasts. We sleep in separate bedrooms."

His words echoed like the retort of a gun. At first, she clutched her chest uncertain if she'd been shot. She breathed deep. The air flooded her lungs, offering reassurance that she was all right. She took another moment to steady herself.

"No," she whispered. Then in a louder voice laced with certitude, she repeated, "No, Jonathan."

He held up his hand. "It's for your own benefit. I'm up all hours of the night with my leg."

The keen sense of disappointment ripped through her. She sat still for a moment considering her next move. She lowered her voice. "I want it all, Jonathan. Everything a marriage entails, including 'sickness and health' and 'with this body I thee worship' . . . which means sleeping together."

His eyes widened.

"Does it shock you that I enjoy the marriage bed?"

~

Shock was putting it mildly. She was talking about consummating their marriage with *him*.

Of course it was with him. She'd married him, not

someone else. He blew out a breath. Simply thinking it made his breeches tighten as parts of him woke that had been sleeping for years. He shifted slightly and crossed his legs to hide the effect of her speech.

Her pleasure was important to her. As it should be, yet he hadn't given it proper consideration. He hadn't been with a woman since his leg injury. Faladen's mocking comments lingered in the recesses of his thoughts. He'd convinced himself it wasn't important.

But now, it was on the table between them. If he were any other person, he'd enjoy the physical aspects of marriage. Truth was, he wanted her. But he couldn't dishonor her. He blew out a breath.

Sleeping together led to the physical act of love . . . which led to feelings . . . and caring . . . all sorts of bother and nonsense. If he was humiliated with a court-martial, then she would be too. Jonathan knew how much the gossip swirling around Meri had hurt her.

Besides, he didn't need the strings attached to it. He didn't want it.

He slid a side-eyed glance her way. She was beautiful and confident and brilliant. A man would count his lucky stars to have her share his life. To wake up with her by his side every day would make life a paradise. Something he didn't warrant in the scheme of the universe.

Perhaps she wouldn't want him? He should have taken off his breeches when he'd first met her in London. The sight alone would have turned her away. But he was familiar and someone from her past. She thought she could trust him. No doubt, her previous husband's action had caused her to be disillusioned with all men. Except she saw him differently.

If she only knew how desolate he really was. Beneath the trappings of an elegant morning suit, he was the definition of dismal. He blew out a breath.

One perfect eyebrow arched delicately in the air. "I didn't know it was something you'd have to consider."

He wasn't fooled by her look of impudence. The narrow lines fanning from her eyes and the glistening of tears betrayed her hurt at his silence. Perhaps it was for the best, but then that part of him he still considered honorable came to the forefront. "It's"—he adjusted himself once more in the chair, his cock still thickening—"not that." He wiped a hand down his face, realizing he was clean-shaven for the first time in months because of her. "You're beautiful and highly desirable."

She didn't move. That perfect eyebrow still arched, but the pain he'd inflicted seemed to have ebbed.

Heat licked his cheeks. He should have poured himself a brandy for this conversation. Poor planning on his part. "My injury . . ."

"There are all sorts of positions . . ." She blushed prettily.

Good God. Just thinking of all the positions they could try was making him even harder. How to tell her his scars were only one part of his failures in life? If the dark truth of his military service came to light, she'd leave him, and he wouldn't blame her. It'd be so much easier if they kept their distance.

"My injury has not only left me lame, but I . . . can't put weight on my knee."

"What does that have to do . . ." she said softly. She clasped her hands and regarded him. "I see. I never thought about that." Her expression wasn't pity, but as if she grappled with a vision of what he'd shared.

Thank God he didn't see any sign of sympathy on her face, but this was beyond mortification if such a thing existed.

"I'm sure we'll figure something out, don't you?" She stood and came to his side. Before he knew what was happening, she knelt before him. The delicate touch of her hand rested on his uninjured knee. "We'll do it together. We won't rush that part of the marriage. We both need to be comfortable with it."

He searched the depths of her blue eyes for any sign of pity. Her gaze was true and honest as if she sought to find answers and solutions to the conundrum that faced them.

There were no answers until he could prove his good name. "You shouldn't have high expectations."

She stood and her gaze landed on the fall of his breeches. The effects of their conversation still left him semi-erect. When their eyes met, she didn't smile as if she'd known she tempted him all along. "I find you beautiful and desirable too."

Her words blasted a new hole in his heart, but the fickle organ mended itself immediately and started pounding against his ribs trying to reach her. Proving that Constance was dangerous to his well-honed existence.

She stood above him, and he had to tilt his head slightly to see her eyes.

The final rule should put distance between them. One day he expected his entire staff to mutiny over his dining habits, but it was best for him and his wife. "There's one more rule that's not negotiable."

"What's that?" she said softly.

"Regina eats in the dining room with me."

"Based upon last night, I expected as much. I concur. In exchange, you agree to my last rule." The directness in her gaze made him straighten in his chair. She didn't even hesitate. "I want you to be a father to my daughter. You accept her as your own."

A father? Him? That would be the day when they served ice slushes in hell. The word *no* was on the tip of his tongue, but the stiffness in her stance took on a significance that held a power of its own. "You mentioned this before. Why are you so adamant?"

For a moment, he didn't think she would say anything. She

grappled with whatever she wanted to say. Finally, she swallowed, the pain evident on her face.

"I want her to have someone honorable in her life. I don't want her hurt. Her own father to put it kindly was a con artist. She'll find out the truth about him one day from others. I believe if she knows a real father's love and support, she'll be strong when she has to face the facts of her birth." Her eyes glistened with tears, and she entwined the fingers of her hands, betraying her turmoil. "I had that, and I want her to have that too. You can give her that security." Before he could respond, she straightened her spine like a newly forged piece of steel. "That is non-negotiable."

"You think me honorable," he muttered. She really had no idea who he was besides a mean, surly, false imitation of a man. If he was brought before the military tribunal, he'd become the antithesis of honorable. He blew out a breath.

She was hurting, and he'd do anything to make her smile again. Even forget all his promises to himself. "All right, I agree to the term."

Chapter Thirteen

She had married a ghost.

For the past week, Constance barely saw Jonathan during the day. Their only interaction was during dinner, then they'd say good night. Which was probably for the best, as Constance had awakened at half past three every morning without fail. Aurelia's sleep was practically nonexistent. Whimpering and fitful, she would be standing in her crib with her arms outstretched for Constance. With such a look, Constance couldn't refuse her and had brought her into her own bed until the poor child had fallen asleep again.

Afterward, Constance would carry her to her crib, then she'd sit in one of the damask chairs in her sitting area and make lists. She lived by lists. Already, she had one started for Sykeston Gardens. Clear the clutter, rooms to right, and gardens to grow. When Dahlia came to sit with Aurelia, Constance made her way downstairs.

Today she'd start tackling her lists.

Her first order of business was the study. She straightened the mess of pillows that were always on the floor. She folded the wadded-up coverlet and tucked it away in the drawer of the side table next to the sofa. Then she set to work tidying and dusting the myriad bookshelves that surrounded the study.

Constance straightened her shoulders before proceeding to Jonathan's so-called shooting area. The black chair reeked of gunpowder. When she inspected it closely, there were hundreds of tiny burn holes resulting from the target practice within the house. She brushed it as best she could, but it still smelled of powder. It was little wonder why Mrs. Butler was up in arms over this room.

After Constance finished that task, she moved to cleaning the windows of the French doors with water and lemon juice. Instantly, it cut through the grime of residue that coated the glass. After drying them with a cloth, she proceeded to the windows and repeated her work.

Next came organizing Jonathan's gun cases. She'd created room on one of the bookshelves to stack them neatly. One by one, she cleaned the inside, mindful of the weapon, then polished the surprisingly heavy cases. Finally, she arranged them in a pyramid shape on the chosen shelf.

She had one more task to complete before she'd allow herself a cup of tea. She made her way to her husband's desk. Carefully, she lifted the inkstand and dusted underneath. The only other item on the desk was a stack of papers. When she lifted them, she gasped and brought her hand to her heart. "He kept it," she whispered. Underneath the stack was her book of essays, the one she'd given him when they parted.

Everything was immediately forgotten as she carefully picked up the small brown book. The worn cover was bent as if he'd kept it in his pocket, perhaps close to his person at all times. Without thought, she sat in Jonathan's chair and gingerly turned the pages.

She bit her lip and took a deep breath as she read the words he'd written alongside her musings. They were dates and remembrances of their time together. She'd written about her parents' home, and he'd carefully written their regular meeting times—each Tuesday and Thursday at one o'clock.

Tears gathered in her eyes when she came across her essay on the beauty of the sea. He'd read it so many times that the page had thinned until you could practically see through it. Her throat tightened as she swallowed the swell of emotion that threatened. She'd written that no matter how vast and turbulent the water appeared, there was a relentless steadiness to its motions, almost as if it represented the universe's heartbeat. Like a restful sleep that cleared the mind of the worries of the day, the nightly tides cleaned the beaches of all the debris and footprints that had laid claim during the day.

Jonathan had written in pencil at the top of the page. "A renewal of man's humanity. She's the sea. I'm the debris. To be swept away in her arms would be my salvation."

She lovingly traced his words, then closed her eyes as a tear escaped. She had no doubt he'd written about her.

Whatever it took, she vowed to give him everything he needed to be at peace. From a hidden pocket that had been sewn into her navy wool down, she pulled out a small bowline knot, one of the most durable knots for sailors. She'd carried it with her ever since he'd left Portsmouth all those years ago. It was the first knot she'd learned to tie from the book he'd given her.

She'd learned how to tie every knot in that book. It was the only way to keep her thoughts from dwelling on Jonathan. She'd followed the London papers seeking news about his sister. Within two months, she'd read about his sister's marriage. That meant there was nothing to keep him in England. Constance had not been able to concentrate on anything that day as it meant that Jonathan would leave for war.

Gently, she placed the knot on top of the small, worn book. She pulled out a sheet of paper and dipped his quill in the inkpot. *For my husband, the bowline, the essential and strongest tie that binds.*

After ensuring the ink was dry, she folded the paper and slipped it inside the book. With her heart near to bursting, she placed the book and the knot on the table, then placed his papers over it just as she'd found them. Though they'd taken two different paths in their earlier lives, they were still bound together.

For a moment, she just sat there. How to break the distance between them? She had the key to unlock his heart. She was sure of it. She simply had to find it.

With a determination that wouldn't contemplate defeat, she made her way to the kitchen for a pot of tea. The cook kept the same early hours as she did.

"Another early morning, my lady?" Mrs. Walmer called out over her shoulder as she kneaded the bread for their daily meals. "Miss Aurelia?"

"I'm afraid so. But she's sleeping now." Constance took a sip of the tea. "This is the most perfect cup of tea I've ever tasted."

Mrs. Walmer chuckled as she pushed the dough into the baking pan. "I thank you. Ever since the earl was a little boy, I've made the house tea that way." She pointed to a cabinet on the other side of the wide kitchen. "There's a special honey in there made from the clover in the north pasture. The earl always said that clover was the sweetest." She shook her head. "Since the war, he only drinks coffee."

Constance gently placed her cup back on the saucer and swallowed the tightness that abruptly appeared. "Have many things changed since the earl has returned?"

"Oh my, yes. He used to see all the tenants weekly. He'd have me make baskets for each family, then he'd deliver them. My kitchen was always busy." She stopped her chores and turned her full attention to Constance. "I miss those days. Now he has Mr. Winstead see to everything. I guess his lordship has more important things to do."

Jonathan's valet entered the kitchen. "Good morning, Lady

Sykeston." He came behind the cook and reached around for a freshly baked bun.

"Ralph Byerly! How many times have I told you not to steal my food," Mrs. Walmer chortled, then playfully swatted at his hand.

By then, Ralph had popped the entire bun in his mouth and couldn't answer.

"I was telling her ladyship how his lordship would visit the tenants regularly."

Ralph's eyes widened in delight as he swallowed. "Remember how the previous earl would host a harvest ball for everyone to celebrate the crops coming in?"

Mrs. Walmer clapped her hands together.

Constance smiled at the joy on their faces. What a beautiful tradition that they could continue in honor of Jonathan's father. "Perhaps we should hold one this year?"

Both of them suddenly grew quiet.

"What's wrong?" Constance asked.

"Nothing," the cook said solemnly.

Ralph was the first to look up. "Well, it's no secret." He turned to Constance. "The earl doesn't go out. He'd never agree to it."

"Hush," Mrs. Walmer scolded. "You need to make the earl's ointment."

"Ointment?" Constance asked.

"Yes." Mrs. Walmer nodded as she kneaded more bread. "The Duchess of Randford has a companion who knows herbs."

Constance smiled. "Willa. She's a good friend of mine."

"His lordship likes to have me massage his leg," Ralph offered, then wrinkled his nose. "I hate making the salve. It stinks."

"I'll make it," Constance offered. When the two servants looked at her with wide eyes, she continued, "If I wouldn't be in the way?"

Mrs. Walmer winked at Ralph, and he smiled in return.

"Your ladyship, that would be remarkably helpful." Ralph smiled.

"How about now?" Mrs. Walmer asked.

"No, she can't do it now." Without breaking stride, Ralph continued, "Your carriage is ready, my lady."

By then, Mrs. Walmer had returned to her bread baking. The conversation among the three of them was clearly finished.

"Thank you, Ralph." Constance stood and gathered her red pelisse. She wore a simple marine blue gown. It was her standard clothing when she went to the dockyard of Lysander & Sons. "I should be home around noon. Would one of you tell my husband and Mrs. Butler? Dahlia will see after Aurelia. When I return, I plan on working in the kitchen, then in the gardens."

"Yes, my lady." Ralph nodded.

Constance made her way upstairs.

Mr. North stood guard over the entry. "Good morning, my lady. Off again so early?"

Constance smiled and tied the ribbons of her hat under her chin. "Today is the monthly bookkeeping. I find that it's easier to stomach if I get the chore over with first thing. I'll be back in a couple of hours."

Mr. North nodded and opened the door. "I saw what you did to his lordship's study this morning. I hope I'm there to witness the look on his face when he sees your work. One can actually see out the windows." Mr. North rocked back on his heels. "A miracle, my lady, in so many ways."

"Thank you." Constance smiled at the praise. "I have even more planned for that room."

With a wave, she was out the door, where a footman waited to help her into the carriage. Within minutes, she was on her way to the docks. Constance leaned back against the black leather bench seat. The leather was cool under her touch. She could smell the sea and brine in the air. She'd always loved to work even when she was a little girl accompanying her father to the docks.

From her satchel, Constance retrieved the journal where she kept her lists. The book naturally fell open to the one that comprised her chores for Jonathan's study. She traced the words with a light touch as a smile fell upon her lips. There were so many things they could accomplish together.

Before she knew it, the carriage had arrived at Lysander & Sons. As soon as Constance's foot hit the ground, Alin Zephyr, one of the longest employed and most crotchety of all her workers, leaned against the building and placed his hand over his heart.

"I must be havin' visions if Constance Lysander is back this morning," he called out to his fellow joiner, James Selwyn. Both men were two of the finest marine woodworkers in all of Portsmouth—no, make that England. She was lucky to have them at her shop even if they did tease her incessantly.

James playfully punched Alin in the arm. "Watch it, old man. She's a countess now."

Alin pulled back in wide-eyed alarm. "I wonder whose nose points higher in the sky? The wife of a duke's son or the wife of an earl?"

"I don't know that answer, but I do know that neither affects my worth around here," she called out.

"Aye," Alin agreed. "You're priceless around here, lass. A Lysander always takes the top spot."

Her cheeks heated at the affection in his voice. Alin may play the grump, but his heart was true and his work was the best—bar none—of any other joiner, including James. "Thank you. Everything I learned about this business came from my mother and father."

"And who do you think taught them?" Alin boasted with a laugh.

They both knew the answer to that question. He had taken

Constance's father under his wing when her father had first inherited the business. Alin had the patience of Job as he taught Constance's father every aspect of the refitting trade. In kind, her father and Mr. Bridges had taught her.

It truly was a family business.

James threw his thumb over his shoulder. "The shipwright and Mrs. Bridges are waiting for ye, my lady. Lord *High and Mighty* is in there with them."

Her smile fell away. "The Marquess of Faladen is here this morning?" He was a longtime customer, but the most annoying and demanding one. Plus, he always paid his bills late.

Alin rolled his eyes. "My work comes second only to my wife, but I could use another year before I have to set eyes on one of his ships again."

"Perhaps he's here to thank us for our efforts the last time." Constance grinned as she unlatched the mighty oak door and stepped into the main office, where silence greeted her. It was like stepping into a tomb.

"Good morning," she said. The discomfort in the room rolled over her in waves. The marquess stood staring out the window. Mrs. Bridges ran her hands down her skirt, while Mr. Bridges fisted his hands.

"My lady." In his early fifties, Mr. Bridges was lean and wiry with a face weathered by the sun. The best shipwright to have graced the Portsmouth yards stood next to a table where a fresh pot of tea stood at attention ready for the morning. The smell of tarts filled the air with sweetness.

Constance's mouth watered. She hadn't eaten this morning as she'd rushed out of Sykeston Gardens after her own breakfast tea. "Oh, that smells like heaven."

"Breakfast needs to wait," Mrs. Bridges said softly. Her eyes were as gray as the North Sea and as turbulent. "His lordship wishes to speak with you." Mrs. Bridges tut-tutted as she rounded the corner of her desk and laid the bookkeeping journals on the large table in the middle of the room. "You might need these, my lady."

"Lord Faladen, how can I help you?" Constance pulled off her gloves then set her satchel down on her desk, which sat in the corner closest to the harbor. Mr. Bridges's desk was directly opposite and faced a bank of windows that overlooked their dockyard. Since he was here every day and all the employees reported to him, it made sense that he be able to view the work being performed. If there were any emergencies or trouble, he would be the first to see it and could lend assistance if need be.

The marquess turned to the couple. "If you don't mind, I'd like a private word with Lady Sykeston."

"I'll fetch you a cup for the tea and a plate for the tarts, my lady," Mrs. Bridges called out.

"I'll stay here," Mr. Bridges offered.

Constance shook her head, never taking her gaze from the marquess's back. "Perhaps it would be best if you keep Mrs. Bridges company."

As soon as the door shut, the marquess turned to face her. A good half foot shorter than Jonathan, the marquess had a normally pleasant but somewhat droll face. Today he wore an intimidating scowl. "Lady Sykeston, to call this a good morning is an overstatement. It's anything but good."

"Oh, why is that?" Constance asked. She sat at her desk and motioned for the marquess to take a seat on one of the sturdy wooden chairs in front of her.

The marquess slid into the seat as if it were a normal social call, but the twitching under his right eye meant he was anything but at ease.

"I'll come straight to the point. My yacht capsized yesterday. I was sailing to the Isle of Wight. By divine providence, another ship was by our side or my men and I could have drowned." He pursed his lips as his face reddened. "I blame you and Lysander & Sons for the catastrophe."

"Us?" For a moment, she couldn't believe her ears. "How do you know it was our workmanship that caused the problem? There were multiple venders that worked on your ship."

He crossed his arms over his chest. The pose reminded her of a child who had a broken toy. "The other work was cosmetic in nature. Your company was the only one to touch the structure of my yacht." He stood, then leaned over her desk. "Lysander & Sons reworked the loose joints and tarred the ship to prevent this from happening."

"Where is the ship?"

He blew out his breath. "*Enchanted Mistress* is unfortunately at the Isle of Wight. This time I've hired a competent refitting operation to assess the damage. They said she can't be repaired." With a crimson face, he pointed at her. "You're going to have to buy me a new yacht." He waved his arms around the office. "Or I'll have my solicitor hire a barrister, and I'll end up owning this discrepant, sun-worn wooden shell of a supposed business."

"I'm sorry this happened." Constance held his gaze and wouldn't look away though he glared at her. "I won't accept responsibility for the damage until it can be proven that Lysander & Sons' performance was the reason that your yacht capsized."

"Typical that a woman running a business wouldn't take responsibility," he spat.

Constance stood up, placed her hands on the desk, leaned forward, then lowered her voice. "Typical that a man would blame a woman without proof."

He hmphed in protest. "I stand by what I said. Let's say you agree you're at fault. How will you pay for the damages?"

"I won't even contemplate such an outcome."

"Listen, I'm a fair man. I don't want to take this from you." He waved a hand around the room. He slid his gaze to hers. "Perhaps you have other assets that will cover the costs."

"Like what?" Constance moved away slowly, keeping him

in sight. This was the only property she owned. Actually, her trust owned it, not her. She could have had it dissolved at any time, but there was never a need. She kept her face a mask of calm, but her stomach churned.

"Perhaps your late husband left you an inheritance? Other property?" He shrugged. "I hate to resort to resolving our differences in court."

"I'm not agreeing to anything until I see the yacht." She tilted her chin upward as she clasped her hands into fists. She'd be damned before she gave him anything.

"Suit yourself. It's at the Redmond dock." He tugged his hat to his head. "If I were you, I wouldn't share this news with your husband. Such worry causes him to become . . . how shall I say . . . more unstable? Unbalanced for lack of a better word."

"Pardon? Are you implying his character is suspect?" She was incredulous that he would even say such a thing, and she wouldn't tolerate one word. "I'll have you know he's the most honorable man I know. Furthermore—"

"Let me explain," he interrupted. "Last year, he received some unsettling news, and I was there. He fell like a house of cards. Required two footmen to help him up. He could barely walk." Before Constance could defend Jonathan any more, he continued, "You'll be hearing from my solicitor."

At the sound of the door closing, Constance collapsed behind her desk. If it became known that he was taking legal action, it'd ruin her business. While many of the refitting companies along the shore came and went, Lysander & Sons had been an institution for generations. She fisted her hand. She would not allow herself to worry until all the facts were known.

The back door opened. Mr. and Mrs. Bridges rushed in. Mrs. Bridges placed the still-warm tarts and a piping hot cup of tea off to Constance's side. The wisps of steam swirled from the cup before disappearing into nothing.

The same as her company if she didn't get the situation with Faladen resolved.

"Thank you, Mrs. Bridges. These look delicious." Constance patted the woman's hand then turned to Mr. Bridges. "Did you hear?"

"Aye," he grunted. "He stormed in here demanding compensation for his damages a few minutes before you arrived." He leaned across the table and glared at the dock outside. "I'd wager my life savings that we weren't the cause of that ship sinking."

Mrs. Bridges tipped her chin in the air, the act of defiance bold on such a small-statured woman. "*Bloody* Lord High and Mighty," she muttered.

Mr. Bridges shook his head once. "Martha, don't let him upset you."

The idea that Faladen would upset Mrs. Bridges enough that she'd curse was beyond comprehension. For as long as Constance had known her she was the most pious, patient, and peaceful person she knew. "Don't worry yourself any further, Mrs. Bridges," Constance said. "The marquess agreed for us to evaluate the damage. We'll know more then."

"My lady?" Mrs. Bridges asked. "Perhaps you should inquire if your husband would intervene. He could talk to the marquess and make him see reason."

"This is my battle," Constance said defiantly and stood a little straighter. She'd learned early in life to take care of matters herself. After her first husband had deserted her, such skills had proven prudent. Now they would serve her well again. "I'd prefer to handle it myself."

Mr. Bridges nodded once. "There's your Lysander side coming out. Your father would be proud of you. Alin and I will sail over and take a look at the ship."

"Once you have an opinion, I want to know immediately." Constance stood and walked to the window. "I'll write to my solicitor in London to let him know the situation."

Finally, she left out a shallow breath. A small bubble of panic burst through her. This was her birthright, one she had every intention of giving to her daughter. She couldn't and wouldn't lose it.

But why did Lord Faladen broach the issue of her husband? Indignant at how he'd slurred Jonathan, Constance silently fisted her hands. Frankly, she didn't trust a thing Lord Faladen said.

Furthermore, her husband had other demons he had to conquer before helping her. The best for all of them including her shipwright, his wife, and the employees who were worked long, hard hours out in the yard was to get this issue resolved quickly.

The lump of disquiet residing in her throat slowly dissolved. She smiled gently. "Everything will be fine."

Chapter Fourteen

Jonathan thrummed his fingers on the desk as he waited for North to attend him. When he'd first walked into his study, the smell of beeswax practically knocked him over. Thankfully, it had diminished in the half hour he'd been here.

Unable to sit still any longer, he stood abruptly and grabbed his cane.

He was more than out of sorts. He was in a foul fit of pique.

What had happened in his study was completely unacceptable. He would not allow anyone, particularly *her*, to nose around in his business.

The cloying sweet smell of floral arrangements filled the room. Regina stuck her snout straight in the air and sniffed repeatedly as if trying to identify the ungodly fragrance.

"You rang, sir?" North stepped into Jonathan's study.

"Tell me who did this." Jonathan carefully made his way to the large table that sat in the middle of the room, then leaned one hip against it in a purposeful show of insouciance.

"Who?"

Jonathan tilted his head and smirked. "Don't act innocent. Was it her?"

"Who?" This time North's brow crinkled in neat rows.

"My compliments on your remarkable impersonation of an owl. I shouldn't have asked. There's only one person who would dare enter this room and interfere." He dropped his voice to the most menacing, gravelly sound he could summon. "Why did you let her in?"

"I beg your pardon." North stood tall and smoothed his hand down his black morning coat. "If you're referring to Lady Sykeston, I didn't let her in here."

"Look around this room. It's . . . it's been obliterated." Jonathan waved a hand around the room.

"You mean obliterated into a semblance of cleanliness that one might enjoy?" North rested his thumb under his chin and tapped his lips with his forefinger. He took a long gander around the room. "Perhaps invite some guests to call upon you?"

"I don't want guests. And I certainly don't want to encourage anyone to call on me." He waved his hand once more, tipping a priceless Sèvres vase given to his father by his mother. With cat-like reflexes, he caught it as it twirled around on its edges.

"A perfect catch, your lordship." The butler nodded approvingly.

"North. I'm serious," Jonathan growled.

"As am I." The butler cleared his throat. "Lady Sykeston is responsible for this. Mrs. Walmer has shared that her ladyship was dressed and downstairs by no later than half past four in the morning. Since she didn't leave for the shipyard until half past seven, she had plenty of time to clean and straighten your study without anyone knowing."

"What about the flowers? Where did she get them?" Jonathan crossed his arms and glared at the butler. "They give me a headache."

"Of course, sir. Everyone is aware you prefer the putrid smell of powder burns mixed with dog." North took a deep breath. "Take a whiff, I beg of you. Isn't this so much more *pleasant* in the morning?"

"No, it's not. You didn't answer my question. *Where did she get them?*"

"From the garden, of course. She cut and arranged the flowers herself. By filling the house with bouquets, the house smells fresher." North wrinkled his nose in pleasure. "And you'll be pleased to know that the garden is already looking better than the overgrown mess you prefer."

At the butler's words, Jonathan's head turned to the French doors to the courtyard to see for himself. He couldn't keep the incredulity out of his voice. "What is that?"

"The courtyard?"

"No. The door windows." Standing in place, he circled the room taking in the travesty of it all. "What has she done? The drapes are drawn and the windows are . . ."

"What, my lord?" The butler hummed. The glee in his voice unmistakable.

"Unusual."

"As in . . . spotless?" North added with a sly hint of pride in his voice.

Jonathan turned and delivered a look designed to impale the brazen butler in his place. "She touched my pistols. She cleaned them and polished the cases." He pointed to the bookshelf. "Look at it. It's like a . . ."

"A tower? Lady Sykeston must have put quite a bit of elbow grease into the endeavor, especially the windows. Perhaps that was the reason for the lemons yesterday."

Jonathan held up his hand. "Wait. She did this by herself?"

"Every bit of it," North rocked back on his heels.

"Without any maid or footman to help?"

North shook his head.

"Was Mrs. Butler aware of this?"

The most aggravating smile broke across the elderly man's

face. "Not until this morning. Lady Sykeston kept the surprise from all of us."

This time he truly was flabbergasted. "She did all of this? For what reason?"

"Whatever reason possessed her, I know the staff is utterly enchanted. She takes tea in the morning with Mrs. Walmer, and Mrs. Butler is delighted with the way the new countess has everything in order. She's taken an inventory of the pantry, the silverware, and has even consulted with me and the cook as to your favorite dishes." He shook his head in apparent wonder. "But to answer your question, if I might venture a guess?" North clasped his hands in front of him in a rather dutiful pose. "I believe she did it because she cares."

He turned to his butler. The infuriating man raised his eyebrows as if demanding Jonathan to guess. "What does she care about?"

"Perhaps she's like the rest of us." He shrugged. "I think her ladyship cares about this great house and the beautiful gardens. The very ones you've ordered not to be attended to. She cares about the wonderful families who have lived their lives here. She wants to honor them," he added softly.

Jonathan pushed back his morning coat, then placed his hands on his hips as he took another glance around the room. It was immaculate, sparkling, and, dare he say it, unusually pleasant. But it didn't explain North's explanation. "Why would she care about my ancestors? It doesn't make any sense." He shook his head.

"Really?"

He tilted his head to the ceiling and stared at those damned cherubs again. "Tell me, North. I trust you to help me here."

"Perhaps she cares because she wants to honor you." His voice was so low that Jonathan wasn't certain he'd heard him correctly. "She cares about you."

Jonathan shook his head and seized his cane. It was impossible what he was hearing. "Our marriage is nothing more than a convenience between the two of us." He gripped the silver knob of the handle so tightly, he was sure he'd leave marks. "You're aware of that."

"I know what I see." North dipped his head and stared at the sky-blue Aubusson rug beneath his feet.

By now, Jonathan's entire routine had been thrown off course by Constance. He could smell her clean scent and slight perfume throughout his home even when she wasn't there. The sound of her laughter taunted him to come out of his study, his self-imposed haven, to find her. Her cheeks would be flushed and bright over something silly like a story one of the maids would tell or a joke one of the footmen would spout. She made people happy.

He didn't like it one bit.

He blew out a breath, hoping it would give him the patience he was in such short supply of recently.

But the real menace was after midnight. His wife haunted him every single night. There was no escaping the effect she had on him when she slept so close. All he had to do was walk through a door, and he'd find her.

And she'd welcome him in her bed.

He wouldn't let her try to conquer him anymore. He had to find a way to create more distance. It was the only way he'd be able to live with her.

"I need some time alone." Jonathan turned to walk out into the courtyard.

"When Lady Sykeston returns, I hope you won't be cross with her," North said in a wry tone. "She's worked very hard to please you."

He grunted in response. The entire conversation was finished as far as he was concerned.

"One more thing, sir. Perhaps with clean windows, you'll

be able to see more things clearly besides the outside." North bowed elegantly, then turned on the ball of his foot.

Jonathan didn't watch him leave. He sat at his desk and stared out the window. No one ever dared disobey his wishes about his study.

Did his wife have any understanding what she'd done to his well-organized world?

He'd have a staff revolt on his hands. Mrs. Butler would want to keep the room tidy. With the window of opportunity wide open, she'd assign maids and footmen to clean.

He practically growled. Regina whimpered at the sound. He soothed her with a pat, but his anger grew. This room was his.

He'd not allow his wife to wreck such havoc. He'd not allow her to destroy his study. If she changed it, then she changed him. Absently, he picked up the papers on his desk. A piece of knotted twine lay on the book that she'd given him. He'd read it every night he was in the army. It was the only thing that kept him grounded and sane. When he opened it, he discovered a sheet of paper inside.

After he read it, he studied the knot, then tested its strength. Resolute and unyielding. With a resigned sigh, he leaned back in his chair and closed his eyes. He refused to think or feel. It was the only way to keep an even keel. Her note with the words *essential and strongest tie that binds* was akin to an attack from all sides. First it was his study, then his pistols.

But the wound she'd inflicted with this note went straight to his heart. The faithless organ tripped in his chest, begging him to accept what she offered. Dare he think it? A real marriage.

He propped his elbows on his desk and rested his head in his hands. He'd not capitulate to his heart or her. The real reason he was angry? It was the state of his life—living

perpetually suspended in midair. There was no chance
of happiness for either of them in their marriage until he
cleared his name.

~⁓

Constance poured a glass of Madeira for herself and a brandy
for Jonathan before dinner.

She normally didn't drink the sweet fortified wine, but
she'd had quite a day. She'd written her solicitor in London
about the Marquess of Faladen's threat, then that afternoon
with Dahlia and Aurelia by her side, she'd made Jonathan's
ointment, then weeded and trimmed a substantial part of the
overgrown courtyard. Though the gardener, Mr. Rowles,
asked if she needed assistance, she'd politely declined, explaining she wanted to do it herself. She was well aware that
the elderly man could hardly dig a hole much less stay on his
hands and knees for hours on end.

After she'd accomplished the task, she'd gone upstairs,
ordered a bath, then dressed for dinner. She'd worn one of
her favorite evening gowns, a pale pink and blue watercolor
silk. Her friend Beth had sewn small beads of crystals of the
same color as the silk around the bodice neckline and short-
ened the sleeves. But the pièce de résistance was a matching
shawl with the same beautiful beadwork around the edges.

Suddenly, Jonathan entered the room.

She came around the table with his glass in her hand.
"Good evening, Jonathan."

"Good evening," he clipped.

By that time, she'd reached his side and presented him with
the brandy.

With a nod of thanks, he downed it in one gulp, and then
placed the empty glass on a side table.

She waited for him to say something about her dress as
she took a sip of her own glass. The cold sweetness of the

Madeira offered a welcome respite from her long day. After she swallowed, she slowly lowered her glass and studied him.

His gaze skated briefly down her dress then back up again. It caught on her bodice but only lingered for a moment until his eyes came to rest on her face. The banked fire in his eyes intensified as it smoldered. Heat, the kind that would combust on its own, sparked between them.

Hopefully, it was a sign that he was pleased with her dress and—just as important—that he was pleased with her efforts in his study.

"Did you have a pleasant day?" She set her unfinished glass next to his.

For an absurd moment, she didn't think he was going to answer her. Unyielding and hard, his face didn't move.

He narrowed his eyes almost as if he was evaluating her before breaking the silence between them. "What do you think?"

She opened her mouth to inquire what had upset him, when the footman came in and announced that dinner was served.

Jonathan waved a hand, and Constance preceded him into the formal dining room. As was her usual custom, Regina sat to Jonathan's right, leaving Constance the other side.

After each course was served, Constance tried to engage her husband, but the effort was futile. Her husband would answer with either a grunt or a one-syllable word. It made the art of conversation nothing more than a long chat with herself.

Finally, the meal was over, and Jonathan nodded for everyone to leave. It was normally her favorite time of the day as they actually talked with each other. But tonight he seemed to be fuming. Discreetly, she waited until the room was empty, then placed her serviette on the table.

"You haven't even mentioned your study." Whatever it was that was bothering him, she wanted to discuss it and clear the air between them. "Is something amiss?"

"That's putting it mildly," he said. For the first time since they sat down, his attention was directed solely on her.

She didn't allow herself to become defensive. Whenever she'd seen her parents disagree, they never raised their voices. They had always been completely focused on each other.

He leaned slightly toward her. His displeasure almost shimmered between them. It was as real and vibrant as if another person had joined them at the table. "I have never allowed the staff to clean my study. It is the one room in the house that is mine. All mine. No one enters unless I invite them in." He softened his voice even more. "What made you think you could cross the threshold and do what you pleased?"

She couldn't concentrate on the words as his voice wasn't a whisper like a lover would utter to another. As if that would ever happen. No, this was a warning hiss before an animal would strike.

Regina whined softly, giving her more evidence that he was furious with her.

His hardened gaze sliced through her, spilling all her good intentions on the floor. "I . . . I thought I was doing something nice for you." She swallowed but didn't turn from him no matter how angry he was.

"Ever since I joined the military, I found comfort in having my things arranged in an orderly fashion, one that suited me."

"And I upset your sense of order?" she asked.

"I don't allow anyone to touch my study, particularly my pistols." His voice grew a little more insistent.

"They're possessions. You make it sound like a shrine."

He arched an infuriating brow. "Precisely. It's my shrine. It reminds me of how excellent I was at my position and my responsibilities." He stood slowly and grimaced.

"I thought if the room was set to rights, it'd make your work easier."

"My work is as I like it. My pistols aren't to be touched." He nodded formally.

"Do your pistols help you with your estate responsibilities? Is that why you rely on Thomas Winstead?" She kept her voice calm, but the challenge was clear.

He stared at the floor for a moment, then shook his head. "Madam, you are unbelievable. There is nothing wrong with how I manage my estates. The next time you have inspiration to do something nice for me, please do us both a favor. Resist the urge." Without taking his leave, he made his way to the exit.

"Wait," she commanded softly. "I didn't mean to intrude upon your privacy. I thought as your wife, I was helping you."

His gaze whipped back to hers. "Helping? Let's not mention it again." With a hand on the doorknob, he carefully turned toward her. "Indeed, you are my wife. God save us both."

Without waiting for a response, he left. The sound of his stilted gait faded as he made his way upstairs.

Regina's big brown eyes focused on her, then she leapt down and followed Jonathan.

Leaving Constance feeling very much alone and bewildered. What had she done?

My God, she never once considered that he might see her efforts as an unwanted intrusion into his life. A wife was supposed to make her husband feel as if he'd entered an oasis of calm and found a refuge from the unkindness and vitriol that was so rampant in the world today.

But what he thought of as an oasis was closer to a pigsty. No matter her own preferences, she should have respected his. In hindsight, she should have spoken to him first. Perhaps she wasn't the first person to intrude in his business or offer unwanted help.

His normal custom was to retire into his private chambers where she wouldn't see him until the next morning. However, she couldn't let this fester between them until she apologized. Otherwise, she'd never be able to sleep this evening.

As she rose to find him, Mr. North came into the room.

"My lady?" He bowed slightly. "Mrs. Walmer informed me that the ointments you made are ready. I took the liberty of having the jars delivered to your bedroom."

"Thank you, Mr. North." The salve provided the perfect excuse to see her husband.

But first, Constance had other matters and little people to attend to. After an hour of playing with Aurelia, then bathing her, Constance put the baby to bed. They said their prayers, then shared a long discussion about how Constance needed her to sleep through the night. With a few flutters of her eyelashes as her answer, Aurelia finally succumbed to sleep.

"One more thing, darling girl," Constance whispered. "If you have any ideas how I can wriggle my way back into his good graces, I'd appreciate your advice. But save it for tomorrow; you need your rest." Constance leaned down and pressed a kiss to her cheek.

As quiet as a mouse, she tiptoed out of Aurelia's room, then closed the door until barely an inch was open. She wanted to hear her if she did stir but didn't want the soft glow from the candles to wake her.

Next door, she could hear someone walking in the dressing room.

She sat in a chair and blew a breath, upsetting the lock of hair that had escaped its hairpin. She would have a better chance of dancing with the devil at the stroke of midnight than giving her husband the salve, let alone a massage this evening.

Constance would have to give it to Ralph. Jonathan would be more amenable to receiving it from his valet. She could imagine the frosty disdain that would radiate from her husband if she suggested she massage his leg.

That thought made dancing with the devil more appealing by the moment. At least, she'd be warmer.

Steps staggered next door in the dressing room followed by a muffled "bloody hell." Before she could rise from the chair to see what was wrong, the walls shook as if a boulder had fallen on the floor.

Simultaneously, a cacophony of noises erupted at the same time. A scratching noise came from the other side of the door along with Regina's distinctive whine. But what worried her the most was her husband's bellowing as if he'd broken his leg.

Chapter Fifteen

⌒

Without delay, Constance wrenched open the door. With his back to her, Jonathan lay on his side gripping his injured leg. She rushed forward and immediately knelt to his side. He wore a banyan, but her focus landed on his colorless face.

"Shall I call for help?"

His arm shot out and he grabbed her skirts. "No. The pain will subside. Damme to hell." He grunted slightly before turning her way.

"Where's your cane?" she asked.

"It slipped out from underneath my hand," he gasped. "Do you think you could push that chair over? I'll use it as leverage to stand. There must be a change in the weather coming. My leg is stiffer than usual."

A staccato knock pounded on his door, then a worried voice came from across the bedroom. "My lord? Was that you who called out?"

She started to stand again when he grabbed her hand with his.

"Don't let anyone in," he commanded softly. His early

anger vanished. "They make such a fuss and bother when they see me like this."

"Of course. I'll see who it is and send them away." She ran across the room, then cut through his bedroom. Without stopping, she unlocked the door, then swung it open.

Ralph stood on the other side, pulling a set of keys out of his waistcoat. "My lady? I was about to open the door myself." He glanced over her shoulder. "Do you need my help? I thought I heard the earl fall."

By now, her heartbeat hammered in double time at the shock of seeing her husband on the floor. Instinctively, Constance brought a hand to her chest as a nervous laugh escaped. "I'm afraid that was me. I was trying to pull a box from a shelf and it fell to the floor."

The valet's brows threaded together. "Must have been a very heavy box. May I offer you some assistance?"

She shook her head once. "No need, Ralph. My trunk of shoes fell. I'm looking for a special pair. I'm sorry if I alarmed anyone."

"Does the earl need me this evening, then?" Ralph peeked over her shoulder into the room. "He didn't tell me if he wanted his shower."

She turned and glanced at the dressing room. "I believe he's seeing to Aurelia. I'll inform him that you're looking for him."

The valet bowed once. "If I can be of service to either of you, please ring for me."

"Thank you."

Ralph turned and started down the stairs to the main floor.

Constance shut and locked the door. Without wasting a second, she rushed back to Jonathan's side.

By now, he was sitting up. "That was fast thinking."

She knelt by his side again. "Do you think anything is broken?"

"No." He pointed to a wall. "I need that chair. I shouldn't have had Ralph move it over there last night." He ran a hand through his hair. "Do you think you can manage it?"

A plain but sturdy oak chair was tucked into a corner of the room. Quickly, she reached it, but when she tried to lift, it wouldn't budge.

"It's too heavy. Push it in my direction."

After a couple of hefty shoves, she'd pushed it to his side.

He turned with his back to the chair and grabbed a low-seated marble commode next to him. "When this happens, I'm usually able to lift my weight of my own accord."

"Has this happened before?" she asked, remembering Lord Faladen's words.

"More times than I care to admit." He braced one arm on the commode, then with his left hand, he grabbed the chair. "Are you keeping count?"

Her eyes widened at his curtness. "Of course not."

He ceased moving to stare at her. "I didn't mean to sound rude."

She nodded. "You're forgiven."

With a grunt, he hoisted himself onto the chair. The joints of the chair legs squeaked under the weight but held firm. Once he cleared the seat, Jonathan collapsed. His chest heaved like bellows from the exertion of lifting his weight with his arms.

He rested his head on the back of the chair and closed his eyes with a grimace. The effort was an obvious attempt to gain control over horrific pain. He constantly rubbed the right thigh of his injured leg. Eventually, he ran his hand over his kneecap. Immediately, another curse escaped.

"Shall I call a doctor? Where are you hurt?" Constance knelt on her knees and lightly placed her hand over his.

Jonathan's eyes jerked open at her touch.

"Come now. I lied to your valet for you. Please don't tell me you're uncomfortable with me by your side touching you."

For an eternity, he didn't say a word, but stared down at her. Without taking her hand away from his, he continued to rub his leg. "It's not that."

"What is it, then?"

He arched a sardonic brow. His voice lowered, and she had to lean toward him to hear. "Very few have seen the gnarled flesh of my right leg. If you faint at the sight, I couldn't pick you up. You'd be on your own."

"I won't faint," she assured him with a smile, then lowered her voice to match his. "But I do have a confession . . . I'm sometimes dizzy at the sight of blood. So, we're both lucky you're not bleeding." She smiled and was rewarded for her efforts when a small grin tugged at his lips.

"Indeed." He chuckled slightly.

"I made your ointment today."

"You made it?" he asked incredulously. "The one Ralph uses for my leg?"

She nodded. "Mrs. Walmer was quite accommodating."

"My cook allowed you into her kitchen." He ran a hand down his face as if trying to reconcile the fact. "I shouldn't be surprised. You could charm a badger to share his burrow." He shifted an inch in the chair, his abrupt exhale ragged.

"Shall I get it?" For a moment, she thought he was going to refuse.

Finally, he nodded. After quickly checking that Aurelia was fast asleep in her room, she picked up the salve, then returned to Jonathan's side.

She knelt again at his feet. She scooted closer until she was practically between his legs. He widened his stance slightly. The subtle movement released the scent of cedar soap. The rich fragrance melded with his own, a potent and virile male who happened to be in front of her.

Constance bent her head, pretending all her concentration was centered on opening the jar of ointment. In actuality, it was to keep from revealing the effect he was having on her.

At the last twist of the lid, the scent of peppermint floated between them.

"Ah." She brought the container to her nose and inhaled. "It's very pleasant. I added peppermint oil. It's still your favorite, isn't it?"

He didn't answer.

She silently exhaled. He should know by now that silence had never stopped her before. "I tried the salve myself. I might make more for my own use." She held the jar out to him.

Without wasting a glance at the salve or her, he said, "You do it."

She swallowed slightly. She never dreamed he'd ask her to help him, but she wouldn't look a gift horse in the mouth. This might be the only opportunity to break down some of the barriers between them. "All right."

He grabbed her by the wrist before she could lift his banyan out of the way. To an outsider, it might have appeared abrupt, as if he wanted to hurt her. Instead, his touch was incredibly gentle, as if holding a piece of crystal. She studied his hand holding her wrist. With the long length of his fingers, he could easily encircle both of her wrists with one hand.

"Are you modest?" she asked gently.

"No. But I'll tell you if your touch becomes too much for me." His gaze never left hers. "I expect the same from you. If it's too much for you, tell me."

The rough and hardened voice infiltrated her chest. Every organ and cell in her body vibrated in awareness. The first time they had truly been alone without another living creature disturbing them. Even Regina had retired for the evening, content that her master was in good hands.

"Of course. But it would be remiss of me not to say that I think you're being awfully squeamish for a man," she teased.

"You're still a minx." When he laughed, the warmth in his eyes reflected a new lightness.

"Always and forever." She scooped some of the salve, then rubbed her palms together releasing more of the fragrance. "This smells lovely."

"I wouldn't care if it smelled like a horse's . . ."

She couldn't help but laugh. "Who would have guessed that the Earl of Sykeston possesses such a vile vocabulary? I'll have to watch that Aurelia doesn't hear such language." The words trailed to nothing as she peeked at him under her eyelashes.

A small smile creased his lips. "Well, if that's all she has to be afraid of, she'll be fine."

"I think I'll start at your ankle, then move toward your knee unless you prefer something else."

"That's what Ralph does too. The worst is above the knee," he answered. "Flesh is missing on my thigh where a ball had to be dug out."

"Are you ready?" she asked softly.

"Yes."

Constance kept her eyes on his as she deftly placed her hands on his ankle. His skin was cool to the touch, and the bones so different from hers. She massaged his ankle down to his heel. His ankle was so large, she couldn't wrap both hands around it. She continued to stroke upward, kneading the tight muscles of his calf. The hair on his legs was smooth but coarser than what she had expected.

He jerked a little when she found the first scar.

"Did that hurt?"

"No. It just surprised me," he murmured.

"What surprised you?" she asked.

"The softness of your hands." His warm gaze captured hers.

The way he spoke the words made her melt a bit. The huskiness of his voice curled around her, and her breath quickened. Somehow, she continued to massage his calf.

"The scar you're massaging felt as if a cup of flesh had

been torn off when the ball hit my calf. A little harder, please. That was the second shot I took. The first knocked me off my horse."

"Then what happened?" She pressed her fingers into his skin, again and again. With the palm of her hand she pushed straight down. She repeated the movement for several more minutes.

He wasn't going to answer, so she reached for more salve.

Then she remembered their stupid rules. "I suppose I wasn't supposed to ask about that."

"What?" He tilted his head as if truly not understanding what she was talking about.

"Asking about your past. What happened on that day certainly qualifies." By then, she'd reached his knee.

He winced slightly at the movement. "I think I might have landed on my knee. I'll have a bruise there tomorrow. Right above where you're rubbing is where the first shot hit. Sometimes, the skin feels numb. That wound is the reason for my occasional instability. Sometimes, it seems as if everything misfires in my leg. The muscles and bone don't work in tandem. It makes sense since my thighbone was shattered." He turned his attention to the window.

Her perfidious gaze dipped to his shoulders, then rose to study his profile. He had grown into an extraordinarily handsome man. His eyes had almost closed as if about to succumb to sleep.

Yet his stubborn pride wouldn't let anyone in. He was hurting in so many ways, more than in a physical sense.

"The surgeon insisted that he had to cut off my leg." He faced her. "I declined."

"Why?" She skated her hands over his kneecap, then swooped back down for another rub lower.

He narrowed his eyes. "I'd seen other men have their legs amputated. Half of them didn't make it through the next week."

"That was very astute to notice that." She scooped another handful of salve. "I must come closer to work on the rest of your leg."

His stare never left hers as he nodded once.

Scooting nearer, she rested on her knees much as if she were in church kneeling to pray. She reached under his banyan, then trailed her fingers across his skin until she found the last injury.

Though this leg was smaller than his other, it was still massive in size and strength, so different from her own. With the tips of her fingers, she could tell where he'd been shot. Angry striations of raised skin accompanied by a depression about an inch deep and several inches wide marked his thigh about his knee. There were more scars from the myriad of stitches the surgeon had sewn to keep Jonathan's mangled skin together. She massaged the area over and over.

With every exhale that escaped from his parted lips, she could tell if she was too rough or too soft. If they were sharp, then she'd pressed too hard. If they were shallow, then her ministrations were perfect.

His breath fanned across her cheek as if kissing her. Memories of their first kiss rushed forward, sweeping her closer to him. This was the worst moment in the world to think about kissing her husband. Constance was supposed to be helping him, not seducing him. She made the mistake of looking down.

God help her. He was aroused. Though his banyan was closed still, the outline of his hard cock resting against his lower midriff was plainly visible.

She closed her eyes, yet the image stayed front and center. She took a deep breath desperate for control. Inside, an incredible heat was building. His scent tempting her to take what she wanted.

"Constance."

She couldn't ignore the low thrum of her name on his lips.

Unable to fight it, she leaned closer and forced her gaze to his. The startling whisky color of his eyes held a fire hotter than the sun. She leaned in an inch, a simple experiment to see how he'd react. If he leaned opposite, he'd have made it perfectly clear he wanted no part of her. He stood his ground.

She wanted to shout to the heavens. But there was still work to be done.

She moved in another inch.

He still didn't move.

Closer and closer she leaned, not giving him any quarter. She moved with a stealth that hunters would have envied. And she didn't stop until her cheek rested against his. She couldn't breathe. How long she had waited to feel this close to him—skin-to-skin. His evening bristles teased her to press closer. All she wanted was to cup his other cheek in her hand, then press her lips against his.

A ragged breath escaped as she tried to tamp down the chaos that had erupted in her own body. Feeling and sensations melded together in a combination primed to explode.

She whispered his name in answer. "Jonathan, do you want . . ." She couldn't be certain, but it was entirely possible his lips brushed against one ear.

"It's quite feasible that I want what you want, but you tell me first."

She refused to move an inch. It was too dangerous for both of their sakes. Though their cheeks touched, several inches separated their bodies. Still, his heat radiated toward her, surrounding her, pulling her closer.

She never wanted to escape.

"Tell me," he demanded softly.

In answer, she moved her hand up his thigh. The muscles underneath her fingers flexed. He placed his hand over hers. Slowly, he pulled it toward his body.

"I want . . ." She slid her cheek across his, the touch incredibly slow and sure and erotic, yet innocent.

A scant inch separated her lips from his. Their breaths mingled in a prelude that they both knew would lead to another wall between them dismantled stone by proverbial stone.

If she had her way, she'd much rather blast it into bits. However, the moment called for patience.

Slowly, she raised her eyes to his. "Let me kiss you."

Chapter Sixteen

Jonathan closed his eyes as Constance's plea stood suspended in the air between them much like those clay disks. Should he shoot it down or reach into the sky and take the gift she offered?

What was he doing?

This was the exact thing he'd promised himself he wouldn't allow. She could not think this marriage was anything different from what he promised. With every intention of pushing her hand away from his leg, he covered hers with his. She tightened her grip ever so slightly, and his own hand did the same.

Her touch nurtured a need within him that he'd denied for ages. The warmth of her hand under his set fire to every desire he'd ached and starved for. Endless nights he'd fantasized of this moment with her. The need for her kiss and touch to absolve him of all of his sins.

God, he craved her.

If he had any honor left within him, he'd push her away and never let her near him again. Not until his name was cleared. He opened his mouth to tell her that.

Instead, his willpower vanished into thin air. He cupped her cheek with his free hand.

Weak. He was always weak when it came to her.

She pulled away slightly. The desire in her eyes set off a chain reaction within him. All reason, wisdom, and sound scattered to the four corners of the room. He didn't take his gaze from hers. Only when she pressed her lips against his did he close his eyes and experience all the grandeur of Constance.

The fullness of her mouth against his was sweeter than late-summer honey. But he didn't move to deepen the kiss. This was hers to give. Her touch was tentative as if she was testing this newness between them. He did the same. When she moaned slightly, he tasted the passion that seemed to ignite between them.

And like the selfish beast of a man he'd become, he'd take everything she'd give him and more. So he wrapped an arm around her waist and hauled her closer until the only thing that separated him from her was the thin layers of material between them. The softness of her breasts crushed against his chest.

She tilted her head and deepened the kiss. Like the touch of a butterfly's wings, her tongue teased the seam of his lips, begging for entrance. He opened to her. When she set to explore his mouth, he groaned. Without thinking of the consequences, he pulled her from the floor and set her on his lap, never breaking their kiss. Her knees straddled his hips. All his prior thoughts forgotten as he canted his hips seeking her heat. His erection thickened at the movement.

Her quick intake of air allowed him to sweep his tongue inside her mouth, stroking it against hers. He brought his hand to her lower back to hold her close. She slipped her hand between the folds of his banyan and rested it over the pounding of his heart. The touch so endearing he lost all thought as he concentrated on the feel of her fingers on his skin.

More than anything, he wanted to pull her into him so that they were one, and he'd never be alone again. Only with her could he imagine a time when he'd been carefree and able to love another person as he'd always dreamed. She was his future and his past.

But it was the present that tore them apart. A cry rent the air, and immediately they both sobered out of their drunken passion. Her eyes searched his for a moment as if she'd forgotten where she was.

"Aurelia," she whispered.

The baby cried out again. At the fretful sound, Regina woke and scrambled out of her bed. She trotted toward the baby's cries.

"I must go," she whispered. "Will you be all right?"

No. He'd never be all right after this night. She'd stolen something very dear to him, and he knew it would be lost forever. She'd stolen his long-protected lie that he didn't need anyone in his life.

Somehow, he found the wherewithal to nod.

Constance searched his face. He blinked in an effort to keep her from seeing how she'd thoroughly wrenched him from his carefully crafted moorings that kept him anchored in solitude.

"I'll be back once I have her settled." She carefully stood, then pressed a quick kiss to his mouth as she cupped his cheeks, a promise that she'd continue to haunt his days and nights.

He didn't answer as she swept from the room. Within seconds, he could hear her sweet murmurings of comfort to her daughter.

He rested his head against the back of the chair and stared at the connecting door.

What had he done?

The unthinkable. Touching his wife and allowing her to touch him had woken a need that he didn't know if he could fight. For both of their sakes, he had to find a way to defeat it.

So he did the only thing he could think of. Gingerly, using his cane, he stood, then walked to her bedroom door.

He called for his dog. Once she was through the door, he softly locked it from his side.

He stood there for a moment, tempted to unlock it and stroll through the room to see how Aurelia was faring.

A father would do that. Jonathan really wasn't her father, and he certainly couldn't stroll.

He leaned against the door and closed his eyes. The cool wood offered little comfort to his fevered brow as the storm he and Constance had created still raged through him. Everything throbbed in his body, including his unruly cock, ensuring he'd not sleep tonight.

For much-needed distance, he returned to his room. His bed matched Constance's except in one thing. Height. He'd had several skilled carpenters raise the massive bed frame to complement his height. He could easily climb in without bending his knee. It allowed him to stretch his body on top of the fine linen duvet without much effort. The windows were open, and thankfully, a cool breeze rustled the curtains.

He stared into the darkness. Unable to help himself, his thoughts wandered to his wife. Her hands had a tender and sure touch. She'd made the ointment for him . . . with peppermint oil, his favorite. The gentle magic in her hands as she rubbed and pressed against his twisted muscles and ragged flesh brought relief. She didn't turn mawkish over his scars. She'd continued to talk as she touched him.

For the first time since he'd been returned from the war, he'd felt connected to another human through the simple act of touch. He didn't even realize how starved he was for such companionship.

But what made every part of him feel alive was the tender touch of her lips against his. He could see the arousal in her eyes. Her heat and scent made his entire body ache to take her.

He parted his banyan and palmed his cock, still hard from their kiss. Semen wet his hand as he pleasured himself. He closed his eyes with a vision of him making love to her. Her arms would hold him as he kissed every inch of her. Her breasts and hips for him alone to taste and worship. She'd cry out his name, begging him to take her. He'd do her bidding and relentlessly stroke inside her until she. . . .

With a final tug, he came, spilling across his abdomen. He groaned her name in the dark like an invocation.

How long he stayed in that position, he couldn't hazard a guess. As he caught his breath, a truth dawned upon him. He'd never be able to conquer his want for her.

The moonlight cast the room in blue shadows. He reached for a handkerchief on the side table and cleaned himself. He rested his arm over his eyes to plunge himself into the darkness once more and allowed sleep to give him a reprieve from his weariness.

The tenacious scratching at Constance's door woke him. He ignored it.

The bed dipped with a groan as his mastiff jumped up. Instead of curling into a ball at the foot of the bed, Regina stood over him, hanging her face right over his. He turned on his side to escape her hot breath. But she wouldn't give up and scratched his side, then whined. When he finally sat up in bed, she jumped down and regarded him with a face that could only be a canine scowl. She took two steps, then twisted to face him again. She wanted him to follow her.

With a sigh, he grabbed his breeches at the foot of the bed, then went through the laborious task of putting them on, then buttoning the placket. He threw his linen shirt from yesterday over his head. Without delay, he grabbed his cane, then followed Regina to the connecting door, where she let out a pitiful whine then a bark. She scratched to get in.

"Shush," Jonathan scolded. "We don't barge into a lady's room without knocking first."

Scratching frantically again, the dog completely ignored him.

Jonathan knocked softly.

With no answer, he unlocked and opened the door.

Regina barreled in without his command to say she could enter. It was completely out of character. She normally waited for him.

"Constance?" he said softly.

When she didn't answer, he glanced toward the bed. Through the moonlight, he found her curled into a pillow. Fast asleep, she appeared younger, reminding him of the girl he'd first kissed.

Another sound flooded the room. A whimper, low and fretful. But it wasn't Regina. It was Aurelia.

With as much haste as he dared, he crossed the room, cautious not to make too much noise with his cane, then pushed the partially opened door wide. Aurelia stood with her arms outstretched. Tears streaked her cheeks. "Da."

Heaven help them both, not tears. What made it doubly difficult was that it was this wee, sweet baby girl. Without another thought, Jonathan reached her side then with one arm, lifted her from the crib.

"What is it?" he said softly. Which was a ridiculous question. If she could talk, she'd call for her mother.

Another half whimper escaped as she tucked herself under his chin and grabbed his shirt with both of her little hands. A new set of tears fell, the big drops instantly soaking through his shirt. But that wasn't the only thing wet.

Her bottom was soaked.

Holding her slightly away from his chest, he found a

washstand next to her crib with clean clothes and a basin and pitcher. "So this is the problem?"

Jonathan laid her on the padded washstand, keeping a hand on her at all times in case she developed a case of the wiggle-worms. But the baby didn't move. She watched him with wide-eyed wonder as he attended to her. Setting aside his cane and leaning against the washstand, he made short work of striping her wet clothing, then cleaning her with water and a fresh towel.

"Now what do I do?" he hummed.

She smiled.

"I expected more instruction than that. The way your mother speaks about your accomplishments, I thought you could conjugate Greek verbs from memory."

She chewed her hand in response.

"Big help you are." He picked up a square cloth and examined it. Precisely how was he supposed to tie this contraption to her? After maneuvering the piece into various positions, he gave up and simply tied it around her waist.

She held up her hands, a command for him to pick her up again.

"I have you," he soothed. The dog stood by his side watching every move.

Aurelia still fretted with little whimpers and a short sob.

Patting her back with one hand, he brushed a knuckle across her cheek. She was hot with fever. "Let's take you to your mother."

In response, the baby grabbed his finger then started to chew.

As he held Aurelia close with one arm tightly wrapped around her, Jonathan considered who possessed the ability to drool more, Aurelia or Regina. His hand was drenched.

Carefully, balancing Aurelia in one arm, he made his way to the bed. "Constance." There was no movement. He bent down with the baby, then touched his wife's shoulder. "Constance, wake up. It's Aurelia."

Constance burrowed into the pillow to escape the pest that buzzed about. But when the thing touched her, she shot up to a sitting position, the pounding of her heart encouraging her to flee. "What is it?" She clasped her hand over her chest, trying to calm the runaway beat.

For a moment, she blinked trying to reconcile the sight in front of her. Her husband stood before her holding her daughter. For a moment, she simply stared at the sweet scene before her, wondering if she was dreaming.

"Aurelia feels hot," he murmured while rocking her gently.

Instantaneously, the dream disappeared. Constance scooted toward him, then held out her hands. In a careful exchange, Jonathan placed Aurelia in her arms. As he sat on the edge of the bed, Constance ran her hand over Aurelia's forehead and cheek. The baby snuggled close and grabbed Constance's nightgown to chew.

"She must be cutting a tooth. I need to get her a wet cloth for her mouth. That seems to help." Constance made a move to get up.

Jonathan stayed her with a hand. "Allow me." He rose from the bed using his cane. Shortly, he returned with a wet cloth.

"Thank you." Constance took the piece of linen soaked in cool water and gave it to the baby, who then released a deep sigh as she chewed. Regina jumped on the bed. She immediately plopped next to Constance with her head resting between her front paws. Constance reached down and patted the dog as she regarded Jonathan. "Was she crying?"

He nodded.

"I can't believe I slept through that. I always get up with her first whimper."

Jonathan reached over and smoothed several blond wisps from Aurelia's face. "Regina was most insistent to come inside your room. I knocked but when you didn't answer, I opened the door."

"The door you locked?" she asked, not hiding the hint of displeasure from her voice.

He leaned away, creating distance between them. "Yes, that one."

She relaxed against the headboard. "You didn't have to lock it. If you didn't want me to return . . . all you had to do was tell me."

"It doesn't matter." He raised his eyes to hers.

If only he had been in a rush to get inside her bedroom for her. "Thank you for helping Aurelia." Constance cradled her daughter and patted her bottom. The movement normally put her to sleep. "Did you change her?"

He cleared his throat softly. "Well . . . in a manner of speaking. I wrapped a cloth around her after cleaning her up." He lifted a brow and waved a hand at the baby. "They should come with instructions. I thought that might have been why she was crying."

For a moment she couldn't speak. Though he acted like a tyrant at times, he was incredibly gentle and caring when it came to her daughter.

"Another thing to thank you for." A fresh breeze blew into the room, bringing with it the floral scents from the garden. With the darkness and him sitting so close, it felt intimate. Or at least, the way she always thought a married couple would interact. "You are a handy person to have around."

"A man of many talents." He sat still for a moment as the quiet surrounded them. "I should go back to my room." He adjusted his position on the mattress and turned to her. "I should be the one thanking you." He cleared his throat. "For my leg. You're much better with your hands than Ralph."

"You are welcome anytime to ask me to massage you. And I mean *anytime*, Jonathan." She stole a peek through her lowered lids. "You should also know that I can massage more than your legs," she said, then bit her lip to keep from laughing.

"I'll keep that in mind," he said huskily.

What else could she say so he wouldn't leave? "Are you sleepy?"

"No." There was enough light from the moon that she could see the puzzlement on his face. "Why?"

"I wondered if we could chat for a while." She swallowed the lump of dread in her voice. She owed him an apology for her earlier actions. Now was the perfect time to say it. "Please."

He smiled slightly. "Only if you allow me to prop my leg up."

In the shadows, he looked like the Jonathan of old with his softened features. She'd wondered where that man had disappeared to. Perhaps he was right in front of her. "If you'd like, you could lean against the headboard." She hastened to add, "It's as soft as a pillow."

"I'll take your word for it." The bed dipped as he positioned himself. "Surprisingly comfortable."

She didn't move from the center, which meant they were side by side, their shoulders barely touching. She slid him a sideways glance. He stared straight ahead as if trying to decide whether to stay or go. If she wanted to say her piece, she should do it before he escaped.

"I owe you an apology." Still holding Aurelia, she turned her face to his. "I shouldn't have barraged into your study without asking you first. It wasn't my intention to disrupt you. Instead . . . I wanted to make the room more welcoming. Make it feel more calming." She adjusted a sleepy Aurelia in her arm, then continued in a softer voice. "What I failed to realize is that what I might consider comforting, you might conceive otherwise."

"You mean the flowers so the room smells like the outside instead of gunpowder? Having the windows spotless so I'm forced to look outside and crave the summer breeze?" He arched a brow.

"Yes." She smiled at the lightness in his voice. "I hope you'll forgive me."

"I accept your apology." He clasped his hands in his lap. "I don't care what you do in the rest of the house." His whisky-dark voice warmed her from the inside out. "I found your note."

A sudden stillness settled between them as she ruminated on his measured words. "Do you think it silly?"

"No." The tenderness in his eyes disarmed her, causing her to inhale deeply to quiet the riot of her speeding heartbeat. "I read your journal every day. The pages allowed me to escape back home even if it was a few minutes before I fell asleep."

Did he ever dare want to escape back to her? If she asked, in all likelihood it would break the fragile accord between them.

"Thank you for the knot." He glanced at his hands then returned his gaze to hers. "You must have found the book useful."

Constance laughed softly. "One of my joiners said I make clove hitch knots faster than anyone. I learned every knot." She swallowed, gathering strength. "I meant what I said in that note. We're tied together by so much . . . our past, our home, and our future."

He nodded once in answer.

She slowly released the breath that she'd been holding. His gesture a declaration they were at peace.

He reached over and patted Aurelia. "Do you think she needs a doctor?" he said softly.

"Let's wait. If she still has a fever in the morning, we'll call for one." The nag of worry that she hadn't heard her own baby crying still rumbled through her thoughts. "I can't believe I didn't hear her," she murmured.

He turned his position slightly so he could see her face. "You may think I'm speaking out of turn, but you don't have to do this by yourself."

"Do what?"

He gestured toward Aurelia. "Be the only one to care for her at night."

Constance shook her head. "I want to be the one there when she cries out . . ." As soon as the words were out, she realized the folly of her answer.

"But you can't be if you're exhausted." The rumble in his voice had returned, and everything within her went alert at the sound. It wasn't the roughness she was reacting to, but the concern. "North told me you rise at a ridiculous hour then are out of the house early for your work at the docks. It reminds me of when we were growing up, and you'd stay up all night memorizing customer lists, shipments, and supply invoices. You wanted to master it all in the shortest time possible, if I recall correctly."

"I don't want to be a parent who has a servant raise my child," she said in defense.

He nodded slowly in understanding. "She appears to be asleep now. Shall I take her back to her bed?"

Constance's eyes slid closed at his words. For all her nights caring for Aurelia alone, this was like manna from heaven. "I think I could hear those words every night and never tire of them." She laughed softly. "For tonight, I think she should be here with me if she wakes again. She was rather fretful."

Shoulder-to-shoulder, hip-to-hip, Jonathan didn't say

anything for a moment as silence settled between them. Yet it was peaceful this time. Then as if preparing to lay down himself, he stretched his arms overhead. Their bodies so close, she felt the movement of his muscles lengthening and flexing beside her.

"You memorized those lists because you wanted to know everything about your company. You didn't have to, because Mr. and Mrs. Bridges were there to help. Yet you were determined." He shifted again until he was leaning on his right side looking at her. "I could lend assistance. We could trade nights. You watch her one night, and I'll do the next."

Constance scooted away to make room for Aurelia. With an accustomed ease, she placed her daughter between them. A contented sigh escaped from the baby as she moved slightly, seeking the most comfortable position.

"Why would you do that?"

"For one, I'm up most nights anyway. It wouldn't be difficult for me. Normally, I'm a light sleeper, so I'll hear if she makes a sound." Through the shaft of moonlight that glowed across his face, a slight grin appeared. "And she reminds me that there's something bigger than my world. I'd like to help."

She shifted her body to mirror his as she tried to decipher whether it meant he wanted a real marriage. "Would we sleep together? Does this mean that you want to change the rules . . . of our marriage?"

"No. I don't think that would be wise." He lifted his hand and for a moment she thought he wanted to take hers. Instead, he gently patted the baby between them. "On the night I watch her, I'll sleep here. You sleep in my bed."

The simple act of him comforting Aurelia undid her, and she gasped slightly. Why couldn't she leave well enough alone?

Because whatever made him believe that he should spend his days secluded away from the world, she wanted to share all of it, the good and the bad. "You don't have to worry about me ravishing you."

"Because of my leg?" His murmur sharp as if warning her away.

"Of course not." She smiled to herself. "You know me better than that, I hope."

He didn't answer, but his exhale meant he'd lowered his guard. "It's not that I don't want to. You surely knew that when we . . ." He let the words trail to nothing.

"When we kissed?" she pressed.

"Yes." He huffed out a breath and bent his head. His hand hovered in the space between them. He couldn't seem to make up his mind whether he wanted to touch her.

His uncertainly emboldened her. Constance clasped her hand with his. She wanted to rejoice when he entwined their fingers together. Perhaps it was an acknowledgment that he faced many demons in his life. But she wanted him to know that she would be there if and when he ever needed her.

"Would you mind if I rested here beside you and Aurelia for a little while?"

Another breeze swept into the room at that moment, but she could hear the uncertainty in his voice. "I would like that," she answered.

"What I said earlier about my study . . . it doesn't mean that you're not welcome to visit."

She nodded, then bent her head to hide her smile. It was a peace offering, something rare and precious. Maybe he was learning about marriage, the same as she was.

Without another word, she carefully arranged herself so as not to disturb the baby, but she turned on her side to face Jonathan. He didn't change his position but had closed his eyes.

In minutes, his breathing matched the baby's. The only sound was the slight snore from the dog sleeping at the foot of the bed.

Sleep turned elusive. But this time, it wasn't due to worry

over Faladen and his threats. She wanted to stay awake as long as she could and relish in the simple comfort of having her husband and child beside her.

For whatever incomprehensible reason, she wanted to be the one awake, the one who stood watch. This was her family now, and she vowed to chase away any and all demons who might dare tear them apart.

Chapter Seventeen

Jonathan eased into his desk chair, then stretched his neck. The cloying scent of florals had completely disappeared, yet the vases in his study were still stuffed with flowers.

He relaxed and took another sip of his coffee. When he'd carefully removed himself from the bed in the countess's suite, Aurelia and her mother were still sound asleep. They didn't move an inch. Proof both had needed a good night's sleep.

As soon as he'd stood, Regina had taken his place curled on the other side of Aurelia so she wouldn't tumble off the bed. He didn't have to give the command to stay. The dog was immediately aware of whom she was supposed to protect.

He'd never slept so soundly since returning home as he had the previous evening. Perhaps it was due to the fact he'd slept beside Constance. This morning, he'd placed a new feather duster on her pillow tied with a ribbon. It was an olive branch, or perhaps an enticement for her to come into his study whenever she wanted.

He should have told her the truth about North's letters. Yet it would have destroyed the newfound peace they'd created between them.

At the sound of the brisk knock, he said, "Enter."

Arkwright popped into the room with a look that reminded Jonathan of a spaniel ready to flush waterfowl from the weeds surrounding the estate ponds. "Good morning, my lord. I wanted to know if you're ready for your morning shoot?"

"Good morning." He straightened several letters and journals on his desk. "I think it's a bit too early. My wife and our . . . her daughter are still sleeping."

He froze momentarily at the slip. Aurelia was not his daughter. She was Meriwether's child and would always be connected to him. The saving grace of her birth was to call Constance her mother, and the Duke of Randford, her uncle. He was more of a father figure than Jonathan could ever be.

He waved a hand at the correspondence on his desk. "I'm expecting Thomas to arrive at any moment. There are several matters on the estate that need my attention. As soon as I'm finished, I'll ring for you."

The brief look of disappointment disappeared from the footman's face. "Of course, sir. Whenever you're ready." The footman glanced around the room. "Have you redecorated since yesterday, my lord?" The footman shrugged slightly. "It looks different."

As if on cue, North entered the room. "Her ladyship began setting it to rights yesterday." The butler smiled as he addressed the footman. "Remarkable, isn't it?

"Indeed, Mr. North." Arkwright's gaze settled on Jonathan. "How do you like it, sir?"

The footman had to wait a few minutes for his response. How polite would it be to say that he'd hated it yesterday, but today it felt like a new beginning of some sort? A beginning that he should push away. Otherwise, like a moth flying too close to the fire, it might singe him. There was an inherent danger of failure when one tried to act like someone he wasn't and never intended to be. "It's fine."

He'd never thought of himself as a hypocrite. Indeed, it was

better than fine. Whatever anger he had over Constance's unwanted good intentions had disappeared much like a puff
of smoke. He'd forgotten most of it as she'd helped him last
night.

She'd been truly remarkable. She didn't fall apart when she
found him on the floor. Nor did she treat him like an invalid
as much of the staff did when they found him after a fall.

Whatever indignation he carried last night had vanished
as soon as she had kissed him. The memory of her sweet lips
against his and her tender hands on his body sent his blood
pulsing with need. He closed his eyes briefly to fight the swell
of desire that thrummed through his veins demanding he go
attend his wife.

"Ring if you need me, my lord." Arkwright bowed, then
left Jonathan alone with North.

"Sir, you are pleased, I take it?" Without a single strand
of his white hair in revolt, he dipped his head.

"Yes, North."

"I heard that you gave her a feather duster." The butler
shook his head.

"Do you and Mrs. Butler share everything?" Jonathan
stiffened his spine. "Can't anything be kept a secret in this
household?"

"It's my duty to know everything that goes on in the
house." North lifted his chin. "A gift is admirable and shows
thoughtfulness. But a duster? If you need suggestions for an
appropriate gift for your countess, allow me. Did you know
you sent her a beautiful scarf for Christmas?"

"How kind." He rolled his eyes.

"Did she apologize?"

"Don't be an ill-bred haggard," Jonathan grumbled.

"You didn't tell her about the letters?"

"No." At his butler's scowl, he added, "The timing wasn't
right."

"Her apology provided the perfect timing." He leaned

slightly and lowered his voice. "It's called creating intimacy between a couple."

"Don't you have responsibilities besides aggravating me?" Jonathan growled.

North smiled demurely. "Of course, sir. Even ill-bred haggard butlers know their duties. It's to remind the dunderheaded lords of the manor what their responsibilities are."

⁓

Constance had been sitting in the salon all morning working, but her concentration lagged every time she caught herself running her fingers through her new feather duster. Looking at it made her smile. It was a key into her husband's world, or at least his fortress, the study. If he'd given her a treasure chest of jewels, it wouldn't have meant a tenth as much.

"My lady, I hate to interrupt you, but there are two gentlemen from Lysander & Sons asking for you."

Constance looked up from her work. "Would you show them in?"

North beamed at her. "The earl's mother always greeted guests in this room. It was one of her favorites," he answered without missing a beat. "Shall I order a tea tray?"

"If you could serve coffee, that would be best," Constance said. "They're not the tea-and-tarts type."

"Of course." North bowed. "I'll order a coffee tray, then escort them into the salon."

Minutes later, North reappeared with two men dressed in working clothes followed by a maid with the coffee tray.

The craggy lines on her guests' weathered faces were a welcome sight, and Constance prayed they had good news.

"My lady, Mr. Henry Bridges and Mr. Alin Zephyr to see you," North said.

Constance glided forward to greet her guests. "Good morning, Mr. Bridges and Mr. Zephyr."

Mr. Bridges returned the greeting while Alin scowled at her. "Mr. Zephyr? I was expecting my da to be following behind me." He looked around the room. "Is that wot you're calling me now, Constance Lysander?"

"It's Lady Sykeston," North corrected.

"Begging your pardon, sir," Zephyr said. "You may call her that ladyship business, but I've known this girl since she could barely walk." He gazed at her fondly. "When she was a poppet, she'd sit on my knee while I told her stories about mermaids and mermen. She will always be Constance Lysander to me."

Constance shook her head. "There were never any mermaids in your stories. You were always telling me that monsters swam in the sea and to stay away."

Mr. Zephyr laughed. "And it worked, didn't it? You stayed away from the dockyard until you were old enough to be there."

"The coffee is on the table, my lady, along with a bit of whisky." North bowed with a smile.

"Thank you, Mr. North." Constance turned to the maid. "Thank you, Lucy."

The young woman dipped a curtsy. "You're welcome, my lady."

"If you need anything, please call," North said before he left the room, leaving Constance with Alin and Mr. Bridges.

"Enough about mermaids, Alin," Mr. Bridges announced. "We've work to do."

"Let's sit." She swept her hand at a small card table in the middle of the room. "I'm anxious to hear what you've discovered."

"Is the husband joining us?" Alin asked.

Constance stiffened slightly, then continued to serve the coffee. She'd never shared anything with Meriwether because deep down she'd never trusted him. Of course, she trusted

Jonathan. However, the timing wasn't right. "This is my business."

Alin stared at her. "Me and my missus share everything. Is it his leg?"

"Why would his leg have anything to do with this?" Constance asked, ready to defend her husband.

"Rumor has it he doesn't go out because he's embarrassed of his limp," Alin explained.

"That's pure nonsense." Constance lifted her chin an inch. "He works on his estate, manages his earldom, and he's newly married with a new daughter. Three very good reasons for him staying busy."

"Lysander & Sons is hers. Leave it be," Mr. Bridges said. He turned his attention from Alin to Constance. "We sailed to the isle yesterday."

Alin took a sip of the black brew. "We had nothing to do with that yacht taking on water."

Mr. Bridges nodded in agreement. "Tell her the rest, Alin."

He stole a glance at Constance, who nodded slightly in encouragement. "Well, the shipwright and I followed the exact course as Lord *High and Mighty*. We sailed straight past the Needles and docked at Cowles. Found several men who knew where the *Enchanted Mistress* had put into port." He leaned back in his chair and rested his clasped hands on his flat stomach. "Cursed name for a yacht if you ask me."

"Alin," Mr. Bridges warned. "That's always been the name of that ship and you know it."

"You don't like it either. Besides, I don't like the man, Henry. Nob or not." Alin set his jaw at a disgruntled angle, then turned to Constance. "Well, Henry and I looked her over. Rumor has it that the captain cut across a shoal trying to beat the other two boats in a race. Damaged the hull."

Constance shook her head in disbelief. "Wasn't anybody watching?"

"Drunk as owls on a full moon," Mr. Bridges chimed in. "The whole lot of 'em. Including Lord *High and Mighty*."

"Well, it didn't take a genius to figure out what was wrong with the ship." Alin shook his head as he told the rest of the story. "Warped the hull out of true. Twisted the knees loose. Even the braces."

Mr. Bridges nodded. "They ran into that bank of rocks close to the east side."

"No wonder it took on water," Constance said, mesmerized. "Are you certain?"

"Aye," Alin pledged. "On the lar side. Saw the scrapes and all."

"My God," she whispered. "And he wanted us to pay for his own stupidity."

The joiner reached into a pocket and brought out a brace. "Here's one of the braces I installed. It has my initials."

"What were they thinking?" Constance examined the mangled piece of metal. It was torn to shreds. She let out a breath.

Mr. Bridges snorted. "It'll require extensive work to make her sail again."

"So." Alin slapped his hands on the table. "What would you like for us to do?"

She released a deep breath. "I want you to go back to the isle and get the names of everyone that might have seen that accident that day. Including the men and women not connected to the docks or ships. They'll be even more valuable as proper witnesses."

Both men nodded.

"Once you have those names, bring them to me," she declared.

"Then what?" Alin asked. He stole a look at Henry. "No offense, Constance Lysander, but this is our livelihoods we're discussing 'ere. Lord High and Mighty is trying to blame our work for his idiocy. What message are you planning to be delivering to 'im?"

"That an apology will suffice as long as it's written, copied, and posted throughout Portsmouth and the Isle of Wight"— Constance glanced at both men—"or do I need to look at the books and estimate the damages?"

"You don't need the books." Henry's patient voice softened. "You know what we lost, Constance."

The room fell into a complete silence except for the tick of the ormolu clock on the mantel. She leaned back in her chair and regarded him.

"We lost the Hartfelds because of him," Henry offered. "They'd been customers of Lysander & Sons since my father was alive. You should tell your husband, lass. All of it," Henry said and patted her hand. "He'd help you."

Alin nodded in agreement.

"I can do this myself." Even she would admit that her tone was defensive, but this was her struggle. To give this worry to Jonathan would be a recipe for disaster. They'd reached a new accord between them last night. Constance wouldn't jeopardize it. She would work through this on her own. She'd always done so before when she was married to Meri.

"All right, my miss. We'll see you at the docks," Mr. Bridges said. The men stood and said their farewells. As if on cue, North opened the door and escorted Constance's visitors down the hallway.

Constance stood and walked to the window. For the first time since last night, things didn't look so bright anymore. She hated to have to deal with Lord Faladen's nonsense. She'd much rather concentrate on her work and home. But she was never one to shirk responsibility. In her heart, she believed that truth, honesty, and her own composure would win the day.

"Did your guests leave?"

She turned around to find Jonathan standing in the room.

"Yes," she said softly. The sight of him stole her breath. His pristine cravat was neatly tied, and his broadcloth morning coat fit perfectly. The rich brown of his waistcoat matched his eyes.

"Do they work for you?" His face a perfect imitation of a mask.

"Yes." Constance debated whether to share their conversation, but decided against it. Her first instinct should be trusted. She wanted to deal with Faladen herself. If she didn't, then every time she had a dispute with a customer, they'd try to take advantage of her.

"It's unusual to see guests being received." His gaze peeled away the layers of her carefully crafted decision not to involve him.

She shook her head slightly to clear the thought. "I thought you wouldn't mind since it was related to Lysander & Sons."

He blinked in reply.

"Much like when your estate manager calls on you."

"I see." He played with an object in his hands. "Fair point."

"What is that?"

"A cartridge. It holds a steel ball and gunpowder. They're typically made of paper, but I'm designing one of metal." He gave it to her.

Constance tested its weight and examined it closely. "Why metal?"

"Paper is unreliable if it's wet. The powder won't light. The metal acts like a flint when struck."

"Rather ingenious on your part." She smiled and returned the cartridge to him.

He grunted in acknowledgment. "The concept may be clever, but I haven't been successful in my designs." He studied the cartridge. "I should return to my study."

"Wait." She took a step in his direction. "Did you sleep well?"

For an instant, he looked stunned at the question. "Yes. You?"

She nodded and smiled as his cheeks reddened slightly. "One of the best nights I've had in a long time. Thank you."

He shifted his weight to his injured leg. "Are you going to the dockyard? If not, I thought . . ."

"Did you want to do something together?" She kept her face frozen preparing for his denial.

"No," he said a little too abruptly. "About last night when you apologized . . . I didn't mention the gardens. I have no objections to you redesigning them. My mother turned it into a thing of beauty, and I know she'd have been thrilled to know that her"—he cleared his throat—"daughter by marriage had taken it over."

"Thank you." It was another gesture on his part, and she would grab ahold with both hands. "I've decided not to go to the docks today. Would you take a walk with me? I haven't seen all of the gardens."

They both knew he wanted to spend the day locked away in his study, yet he nodded. "Of course."

Constance went to his side, and when he held out his arm, she wrapped hers tightly around his.

When they were outside, Jonathan surprised her with his knowledge of the plants in the courtyard and the surrounding park. His mother had been planting the flowers for years. Constance had never seen such variety.

"I hope we can do this every day," she confided, squeezing his arm. "I find a walk helps clear any worries or bothers."

He drew her to a stop. "Speaking of 'bothers,' if something were upsetting you, you'd tell me."

Though it sounded like a command, she could hear the question lying within. "Why would you ask?" she responded as nonchalantly as she could.

"Because I was trained to discover people's weaknesses and vulnerabilities."

For a moment, she saw his past in his serious nature, and her heart skipped a beat in empathy. She had no idea what he'd been through during the war, and she wouldn't ask about it until he was ready to tell her. Whatever it was, it had taken the jovial, loving young lord from her youth and turned him into a man who preferred to distance himself from everyone and everything.

"I would tell you if it was significant or if it concerned us." She pushed back a wayward lock that had caught in the wind. "It's something at the dockyard."

His eyes tracked her every movement. When the wind caught another lock, he was the one that smoothed it for her, his fingers brushing against her skin. "Though I'm a beastly bear to most, when it comes to you, I can be a good listener."

A wave of sentimentality threatened to throw her under as they continued on their way. She leaned into his touch. "I used to bore you with my tales."

"Constance Lysander never bored me," he objected softly. "And neither does Constance, the Countess of Sykeston. You might not believe this, but I remember our past conversations. I meant what I said. Whatever you need, I'll help you find it."

"I'll remember that, and I'd do the same for you." The graze of his shoulders against hers kindled memories of last evening's intimate conversation, and she smiled. "If you like, after your evening shower, I could massage you again."

"Would you like that?" he asked with a boyish grin and leaned close.

She couldn't help but laugh. "I think we both know the answer to that, especially if more kisses were involved."

A twig broke. Immediately, he pulled away.

"It's nothing," Constance said softly. "Probably a squirrel."

He surveyed the grounds. "I've trained myself to know when an animal breaks a stem versus a person. These particular squirrels bear an uncanny resemble to North and Mrs. Butler. They're spying on us." He pulled away with a deep breath. "Let us return to the house. My leg feels temperamental."

She groaned silently. Those two had the best of intentions, but they needed to work on their timing.

"Good morning," Mrs. Butler called out.

Constance and Jonathan turned in tandem to greet the two.

"Beautiful day for a walk, isn't it?" North grinned.

"It is," Constance answered.

Jonathan simply grunted.

"We're . . ." Mrs. Butler turned to North.

The butler's brows knitted together in confusion, then a sudden smile lit his face. "Mrs. Butler and I are off to throw some netting over the estate's gooseberry bushes."

Mrs. Butler nodded a little too vigorously at his explanation. "The birds will eat them otherwise."

"Excellent idea. My mother had those bushes planted for my father." Jonathan turned to Constance. "Gooseberries were his favorites for jelly and pies." He dipped his head slightly, indicating they were finished with the conversation. "Lady Sykeston and I are heading back to the house."

As soon as they passed the butler and the housekeeper, Jonathan paused, then turned around. "The task might be a little easier if you'd brought nets with you."

Instantly, their eyes widened with their mouths gaping.

Without another word shared between them, she and Jonathan walked back to the house and soon stood by the steps outside his study. All the while, she couldn't quiet her thoughts.

"Speaking of your father, some of the staff mentioned that he used to have a celebration for your tenants at the end of the harvest. I thought it might be lovely to host such an event. My father always insisted we have one at the end of the summer as a thank-you for his employees' hard work. I continue that tradition. We could combine the events. The garden will be finished, and we could host it outside here."

"My first reaction is no."

"Will you consider it?" She didn't keep the pleading out of her voice.

"Yes." He pulled away, creating distance.

She was desperate to reclaim the earlier ease between them. "Your question about something bothering me?" She paused for a moment, considering how much to share. "A longtime customer is unhappy with a project we did for him. His ship was damaged, and he claims we're at fault. Alin and Mr. Bridges came to tell me that it had nothing to do with our work."

"You're satisfied?" he asked. His formal tone returned.

"Yes." It was true. The information she'd discovered today would put an end to Faladen's machinations. She'd write him and her solicitor today with her findings. Before she could say more, Arkwright appeared.

"My lord, target practice today?" he asked.

Jonathan shook his head. "My study calls." He turned and took her hand and brought it to his lips, his gaze never leaving hers. "Thank you for the walk."

She managed to smother her frustrated groan as a green wave of envy flooded her thoughts.

How ridiculous that she was jealous of a room.

Chapter Eighteen

When Constance left for the market that same afternoon, North strolled into Jonathan's study and closed the door. "Sir, did you by chance happen to notice that your wife had visitors this morning? Male visitors?"

One of Jonathan's eyebrows shot up at the question. "I did."

One thing about North that didn't irritate Jonathan was his butler's innate sense of loyalty. A titled gentleman wielded great power, but a reclusive earl was a whole different beast. He needed help in discovering what happened in the outside world.

Jonathan motioned to the chairs that surrounded the library table. With a relative ease, North lowered himself into a chair. He tapped his chin in contemplation. "Don't worry about secret liaisons. Those men were old enough to be her grandfathers."

"This is not humorous," Jonathan growled.

North shrugged. "That walk in the garden gives me hope. An excellent start if I do say so myself."

Jonathan put both elbows on the table and leaned close. "What do you want?"

North hmphed, then grinned. "You actually took a stroll for pleasure. *Outside*."

Jonathan relaxed against his chair. "I enjoyed myself." His gaze drifted to the courtyard. He found pleasure in her company and always had.

"As Lady Sykeston's guests were leaving, I heard them mention Lord High and Mighty and the Isle of Wight." North lowered his voice. "They were worried, by the expressions on their faces."

"Do you think they were referring to me as Lord High and Mighty?"

North shook his head. "They mentioned you by name to me. Asked if I would pass along their best wishes on your marriage. The salty one by the name of Mr. Zephyr said they're quite fond of your wife, and if you ever hurt her, then you'd face his wrath."

"Thank you for the warning," Jonathan murmured.

"I think it speaks well of their loyalty to your wife," North said softly. "Are you worried about her?"

"She shared they were having problems with a longtime customer." He thrummed his fingers. "She didn't identify the customer, but said the matter was resolved." He picked up the estate bookkeeping Thomas had dropped off earlier and started perusing the numbers. "It's her business."

North's calm reserve should have warned Jonathan that he wasn't going to like what the man had to say. "Have you told her about your letters?"

"You mean, the ones that you wrote." Jonathan lifted a brow.

North nodded without a hint of contrition. "If you show her a little bit of yourself, she'll do the same. I'm confident of it."

"Oh, I can see that conversation right now. After I tell her that my staff revolted behind my back, I'm sure she'll be thrilled to hear that I wasn't traveling and working for the

Crown. Once I tell her I was in Portsmouth the entire time, she'll be livid." He shook his head. "Look at the blunder you've put me in."

"I don't think it's a blunder if she's here now." North's face softened. "You said you enjoyed the walk. Today you acted like the earl you were before the war. He would never keep a secret from Constance Lysander."

Jonathan answered with a small nod. "But you're forgetting something. I'm not that man anymore."

~

After their evening meal that night, Constance had donned her dressing gown. Since Aurelia had fallen asleep early, Constance finished another letter to her solicitor explaining what Alin and Mr. Bridges had discovered. Afterward, she started a draft to Faladen but set it aside. She needed to write both Beth and Katherine and ask their advice about the troublesome marquess. She blew out a breath. She missed them so much, and if they were here in Portsmouth, they could help her work through the issues. She smiled to herself. They could also see how her marriage thrived.

Yet she wanted more. Perhaps she was expecting too much from her husband in such a short period of time.

Constance lit the candles on the side table, then made her way to the small writing desk that overlooked the garden. It would be a perfect place for a party. Several lanterns were lit around the center fountain. Their light flashed upon the water like an evening gathering of fairies frolicking among the gentle fall of water.

If only there were such things as fairies and fairy tales, then perhaps with a little guidance from them she could settle all the unrest in her life. She turned to her desk, then stopped when something gleamed across the floor next to the bed. When she went to pick it up, she discovered it was one of

Jonathan's cuff links. Half a foot away, its mate lay buried in the carpet almost as if hiding. They must have fallen out of his breeches when he'd lain on her bed last night.

She knocked on the dressing room door. Jonathan's valet was the one to answer.

"Ralph, I didn't expect you." She peeked around the corner, hoping for a glimpse of Jonathan.

"Good evening, my lady." With an armful of laundry, he bowed slightly and stepped out of the way to let her in. "I hope it wasn't too loud. The footmen filled the overhead tub with warm water. Lord Sykeston is preparing to take a shower."

"I don't want to interrupt him." She extended her hand palm up. "I found these in my room."

Ralph glanced at the cuff links, then smiled slightly. At his expression, heat swept across her cheeks. The man obviously had the wrong idea, but she wouldn't correct him. Whatever went on behind their bedroom doors was their business.

"I don't think you'll disturb him at all." A wry grin appeared, but he turned and pointed to a short commode. "The top drawer on the right-hand side is where he keeps them."

"I can return them," she said.

"Thank you, my lady." With a farewell grin, he turned and walked back into Jonathan's bedroom.

She walked to the commode, then opened the drawer. The left side held a neat stack of fresh cravats. The other side was lined in black velvet and contained the few pieces of personal jewelry he wore.

The cold metal had slowly warmed in the palm of her hand. They were gold inscribed with his captain's insignia. Jealousy, faster than lightning in a midnight sky, streaked through every ounce of her. Those two pieces of metal had been with him when he'd been in France. They'd been there with him as he lay injured and near death.

The cuff links would have offered no comfort.

But she would have, if she'd been there. She would have stayed with him through every horrible hour that he suffered. It wouldn't have been a hardship. In fact, there was no other place she'd rather have been than there helping him through his pain and recovery. The truth was she would have sold her soul to have had the chance to nurse him. Even if she'd been dropped into a raging battle, she'd have stayed by his side.

He'd have done the same for her. She'd always known he was a man who felt deeply, one who vowed to protect those he loved. Though he'd always promised to be there for her when she needed him, it didn't mean that he loved her. She was no wide-eyed romantic. However, he had a deep regard for her. She had little doubt. What other man would have married her with scandal swirling around her and her daughter?

Only Jonathan.

Well, she felt the same for him—perhaps it was more than a deep regard.

She placed the links in his box. Before she could return to her room, the bedroom door opened. Expecting to find Ralph, she turned to tell him that she'd replaced the cuffs only to find Jonathan standing before her.

Naked.

He saw her the instant she saw him. Her perfidious gaze swept down his body. His wide shoulders, the muscular chest with a smattering of black hair that tapered into a narrow waist. His cock nestled between his thighs was thick and long.

She gasped silently as her gaze slid down his muscular legs. His right leg was mangled, but it was a symbol of his courage and his valor. It made him all the more attractive to her. There was something raw and primitive about him standing in the room without a stitch of clothing on. She couldn't breathe.

With reddened cheeks, he ran his hand through his hair while the other hand squeezed the top of his cane. Abruptly, he set aside his cane, then grabbed a linen toweling close by. Quickly, he tied it around his waist. "Would you like for me to come closer so you could have a better look."

The anger in his voice was unmistakable. For a moment, she couldn't think of a response. "I wasn't staring at the scars."

"I don't believe you," he practically growled.

"I was . . ." Her gaze dipped to the floor as she decided to confront him with the truth. She'd not let him think she was disgusted by him. It was quite the opposite.

With a defiant tilt of her chin, she met his stare with one of hers. "I was . . . admiring you. I did the same thing in London the day before our wedding if you recall."

"Broken as you'd thought I'd be?" he asked, the sarcasm clear.

"Don't say that."

"Perhaps *destroyed* is a better word."

Though he acted offended at her thorough perusal, she recognized the anguish in his voice. "Hardly," she countered. "You didn't let me finish." She took one step closer as she lowered her voice. "You're every bit as attractive and handsome as I'd always imagined."

He huffed out a breath in disbelief.

She collected every piece of courage she possessed and gathered it into a surety that she was doing the right thing. With her newfound strength, she walked toward him, not letting him look away. When they were no more than two feet apart, she stopped.

"I've imagined all sorts of things we could share with each other." She untied a ribbon at the top of her dressing gown. "The kiss we shared last night? It was one of those things."

She traced her collarbone; one finger meandering across her skin before trailing it down her cleavage. Determined to

make her husband understand what she felt called for a boldness that she'd never shown a man before.

His eyes widened in shock, but still he watched her every
move.

"Do you know what else I imagined?" She focused on his
lips and waited.

An unsteady breath escaped. "No," he said softly.

She huffed a breath and smiled. "I've imagined pleasur-
ing you." Her eyes dipped lower, where she discovered his
cock thick and hard. The telltale ache of arousal spread
throughout her. He would always have that effect on her, she
was certain. She had always desired him. Like a slow boil,
this yearning for him had simmered. But at the sight of him, it
had quickened with heat, like water hitting the boiling point
that refused to be contained. No matter how he rejected her,
she'd push through until he understood her deep regard.

"I want us to do things with each other that we've never
shared with anyone else. I want to leave my mark on you, and
you to do the same to me."

How often had she dreamed of claiming him as her own
as she made love to him. Not the other way around. She would
prove to him how beautiful he was inside and out.

"Such as?" His eyes smoldered with intensity, the kind that
could burn them both.

"Come closer, and I'll tell you," she whispered.

He took a step forward, and she did the same. Her dressing gown swooshed forward, the movement causing her skirt
to wrap around his legs as if refusing to let him go.

He was so close that their breaths mingled.

"I've always wanted to swim with you in a lake on a summer day. Then I'd take you to shore and kiss every inch of
you." She leaned close and whispered, "Bend down, please."

He did as she asked.

"I'd kiss every part." She clasped his earlobe with her teeth and gently tugged before pressing a kiss on the tender skin below his ear. "I want us to sleep naked under a tree, then wake up and make love again."

"You've thought that?" He pulled away and searched her eyes, his gaze hooded as if not believing her.

"And more," she whispered. He was so tall that when she stood on tiptoe, she could barely look him in the eye. "Would you let me show you . . . tonight?"

He looked away as he let out a breath. His indecision was clear to both of them.

"You must know how much I desire you. If you don't want . . . me, I'll not ask for something you'd regret. It has to be something we both want."

"It's not that." One of his rare, gentle smiles, the kind filled with tenderness and seasoned with fondness, appeared, and she wanted to capture it in a bottle and keep it forever. "I'm not the man you think I am."

"You're wrong. I know who you are," she answered. She closed her eyes and inhaled the air filled with their scent. Memories of their tender affection for each other when they were younger crept into her thoughts. It was like finding the pieces of your heart that you'd thought lost forever.

"Christ, Constance." The warmth in his deep voice made her ache. He trailed the back of his hand across her cheek. "You make me forget everything."

"That's quite a compliment," she said softly.

"It is. I need to forget." The acute ache in his voice clear. He bent and pressed a kiss across her cheek. "May I take your hair down?"

She nodded.

Carefully, he pulled the pins one by one by one, then placed them on a table beside them. The weight of her hair finally succumbing to its freedom in a free fall. With his hands framing her head, he combed her hair with his fingers, his touch incredibly tender. "I've wanted to do this since I first saw you in London. Your hair is softer than silk." He brushed his lips against hers.

It took every strength she possessed not to wrap her arms around him and pull him close. But he had to make the decision that he wanted this. Her entire body quivered, overcome with this man.

A man she'd wanted in every aspect of her life.

"I don't have a lake or a pond handy, but I have a shower." He brushed his nose against hers. "Have you ever experienced a warm waterfall?"

She shook her head, suddenly losing the ability to talk as his mesmerizing gaze held hers. She took his hand in hers and brought it to the remaining tie of her dressing gown.

"Shall I undress you?" he asked.

"Please."

Almost as if in slow motion, he pulled the ties apart. A sudden rush of cool air hit her chest, pebbling her skin along with her breasts and nipples.

When he stared at her exposed skin, her breasts grew heavier and tighter, begging for his touch. Her body had changed since giving birth. Her stomach was rounder and her breasts bigger, a mark that her entire life had been transformed. It was who she was now.

Jonathan seemed mesmerized by her body. He gently trailed his fingers over her chest, learning every inch of her. Her gaze never left his face as his touch meandered down the slope of her breast. She inhaled sharply at the sensation.

"Constance?" he asked softly.

"More, please," she answered.

Instead of touching her with his hands, he pulled her into his embrace with one arm. When his lips met hers, it was undeniable that he hungered for her the way she did him. Their kiss turned rapacious, their teeth clashing as they adjusted their positions desperate to fit with each other. Finally, they settled into an embrace, a perfect position to feast on each other's mouths.

She moaned softly, and his tongue entered her mouth. His moved with hers, exploring and relentless. Their tongues mated and conquered each other. Sometimes their kiss turned gentle, with nips and lips pressing against each other.

Then, without warning, their kiss turned savage. They were hungry, greedy for each other. It wasn't an exaggeration to say they were lost together in an eddy of passion that neither wanted to escape from.

This was the kiss she'd wanted her whole life from him. She moaned his name softly as he untied the toweling from his waist, then slid her dressing gown off her shoulders. His gaze caressed every curve and dip of her body. When his eyes finally met hers, he grimaced as if in pain. "My God, you're more beautiful than I ever imagined. I never knew such perfection exists."

A blush heated her cheeks.

He took her hand in his and led her to the monstrous shower. "Come. Let's get you under the warm water."

Every time she'd been in this room, it'd been hidden by curtains. But not now. A huge wooden tower at least ten feet tall stood in the middle of a basin. On top of the tower was a leather tarp. A wooden door opened, revealing three marble stairs and a handrail into the basin. It had to measure at least ten feet wide and two feet deep. Perfectly matched tiles paved the bottom. A wooden stool sat in the center under the spout.

"I've never seen the like." Her voice filled with awe.

"That leather bladder is filled with water." He pulled her close and pointed to a valve directly above them. "The water falls from there. Afterward, there's a drain underneath that opens and the water is released outside. Ready?"

She nodded.

With his left hand, he entwined his fingers with hers. Holding the rail with his other hand, he preceded down the steps, left leg first. Once they were in the basin, he pulled a cord above them. Soft, warm droplets of water fell like summer rain on their heads. More and more drops cascaded down their bodies until they were both soaked.

She laughed at the sensation of water drops hitting every inch of her. It was freeing and wicked and she could experience this every night and never tire of it. Jonathan joined her in laughing as he gently sat on the stool. The mirth in his eyes making them flash.

Eventually, their mutual laughter melted as desire ignited between them again. He pulled her in his arms again to kiss her. They parted, and Jonathan reached for a bar of fine-milled soap and rubbed it between his hands. "Let me wash you."

"As long as I can return the favor," she quipped.

"I was hoping you'd ask," he replied with a devilish glint in his eyes.

She bit her lip and flirted with him in return. "Your stool is the perfect height. I don't have to look up when I kiss you."

He swept his lips against hers. He tasted of water, wine, and Jonathan. He pressed the soap into her hands. "Now kiss me to your heart's content."

How to say that there would never be enough kisses for that? After she'd lathered her hands, she placed them on his chest. The scent of fresh pears mixed with the scent of water. With her fingers, she traced the contours of his arms and shoulders before coming to his chest. His brown nipples were compact and the skin surrounding them tight. He felt like heaven. The fine black hairs that swirled in a pattern on the upper part of his chest tickled her hands. She caressed every cord, sinew, and muscle she could find. His sudden intake of breath made her smile. He placed his hand over hers, keeping it in the center of his chest.

She tipped her head, the water falling gently on her face,

and gazed at him. The illuminating gleam in his eyes told her so much. Through the power of her touch, this moment that they shared was a new beginning for them. She leaned in for a kiss, and he met her mouth with his.

"My turn," he said. With his soapy hands, he mimicked her movements on her chest, paying special attention to her hard nipples. After the water had washed off the soap he'd so carefully applied, he tilted her in his arms as he took one nipple into his mouth and sucked.

She gasped, and he sucked harder. Happily dizzy, she grasped the solid mass of his shoulders, then leaned back further, relying on his strength to keep her standing. When he had his fill, she straightened, then trailed a hand down his flat abdomen and took him in hand, marveling at his strength and heat.

The water stream diminished, signaling the tank was almost empty. His hand covered hers where she gripped him. "Let go for now."

She did as asked, and he brought that hand to his mouth then pressed a kiss.

"Let's get dry before you catch a chill," he said, extending his hand. Together they exited the shower, and still holding her hand, he took his cane in the other hand.

The warmth of his skin contrasted with the cool air that surrounded her body. Soon they stood in front of each other. He handed her a toweling for her body, then grabbed another. When she was finished, he gave her the extra. "For your hair," he said.

Only then did he dry himself. He scooped her discarded dressing gown with the tip of his cane, then draped it over her shoulders before wrapping another toweling around his waist. If it was physically possible, his erection was even larger than it had been before.

She closed the distance between them. Several trickles of

water trailed down his chest. She bent and licked the first. His stomach muscles tightened from the touch of her tongue.

She did the same for the second stream. For the third, she untied the linen toweling around his waist. With her gaze, she tracked the water's trail down his stomach, past his hips, to the nest of curls where his bold erection stood at attention as if waiting for her attention.

She gazed up at him to find Jonathan's nostrils flared. A smile tugged at one side of her lips. "Do you know what else I imagined?"

"Do tell," he answered.

"I'll show you instead." She retrieved the salve from a table, then slid a small chair closer and pointed to it. "If you please?"

With an adorable grin on his face, he sat down.

"Will you part your legs?"

"Constance," he warned. "What are you planning?"

"Heaven," she answered. "If you'll allow it and you feel comfortable with me."

Slowly, he nodded, then leaned back in the chair. He widened his legs. His rigid cock rested against his flat stomach.

She settled between his legs on her knees. Every night when he'd allow, she'd applied the salve and kneaded his muscles. Always before, he'd worn his banyan. But tonight was a cause for celebration as this was the first time he'd trusted her enough to show his scars.

Like before, she rubbed the salve into her hands, then massaged his legs. With each stroke of her hands, her breath grew more ragged. Their gazes never left each other until she found a scar. With each one, she pressed a kiss, a pledge of her fidelity and commitment to him.

When she finished, she trailed a finger down his chest where a remaining trail of water trickled. "Did you know that water always seeks the lowest level?" she asked.

His eyes grew hooded as she tongued the nipple of his

chest where the water had first tumbled, then she followed its path all the way down to his member. With the press of her lips against him, he groaned, the sound a plea for more. This was what she'd dreamed of since she'd been back in Portsmouth. To be with him in every way. She circled the crown with her tongue.

When she moaned her delight, Jonathan carefully tangled his fingers in her wet hair and brought her closer. She sucked repeatedly while she wrapped her hand around the base of his cock and pulled and squeezed in a rhythm that matched the movement of her mouth.

The whisper of her name across his lips sounded like a prayer. She drew him deeper in answer, then swirled her tongue around the head.

"I'm going to come." He tried to pull her away, but she'd have none of it.

She turned her gaze to his. Now she was the one pleading. "I want this."

With a shuddered breath, he nodded. She returned to her ministrations, and soon, his hips bucked wildly, but she refused to let go. When she tasted the musky and salty fluid on her tongue, she groaned in triumph.

She looked up in time to see his eyes clenched, lost in the sensation. As she lapped his essence, he opened his eyes and crooned her name.

Never had she witnessed such power and beauty in such a carnal act.

For as long as she lived, she'd remember this moment.

She'd been on her knees before the elusive Jonathan Eaton, the Earl of Sykeston, but he'd been the one at her tender mercy.

And they were both the richer for it.

Chapter Nineteen

❦

Jonathan's heart threatened to bust through his ribs.

He'd lost such control, something he never let happen in his everyday life. But this was anything but ordinary; his wife had pleasured him like a virtuoso making music. For a moment, all the reasons for staying away from this woman, his wife, had evaporated like water on the hottest summer day.

As he struggled for breath, the incessant pounding of his heart slowly returned to normal.

But that was the only thing normal in this room. *Damnation*, it was the only thing normal in his life at the moment. Gently, he tugged Constance from her kneeling position until she stood before him. He grabbed a towel, then wiped her chin and mouth. With the utmost care, he reached for her and pressed his mouth to hers, the taste of him still on her lips and tongue. She'd taken everything he'd given her, all his abruptness and his scars, and amazingly she was still here by his side.

When they broke apart, he brought her close and settled her on his lap. She nuzzled her head under his chin, then pressed the lightest of kisses like the touch of a butterfly's wings against his skin.

"Did you enjoy it?" A saucy smile lit her face. Pleased with herself, she was irresistible, and he smiled in return.

"What a question?" he parried as he caressed her breast, her nipple tightening into a bud.

She bit her bottom lip and swirled her finger around one of his nipples. "Well, I did." Her gaze slowly rose to his. "I hope you enjoyed it."

"You know I did." He pressed a light kiss to her cheek. "Now, how shall I give you the same?"

She wiggled on his lap, the movement causing his cock to once again thicken. How long had he dreamed of holding her, teasing her, making love to her like this? *Since forever* didn't sound long enough. Such was the power of Constance. Only the present mattered when he was with her. He'd swallow every bit of light and goodness she offered and would save it for when the darkness threatened him.

"I don't think you can give me the same pleasure." Entirely serious, she blinked.

His brow crinkled. "I don't understand."

She waved a hand in the direction of his erection. "I don't have one of those."

He couldn't help but laugh at the tart-tongued response. "Hmm, I suppose not, but you do have some exquisite parts I'd like to explore, if you'd allow?"

She nodded and a breathless exhale escaped.

God, how he wanted to spread her out on the floor where they were and bring her a completion that would rival anything she'd experienced before.

If only he could. He did his best to push away such negative thinking. The only thing was to be completely honest with her.

Merely thinking the words *court-martial* turned his stomach over. Never had he missed holding a woman or even making love to her until Constance had come back into his life. Why was he even contemplating such a thing?

God, it sickened him to think she might one day be ostra-
cized from society because of him.

Constance's gaze never left his. It was as if she could hear
his unease. "We don't need a bed." The soft challenge in her
voice clear.

"Of course we don't." The words sharper than he would
have liked. He ran a hand down his face. "Listen." He lowered his voice. "I want to pleasure you, the same as you've
done for me."

A pretty blush brightened her cheeks.

"But right now, you should run from me and never look
back."

A medley of emotions crossed her face. Confusion, doubt,
but never fear. He released a silent sigh. What was that saying
about fools and rushing in? The sincerity on her face gouged
his heart. She'd be the one determined but misguided angel
to lead the charge for him.

Her gaze skated across his features until it locked with his.
"Jonathan"—she ran her hands through his hair and gently
tilted his face to hers—"I don't know what's swirling in
here." She pressed a kiss to his forehead. "But I know one
thing. You'll not hurt me."

He closed his eyes as she placed her hand over his heart.

"Because I know what's in here," she said, her voice soft.
"You're the same man I've always known. Just more handsome, truth be told."

Suddenly, she pressed her lips to his. Like kindling to a
flame, he ignited with the need for her. When she moaned,
he took advantage and swept his tongue into her mouth, showing her the hunger and wicked craving he felt for her.

He pulled away and stared into her desire-filled eyes.
He couldn't resist her and wouldn't try. Without hesitation,
wherever she wanted to go, he'd follow without complaint
or question. He had a hunch that after tonight, whatever she

wanted him to do, he wouldn't be able to resist. She was his ultimate weakness.

She placed one hand on his shoulder for balance, then straddled him. Lifting on her tiptoes, she positioned herself over his erection. Then the minx took it in her hand with a little squeeze.

"Careful," he groaned. He gripped her hips to steady her.

Without her gaze leaving his, she lowered herself inch by incredible inch. Letting her head fall sideways, she closed her eyes as she seated his entire length within her.

The slick heat of her center felt like heaven. Hell, holding her body by her hips felt like paradise, a rapture he didn't think he'd be able to withstand. Unable to bear it any longer, he took her in a soul-confessing kiss. He needed to feel every inch of her.

Christ, he needed *her*. Only she could cast out his demons, if only for a few hours.

Her tongue slid against his as she moaned her pleasure. She lifted herself on the balls on her feet, then lowered. The motion sent staggering pulses of pleasure throughout his body. She continued the up-and-down movement, her breath coming faster as her pert breasts bounced in a perfect cadence with her movements.

It would take little for him to come again, but this wasn't for him. It was for her. He wrapped his arm around her waist and brought her close. Not breaking their kiss, he slid his hand down her torso. His fingers combed through her tight silken curls, then slid lower.

Her sex was incredibly wet, and he glided his forefinger through its soft folds until he found the nub. She gasped as his finger pressed against it. He broke the kiss and trailed his lips across her cheek.

With his mouth against her ear, he whispered, "Tell me what you like."

In turn, she pressed her cheek against his. "Swirl your finger. Don't stop until I tell you."

"I've always found a confident woman incredibly arousing." He chuckled gently.

"Good," she answered. "I'll tell you when to change your movement."

He slid his mouth to hers. "Your command is my greatest wish."

Her eyes reminded him of a thousand brilliant sapphires glittering under a midnight moon. Each gem designed to mesmerize a person who gazed upon its glow.

As he circled the sensitive bud over and over, he listened to her body, learning what she liked. The increase in breath, the little gasps she made when he touched her in a particular way. Every part of it he memorized. More than anything on this earth, he wanted her to come.

Needed her to come.

In response to his touch, her movements increased. Blood thrummed through his veins. Shards of sensation gathered in his spine as his bollocks tightened in preparation for another orgasm. With her every movement on his cock, he fought the urge to come.

His kiss turned savage as he sucked her tongue and mated his with hers. Little sighs of pleasure escaped from her, but he gave her no quarter. Tonight he wanted to eliminate her memory of any other before him as he marked her as his just as she'd marked him as hers earlier.

"Touch me," she whispered.

She didn't have to ask twice. He gentled his kiss as he stroked her with a touch designed to send her over the edge.

"Yes, there." She sighed then whispered his name.

At the same time, every muscle of her center tightened around him. Each vivid sensation unhinged him as everything within him exploded. This climax more powerful than the one she'd given him with her mouth.

She stopped all movement while her muscles clenched as if never letting him go. Her forehead rested against his heaving chest as they both struggled to regain their equilibrium.

He wrapped both hands around her, not certain if it was to keep her steady on his lap or as a way to never let her go. She'd completely destroyed him tonight. There were no thoughts of never touching her again.

But did he please her as she'd done for him? It was a nag that refused to be silent.

"How was it?" he asked, pressing a kiss to her temple.

"Adequate," she answered.

His heart stood suspended in his chest.

She gazed at him with a dreamy smile. "It was more lovely than I ever could have imagined, and we both know it."

He exhaled slightly in relief. He smiled while his heart resumed its pounding in some ancient primeval beat of self-satisfaction at her words. For him, what made it all the more wondrous was that it was Constance in his arms.

She made a move to stand, then wobbled on her feet. He took her arm to steady her. "Careful." For some absurd reason, he relished that she was physically affected by their lovemaking. He picked up a fresh linen toweling and looked up into her eyes. "It'll be my turn to care for Aurelia tonight."

"In my room?" She ran her fingers through his tousled hair.

With a slow reverence, he gently cleaned away the remnants of their lovemaking. "We didn't discuss this before, but I came inside of you. We should have—"

She pressed her forefinger against the center of his mouth to silence him. "I don't mind another child. Do you?"

His mind screamed the word *yes* but his heart sounded a fervent *no*. He had no business bringing a child into this world—not until his own life was in order.

But when it came to Constance, his heart always ruled.

"No," he said softly.

She took the towel and cleaned him like he'd done for her.

He felt himself stiffen again at her unbearably erotic touch. When she saw the effect she was having on him, she smiled as her gaze met his.

Constance handed him his cane, then took his other hand in hers. "Let's go to bed."

Without objection, he picked up his cane, then followed her into the countess's bedroom. A vision of her round with his child sent his thoughts reeling. Things between them were becoming clearer and at the same time, murkier. He still had to tell her the truth about the letters.

More important, he should tell her the truth about what was hanging over his head.

Couldn't he have one perfect night with his wife before he ruined everything?

Chapter Twenty

The next morning, Constance carefully untangled herself from her husband's arms, then stood by the side of the bed. From the pink and orange ribbons in the sky, they'd slept late. Or at least, she had. She normally had several hours of work in by this time.

In sleep, he had his arm thrown over his eyes as if avoiding the inevitable morning sunrise. Black bristles shadowed his cheeks. It amazed her every time she saw such a sight. In her estimation, he was even more handsome in the morning than the night before. She loved the feel of his whiskers against her skin even though they were prickly—much like her husband.

Jonathan resembled a fortress, one that she was slowly learning how to raise its gate. She had a hunch that the portcullis hadn't been drawn in a long time. Patience was the key to getting him to lower his barriers and open his heart.

After checking on Aurelia to discover Dahlia had already taken her to the nursery, Constance made her way to the dressing room only to spot a gardening basket with a new spade and a pair of gardening gloves wrapped in satin. There was no note, but she knew who'd given her such a lovely gift.

She tiptoed back to the bedroom, then bent over and pressed a kiss to his cheek. "Thank you. It's beautiful. Does that mean we'll have the party?"

With a mumble for answer, he turned away from her. A rueful smile tugged at her lips. She wanted nothing more than to climb back in bed and curl up next to him, but she had work to do.

After Constance dressed, she headed to the library with her gift basket by her side. She'd work in the garden after she dealt with the next project. She spread out the myriad of receipts Meriwether had given to each of his wives after his death.

Though there were no letters of instruction, Constance was convinced that the receipts held the key to where the three wives' dowries were. She had to figure it out. Those monies represented their financial security in case of Meriwether's death, but they all suspected he had gambled the proceeds away. Yet no one could ever find the amounts in the expenditures. Kat's dowry had been two hundred pounds; Beth's dowry had been twenty thousand pounds; and Constance's had been a respectable two thousand pounds.

She organized the receipts by wife and date. If she could untangle the riddle, then she could help Beth escape from the seventy-eight-year-old suitor her brother had arranged for her to marry.

There was no logical explanation for any of the expenditures. She decided to look at the puzzle a different way. Carefully, she organized all three piles into one by date, starting at the beginning.

Since she'd been sitting there for over two hours, she stretched her hands overhead. The movement caused her blue and cream colored silk floral wrap to fall to the floor.

As she reached to pick it up, a large masculine hand met hers.

"Allow me."

She looked up to see Jonathan before her. Clean-shaven

and dressed to perfection like another present to unwrap, he stood before her. Everything within her tingled. Even the chandelier above her twinkled a little brighter in his presence.

With the tip of his cane, he picked up her shawl, straightened it, then held it in his two hands. "May I put it around you?"

"Please." His eyes never left hers. But the heat of his stare reminded her of a hunter, one who wanted to devour her. She leaned back in a way that gave him an excellent view down her bodice.

His deep inhalation sounded. He squeezed her arms after draping the wrap around her. "A tempting sight for me this morning."

"You're the same for me." She picked up the basket. "Thank you for the thoughtful gift."

"Do you like it?" Wariness lined his brow.

"Very much. I planned on working in the garden later today." When his wariness melted into concern, she asked, "What is it?"

He pointed to the pile of papers. His gaze glued to the receipts in front of her. "What are those?"

"Receipts that Meriwether left for all of us." She straightened them in front of her. "I'm trying to make sense what they mean."

"For what purpose?" The sharpness in his resonant voice was unexpected.

She stood to face him. "Kat, Beth, and I believe that these receipts are the key to what he did with our dowries."

His gaze latched onto hers. "Didn't Randford pay you all?"

She nodded, then picked up a receipt that belonged to Beth's pile. "He did, but unfortunately for Beth, she decided to give the money to her brother, the viscount, after he shared how destitute he was."

"St. John Howell," he growled, the disgust palpable. "Why are you the one with this task?"

She pursed her lips at his tone. "Because I offered to do this for Beth. Besides, Kat and I would like to know what happened to our monies. If we're successful, then it's one less thing that Meriwether took from us."

"Perhaps it would be best to leave it all in the past." He switched his cane to the other hand.

"No. This mystery must be solved." She spread the pile like a deck of cards, then pointed to several receipts. "Do you see this? It's a transaction for a prize Hampshire pig." She pulled one out and handed it to him. "Meriwether traded some type of statue, perhaps one of his renowned erotic sculptures, for the animal." She pulled out another one. "This is the delivery receipt. The pig was delivered to Kat five months ago." She shrugged. "We didn't think he left us anything. Yet Kat received a bequest months after the reading of his will. None of it makes sense. There were so many loose ends. It's like a cloth unraveling before me. If I can simply grasp what all these transactions are, I'll find the money."

"I can send these to my solicitor's office. He's an excellent puzzle solver. He can figure this out, if there's anything to figure out." He smiled as if he'd found the way to turn lead into gold. "You don't need to do this."

The urge to reject his offer out of hand was on the tip of her tongue. Constance had been making her own decisions for the majority of her life. Husband or no, she would decide how to handle this. She placed her hands on her hips and shook her head. "Thank you for the offer. I promised Beth and Kat, and I plan to continue."

"May I point out several things?" He arched a brow. "You're already overcommitted as it is. You work at the dockyard practically every day, then you come home to Aurelia."

"And you," she said.

"And me," he agreed with a smile. "By night, you're exhausted."

"All you've pointed out is that I like to work and play with the baby." She lifted her own brow in answer. "Obviously, I'm not too exhausted if I want to make love to you."

His cheeks reddened slightly. "Lucky for me."

She laughed at the sudden cocky grin on his face. "And for me."

"But did you hear Aurelia last night?" His expression turned innocent.

Her hand flew to her chest as her heart tumbled in a free fall. "Please don't tell me she was up last night," she said softly.

He smiled much in the manner of *I have a secret.* "I won't."

"Out with it," she softly commanded.

"Twice."

She slid her hand from her chest to her stomach to tame her disquiet. What was happening to her? What if Aurelia had been in true distress or, worse, injured? She would feel abandoned, and Constance more than anyone knew how that could wreck someone's confidence and trust. "I'm the worst mother."

He circled around the table, then sat directly across from her. "No, you are not."

She shook her head in denial, but he raised his hand stopping any protest on her part.

"However, you're bone-tired." He reached across the table and took her hand in his. "When you're like this, you become ill. Remember after your parents passed, you took your daily lessons, then worked at Lysander & Sons, before coming home to take care of Aunt Vee and straightening out your parents' estate matters. You developed a severe lung ailment. That's what happens when you work yourself to exhaustion."

"I can't believe you remember that." Even she had forgotten how ill she'd become. But he hadn't.

"I consider myself an expert on you and your habits. You shouldn't be taking on another project, particularly for Kat or Beth. Kat is married to Randford. She doesn't need the money."

"Kat saved that dowry amount for herself."

He looked at her askance.

She tilted her chin an inch. "It represents her accomplishments. If it was me, I'd want that money returned too. She can invest it for her daughter if she ever has one. I'll do the same with my dowry."

He squeezed her hand. "I have plenty of money. You don't need to worry about your two thousand pounds. I'll provide a dowry for Aurelia."

How could she not soften at that endearing statement? "I can't tell you how much that means to me. I could kiss you right now."

"Tempting offer, but first let me ask you another question." Jonathan fixed his gaze to hers. "Do you need additional funds for Lysander & Sons? Is everything in good order there?"

The questions hung heavy between them, and for a brief second, she debated whether she should share more, then dismissed the thought. "I'm doing this"—she waved a hand over the receipts—"for my friends."

"They don't need your help. You work as hard if not harder than they do. They shouldn't take advantage of your kindness."

She entwined their fingers. "These women are more than friends to me. They're my family. I write to them every single week." She tugged their hands closer until they rested against the beat of her heart. "I'm doing this for Beth. She works with Kat and adores it. Can you blame her for wanting to get out from under her brother's thumb?"

"You have to protect yourself from such exploitation. Trust me on this point." He released her hand then leaned back in his chair.

"Jonathan, if I try, and fail, then I'll think of something else." She tilted her head and regarded him. "I feel as if we're discussing two different things."

He pushed the chair away and stood. "People are not to be trusted, and failure is not easy to live with."

She stood the same as he did, then lowered her voice. "What are you referring to? What's happened?"

An icy chill permeated the air. "Nothing. However, I've discovered that sometimes life is so much easier if you don't bother with others. Particularly so-called friends. It's the natural order of things. People take advantage. I don't want you to worry about money. I'll direct my solicitor to transfer two thousand into your operating account. Do with it what you like."

"I don't understand . . ."

He'd already left the room and didn't hear her answer. He was hurting more than she ever suspected. And she had no idea how to help him.

Chapter Twenty-One

The next morning, Constance woke to a rousing chorus of wrens and warblers vying for a mate—and to an empty room. She didn't tarry. She rose from the bed, finished her morning ablutions, then dressed to greet the day. She stole a peek at Aurelia, who was still sleeping. With a kiss on the baby's forehead, she returned to her room. Amazing what another night of sound sleep could do for a person's attitude. She felt as if she could conquer the world.

Or at least her husband. Last night, she'd decided that a picnic would be her next effort in breaking down Jonathan's defenses. She and Aurelia loved the garden they'd worked on, and Constance couldn't wait to show him. Those were the moments that brought a family together.

She rang for Dahlia, then dressed. As soon as the nurse-maid arrived, Constance rushed to her husband's study. With a quick knock on the study door, she walked inside with a smile on her lips.

Immediately, it faded on finding the room empty.

"Good morning, Lady Sykeston," Mr. North called out as he walked to her side. "If you're looking for his lordship, he's visiting a couple of tenants this morning."

The butler was practically beaming.

"Good morning, Mr. North." She grinned in answer. "So early?"

The butler nodded. "Indeed, my lady. Several of the tenants had asked for his assistance this morning." North leaned forward and lowered his voice. "It's excellent news. He hasn't seen any of them since last year."

"How did he arrange his business before?"

"He'd send Thomas," North offered. "I expect Lord Sykeston to return in several hours."

Hiding her chagrin, she nodded. "Thank you."

It was silly to feel disappointed. She needed to set clear boundaries about her expectations. Marriage wasn't something that bloomed overnight. It took time and effort on both parts. Not every hour of the day belonged to them. Jonathan had responsibilities and so did she.

There was one way to change her mood.

She set off to tackle the various tasks she'd need to complete before she could take Aurelia on a picnic. After working for a couple of hours on Jonathan's study, she turned to some correspondence. With that finished, she visited the kitchens for the basket and took it outside. Afterward, she retrieved her daughter.

Then she made her way to retrieve her husband.

With Aurelia carefully balanced on one hip, she knocked on the study door with her free hand. When Jonathan looked up from his desk, she strolled inside. "May we steal you away for an hour or so?"

As soon as they walked into the room, Regina looked up from the black velvet sofa. Aurelia demanded to touch the dog. As soon as Constance set the baby down, Aurelia crawled to the dog's side, then used the sofa to pull herself to a standing position.

Jonathan stood and watched them interact as a slight grin spread across his face.

"Imagine the trouble these two will find when Aurelia is a little older," Constance said.

"I suppose so." He narrowed his eyes and looked at her. "You were in here this morning working, weren't you? It looks freshly dusted and straightened. When I first walked in, I thought I had the wrong room."

"Are you upset?" She calmly clasped her hands in front of her while her heart stumbled in her chest.

"I'm pleased, but you're Lady Sykeston." He took her hand and brought it to his lips. "You shouldn't be cleaning."

"I'm also your wife. This pleases me."

He squeezed her hand. "Thank you. Now, to what do I owe this honor?"

"Aurelia and I want to share a picnic with you." Her smile stiffened when he frowned.

He glanced at the papers that were strewn upon the desk. "Picnic," he murmured. "I'd planned to work in here all day."

"If you're too busy, we understand." She tried to sound cheerful, but the effort was unsuccessful based upon his frown.

"I have to finish a task or two, then I'll try to join you." His gaze drifted from hers to the duo on the floor. Aurelia was pulling the dog's ear, while Regina licked the baby's face amid giggles.

She walked to the sofa and scooped up a giggling Aurelia, who was covered in dog slobber. With a half turn, she waved, keeping her face hidden.

The nag of discontent that tugged was completely unwelcome. Constance had to remember that Jonathan wasn't Meri. She might be alone with Aurelia on the picnic, but he hadn't abandoned Aurelia or her. It was admirable that he was working on the estate.

"We hope to have your company, my lord," she said with a breeziness in her voice to hide her disappointment. As she strolled out the French doors of his study and down the steps into the newly groomed courtyard, she felt something at her back.

She turned slightly to see what could possibly cause such a feeling. From across the way his eyes bored into hers.

He'd likely been staring at her the entire time she walked out of the room. She'd bet Lysander & Sons' next month's profits on it.

⸺

Jonathan may have been a recluse when it came to society, but he had enough past experience with his sister and mother to know when a woman possessed the deadly combination of disappointment and irritation. One by itself was trouble enough, but when they twisted together? It foretold calamity if not rectified quickly.

Unfortunately, there were only a couple of outcomes that could tame those demons.

Either an apology or set aside his tasks and join the ladies in his life for a little respite. He let out a deep breath. As soon as he finished the work before him, he'd join her.

First, he had to review the rent rolls, approve them, then ask Thomas to deliver them to his solicitor in London. The Sykeston earldom had successful farming operations across England. It was Jonathan's preference that Thomas traveled and met with the earldom's solicitor instead of him.

It had the added benefit that Jonathan didn't have to entertain anyone when he was there.

But today after meeting his tenants, he'd regained a sense of responsibility to them. These people and their families had worked together with his for generations. Every family and he were connected. He smiled slightly. They were happy to see him. Practically all of them had asked how he was faring and even offered congratulations on his marriage.

He could not think of the future as something to be

dreaded. He would continue to try to find Jean Davout. From the mere moments he'd spent in the man's company, Jonathan was convinced he was a man of honor. He would tell the truth.

Though he thought his legacy was in perfecting his cartridge design, he owed his tenants more of his attention. He had promised himself on the way back to the house that he would make the effort to see them more often. Next time, he would take Constance with him and make the introductions. She would enjoy being a part of that, and he'd be proud to introduce her as his wife.

The sweet resonance of giggles rushed to meet him. He looked up from the papers and smiled. He didn't want to think too much about the cause of his new mood, but the cavorting in the courtyard was a sound reason for it.

Funny, he would have never thought to visit the tenants around his estate without it being a necessity. But waking up next to Constance had brought a surge of energy, one that had been lacking in his life since he'd returned home.

After he signed the documents and left instructions with North to give them to Thomas, he made his way to join Constance and Aurelia. Even his leg seemed to be cooperating with him and his fine spirits today.

"Room for me?" Jonathan called out. "More important, is there food left?"

Constance waved him forward. Regina didn't budge from her position on the blanket next to his wife, but the baby stood precariously on the uneven ground and stretched her arms to him. "Da."

Constance splayed a hand across her chest. "What did you say?"

For a moment, he didn't breathe as the wonder on Constance's face turned to shock.

The baby ignored her mother as Jonathan laid his cane on the ground, then picked her up as she commanded. Leaning against the tree to keep his balance, he lowered them both to the ground by stretching out his right leg and using his left to bear his weight. Once seated, he scooted next to his wife with the baby on his lap.

"Did she say what I thought she said?" Constance asked, not looking at him as she prepared him a plate of cold chicken, sliced cheese, bread, fresh berries, and apple tarts.

"I think she's saying dog. When I went to her the other night, she did the same thing." He took a bite of chicken and chewed.

Constance poured a glass of lemonade, then set it beside him. "Did she hold out her hands to Regina like she did now?"

"No." He swallowed a piece of cheese.

"I see." She looked to Aurelia then back to him. "So, she's calling you Da."

"Hardly," he objected. "Regina was with me too. Maybe she's saying dog."

His wife chewed on her bottom lip, the one he'd feasted on the other night. "I've heard her refer to Regina as Gee."

An absurd grin broke across his face at the thought that Aurelia thought of him as her father. But at the sight of Constance's pursed lips, he immediately sobered. "Don't be jealous."

Her hand flew to her chest again. "Me? Of course not. I've heard her say all sorts of words. Or what could plausibly pass as words."

Jonathan leaned close as Aurelia bounced on his left leg. "Has she said Ma or Mum yet?"

"What a ridiculous question," Constance murmured as she unwrapped several slices of fruit cake. She handed a small piece to Aurelia.

"Has she?" he whispered.

Her gaze flew to his. The fire in her eyes betrayed her agitation at his teasing.

He took her hand and dipped his head until they were eye-to-eye, then leaned closer. Only an inch separated them. "This beautiful, vibrant girl"—he looked down to see Aurelia smearing fruit cake across his navy wool breeches—"knows exactly who the most important person is in her world."

Her eyes glistened with emotion.

"It's you." He squeezed her hand. "Only you. Her mother."

"That's sweet." A sheepish smile graced her lush lips. "Thank you."

"I'm glad I could be of service, madam." He brought her hand to his mouth, not failing to notice the soft skin, cool and inviting. "Do you know what else?"

A blink was her only answer. He could lose himself in the blue depth of her eyes and never want to be found. "I apologize for being late to this." He squeezed her hand once more, then let go as Aurelia threatened to fall off his good leg. He balanced her by wrapping his arm around her tiny waist. "Something happened this morning. I woke up with an energy I hadn't had in ages. I decided—"

"My lady, might I have a word with you?" Standing in the courtyard not more than ten yards away, an upstairs maid called out in a breaking voice. "I broke a vase."

"Of course, Lucy." Constance made her way to stand. "She sounds upset. Would you watch Aurelia? I'll be back as soon as I can."

He nodded as the baby stood on wobbly legs, and he helped her balance.

Constance practically glided across the courtyard. Looking at the ground, the maid stood with her shoulders slumped. When his wife reached Lucy's side, the woman glanced up with tears running down her face. Immediately, Constance took the young maid's hands in her own.

He couldn't hear the conversation, but he had little doubt that his wife was comforting the woman. He was struck by the caring concern that crossed Constance's face. That's what a good mistress of the house did. She comforted and counseled the people who worked there to ensure that everyone felt their efforts were vital and that they belonged.

Something he'd never taken the time to do before. But he'd watched his father and mother do the same countless times in the past.

A squeal sounded, and Jonathan glanced across the courtyard only to see Aurelia toddling toward a small decorative pond that bordered the courtyard. It was deep, and there was no ledge to keep the baby from falling in. It drained into a stone stair-step fountain. If she fell in and made it to the fountain, she'd crack her skull open.

Regina trotted beside her, unaware of the danger—she saw it as play.

Jonathan grabbed his cane and pushed to his feet using the tree as leverage. The quick movement sent an avalanche of jarring pain through the knotted muscles of his thigh. With the first step he stumbled but regained his balance.

"Aurelia, stop."

Only Regina halted on his command. The baby glanced his way yet kept her course, all the while wearing a near toothless, lopsided grin. She sped up as best she could, thinking he was playing a game by chasing her.

For the love of God, she's within thirty feet of the pond.

Using the cane as leverage, he crossed the ground in the longest strides he dared without falling. The baby still trying to outrun him.

"Aurelia," he scolded. Out of the corner of his eye, he saw Arkwright and Constance running toward them.

"Stop, Aurelia," Constance cried out.

By then, Jonathan was within a couple of feet of the baby. As he reached to grab her, she tripped and landed hard on her face.

In seconds, he scooped her small body up in one arm. He juggled her to look at her face. Blood mixed with saliva seeped from her mouth while her lips wobbled as if not knowing what to do. Claret-colored dots bubbled from a scrap down the right of her cheek. Her eyes searched his as if trying to understand what had happened.

"Aurelia, that was quite a tumble," he soothed.

The offer of comfort was lost in a bloodcurdling scream that erupted from her little mouth. He winced at the horrific sound of fright.

By then, Constance was by his side and grabbed the baby from his arms. The child was crying so hard, she couldn't seem to breathe.

Every organ within him slowly curled into nothing. For the love of God, he'd failed to watch the child as Constance had asked. Aurelia could have been badly injured if she'd toppled into the water. Now the baby was in distress, and it could have been avoided. Aurelia gasped in a stutter, desperate to catch her breath.

Numbness held him hostage just like it did that day he fell in Faladen's study. Christ, he couldn't even manage the simplest things, such as watching a child. All he was good at was shooting. His vision blurred and darkness seemed to threaten to swallow him whole. He teetered slightly but caught himself before he fell again. Why did he think he could have a normal life with his wife and daughter? He couldn't protect himself, let alone his family.

"Forgive me. I wouldn't have hurt her for the world," Jonathan murmured.

Constance either didn't hear him or didn't think he deserved an answer. All her attention was devoted to Aurelia.

An odd sensation of weightlessness surrounded him as if he were about to float above the fray. "Forgive me," he murmured again.

Constance finally turned toward him, holding Aurelia tightly against her chest. "Jonathan?"

Smears of crimson stained his wife's cream-colored dress

where the baby had laid her head against her mother's breast. They looked like they'd been through a war.

He'd done that to them.

Her brows knitted together as she stared at him. "What happened?"

"Forgive me." He stumbled back a step as he said the inane words. Begging for absolution meant nothing. What he wanted was to bring them back to where they were five minutes ago, a family growing the bond between the individual members. A newly minted husband and wife finding their way in marriage.

Aurelia hiccupped again. The worry that flashed across Constance's face as she leaned back to examine her daughter threatened to knock him to his knees.

Unable to look at the macabre scene any longer, Jonathan relied on his old ways. Whenever he had created chaos on the battlefield or a dueling field, he disappeared. As steadily as he could, Jonathan made his way from the group. He looked toward his study only to discover Mrs. Butler and North standing together on the terrace wearing identical expressions of worry.

Jonathan made an unobtrusive beeline toward the side of the house away from the crowd. Because of his damned leg, he wasn't fast enough. North cut him off, but at least they were far enough out of the way no one would be looking for them.

"My lord, what happened?" North's gaze drifted to the group assembled around Constance and Aurelia.

"I . . . I didn't protect her. When she ran, I couldn't catch her." He straightened his shoulders and stared at his loyal butler. "My wife asked me to watch Aurelia while she spoke with Lucy. I didn't and now the child is hurt because of me." He turned to leave.

"My lord?"

Jonathan looked over his shoulder at the butler.

"You fell once when you were about the same age as Miss Aurelia. You bloodied your lip. Your mother did the same thing as the countess. She wouldn't let anyone near you until she could determine for herself that you were all right." North glanced again at Constance then back to Jonathan. "Children fall, my lord. They always have."

"Not much has changed over the years. I still suffer the same affliction as I did when I was a toddler." Jonathan didn't wait for a response but headed off to the side of the house.

He wasn't referring to merely a physical fall, but a fall from grace. That tumble would hurt more than just himself. It would devastate Constance and Aurelia once the gossip rags got ahold of his downfall with their rabid teeth.

Chapter Twenty-Two

With a smile and a wave to Dahlia, Constance quietly slipped from her daughter's room. It had taken Aurelia only a few minutes to fall asleep. After her crying spell had subsided, the baby had yawned repeatedly. There had been no need for a doctor since Aurelia's injuries were superficial.

Constance crossed her room to the shared dressing room, then removed her soiled dress and undergarments. She could still hear Aurelia's screams echoing in her brain, and it had been at least an hour since she'd brought her inside and cleaned her face, looked at her mouth, and changed her.

After washing her arms and hands, Constance donned a fresh chemise and dress. It was time to find Jonathan. The shock on his face had matched her own, but with one difference. She'd actually held Aurelia and discovered that the mouth wound was caused by her biting her lip. The scrape looked worse than it actually was once it was cleaned.

She'd never heard such sorrow in Jonathan's voice as when he said, "Forgive me." The key Mr. North had given her in the courtyard lay on the table beside her. She picked it up and slid it into her pocket. It was the exact one that Jonathan's mother had always carried on her person when she lived here. It would unlock most of the inside doors, including Jonathan's study.

As she went to knock on his bedroom door, the crack of pistol fire echoed through the house. This was the first time since she'd arrived that he'd started shooting in the house again.

Another blast cracked the quiet. In record time, Constance stood outside his study door. With her knuckles she rapped the hard oaken panel of the door. When she reached to open it, she discovered the door was locked.

She knocked again, but a gunshot canceled the sound. Without second-guessing herself, she reached for the key in her pocket and unlocked the door, then stepped in.

He sat in his favorite black chair with smoke swirling around him much like the primordial deity Erebus and his accompanying darkness. The sense of loneliness and morosity weighed heavy in the air.

"Jonathan?"

He didn't answer, preparing his pistol to shoot again.

"Please don't do that," she said as she approached him. "Aurelia is asleep."

Finally, he made some type of a sound. It might have been a grunt, but she'd accept it as a positive answer.

"I thought you might like to know how she is." She came to his side and placed her hand on his wide shoulder. Through his morning coat, she could feel the shift of his muscles beneath her touch. He had the same effect on her. Whenever he touched her, every inch of her body seemed to vibrate in awareness. She didn't look down at him. Instead she surveyed the courtyard. Arkwright was nowhere to be found. "What are you shooting at?"

"Leaves."

"Isn't it hard with the wind blowing?" she asked.

"Not really. I'm good at it, and I can control it."

She nodded, then knelt by his side. "Why did you leave the courtyard?" She kept her voice purposely low.

"Because I had no place there." He emptied the remaining powder from the pistol, then placed it on the side table away from them.

"I beg to differ." They had never argued, but they needed a very pointed conversation now about how they would go forward from here. "This was one of our rules. We're a family, and you don't leave in the middle of a crisis."

He studied her face, then leaned back in the chair. "You shouldn't let me near Aurelia. I should have trusted my instincts. I didn't think I was capable of holding her if she needed me, and I was correct."

Constance tilted her head. "Help me understand."

He waved a hand down his leg. "I can't protect her if she's in danger. I can't reach her in time."

"But you did. She was headed straight for the fountain, and you kept her from falling in."

"She fell in front of me, and I couldn't stop her." He was practically yelling at this point. "If you haven't noticed, I'm an invalid. I can barely walk."

"That's not true. You walk just fine," she argued. Her own voice grew louder. "What I notice is that you shy away from being close to people . . . people who care deeply for you. Your own family."

"Is that what you want in your marriage? Take care of a cripple?"

"Don't say that," she answered.

A sneer tugged at one side of his mouth. "Rubbing my leg every day to keep me somewhat mobile."

"I would do it twice a day if you desired. I'm your wife." The last words hitched in her throat.

He leaned in and lowered his voice. "Will you take an honest look at me? This is as well as I'll ever be. As I age, it will only become worse. I'll be forced to rely on footmen and a three-wheeled bath chair. Perhaps I'll have a sedan chair made for the house."

"Stop it. I think you're trying to push me away." She lifted her chin. "If you're feeling guilty, don't. She's been injured before when I was with her, and I daresay it will happen again." She softened her voice. "Jonathan, no matter how much you or I try to protect her, accidents happen."

A twisted smile creased his lips. "That's where you're wrong. You see, I wasn't protecting her, because I wasn't watching her as you'd asked."

She opened her mouth to deny what he was saying. He wouldn't hurt Aurelia. Not for the world.

Jonathan ground his fist into his injured leg. "Instead of tending her, I was watching you. Thinking how my life had changed since you've been here."

Silence descended between them. "Are you happy your life has changed?" It was difficult to tell. Earlier with his easy smile and happy attitude, she'd have said yes. But now he'd withdrawn behind a proverbial screen. The blaze in his eyes had died to embers.

He leaned back and rested his head on the back of the chair.

"It's all right," she said softly.

"Maybe for you, but not for me." He exhaled as if defeated. "What if something horrid happens?"

"We'll deal with it as a family. You and I. Together." She smiled slightly, but sensed he was referring to something else besides Aurelia's fall. "No matter what life throws our way, we'll manage it. Remember, you said she made you realize that there was something bigger than your world."

"Today taught me that I don't belong in her world." Before she could respond, he continued, "How is she?" The low thrum of his voice had lost its earlier vibrancy, as if he'd run out of energy.

"She's fine. A scrape to her cheek and a cut on her lip. She'll be back to her old self tomorrow."

Jonathan nodded distractedly. "If you don't mind, I have quite a bit of work to do this evening before tomorrow breaks. I plan on eating here while I work."

"May I join you?" His desk was perfectly clean as if he'd already finished his work for the day.

He turned that dark-as-midnight stare her way. "I think after the day we've all had, it would be best if you stayed with Aurelia tonight.

The sudden matter-of-factness in his voice stopped her cold. With his face blank and his eyes vacant, all emotion had disappeared.

He had turned into an automaton.

The jangle of the horses' harnesses woke Constance up from a sound sleep. She walked to the window in time to see Jonathan step inside. Within seconds the coach-and-four lurched into motion.

She rang for Dahlia to watch Aurelia, then dressed and departed for downstairs. When she reached the ground floor, North stood at the bottom of the steps waiting for her. Thankfully, none of the other servants were there to hear their conversation.

"Where did he go?" she asked. It was rude not to say good morning, but the sun had not yet risen, the sky still dark as night.

North acknowledged her with a bow. "London."

Her hand flew to her chest. The butler couldn't have shocked her more if he'd said her husband had flown to the moon. As she struggled for a response, she tried to tame the sudden fear that rattled her very core. What if Jonathan had left her for good?

Oh, she had every right to feel that way. This was exactly what her first husband had done after staying with her for a month. Without a single word, he'd bolted for Cumberland in the dead of night, leaving her pregnant.

Dear God. It was possible she was carrying now.

"I see," she uttered. What a pathetic response.

"He only decided half an hour ago," North offered. The sympathy in his voice made her feel even worse.

"Did he say when he'd return?" As soon as she'd uttered the needy words, she wanted to withdraw them.

"He did not."

Inwardly, she flinched at the butler's kind eyes.

"Nor did he say what his business was."

She cleared her throat. "Thank you, Mr. North." She turned to leave.

"My lady?"

She stopped on the stairs to face him.

"Only his valet and I are aware of the haste of his travel plans. No one else will know what we've discussed."

Desperate to keep what remained of her dignity close at hand, she nodded brusquely. "Thank you."

His eyes never left hers. "Perhaps I'm speaking out of turn, but I believe your marriage and Miss Aurelia's accident are the impetus for his unusual behavior. He appears lost and grasping at whom he's become."

"Who is that, Mr. North?"

"A man with a family, one he doesn't believe himself deserving," he answered. "You're stretching his limits." The butler shrugged, then smiled. "He's been in the cold so long he doesn't understand what comfort and warmth feel like." He sighed gently. "However, he's a smart man. He'll be more miserable once he concludes the answers aren't in London." With that, the butler bowed slightly.

Leaving Constance wondering exactly what the question was that her husband was trying to answer.

⁓

As the days slowly passed following her husband's abrupt desertion, Constance's earlier shock had transformed into worry. By the third day he'd been gone, all that worry had morphed into anger. It wasn't as simple as leaving; he'd fled from her.

He'd even taken his dog with him, leaving Aurelia sorely aggrieved. Every night, the baby had cried herself to sleep while woefully calling out, "Da, Da" and "Gee, Gee." Each time, Constance's heart had squeezed at the pitiful sound.

It had been five days since his departure. That night, as Constance soothed her daughter with gentle pats, she straightened her spine. This was the last time she'd allow herself to be vulnerable to the whims of another, particularly a husband. Tears threatened as Aurelia called out again. It wasn't fair to her daughter or her.

"It's all right, love," Constance whispered. "We have each other." She hummed Aurelia's favorite lullaby. In minutes, the baby had calmed. Within a quarter of an hour, she'd fallen asleep. Carefully, Constance carried her to bed. As she stared down at the sweet, tear-stained face of her daughter, one of her own tears fell.

All the sentiments of hurt and abandonment she'd vigilantly tamped down woke from that deep place she'd thought conquered. No matter how she tried, she couldn't ignore it. She brushed the bothersome evidence of her pain away. He couldn't leave them like that. She wouldn't allow it.

She closed her eyes and smoothed a hand down her stomach. Jonathan had promised to be supportive and share whatever bothered him. How could they have a marriage and a family if he didn't trust her enough to share his pain?

She pressed a kiss to her daughter's forehead, then quietly returned to her own room and settled behind her desk. She hmphed silently as she pulled out their rules for marriage from the top drawer.

The cad had broken his own rules of engagement.

If she ever saw him again, she'd not let him forget it.

Chapter Twenty-Three

"Welcome home, my lord." The butler's quiet voice met Jonathan in greeting as he climbed the stairs to the house.

"North," he answered. Every part of him ached even with the excellent suspension of his coach. His leg throbbed, but not even that inconvenience could convince him to rest at a coaching inn for the night.

Though it was late, nothing would keep him from seeing Constance. Five days away had felt like five years. He had no intention of interrupting her sleep, but the need to feast his eyes on her sleeping form would be the medicine he'd need to rest.

"I hope your trip to London was successful." North bowed slightly, but Jonathan could still see the slight grin that stretched across his lips.

"It was." Jonathan stopped inside the entry to catch his breath. He'd picked up a couple of necessary items and brought them back to Portsmouth. But more important, he'd come to realize that only a coward would run from the truth. "Everyone in bed?"

North's busy white eyebrows shot up. "Lady Sykeston retired shortly after the dinner hour."

"Thank you." Jonathan smiled. It felt rejuvenating to be home. Simply knowing she was here made him relax. However, he aware of what he'd done. He should have never left for London without discussing it with her. He carefully removed his gloves, then handed them to North. "Good night." Jonathan took a deep breath then released it. Time to tackle the remaining staircase.

It wasn't trepidation that sang through his veins, but something else. *A reckoning of some sort* was a better description. As soon as he'd set off for London, his determination to stay in the city for a while had vanished. He'd made a grave mistake leaving Constance without imparting his plans.

He'd had the best of intentions for leaving before dawn. When Aurelia had looked up at him with an expression of betrayal, he knew exactly what she felt. He'd been betrayed by people he trusted too. But Faladen and Peterson had never caused him physical harm.

Over the miles he'd traveled, Jonathan had struggled mightily with his failure to protect his family. They should have expected better of him. He'd expected better of himself.

There was only one way he knew how to protect them after Aurelia's accident. That was by disappearing.

Yet he couldn't stay away. It was as if the poor excuse for his soul had been voided without Constance. He'd felt emptiness before, but nothing like the searing loneliness that burned through him these last several days. As soon as Jonathan entered his room, he discovered his trunk unpacked. It looked as if he'd never left the house. If only that were the case.

After undressing, he donned his banyan, then with as much stealth as he could muster, he crossed the dressing room to Constance's door. He placed his hand on the cool wood panel and closed his eyes. If he were a praying man, he'd ask for help, though it was probably a worthless cause.

Even the so-called man's best friend couldn't be found to

stand beside him. There was nothing else to do but go forward.

He gently knocked and waited. A murmur sounded behind the door, an obvious signal to come in. He depressed the latch, then entered the room.

Constance sat at her desk gazing directly at him. Her blue eyes glistened, and the moue of displeasure on her lips was unmistakable.

"How was London?" The anger in her clipped voice unmistakable.

"Short."

A wagging Regina lay on Constance's bed not bothering to get up. She didn't even lift her head.

"How long has she been in your room?" Jonathan pointed at the traitor.

"Quarter of an hour," Constance answered. "Shortly after your carriage pulled to a stop, she was scratching at the door begging to be let in."

Much like he was now.

Constance placed her quill in its stand. "Why are you here?"

He rubbed the back of his neck. *I can't go to sleep without you. Or the perennial favorite, I'm lost without you.* "I had to see you." The words sounded trite to his own ears.

"You didn't need to see me the morning you left." Her eyes sparked with a renewed vexation. "So how have your circumstances changed?"

He could feel the electrical current between them. It pulled and pushed, bringing them together, then forcing them apart. He wanted to close the distance, hold her, then beg forgiveness. Kiss her until neither remembered their names, then make love to her all night as a way of atoning for his sins.

With an ease that told him to beware, she pushed up from the desk, then walked around it. His gaze skated down her face and dressing gown. Her dark tresses were loosely pinned atop her head, but damp ringlets frolicked around her face. She must have taken a bath or shower earlier.

Bloody fool that he was, he could have joined her if he'd been home.

She rested her backside against the desk facing him. In her hand she held a piece of paper. Briefly, she glanced at it, then crossed her arms and regarded him. "Do you know what this is?"

He shook his head.

"It's your rules of engagement," she said bitterly. "Your own *bloody* rules that you broke." She regarded the paper and read aloud. "*We shall be supportive of each other's goals and dreams.*" She looked up over the paper. "Those were yours. Here are mine. *We make our marriage a priority. If something is bothering one of us, we tell each other.*"

"You don't have to repeat them." He released a breath.

"Why did you leave without telling me?" She threw the paper on the desk. Her gaze was an examination like none he'd experienced before. It was as if she could see every misdeed and mistake he'd ever made. With others he wouldn't give a damn, but this was Constance, and she deserved better.

Specifically, she deserved better than him.

"I had to leave. I had to get away." He wanted to pull his hair. The excuses were lame.

"From what?" Her anger deflated before his eyes. Before he had a chance to answer, she asked in a quiet voice, "From me?"

"No." This time he did run his hands through this hair. "From me."

Besides the fact that he'd endangered Aurelia, how could he explain that he didn't deserve Constance, her daughter, or any of the comfort they provided?

She cocked her head and stared. "Why?"

"That's my past." He shook his head. "It's not allowed for discussion as per our rules."

"We've already broken that one, haven't we?" She arched a perfect brow. "You told me about your wounds. I told you about my first husband leaving me without a note or a word. Much like what you've done."

A wild surge of anger coursed through his veins. "I wish I'd found him before he drowned in that mud puddle. I would have had no qualms challenging him to a duel then and there." He huffed out a breath.

That was the past, and he couldn't change it.

But he could change this moment between them.

"Let me hold you," he said softly. *Forever.* "Forgive me."

"You shouldn't have left," she answered in the same sotto voice as his. "I wouldn't have done that to you. Do you have any idea how much that . . . hurt?" She turned and faced the windows where the darkness held all their ghosts and the reminders of their wretched respective pasts.

His arms fell to his sides. He didn't think about the hurt he'd caused her because he was a selfish bastard. A need broke free in his chest, that indescribable want to have never, ever left her side all those years ago. When it reared its head, it never took him long to squash it like a beetle beneath his foot. His past couldn't be changed. But this time, it hurt ten times more than it ever had before. It threatened to drown him.

Because he'd wanted to be better for her, and he'd failed.

She'd buried her face in her hands. The small shake of her body betrayed her tears. He damned the consequences of touching her. Of all the people in the world, it was Constance who deserved better. When he'd lain on the surgeon's table praying for death to take away his pain, she'd been his champion in all his dreams. She was the one who brought him back from the edge of hell each time.

Though he was a poor excuse for a husband, he vowed to become the one who gave her the sense of security she needed. By then, he stood behind her and rested one hand on the desk close to her hip. He reached into his pocket and pulled out a black leather case, then set it in front of her. "Open it."

With a trembling hand, she pushed it aside.

A soft sob broke, then she turned in his embrace. Though she hurt, Constance continually proved her strength. She wiped her eyes, then stared into his. "I don't want jewelry. I want you."

When she grabbed the lapels of his banyan, he didn't move. Her lips quivered as she searched his face. "Don't ever leave me again without telling me. I've been in a fog these past days reliving the nightmare of my previous marriage. It felt as if you'd abandoned me like he had done, only it was worse."

He grimaced at the pain in her voice as he brushed a renegade tear with his knuckles. "How so?"

"Aurelia didn't meet Meriwether, but you . . . you're in her life. Every day, she sang 'Da . . . Da . . . Da.' At night, she cried for you."

He cringed at the pain he'd caused the baby.

She shook her head as if damning him, which was what he rightly deserved.

"She's probably saying the words as a curse." He dipped his head to meet her gaze, then smiled. "I wouldn't find fault in that. Nor would you, I fear."

"Stop making me want to laugh." A groan of frustration escaped, and she leaned forward resting her head against his chest.

That all-consuming want to hold her could finally be satisfied. Slowly, he embraced her and kissed her head. When she leaned back and met his gaze, he took her hand in his and brought it to his heart.

"Please, forgive me. I want to be a father for Aurelia, and more, I want to be a better husband to you. Let me try?"

Without waiting for her answer, he bent down and pressed his lips to hers, almost making him feel human again. Funny how the simple uncomplicated touch of his mouth against hers brought forth the need to never leave her side again.

As he went to deepen the kiss, she bit him. Not a tug of his lip with her teeth. This was a bite-down-hard take-no-prisoners assault.

He leaned back to lick where her teeth had twisted the skin of his bottom lip. The metallic taste of blood slid against his tongue.

Her nostrils flared. She was riled.

Constance leaned in, and he pulled away slightly, not ready for another attack. She stood on the balls on her feet, then like a thief, she swooped in and licked his mouth where she'd bit him. "I drew blood."

Those brilliant blue eyes of hers reminded him of the witching hour, when all sorts of mischief and mayhem prowled through the night. She slowly closed the space between them, the scent of orange blossoms wrapped around him, keeping him captive. His own nostrils flared at the scent, but this time he didn't move.

A wicked grin tugged at her lips right before she pressed her mouth to his and took her fill. She pushed her tongue into his mouth, the movement like a sword-wielding Valkyrie sworn to vanquish all enemies. It wasn't gentle, kind, or soft.

She pulled his hair, holding him in place as she had her way with him. Her tongue lashed against his. She inhaled him, and he couldn't breathe. But he'd give her his last breath if she continued to kiss him like this.

Savage. Raw.

He lost his bearing at the unexpected fierceness of the kiss. But the ever-present desire he possessed for her grew from smoldering embers into an uninhibited blaze.

While she held his head, he brought her tight into his

embrace. He was not going to let go of this hellion anytime soon. Not until she was finished with him. His tongue chased after hers, and a moan erupted.

He'd never been so aroused in his life. The pounding throb of his cock kept time with her punishing kisses. She canted her hips toward him as if demanding that he relieve her ache. He ground his cock against her, the relief slight. If anything, he wanted more.

Suddenly, she broke the kiss and blinked.

He'd never seen her more beautiful. Like a siren demanding his downfall. He would go down without a fight as long as she continued to kiss him like he was the only thing she needed.

"Undress, then lie on the bed." Her gaze nailed him in place.

His pulse raced as he panted at the iron will in her voice. "Are you asking or telling me?"

"It's a command," she answered pushing him in the chest toward the bed.

Chapter Twenty-Four

Watching Jonathan's every reaction, Constance reached up and let her hair down. Her husband's gaze was riveted to her. She taunted him by shaking her head, the movement causing the waves to cascade down her back. With her fingers, she fluffed it until it had to resemble Medusa's many snakes.

Which was an appropriate comparison as Jonathan lay on the bed as still as stone. Only the flash of desire in his eyes and the heat coloring his cheeks betrayed him. Of course, his erection bobbed as if straining to reach her. She boldly stared, contemplating how she would have her way with him.

She lifted her gaze inch by inch to his. They held each other's stare, neither blinking. His chest heaved as he waited to see what she would do next. She prowled toward the side where he lay, released the tie of her dressing gown, then slid it off her shoulders. The fabric floated to the ground, where it pooled in a silken puddle at her feet.

With her fingers, she traced an imaginary line up the middle of his foot, over his ankle, calf, and thigh. Her touch light and sure, she continued around his hip, then allowed her fingers to meander through the nest of curls at the base of his cock. It jerked in response to her touch, and she wrapped her hand around it then tugged. He moaned in response.

As he went to reach for her, she released him, then stepped away. "After everything you've done, you're not allowed to touch me until I say you can."

"I'm being punished." His nostrils flared, but his gaze never strayed from hers. "I deserve it."

"You do." Little frissons of awareness prickled through every part of her. It was that deep voice of his and his hawk-like stare that caused such a chain reaction. She lifted her chin in defiance. "I've given thought to how you could pleasure me."

"Tell me what you want," he rasped. "I'll give it to you."

The sound reverberated through her chest. If he'd read a poem of seduction in that same roughened voice, it wouldn't have had the same effect on her. Silken heat slid through her abdomen, collecting between her legs.

He was restless and practically begging for her. Without another word, she climbed on the bed and straddled him. Hip met hip as she rested her weight on her fists, framing his chest. "I'll show you."

Leaning down, she rubbed her center against his cock. He hissed as it easily slipped through her wet folds. He reached for her.

She drew back. "Do not touch me until I say."

He stared at her before nodding. "May I speak?"

"No." She ground against him, not letting herself blink as she watched him fist his hands in the covers fighting the need to hold her.

She did it again, then closed her eyes on a moan. She crawled up his body, taking time to lick the sensitive nipples on his chest.

"Let me kiss you," he groaned.

"When I say," she answered. She tasted him by licking and sucking various parts of him. She feasted on his hard biceps, nipping him playfully, then soothing his skin with her tongue. She bit his shoulder, savoring it while marking him. Reverently, she kissed the hollow of his throat, then licked his neck, tasting his salty skin.

As he rested his head on a pillow, she continued by flicking her tongue at the indentation of his chin, the one that had always been irresistible to her. She bypassed his mouth, and with her nose trailed a path up his face. He groaned in response.

Then with a newfound boldness, she straddled his shoulders, placing her center right before his mouth. She ached for him with a need that had her legs shaking. "Now kiss me."

Hotter than fire, his eyes blazed as he watched her. A growl escaped as he put his mouth on her. His tongue breached her slick folds, then swirled around her sensitive nub. She bucked her hips against his mouth as an indelicate moan spilled free. She was in the sweetest agony as he feasted upon her like a starved man.

"You taste like honey and fire and decadence." He sucked the nub and lightly grazed it with his teeth. "Sweetness for me. Only me." His eyes bored into hers.

Unable to answer as another indelicate moan decided to escape at that moment, she pressed harder against him.

He gentled his kisses, and she cried out. Somehow he'd moved his arms. With his hands, he steadied her hips as he slid down the pillow farther. His tongue entered her, pushing through the slickened walls ready to claim her as she demanded. It was primitive, primal, like an offering to an ancient goddess with her being the deity. She gasped as she clutched the headboard, hanging on for dear life. Her hips undulated against him as the muscles inside of her contracted, a signal she was ready to come.

Constance rested her head against the headboard and closed her eyes. His mouth was everywhere, firing every nerve she possessed. Her thigh muscles trembled, unable to withstand the monstrous pleasure he was giving her.

Time and thoughts swirled together. Aloft in another world, she felt her body grow lighter, climbing higher until she faced the peak her body desperately sought.

At the precipice everything stilled. She let go, setting off a chain reaction. Her orgasm ripped through every particle of her, sending her over the edge. The sheer drop as exhilarating as the climb. In that split second, she cried out his name when her heartbeat tripled, threatening to break through her chest.

As she grappled with the aftermath, a quiet gasp drained the last remaining bits of her. Boneless, she slumped to the side. Instead of falling, she found herself on her back with a very aroused Jonathan hovering over her, his hand stroking his cock. His gaze caressing every inch of her skin. He nuzzled her neck, then trailed his mouth to hers. Her eyes searched his, and a smile, the kind that promised all sorts of enchantment, glittered from his whisky-dark orbs.

Oh, she wanted everything he promised in that smile. She lifted her mouth to his.

He was the one to tease now. He pressed a light kiss to her mouth. She groaned.

He reached down between them and slowly swept two fingers through her folds, coating them with her arousal. He brought those fingers to her lips and pressed them into her mouth. "Taste."

She closed her lips around his two fingers and sucked. She'd never done anything so lustfully wicked in her life. Emboldened, she swirled her tongue.

He groaned in answer. "After having you, I'll be your prisoner from now on and never beg to leave."

"Hush." Unable to deny herself any longer, she molded her mouth to his. He parted his lips, and she didn't need any further invitation. She slid her tongue inside and met his. With each stroke, they learned anew the rhythm they both needed. He pressed his hot length against her.

"Constance," he whispered against her lips. "What do you command now?"

"Inside me." She canted her hips in invitation.

Without any indication he was tiring, Jonathan straightened his right leg, then brought her left leg over his right shoulder, leaving her open and exposed.

She frowned slightly, not understanding what he was doing.

"It'll keep my weight on my left leg." With his right hand grasping the headboard, he bent and took one of her breasts into his mouth. His tongue swirled her swollen nipple repeatedly. She arched her back, giving him greater access.

He chuckled slightly, then turned his attention to the other.

Every inch of her skin tingled at his ministrations. When she groaned for more, he positioned himself at her entrance. In one push, he was inside of her. When he was all the way in, she tightened her muscles around his cock.

He hissed in pleasure. "Sorceress."

"You think I'm a witch?" She laughed and tightened around him again.

He swirled his tongue around her nipple while watching her reaction. At her sharp intake of breath, he smiled. "An enchantress whom I pray will continue to cast her spells on me."

"Only if you behave." She lifted her hips.

He withdrew until only an inch was inside of her. With a roll of his hips, he slowly entered her. His cock pushed against an especially sensitive area of her core.

She stilled, trying to hold the sensation for as long as possible.

He huffed a breath. "Does that please you?"

She nodded. "Do it again."

"Such a demanding piece in bed."

"Lucky for you," she retorted.

He repeated the movement, and she squirmed as a wave of pleasure rolled through her. He rolled his hips again.

She cried out, unable to bear the intensity but craving it at the same time. He continued as he watched her reaction to his every move.

It didn't take long, and she was ready to come again. "Please," she begged.

In answer, his movement quickened, turning his hips into pistons. Each perfectly orchestrated movement created for her pleasure.

"Jonathan," she cried.

"I have you." He wrapped his free arm around her, a haven from the outside world.

As she climaxed, her muscles flexed. She pulled him tighter, never wanting to let go.

In answer, he cried out. Closing his eyes, he threw back his head. The moment of his crisis was evident as the muscles of his neck lengthened, and he spilled his seed inside her.

They were both panting by now. He burrowed his head into her neck desperate to regain control of his body. All the while she held him close, providing a sanctuary for him to rest and find relief from whatever pain seemed to dog him every hour of his day.

Like a chant—or perhaps it was a spell—she whispered his name through the stillness surrounding them. She never wanted to let him go nor leave this bed without him by her side. That's how greedy she'd become for him.

Jonathan shifted his body to stretch out beside her, putting his weight on his left side.

He trailed a finger down her face, the act endearing. His eyes softened as he grinned. Never had she felt this cherished. Whatever demons he possessed, she would cast them out of his life. She cupped his face, the contour so familiar. Then she trailed her thumbs over his evening bristles and the sharp angles of his cheeks.

"I would do anything for you," she whispered. For a moment, her words lingered in the air between them.

He brushed back a lock of her hair against her brow. "I've never seen this side of you."

"Meaning?"

He pressed a kiss against her nose, then pulled away. His eyes searched hers as his brow wrinkled. "First, you're livid with me, kissing me with all the anger and passion you possess, then you would do anything for me."

The baffled look on his face would have been endearing if she hadn't wanted to scream in frustration. "You truly haven't a clue, do you?"

Jonathan leaned back but kept his body touching Constance. He waited for the chronic pain from his twisted muscles to seize his leg. Frankly, he was amazed that he wasn't howling in agony.

He caressed her elegant foot with his as he rested his head on his bent arm. "I admit that I'm not clearheaded when it comes to things outside my domain," he whispered in her ear. "But you keep me in a perpetual state of topsy-turvy."

Constance let out a soulful sigh, then turned in his direction. "I didn't share with you everything about my previous marriage." She drew a design on his chest, the touch endearing and erotic. "I thought it best to let the past stay buried, but it's coming between us."

At the dulcet tone of her voice, Jonathan placed his hand over hers, keeping it anchored to the middle of his chest where his heart pounded. She smiled then grew somewhat wistful. She had to be thinking of Meriwether. Both of them had opened the gates to their past. He'd never pried, but after they'd made love, now was the right time to seek the answer to the question that lurked in their shadows.

"Did you love him?"

She lifted her gaze from their entwined hands to his. "No."

He exhaled silently and squeezed her hand. For some odd reason, the answer gave him comfort.

She blinked slowly. "He was charming. He was attentive. And he'd possessed an irresistible laugh. I thought he'd be a devoted husband." A frustrated breath escaped. "I didn't meet anyone else I could ever imagine marrying until Meriwether. Yet he was constantly out, supposedly conducting business. One morning, I woke and he was gone. I didn't think anything of it until I went to dress, and realized he'd taken everything with him." Her eyes narrowed as she looked past Jonathan's shoulder, lost in her memories. "He didn't even leave me a note." She shook her head, then turned to him. "I was that inconsequential to him."

He brought their entwined hands to his mouth. "You never saw or heard from him again?"

"No. A month later I discovered I was with child." She rested her head on the pillow and put her hand over her eyes as if hiding from him. "I was completely bereft at the news. When others asked where he was, I made up a story that Meriwether had to oversee some of his brother's businesses."

"Did anyone believe it?" He placed his hand on her cheek and gently urged her to turn his way.

"Everyone did. However, I did tell Mr. and Mrs. Bridges he'd left. In many ways, they're my second family. They had a right to know." She looked to the ceiling then returned her gaze to his. "It was humiliating. He deserted me, then didn't care what kind of aftermath he left for me to face."

Jonathan was struck by the bare emptiness on her face. Everything that made Constance shine like a perfectly cut jewel had dulled. "I wish I'd known."

"And do what?" She bit her lip. "I'd been in Portsmouth practically the entire time since you'd returned from the war. I called on you, but you were never at home."

The unspoken words lay between them. If he'd only come to her when he returned, their lives might have been so different. At least, hers would have been. He would have made damned sure of it.

"I don't regret any of it." She turned on her side and faced him. "Not a single moment. For without Meriwether"—she pointed to Aurelia's room—"I wouldn't have that brilliant little girl. She's rescued me more times than I can count with a smile or a giggle or a simple coo when I've felt my world torn asunder. You have no idea the ridicule and gossip written about me and my friends when it was discovered we'd married the same man." Her voice vibrated with emotion. "*Our* daughter was the best thing that resulted from my marriage. Aurelia was my refuge during that unbearable storm." Her chest heaved as if she'd run a mile.

"I failed you when I didn't seek you out in Portsmouth."

Constance threw her head on the pillow as soon as the words left his mouth. She growled slightly under her breath, then faced him. "That's my past. I don't want it to change."

Then a new tenderness and, dare he hope, affection shone in her eyes.

Constance brushed back the hair that had fallen across his brow. The smile on her face reflected forgiveness. "She's *our* daughter. She deserves more from her father. She needs a father who believes he deserves her. Don't you think?"

His chest tightened at the hope in her voice.

"If I didn't think you could be that man, I wouldn't be in this marriage. Nor would I be in this bed." She pressed a kiss to his cheek that twisted his insides.

If only she knew how much he wanted to believe he deserved this family. "Remember when I fell in the dressing room?" His voice cracked on the last word. This was his biggest humiliation, but she deserved to know how he was perceived in the outside world.

"After I came to your house that first day, I was knocked

to the ground by three children chasing a cat. I couldn't get up without Arkwright's help. As it happened, the children belonged to Colonel Peterson, the man who'd recruited me for service. He apologized, then introduced me to a Lieutenant Roth." God, every time he thought of the exchange, his heart pounded in fury. "I discovered that Roth had been selected to take over a project that I'd created. No one knew about it except for my former commanding officer. I'd spent over a year designing it. I personally wrote every lesson and had even determined how to select and train the most talented men in the country to become marksmen like myself."

Constance scooted forward and laid her head on his shoulder as she rested her hand over his heart. The heat of her body reassuring much as she had in all his lonely dreams.

She curled up closer to him. "Go on."

His throat had thickened so he couldn't immediately answer.

He closed his eyes and pressed his hand over hers, drawing from her strength. "Much to my shock, Colonel Peterson told me that my former commanding officer was the one who'd created *my* project and curriculum. The colonel said both of them thought me too damaged to lead the men. That's why I was distracted and surly on our wedding day. But the sense of betrayal felt like a knife stab." He turned to her. "I'd discussed my plans with my commanding officer, and he stole them as his own."

"What did you do?" Her eyes were wide in astonishment.

"After I left our wedding, I arrived in Portsmouth. The next day I confronted him. He didn't deny that he'd stolen my idea, but said he'd made changes to it, so he claimed it as his work." He forced himself to look her in the eye. "There's more. Once you hear me, if you leave me, I will understand." He swallowed the emptiness he felt but locked his gaze with hers. "Frankly, I think you should leave me."

"Jonathan, you're scaring me," she said softly as her eyes searched his.

"My former commanding officer has a charging order in his possession. He's ready to submit it to a tribunal for a general court-martial of me for desertion and dereliction of duty." He linked his fingers with hers selfishly, desperate to keep her by his side. "My last assignment, I found my target. He was unarmed. As soon as he saw me, I retreated. We both knew that I wouldn't shoot without him having a weapon."

"What happened?" she asked, placing her other hand over theirs.

"I returned to camp and informed my commanding officer of the event. It was just the two of us in the tent. He dismissed me." He blew out a breath. "In no time, rumors started that one of the men in my company would be court-martialed. I thought nothing of it. Then I was injured. Right before I came home, my commanding officer sent for me and said the rumors were about me. He ordered me to go home, accept half-pay, and keep a low profile."

"Desertion?" Her brow furrowed into neat lines. "Where did that come from?"

"My commander said when I left my unarmed target, I was derelict in my duties and deserted my post." He shook his head at the travesty of it all. "Constance, I did everything right, and now I'm being blackmailed because my commanding officer wants to take over the training of recruits for some reason. He said if I took it to someone higher up, he'd submit the charging order. It's his word against mine. He's of a higher rank. They'll believe him. I'll be ruined." He forced his gaze to hers. "By association, you and Aurelia will be ruined."

"What a horrid, horrid man." She sat upright. The flash of her eyes exposed her outrage on his behalf.

"I've written several French envoys I'm acquainted with.

They've been trying to find my target for the last two years. I believe he'd testify on my behalf, but I can't find him. I'm afraid he's dead." He blinked, trying to rein in his emotions.

"No one will believe such a tale. You're an honorable man and a symbol of the brave men who serve our country," she offered in that honeyed voice of hers. "We'll fight this, Jonathan, together."

He couldn't resist such sweetness and stole a kiss. Only she would think of him this way. Her cheeks deepened in color and he ran his hand down her arm, only to discover her skin pebbled.

"You're cold." He shifted and pulled the covers out from underneath him, then pulled her next to him. The movement put them on her side of the bed. Soon they were nestled under the luxurious linens. "Better?"

"Much." She snuggled against him and returned her hand to his chest. "Tell me the rest."

"I challenged him. He practically laughed at me."

"What do you mean?" She looked up at him.

"I told him that his dishonorable actions wouldn't stand. I said he didn't want to confront me over the betrayal. He called my bluff then demanded I leave. There wasn't anything else for me to do, so when I started my grand exit, I fell on my face in front of him." He rubbed his fist down his right thigh. "He told me I was broken. He was correct. I am damaged. It's a hard lesson to learn."

Tears welled in her eyes, but Constance didn't turn away. Instead, she comforted him by stroking his face as he told the gruesome story. "You're not broken." She caught his gaze and smiled. "Or even bent. Not in my eyes, and not in the eyes of your friends."

He tried to smile, but it felt more like a grimace. "That's why I left after Aurelia was hurt." He took her hand and squeezed as he remembered when that precious baby viewed him as a monster. "I can't protect her, nor can I protect you.

I can't even protect myself from these charges." He cleared his throat again then wiped his hand down his face, trying to erase the grief that bubbled inside but would never burst. He looked away trying to compose himself.

She propped herself on one elbow. Her gaze turned incredibly tender. "You should let me be the judge of what's good for me." The kind smile she offered wasn't of pity but of understanding. "I'm not looking for a protector. I want a husband and a father for my daughter."

Every inch of her face, he memorized. Though he had a deep hole in his heart, he'd think about this moment when he faced the darkness. Never before had he been close enough to anyone to share this sordid tale. Not even North. She listened without judgment as he aired his failures.

She reached up and pressed her lips to his. Her eyes like a beacon drawing him home to a place he didn't deserve. "My first husband could ride, run, and dance. But do you know what he couldn't do?"

The humiliation and anguish ripped him apart. He couldn't bear to look at her. A tear ran down his cheek. The first ever. When he tried to turn from her, Constance wouldn't let him. She leaned in and kissed it from his cheek.

"He never came home because we didn't matter," she whispered. Tears glistened her eyes. "He didn't want us." She brushed her hand against his cheek. "But you did." A heartfelt smile appeared, one so sweet it stole his breath. "Your letters . . ." She pressed a single kiss against his lips. "Your letters gave me a sense of security, one I hadn't had since my parents passed."

Guilt threatened to swallow him whole. She'd been hurting for the past year, and he'd been safely ensconced at home.

Swiftly, he leaned back and took her hands from his face and held them. "Don't you see? Aurelia was hurt because I couldn't protect her. I'll be an embarrassment to her."

"Hardly," she whispered. "Aurelia's hurt because she fell.

That's all. You have to believe me." Her eyes searched his. "Your written expressions of affection for me and Aurelia . . . well, they made our year apart bearable. We're connected because of them. That to me is worth more than gold, or the ability to ride and dance."

He brought her close, then stretched one arm beneath her pillow only to discover a round object. He pulled his hand out with a sixpence in his palm. "What is this?"

Her eyes widened, and she extended her hand. "It's merely a coin."

"Really?" He examined it, then placed it in her palm. He closed her fingers around the coin, then brought her fist to his mouth for a kiss. "What's special about this particular one?"

Heat, the kind that told so much, flooded her cheeks, making her look like the girl he'd kissed that day so long ago. "My aunt gave it to me the day we married," she said softly.

He lifted his head and captured her gaze. "Why sleep with it under your pillow?"

Her lashes fluttered closed as she tipped her gaze to the ceiling as if looking for divine intervention. "It's for good luck."

She was beautifully stunning tonight, and the pink that stained her cheeks made her even more so, but he didn't want to embarrass her. "I think I'm the one who has found good fortune. I get to hold you in my arms all night."

They curled around each other. In a way, it was as intimate as when they'd shared their bodies with each other.

"I'm a good listener," she whispered, then pressed a kiss against his heart. "Any time and any subject you want to discuss, I want that conversation."

He hugged her tighter in answer. When he told her the truth about the letters, he would disappoint her just like her first husband had done.

"The reason why Aunt Vee gave me the sixpence"—her

words were soft and sweet like a lullaby—"was for luck in our marriage. I think it's working."

He held his breath for a moment as he contemplated the significance of the statement. "I'm hoping it'll give me luck tonight," he whispered. For a moment, he wrestled with how much to say. For the first time since he had returned home, Jonathan felt Constance's essence, her light for a better description, and it was leading him to a place of peace. It was because of her and the faith she had in him. It was now or never. "If you think me an honorable man, then I need to share something about the letters you received from me."

Her even breathing of sleep was the only answer he received.

Chapter Twenty-Five

The next day brought a truth that smacked Jonathan in his chest. He was drowning in his wife, and he couldn't be happier. Without her even knowing, Constance had somehow tangled herself in every aspect of his life. With a deep breath, he glanced around his study. Everything was perfectly dusted. She'd rearranged the furniture, and he hadn't even noticed until now. Gone was his black velvet chair that he used to sit in when he took his daily target practice. The smell of wet dog had dissipated from the room. Funny thing, even his disappointment when his cartridge designs failed had waned.

Even today's letter from the American ambassador to France stating that his inquiries for Jean Davout's whereabouts had come to naught didn't dishearten him.

Distractedly, he reached for Regina. The loyal hound nestled his palm, then settled beside him with a loud sigh of gratification. He knew the exact feeling.

"My lord?" The footman Fred Loring stood inside the room jiggling Aurelia. "I beg your pardon, sir, but I'm to make a trip to the market for Mrs. Walmer. Miss Dahlia isn't feeling well today, Mary has laundry duty, and Lady Sykeston is off to the dockyards."

"All right." Jonathan enunciated slowly while wondering what the footman wanted. "Why are you holding Miss Aurelia?"

"Well, I've asked around, and no one can watch her as they've tasks to complete this afternoon." He adjusted the wriggling baby in his arms.

With waving arms, she reached toward Jonathan and proclaimed, "Da."

With her adorable little toothy smile, she instantly became the centerpiece of attention.

Fred grinned down at the baby. "I'll need to take her with me, but I thought I should inform you since you're her father."

Jonathan stood from the desk, and immediately, Regina stood also.

Aurelia's eyes grew round, and she exclaimed, "Gee." She pushed against the footman's chest with her tiny hands, a full-on assault to be put down.

"No need to take her. I'll watch her until you get back." Jonathan grabbed his cane and moved around the desk, then held out his arm.

"If you're sure it's no trouble, my lord." Fred was already by his side handing off the baby. "Without the little one, I can be back in half the time."

"Go." Jonathan felt a surge of something as the baby calmed in his arms.

She cuddled under his neck and released a deep breath. She apparently was as content as Jonathan with their arrangement. She turned her attention to the dog. "Gee," she squealed as if reunited with her best friend.

Jonathan chuckled and waved for Fred to leave. "Regina and I have the situation well in hand."

With a nod, the footman took his leave.

"Well, my little miss, it's you and me for the time being." He pressed a kiss against the top of her head. The sweet smell of baby filled his lungs. She turned her head and caught his gaze, then smiled as if truly delighted to be with him.

"You'll be a heartbreaker, just like your mother." He brushed his fingers across her small cheek, the scraps barely visible. "I'm sorry, sweetheart."

She stared at him as she stuffed her fist in her mouth. Her innocent expression encouraged him to spill his secrets.

"You mother thinks I was doing something noble the past year, when I was here the entire time. I need to tell her, but she'll hate me."

That confession earned a wrinkle of her tiny nose.

"Did you know she was my best friend growing up? Of all the people in this world, I don't think I could bear it if she was ever repulsed by me. I tried to keep her at a distance, but the truth? She's like the air I breathe and the water I drink every day." He let out a painful exhale.

Regina and the baby did the same in empathy.

"I would never in the world hurt her, just as I'd never hurt you." He gazed into the baby's eyes, and she smiled again. "Do you know how to swim?" He lowered his voice. "I have a special place, a beautiful pond just for swimming. I'll teach you as soon as you master how to walk." He lifted his right leg in front of him to show her. "Though I can't seem to manage the fine art of ambulating with any regularity, I can swim like a fish. I have a feeling you'll be a natural at it."

She bent over his arms to examine his leg, then a lopsided drooling grin appeared on her face. "Gee."

"Yes, Regina may accompany us. She's a fine swimmer too. We'll go to the pond"—he kissed her nose—"when you grow up a bit more."

Satisfied with his promise, she snuggled her head under his chin and yawned.

"Nap time already?" he asked softly, then glanced at the clock where the cherubs proclaimed with their twirling arms that it was half past three in the afternoon. "Shall we rest for a while?"

With the utmost care, Jonathan carried her to the sofa and relaxed into a reclining position. He tucked Aurelia close. Within seconds, Regina hopped up and circled into a position by his boots. Half guard dog and half nursemaid, she kept a close eye on the pair of them.

"Good girl," he murmured to the dog.

Aurelia seconded that thought with a soft, "Gee."

"That's right. Gee's a good girl. You're a good girl. Your mother is a good girl."

The baby lifted her head and regarded him.

"All right. I stand corrected. Your mother is better than good. She's like the holy grail of women."

"Ma." The baby grinned in approval, then plopped her head down again against his chest. "Ma-ma."

"Indeed." He hugged her a little tighter, and the soft rise and fall of her chest against his caused satisfaction to well within him. Jonathan, the self-proclaimed hermit, could never have imagined himself falling in love with this one-year-old bundle. The sight, smell, and feel of her little body next to his released a sea of contentment. In that moment, he knew he'd lay down his life for Aurelia. Though they didn't share any blood, he felt deep within his heart that she was his. The need to be the first worthy man in her life scared him senseless. But the overriding desire to fill the shoes of her father was a commitment he'd make.

When the time came time to walk her down the aisle and give her hand away to the man of her dreams, he'd make certain the gentleman was worthy of her. That's what a father would do.

He closed his eyes and let the unfamiliar feeling of happiness permeate his thoughts. Though it was fleeting, he'd remember this moment for the rest of his life. The simple joy of holding this precious girl in his arms.

He pressed another kiss to Aurelia's head. "I'll try harder to be better for you and your mother."

The baby sighed in sleep as if accepting his promise.

It was enough for the moment. Jonathan's own eyes grew heavy, and he resigned himself to rest. How long they laid together in that position, he had no clue. Upon waking, he became aware of several things. Regina had her weight on his feet, and they'd gone numb.

Someone was in the room with him.

"Is he snoring?"

The voice belonged to a man, but it was too soft for him to identify.

"No," said another.

Bloody hell, there were two of them.

"It's the dog," the second voice added.

A gentle laugh came from the first. "I wish I could draw worth a damn. This would be a great extortion piece."

"Not wise, my friend. Why would you even think of black-mailing the best shot in all the kingdom."

He finally recognized the trespassers in his study. "What malfeasance have I committed that warrants having the two of you in my house?" he said softly so as not to wake Aurelia. He turned his head to find the Duke of Randford and the Marquess of Grayson sitting in two chairs directly across the sofa from him.

"Sleeping Beauty wakes," Randford quipped with a blinding, bright smile. He'd worn the same infuriating expression the day Aurelia had been born.

"More like the sleeping beast," Grayson chuckled.

"If either of you wake her because of your incessant chatter, I'll shoot you both."

"Always the consummate host, Sykeston." Not at all intimidated, Randford leaned back in his chair with a relaxed stance.

"I'm not your host," he growled.

"Tout au contraire." Julian Raleah, the Marquess of Grayson, mangled the words.

"Your French is atrocious, and I didn't invite you." The baby in his arms jerked slightly in her sleep, and he tightened his arms around her. Speaking softly didn't have the same lethal effect as a full-throated growl would have, but Jonathan wouldn't wake her though he longed to give a proper dressing-down to his friends. "If you think I'm not serious about shooting someone if she wakes up, try again," he whispered.

Randford leaned his long body forward to see Jonathan and Aurelia better. "I swear they can sleep through anything."

"Your son slept through that dreadful trip from London." Grayson rubbed his lower back. "I'll be in bed the entire week."

"Week?" Jonathan forgot about the baby and abruptly sat up. Realizing his error, he cooed to her as he gently patted her back. He regarded both of them. "What do you mean a week?"

The marquess's brow wrinkled into neat rows. "We're on our way to Brighton. Kat and Beth have business there. We thought we'd spend the week here with you and your lovely countess, then travel to our destination."

Jonathan hissed, still comforting Aurelia. Thankfully, she'd fallen back to sleep. A week was an eternity. He swallowed the thickness that had started to congeal in his throat and asked the question though he dreaded the answer. "How many of them are you?"

"I'm rather offended. You make us sound like a gang of highwaymen," Grayson said.

"Par for the course with Sykeston," Randford said. "Your guests include my wife and our son, Miss Howell, Grayson, and me."

"Did you bring staff?" Jonathan's skin crawled with the vision of the house being overrun with guests and their servants milling about. He had little doubt that rumors about his idiosyncrasies would be spread throughout society in a matter of weeks. He didn't care about himself, but he didn't want Constance or Aurelia to suffer because of him.

"No servants accompanied us here. My valet Morgan and Kat's companion Willa went ahead to Brighton. We wanted to see Constance, and of course you."

His name definitely sounded like an afterthought.

The heat of Randford's stare seemed to smolder in awareness that something was off.

To have his two friends here for a week was as painful as inviting them to stay for the next year. "How long have you been sitting there watching us?"

"Long enough to know you're smitten with that wee child," Randford answered. He leaned forward with his elbows on his knees. "I cannot believe the difference in her." His face alighted with an affectionate smile. "She looks exactly like Meriwether."

Jonathan grunted noncommittedly. It was only natural that Randford would see his half brother's resemblance in Aurelia. However, anyone with an exacting eye could see the child was the spitting image of her mother.

"Did my housekeeper see to your rooms?" He had no idea whether the rooms had been cleaned. But then he relaxed. Constance would ensure everything was in proper order for *her* guests.

That's what his wife did. She took care of others. He didn't.

Randford nodded. "The accommodations are perfect. Mrs. Butler has assigned a maid to help my wife and Beth."

"There you are," Randford's duchess announced while holding her baby. Another woman followed.

Instantly, Randford and Grayson stood with an ease that made Jonathan want to throw something. There was no earthly way for him to stand quickly and safely while holding Aurelia. Before he started the slow tedious process, Randford's duchess sat beside him cradling the baby.

"Please don't stand on our account," she said softly for the babies' benefits. "Lord Sykeston, this is our son, Lord Belton, but we call him Arthur." She nodded toward the other woman. "This is Miss Beth Howell."

"Your Grace. Miss Howell." Jonathan bowed his head in acknowledgment. "My lord, the pleasure is all mine," Jonathan said solemnly to the sleeping baby.

The duchess winked his way as if delighted he'd acknowledged the baby. "You must call me Kat. All my friends do."

Jonathan took a deep breath and exhaled. Aurelia snuggled against him, waking from her nap.

Kat turned her attention to Miss Howell. "Aurelia looks simply adorable."

The other woman came forward. "She does." She placed a hand over her heart. "May I hold her?"

Without waiting for Jonathan's permission, the woman placed her hands around the baby.

Jonathan twisted at the waist, thereby freeing Aurelia from the woman's grasp. "Do not touch my child." His voice lashed a chilling rebuke. He hugged her close, cradling her head to his chest. The baby whimpered at the sudden movement.

"Sykeston," Grayson barked a rebuke.

"Sykeston, bad form," Randford snapped in a low voice.

Both men said it at the same time. A sudden silence filled the room, and all eyes turned his way. The air around him turned oppressive.

Miss Howell sent Grayson a glare that should have incinerated him on the spot as she held out her hand to stop any further outbursts. "I'm perfectly capable of handling matters for myself."

"I didn't mean it as an insult," Grayson offered.

"He's protecting her." Without another glance to Grayson, Miss Howell continued, "Lord Sykeston, I beg your forgiveness. I shouldn't have been so forward. We met years ago, but you may not remember. I'm Miss Blythe Howell. But please call me Beth. Thank you for having us."

The woman was a dear friend of Constance's, and he'd insulted her with his rude behavior. By some miracle, the rules of etiquette were remembered.

"I'm the one who must beg forgiveness. My wife considers you family." His cheeks heated with licks of humiliation. "I don't know what came over me."

Randford acknowledged the apology with a nod. Grayson shook his head as if he were debating whether to tackle Jonathan. Kat's gaze was glued to Beth's.

Jonathan didn't care about the others. It was Beth's apology that mattered.

"Indeed, Kat and I consider our friendship with your wife to be closer than sisters, which makes you family." Beth smiled gently, and the tightness in Jonathan's chest eased somewhat. "Family forgives family."

"Thank you, ma'am." At his words, the others relaxed.

Aurelia rubbed her face against his waistcoat in an attempt to wipe the sleep from her eyes, then peered at the others.

Jonathan cleared his throat. "Do you still want to hold her?"

Beth's eyes brightened. "Please."

Her hands were already outstretched. With reluctance, Jonathan lifted the baby to the woman's waiting arms.

Beth wrapped Aurelia in a tight embrace. "Hello, my precious," she cooed.

Aurelia answered with a gurgle. Sniffing the baby in Kat's arms, Regina leaned over the sofa.

A sound, much like a low growl, erupted from Randford.

Jonathan signaled for Regina to jump down. When she did, dog hair danced with the dust motes in a ray of sunshine that had decided to take up residence beside Jonathan.

The duchess sneezed delicately, then stood with her baby.

"Perhaps a little sunshine might be good for all of us. Would anyone care to join me in a walk?"

They all rose to their feet at the suggestion. Jonathan closed his eyes at the word *walk*, a simple entertainment. This was why he hated guests and visits.

Beth went to hand Aurelia to Jonathan, but he shook his head. "Please take her with you. She enjoys the outdoors. But you'll need to watch her. There's a pond in the courtyard." He was dribbling on like an overprotective nursemaid.

Beth smiled in reassurance. "I won't let anything happen to this darling girl."

Jonathan had debated whether it was wise to let Aurelia go, but the steadfast assuredness in Beth convinced him. "Excellent. While you're walking, I shall check with Mrs. Butler and ensure everything is in order."

Randford went to his wife and kissed the baby. "You go, and I'll join you shortly."

After the others left, Randford stood in front of him. "It's one thing to be cross with Grayson and me, but Beth didn't deserve that barbaric show of uncouthness."

He forced his gaze to the duke. "She took me by surprise. I haven't . . ."

"Been around polite company?" Randford offered. "Perhaps you suffer from a lack of sleep." He huffed out a breath. "Whatever bee has taken residence in your bonnet, I hope you can tame it quickly."

Jonathan exhaled, wishing he could go back in time for twenty minutes and react differently to Beth. Well, if he were asking for time, he might as well wish for ten years. He'd never have left Portsmouth. "My wife would have been mortified at that exchange."

"Indeed, she would have." Randford lowered his voice. "As Beth said, we are Constance's family. Beth's kindness toward you was due to her affection for your wife. If you are treating your wife in a manner similar to Beth, I hope you've asked God for mercy. We love Constance, and there is not a one among us who would tolerate such behavior directed toward her."

Jonathan stared at the duke, grasping for words. How to explain that he didn't want guests. He didn't want them here if a charging order was delivered to his doorstep. Not after last night when he'd held his wife in his arms, and she'd said they'd fight against the injustice together. He wanted to believe Constance and not the irritating voice inside that said otherwise.

"We're your friends. Grayson and I knew you before the war and after. I saw you at your worst."

"No, you didn't. I was at my worst lying on that cot unable to move and waiting for death," Jonathan murmured.

"You are fortunate to have survived," Randford answered with a gentle smile. "You have a beautiful wife and a lovely child that I heard you refer to as yours. Let's start anew, my friend. We've all been looking forward to this visit."

Randford left without another word.

Jonathan scrubbed his hand down his face. What the hell was happening to him?

There was only one explanation. He wasn't fit for proper company anymore.

Then and there, he decided that for the next week, he would avoid any and all engagements with his wife's guests. Which begged the answer how his wife would take such news. Jonathan had little doubt her response.

Constance would understand.

Chapter Twenty-Six

As soon as Constance arrived home from work and saw the Duke of Randford's carriage, she rushed inside.

As customary, Mr. North greeted her at the door. "Welcome home, my lady."

"Thank you, Mr. North." She whipped off her hat and pelisse. "Where are they?"

"Your guests are waiting in the family sitting room." North took the hat and light summer coat and gave them to the footman who stood by his side. "I believe you're in time for tea."

"Thank you," she said breathlessly, then practically ran up the stairs to the sitting room across the hall from her and Jonathan's chambers.

At the sight of her two dearest friends, tears of joy sprang in her eyes. "You're here."

"Constance," Beth cried, holding Aurelia.

"There's our countess." Kat smiled, rocking Arthur.

Holding her hands out, Aurelia joined in the merriment by shouting, "Ma."

Constance took the squirmy baby, buzzing a kiss on Aurelia's, then Beth's cheek. "Beth, you're more beautiful than the last time I saw you."

Beth leaned back to thoroughly examine Constance. "The same goes for you, my darling."

By then, Kat was by her side, and they repeated the ritual. "Constance, your husband is a lucky man."

She immediately blushed. She felt lucky too.

"What a lovely surprise. Sit, please." Constance waited until her friends were seated before she did the same. "How was your travel?" Immediately, she picked up a shortbread biscuit and gave it to a clapping Aurelia.

"Fine," Kat answered.

"Pftt. It wasn't at all fine. As soon as we arrived, I had to help Kat out of her dress and stays." Beth sat leaned back in her chair and popped a petite tart into her mouth. "She's not even wearing any now."

"Why?" Constance looked at Kat. Even without the undergarments, Kat's figure was lean. It was hard to tell she'd had a baby only several months earlier.

"They became unbearable on the way down." Kat waved a hand in dismissal. "You know how uncomfortable travel can be."

Beth shook her head, then leaned close to Constance. "Randford insisted on driving part of the way. He hit every hole in the road while trying to avoid them." She pointed to Kat. "Every time the carriage hit one, it threw us up in the air. She has bruises where her stays dug into her skin when she landed on the bench seat."

"Good heavens." Constance winced. "That sounds excruciatingly painful."

"When Christian discovers the bruises, he'll be angry at himself." A devilish smile tugged at Kat's lips.

"Well, proper atonement should require two kisses for each bruise," Beth announced with a vigorous nod.

"He needs to grovel. At least three kisses for each bruise." Kat winked.

Constance laughed. "That won't be a punishment for him."

Kat waggled her eyebrows. "I'm counting on it."

"How long can you stay?" Constance asked.

"We were thinking a week," Beth said.

Kat laid her son in a beautiful wicker basket by her feet. "Morgan and Willa have gone ahead to make preparations for our arrival. The Prince Regent will be in residence sometime this week. We don't want to arrive before him." She shifted slightly in the chair as if the bruises were more painful than she let on. "Tell us how marriage agrees with you."

Constance hugged Aurelia a little tighter and glanced outside to avoid looking her friends directly in the eyes. How to explain that her marriage to Jonathan was like a seedling that was groping to find its roots?

"As all marriages are at the beginning, I suppose." She shrugged and forced herself to look directly at Kat. "Everything is new, and we're learning about each other."

Beth scooted forward to the edge of her seat. "What I want to know is whether you are happy?"

"Yes," Constance said softly. These two women were her best friends. If Constance couldn't confide in them and ask their opinion, then she was truly alone. Yet she'd safeguard her husband's secrets. Because when he shared them with her, it'd become an act of trust and intimacy between them. That also meant they'd become her secrets.

Constance gave Aurelia another biscuit to replace the one that had fallen on the floor. Thankfully, the small action gave her a chance to collect her scattered thoughts.

Like clockwork, Regina had sniffed out the lost biscuit then munched it in one gulp.

With a deep sigh, she turned her gaze to her friends. "I'm happy. Jonathan is . . ."

"An acquired taste?" Beth offered with a laugh.

She didn't trust herself to speak for a moment as heat spread across her chest with last night's memories of his kisses and the taste of his mouth against hers. Then the inevitable happened. Those thoughts of kisses led to thoughts of embraces which led to thoughts of their lovemaking. When he held her, the tenderness and care he gave proved he had affection for her. By then, the flush had marched straight from her chest, up her neck, to her cheeks.

"He's not an acquired taste for me," she softly defended. "I've always cared for him."

Kat's eyes twinkled with emotion. "You've always loved him, haven't you?"

"I have." She glanced at Aurelia, then smiled. It felt wonderful to admit it aloud. "I don't want to tell him until the right moment. Does that make sense?" She looked to Kat, then Beth.

Kat nodded once, then reached over and grabbed her hand with hers. "Darling, I hate to be the spreader of tales, but you need to hear this."

"What?" Her heartbeat slowed to a pace that a turtle could outrun as she waited for the bad news.

"Christian was leaving his solicitor's office as the Marquess of Faladen was entering. One of the clerks called out that he had the petition for damages drafted." Kat's eyes narrowed in pain. "When Christian inquired, Faladen said he is bringing a suit against your trust. He believes that's the only way to receive his due compensation for the damage to his ship."

Thankfully, a ringing pinged in her ears. If only a little louder, it would drown out Kat's words. "I'm at a loss," she finally said. "I sent Faladen a letter refuting his claim. He ran that yacht into a bank of rocks."

"Grayson heard it too at an event he attended," Beth added gently. "I believe they're both going to discuss it with Sykeston sometime during the visit."

"Jonathan doesn't know. I didn't want there to be another burden on us now." Constance leaned her head against her daughter's as she tried to grapple with the revelation. "If Faladen wins, my employees' livelihoods are at risk."

"You should tell Jonathan," Kat said.

"You should," Beth agreed.

Constance pressed a kiss to Aurelia's soft blond curls. Perhaps she should. He'd always been a brilliant strategist. "Let me speak with him before Randford or Grayson say anything."

"I know it's upsetting, but perhaps the gentlemen can come up with an alternative." Beth patted her arm again.

"Such as?" Constance lifted an eyebrow. "Aurelia and I can't afford any further rumors attached to our names. This is my problem. Next week, I'll go see Faladen myself."

Aurelia patted her mother's cheek in comfort. Constance kissed her cheek at the gesture. Then her daughter offered her a bite of biscuit while chanting, "*Yum-yum.*"

"No dearest. That's for you," Constance murmured as she darted out of the way of the biscuit, which barely missed her chin.

"Seeing Faladen is brilliant. With your persuasion skills, you can convince him to see reason." Beth leaned down and pretended to take a bite of Aurelia's biscuit. "I'm hungry, darling girl. I could eat you up."

Aurelia smiled, then attempted to stuff the whole biscuit in Beth's mouth. "*M-num. M-num.*"

Constance's friend laughed, then wiped her face before she did the same for Aurelia. "If you don't mind, perhaps you'd allow me to hold her?"

The entreaty in Beth's voice made Constance take notice. "I'd never mind, dearest."

"I don't want to make presumptions or be considered too forward," Beth said.

Constance shook her head. "Stop that. I consider you her aunt."

Kat's cheeks heated at the words and she bent down, suddenly finding interest in Arthur's hands.

"Just as you are, Kat." Constance glanced at both of them. They were both acting extremely awkward in her presence. "Is something amiss?"

Beth shook her head in denial.

Kat turned to Beth. "If it was me, I'd want to know."

"It's nothing of import." Beth shook her head in disagreement.

"Did someone say something unkind or rude?" Constance ran through the servants at the house. There wasn't a one that would insult her company. In fact, the entire staff was probably in a celebratory mood over their arrival. According to North, it had been ages since company had been entertained at Sykeston House.

She rested her head in her hand to suppress the need to groan. It wasn't the staff.

It was her husband.

She closed her eyes desperate to keep her temper.

"It's Jonathan you're discussing, correct?" She kept her voice even so as not to upset Aurelia. "What did he do?"

~

Later that evening, Jonathan entered his study and closed the door. He'd steal as much solitude as he could during the upcoming week. A stiff drink might help him gird his loins for the entertainment Constance had planned for her guests after their excruciatingly long dinner that evening.

His wife had been in grand spirits, chatting and laughing. It wasn't an exaggeration to admit she came alive in a way he'd never seen before. She actually enjoyed these people. With a painful exhale, he petted Regina, who'd been exiled to the nursery during dinner. He felt the same way. Ignored and relegated to playing a reluctant host. It was selfish, but he wanted his wife's attention on him and not their guests. He now looked forward to their evenings together. After dinner, they'd go upstairs, and she'd massage his leg after they said good night to Aurelia. Then they'd make love. He grinned. His wife possessed an uncanny ability to devise all sorts of positions they could try in bed.

The soft jingle of the pianoforte sounded in the distance, his cue to attend Constance's guests again. Perhaps they'd call it an early evening as they'd traveled all day. He could only pray. With a weary sigh, he stood and made his way to the music room with Regina by his side.

Aunt Vee sat at the pianoforte playing a spry little tune. Her husband, Lund Bolen, sat beside her and turned the pages of the sheet music. Naturally, they'd been invited tonight since Aunt Vee was close to the other two wives. One side of Jonathan's mouth tugged into a sneer at the jovial faces that surrounded the piano. Such a commonplace event, but so utterly useless in his estimation.

"There you are," Constance exclaimed as she made her way to him. She wrapped her arm around his. "Isn't this divine to have the house full?"

Only if you were stuck in the first two parts of Dante's *Divine Comedy*.

He grunted in response as she squeezed his arm. North stood inside the room and grinned like an adolescent at his first dance. Naturally, he'd think the evening grand. By then, Constance had led him straight to Randford's and Grayson's sides.

"Marvelous meal," Randford acknowledged. "Thank you for having us. Mrs. Walmer still makes the best Welsh rarebit I've ever tasted."

Grayson held his hand to his stomach. "I haven't eaten this much since the last time I visited."

Aunt Vee stood and clapped her hands. "Shall we dance?"

While the men groaned quietly, the women, save Constance, cheered.

"I'll play," Constance insisted. Her gaze caught Jonathan's, and she smiled.

As Katherine, Beth, and Constance's aunt lined up, the men slowly followed.

Mrs. Butler marched into the room with a huge grin. She conversed with North, then they strolled to Constance's side. By then, Jonathan had sat at a table, a deck of cards spread out before him.

Automatically, he shuffled the cards and laid them out in a formation. Absently, he started to play a game as the music began. He tried to ignore that their friends were dancing in his home. Two weeks ago, he'd have railed at anyone who had even suggested such entertainment. But Constance wanted them here.

As the music increased in tempo and the dancing grew more boisterous, his misery swelled, suspended in a perpetual darkness that couldn't be cast aside. He swallowed a gulp of brandy hoping for a distraction. His gaze wandered to the tableau before him. A chandelier cast the room in a glowing brightness that would make the midday summer sun envious. The laughter, the claps, and the smiles on Constance's and their guests' faces were brilliant as they reveled in the entertainment.

The irony didn't escape him. Surrounded by light, he still felt the darkness rise within him.

How could he ever be that gay and carefree again with the accusations against him looming close, ready to snatch the brief happiness he'd shared with Constance? His chest tightened painfully, making him gasp. If the worst happened and he was found guilty, every single person in this room would have to shun him except Constance. She would be shunned right alongside him because she was his wife. He had to protect her the best he knew how.

He couldn't allow her to stay.

"Sykeston, am I allowed to partner your wife in a dance?" Grayson called out. He lifted an eyebrow.

Before Constance could decline, Jonathan plastered on a smile that probably looked more like a smirk. "My wife makes her own decisions. You'll have to ask her if she's amenable."

He returned to his cards, but not soon enough. He'd seen the frown on Constance's face.

When he couldn't take it anymore, Jonathan looked up to find her dancing with Grayson. Mrs. Butler sat banging on the keys of the pianoforte. Randford danced with Miss Howell, and North danced with Katherine.

A red-hot poker thrust into his gut would have hurt less than the sight before him. His beautiful wife, *his* Constance, moved with an innate grace like poetry set to music. Her reddened cheeks and the brilliance in her sapphire eyes enhanced her beauty. She was in her prime and married to him, a cannon ready to explode and destroy everything within its path.

He dug his fist into his injured thigh, pain radiating upward. He couldn't help but compare himself to his two friends. Grayson hadn't served in the war, and Randford had returned home a war hero duke. All of them respectable and welcomed members of society.

Such a spectacle reminded him of the peril Constance had put herself in when she married him.

He glanced down at the cards. He'd laugh if it wasn't so dreadfully ironic. He hadn't even noticed, but he was playing solitaire.

"Jonathan?" Constance placed her hand on his shoulder.

Immediately, he tilted his gaze to hers and drank in the sight of his beautiful wife. She was slightly flushed with her brow glistening.

"Will you join us?" She bent down and whispered in his

ear. "I'll encourage Mrs. Butler to dance, then you and I can sit at the piano? I'd enjoy your company."

The entreaty in her eyes reached deep into the middle of his chest and squeezed. He looked his fill, studying her face and the affection in her eyes. "Sweetheart, I'm tired." He cupped her cheek and ran his thumb gently over her cheekbone. "If you don't mind, I'll retire now."

"Shall I come with you?" The concern in her sapphire eyes made the color deepen even more.

"Stay with your guests." Carefully, he rose. Away from the others and hidden in the shadows created by the candlelight, he pressed his lips to her cheek. "I'll check on Aurelia." He took her hand in his and squeezed. "Enjoy yourself."

She studied him a moment more, then nodded. As soon as she returned to the piano, North asked her for a dance.

Let her enjoy a night of pleasurable diversion without having to attend him. He watched the two dance for a few moments. Without delaying anymore, Jonathan took a side entrance, escaping anyone's notice.

Tonight, he'd give her the gift of not having to worry about him.

Chapter Twenty-Seven

When Constance had retired, she'd found Jonathan asleep in her bed with Aurelia tucked next to him. His arm had been wrapped around her tiny waist. Happy tears had blurred her vision, an overwhelming emotion tugging at her heart. In that magical moment, everything in the world had fallen into a perfect order.

But when dawn came, things were chaotic once again. Jonathan could have joined the circus, as his disappearing act was quite phenomenal. For the remainder of the day, she hadn't laid eyes on him. When she'd asked North about Jonathan's whereabouts, the butler had been purposely vague.

Tonight's dinner was about ready to start, and Jonathan still hadn't appeared. Aunt Vee and Uncle Lund had arrived. Aunt Vee had been beside herself when North had informed her that there would be dancing once again this evening. Randford had asked to partner her in at least one set.

Everyone had taken their seats at the elegantly set table. Constance was about to signal the footmen to start serving when her husband finally made his entrance. It wasn't grand or loud. But because it was him, she realized the moment he entered without having to turn around and look at him.

She sat at the end of the table with her back facing him. It was the customary seat for the lady of the house when entertaining. Jonathan would take his seat at the head of the table. A ridiculous sense of excitement came from nowhere, and her skin suddenly tingled in awareness. Heaven help her if he gazed at her with that expression that said *I want you*. She wouldn't be able to eat a bite. There was only one reason for such thoughts.

Everything between them was perfect.

With his cane, he made his way to his end of the table where Kat and Christian sat. The footmen who would serve them stood absolutely motionless. North stood by the marble console supervising. When Jonathan pulled out his chair, she slowly raised her eyes to his. Staring at the unfathomable depths of the deepest ocean would reveal more than her husband's current expression.

He nodded with a slightly bowed head.

She nodded in return.

"Good evening," he said to the rest of the table. Murmurs of greeting floated his way. Carefully, he eased himself into the seat at the head of the table.

With uncanny timing, Regina loped into the room with an eye on the prize. Dinner.

Every guest's gaze followed the dog as she slid to a slightly off-kilter stop between Jonathan's chair and Katherine's chair, Regina's customary seat.

Oh, for the love of all cats everywhere, the dog wanted to eat with them. Constance had specifically instructed Dahlia not to let Regina out of her sight until dinner was over. She motioned to Fred, the footman closest to her. "Will you take Regina—"

At the sound of her name, the dog barked twice.

Jonathan whipped out his serviette and placed it in his lap without a hint of disquiet. He looked around the room at the startled faces and smiled. "She eats with us every night." With an unabashed effort to foment the dog into an excited frenzy, he patted his leg.

Naturally, the well-trained Regina obeyed by hoisting herself to the table and resting her massive front paws near the edge.

Randford's gaze swiveled from the dog to Jonathan's as the volume of his disbelieving voice rose. "How does it eat with you?"

"It's a she for your information." Jonathan patted Regina. "She sits at the table."

Constance wanted to bury her head in her hands at the complete and utterly mitigated disaster unfolding before her. If there were such things as fairy godmothers, she wished hers would have arrived five minutes ago with her magic wand waving.

However, with no fairy godmothers in sight, Constance would have to be the one who saved her husband from himself.

Behind her, the footmen were whispering what they should do. With Regina's bulk crowding Katherine, the duchess had been forced to lean against Grayson to escape being knocked out of her chair. Aunt Vee's eyes threatened to pop out at the spectacle before her. Poor Uncle Lund was trying to calm her by patting her hand.

"No, Regina." Constance stood and pointed to the floor.

Jonathan turned his attention to Kat. "I'm sorry, Your Grace. You're sitting in her chair. Last night, she thought she was being punished when she couldn't join us." He lifted one hand to his heart. "I couldn't do it to her again." He picked a piece of cheese from the hors d'oeuvre tray and fed it to his dog at the table.

If canines could smile, Regina was practically giddy at the commotion. She barked joyfully at the ruckus.

"You let that mongrel sit at the table with you?" Uncle Lund asked.

"She's a mastiff, not a mongrel," Jonathan replied.

"My lord," Constance said through clenched teeth. "Get her away from the table."

"You mean the duchess?" Jonathan furrowed his brow. "That's not necessary." He turned to Fred, the footman. "Would you bring another chair? Regina can sit between the duchess and me."

Grayson threw his serviette on the table. "Get that animal out of here."

The footmen hesitated for a moment, but when Grayson snapped his fingers, they all rushed to assist.

"Or what?" Jonathan asked with a slight menace in his voice.

"Are you all right, love?" Christian asked his wife.

Kat laughed. "It's a dog. I'll survive."

Randford held his wife's gaze for a moment.

"I'm fine, Christian," Kat whispered to pacify her husband.

The duke exhaled a relieved sigh, then leaned back against his chair. He shook his head in disbelief.

"I'm so sorry," Constance offered. She moved to make her way around the table. "I'll take Regina back to the nursery while you continue with dinner."

"Stay with us, Constance." Clearly bemused by the frown on his face, Randford turned to Jonathan. "Would you please instruct one of the footmen to remove your dog from the dining room?" With his hand, he motioned for the marquess to sit.

As Fred came to lead Regina away, Jonathan stayed the footman with his hand, then turned to Randford. "I thought it was supposed to be a party?"

Christian's eyes never left Jonathan, but he smiled. It was one of those smiles that reminded Constance of a dog wagging its tail as it bared its teeth. "Grayson, why do you suppose he's doing this?"

"Because he's a beastly philistine," the marquess growled. "When I was here six months ago, Mrs. Butler refused to allow that dog to eat with him when he had guests."

Everything stilled within Constance as a sudden chill wrapped around her. Six months ago, she and Aurelia had celebrated Christmastide with Kat and Randford. During that time Jonathan's letters had been filled with wistful musings about how he'd regretted that they were separated during their first Christmas as husband and wife. He'd written tenderly about Aurelia's first Christmas and how he longed to see her. She'd tearfully read his beautifully crafted thoughts that they'd be together soon.

Constance brought her hand to her chest hoping to calm the tripping beat of her heart. She forced her gaze to the table and studied the Sykeston family crest on her plate. She swallowed the vile disbelief lodged in her throat.

He wouldn't have purposely lied to her. Or would he?

Yet Grayson's declarations had made it clear. She closed her eyes desperately searching for a reasonable explanation.

"A beastly philistine makes sense, but I also prefer a boorish beast," Randford agreed. "I believe the real reason he's acting this way is that he wants us to be appalled by his behavior and leave."

She opened her eyes when she couldn't find a reasonable explanation. Time slowed to a crawl. Constance couldn't breathe until she gasped, breaking the spell. "Would everyone leave except my guests?" Her voice had dropped an octave of its own accord. Unable to look at her husband, she stared at her wedding ring for a moment. "Mr. North, that includes you," she said softly, watching the butler out of the corner of her eye.

With a barely perceptible nod, the butler did her bidding, being the last to leave.

Constance waited until the click of the door sounded. An eerie silence blanketed the room. She needed a drink of water to ease the ache in her throat, but her hands trembled to such an extent that she didn't think she could accomplish it without spilling it. She didn't want to believe it, but she had to find out the truth.

"Constance?" Kat asked softly.

Instead of answering, she turned her attention to the marquess. "When exactly did you last visit my husband?"

The marquess hesitated before finally replying, "Christmastide."

A sudden pain pierced her chest. "Here at Sykeston Gardens?"

Grayson didn't take his eyes off hers. "Yes."

Under the table, she clenched her fists so hard that her nails dug into her palms, no doubt leaving marks. "My husband said he was traveling. Was he here?" She kept her gaze trained on the marquess. When he didn't say a word, she continued, "Why did you visit?"

Grayson shook his head, the anger slipping from his face. "My lady, I shouldn't have spoken so freely. Forgive me. I was angry about the dog."

"It's all right," Constance laid her serviette on the table and straightened her shoulders. Her voice turned surprisingly steady. "I must know."

Quiet hung heavy in the room, trapping everyone in place.

Eventually, her husband broke the silence. "He came here to cajole me into bringing you home," Jonathan replied softly.

She swept her gaze down the table, past the serving dishes, the wine goblets, the silver, and the plates arranged neatly for a formal dinner. An extraordinarily beautiful sight in a bizarre setting and time. Everything suddenly seemed strange, as if slanted sideways. Finally, she forced her gaze to her husband's. She really didn't know what she expected, but it certainly wasn't panic. The whites of his eyes were visible clear across the table. It was if he were in shock.

That made two of them.

⁓

"Constance," Jonathan said softly. Dante's hell was child's play compared with what was unfolding before him. "Let me explain."

Aunt Vee turned to Constance. "I thought you said he was doing secret work for the Crown." She turned to her husband. "France, Italy, and Elba, wasn't it? Something to do with Napoleon?"

Lund blinked slowly twice as if trying to get his bearings. "How he had escaped?"

Constance looked to Randford. "Did you know?"

"For the love of God, no." He slowly shook his head. "If I had, I would have brought him back to London, then I'd have beaten him to a bloody pulp." Randford swore and rested his head in his hand. "What have you done, Sykeston?"

Before Jonathan uttered a word, Aunt Vee continued, "I don't understand."

"I don't either," Constance said softly.

"Oh, love," Beth said. Her sympathetic smile mirrored the pain on Constance's face.

The table had quieted to an unnatural silence, but Jonathan petted Regina as if she were the safety line keeping him from drowning. Yet he couldn't turn away from his wife.

"Why?" Her voice was so low he wasn't certain he'd heard her clearly. But everyone else had.

All eyes turned to him.

"Why did you tell me in those letters that you were on a secret assignment for a year?"

For a moment, he couldn't catch his breath. Why hadn't he told her the truth?

Because at first, he'd been certain she'd leave him. Now it was inevitable.

"Let's talk in private." Jonathan ran a hand down his face, but it wouldn't wipe away the shame that was his due. She didn't deserve to find out this way. With every ounce of strength, he forced his gaze to hers. "I should have told you earlier."

"The entire staff knew." Her hand flew to her chest. "You were here the entire time, and no one said a word before or after I arrived." She released a breath as she stared straight through him. The betrayal in her eyes hurt worse than the bullets he'd taken that day. "Did you even write those letters?"

"Constance, not here," he implored.

"You've already embarrassed me in front of my family and friends. I told them all the heroic things you'd done. I spoke of your lovely letters and your travel. I was so proud of *you*." The agony in her voice cut straight through him, baring every single fault and failing he possessed.

"It wasn't designed to hurt you." The pain on her face tore him apart inside. No matter his intentions, he'd wounded her by not being forthcoming with why and by whom those letters were written. "I tried to tell you."

"But you didn't." Her cheeks blazed in anger. "Who wrote the letters you supposedly sent me?"

Not a single person moved or said a word. They stared at their plates hoping to avoid being in the direct line of fire when he was annihilated.

"At least tell me it wasn't you." Her sharp rebuke skewered him. "I deserve the truth."

"It wasn't me." He forced his gaze to hers, willing her to give him the benefit of the doubt.

She was motionless except for a slow blink.

"Let me explain." He didn't care if he was pleading in front of everyone. He had to make things right between them.

"Things are starting to make sense now. Why you were so shocked when I arrived. You didn't want me here. Nor Aurelia." She searched his face, seeking an understanding or perhaps wanting to know what he wanted.

Christ, even he didn't understand. "I would never purposely hurt you. Back then, I didn't know what I wanted. But that's not the case now."

Her gaze dropped to the table. For an eternity she didn't say a word. The silence in the room magnified until it threatened to explode. Finally, she lifted her head. The look of utter disappointment was there for all to see.

He'd done that. His actions had caused her this incredible pain tonight.

"I feel as if I've been hurled onto a stage in the middle of a play, and I have no idea what the next line is or even if I'm supposed to be here," she whispered.

He looked around the room. None of the ladies were looking at him, their embarrassment obvious at the situation he'd put his wife in. Whereas the men's expression of shock had frozen on their faces.

Uncle Lund stood. "Come, Venetia. We should leave."

"I beg you to stay." Jonathan stood.

Constance pulled herself from her reverie. "Yes, please stay." She looked around the table at her guests. "I want all of you to stay." She finally turned her gaze to Jonathan.

He stared at her for a long moment. It was the only thing he could do in this absurd moment that he'd created.

Her lips trembled. Instantly, she brought her hand to her mouth.

Slowly, her expression changed into a mask of indifference, which meant she didn't want anything to do with him. His heart lurched in its beat. Since he'd returned from the war, he'd only ever felt comfortable in her company. She was the only one he'd ever allowed to hold him. He'd thought keeping himself distant from others was a way to protect them and him. By not following his own rules, he'd hurt the most important person in his world. The undeniable need to go to her side and offer comfort became overwhelming. When he moved to do just that, she held up her hand stopping him mid-step.

He forced himself to remain still when she straightened her shoulders and regarded him as if he were the only person there.

"What I've feared the most has happened. Once again, I've failed to see the future consequences of marrying a man whom I thought I could trust. I believed you to be a man who would respect and honor me." She waved a hand at Randford and her uncle Lund. "These men are perfect examples of good, kind husbands who love and cherish their wives." She locked her gaze with his. "It's my misfortune that I find men who fail me. I found it with Meriwether, and now I found it with you."

He didn't move a muscle. Nor did he defend himself. What she said was the truth. Tonight's actions proved he wasn't honorable or good—not anymore.

"But there is one monumental difference," Constance said, her voice quiet but steady.

He could see the pity in her eyes. This was the worst hell he'd ever experienced in his life. He cleared his throat, hoping the earth would open up beneath him.

"I was never in love with Meriwether."

He sucked in a breath. For a moment, he'd thought he had been run through with a bayonet.

Only he would feel as if he were gutted when his wife told him she loved him.

Chapter Twenty-Eight

Constance closed her eyes and a single tear fell. Willing the rest of them away, she vowed not to appear wounded by her husband's outrageous behavior.

Not tonight. Not tomorrow. And most assuredly, not ever again.

Jonathan nodded once, then left the room. She watched his slow progression to the hallway. Regina followed. For whatever reason, the sight of his dog accompanying him relieved some of the tightness in her chest. She chided herself for even thinking such a thought. She shouldn't care. With as much grace as she could muster, she called the footmen back into the room to serve dinner.

It proceeded with an unearthly quiet, and thankfully, it was over quickly. Hasty goodbyes and good nights were exchanged.

Afterward, Constance returned to the family sitting room. Surrounded by Kat and Beth, it had turned into a somber gathering. She clutched the satchel next to her chest, then handed it to Beth. "I'm sorry that I couldn't figure out what Meriwether did with our dowries, but I've written one list of the transactions in chronological order. The first date is from

the day of Kat's marriage, and the last one was the day before Meriwether died."

Dressed in a retiring gown, Kat placed her empty teacup
on the table before her then twisted to face Constance. "That
was a monumental task."

She nodded. "I spent several days on it, but I still can't
make heads or tails of it."

"I appreciate all you've done. I'll study it when I return to
London. Perhaps I'll see something." Beth sat on the other
side of Constance and squeezed her hand. "A common ven-
dor or perhaps a pattern to his purchases."

"A sound plan," Constance agreed without much enthusiasm. All of her earlier excitement for her friends' visit had
dimmed. Her husband had stolen that from her this evening.

"Please don't worry with it anymore." Kat patted Constance's hand. "With Lysander & Sons and Aurelia, I don't
see how you could devote any time to those receipts anyway."

"When do you sleep?" Beth's look of concern ripped a new
hole through Constance.

She smiled slightly. "I sleep every night. In fact, when I
go to bed, I don't even hear Aurelia cry in the next room."

"I'm sure Dahlia takes excellent care of her," Kat answered.

Constance shook her head. "Dahlia doesn't stay with her."

"When she cries, who hears her?" Kat took another sip
of tea.

"Jonathan," she said softly and closed her eyes, unwilling
to see her friends' expressions. "Believe it or not, he's marvelous with her."

Beth knelt on the floor and sat with her legs tucked under,
facing both Kat and Constance. "Jonathan? The liar obsessed
with his dog?"

"He's not obsessed with her." Constance didn't deny the
rest. But Beth's look of *don't try to defend him* spurred Constance to reveal more. "She's helped him with his loneliness.
Haven't you ever had a pet that was part of the family?"

"Oh yes." Beth nodded. "Every one of my brother's race-horses. They're practically family since he has breakfast with them in the stables. He prefers their company to mine." She took a sip of her port. A moan of appreciation escaped. "Seems a pity that we can't imbibe port after dinner with the gentlemen. The male species could learn a thing or two about deportment."

Kat's smile reeked of sympathy. "Speaking of dinner and deportment . . ."

Constance sucked in her stomach to steel herself. "I owe you an apology for tonight's spectacle. I know you're leaving because of my husband's abhorrent behavior. Frankly, I can't blame you."

Kat glanced at her clasped hands, then looked to Constance. "Why don't you and Aurelia come to Brighton, then travel back to London with Christian and me. A little holiday of sorts."

An exuberant smile spread across Beth's face. "*Yes.* Once you tire of Kat and Randford, you can stay with me. I'll watch Aurelia for you."

Tears welled in her eyes. "You're trying to shield me from the fact that my husband didn't want me." She bit her lip and forced her tears back. From nowhere, the guilt that she'd failed her daughter and herself threatened to steal her breath. "I'm not a very good judge of men."

"Constance," Kat soothed. "What happened isn't a reflection on you."

She lifted a brow contesting that statement. "It's a reflection on my marriage, and I'm half of that equation. You'd think I'd have learned my lesson after being hoodwinked by Meriwether and his lack of regard for me. Instead, I walked into an even worse marriage, because I brought my daughter into it."

"Don't say that," Beth crooned in sympathy. "Meriwether was the master of delusion. All three of us were his victims.

And not to mention, we're all three intelligent, responsible women."

"She's right." Kat shrugged slightly. "Don't take that guilt as yours to bear, darling. And Jonathan?" She placed a hand on Constance's knee. "Time will tell."

"I can only draw one conclusion." Beth stuck her nose in the air like a high society matron. "If your husband continues to act like a mad hatter, then you need to leave him."

Heat bludgeoned her cheeks as her heart ached.

She took a sip of port to hide her own uncertainty. The idea of leaving Jonathan made her stomach clench into a knot. How could she do that to him after he told her about the court-martial? How could she do that to Aurelia? Her daughter loved him, and Constance had loved him ever since they first kissed. She'd experienced loneliness after the shambles Meriwether had left in his wake, but not with the starkness she faced now. It left her utterly bereft and cold.

Kat shook her head. "Only you can decide if it's in your and your daughter's best interests to stay here."

Constance opened her mouth to object, but Beth clasped her hand and squeezed. "What do you want?"

Kat's eyes softened.

Constance closed her eyes, staying the tears. "I'm trying to decide."

$\backsim$

Jonathan's time alone in the courtyard with Regina by his side did little to relieve his anguish. The look of suffering and betrayal on his wife's face this evening tore him apart. It reminded him of how he'd felt when he'd confronted Faladen.

Mayhap, it was fortuitous that fate had stepped in and ruined him. To believe otherwise was to believe in fairy tales. They were light and fluffy on the outside, but horror burrowed deep inside. Anyone that examined those stories closely would see the truth revealed.

In those fanciful tales, beautiful women, much like his wife, had their lives torn asunder by some magical being. Only when they found a way to ultimately break the enchantment did the women find freedom. Of course, a rich, handsome prince would arise from the ashes of the mystical creatures destroyed. Then both the beauty and prince would declare their undying love for each other.

Jonathan huffed. What *bloody* nonsense. Oh, he could see the similarities between himself and Constance and the aforementioned stories. She was more than beautiful. Simply put, she was stunning and had a heart that would give and give even to her own detriment. He was rich and lived in an exquisite house fit for royalty. As he'd proven tonight, he was a creature who would forever be damned to live his days alone after destroying his wife's affection for him.

Jonathan carefully made his way from the courtyard to his study. Randford waited with a glass of whisky in his hand, watching his every step.

"Why are you here?" Jonathan ensured that he delivered his best sneer as he carefully lowered himself to his sofa. Regina dutifully jumped up beside him and curled into her favorite sleeping position.

"I wanted to see the carnage up close." Randford poured another whisky and set it on a side table beside Jonathan. Settling into a chair, the duke took a sip and regarded Regina. "Your dog is bigger than most people. It must eat more than the entire household."

Jonathan smiled briefly. "She does have a healthy appetite."

The duke examined his glass. "In the past, your wife shared that she had one when she was younger." His gaze slowly rose from the amber liquid and regarded Jonathan. "You knew each other well?"

Jonathan grunted noncommittally as he took a swig,

savoring the smoky taste. As it slid down his throat, the
sting reassured him that he wasn't completely numb.

Another knock sounded with Grayson entering without permission. He stared at Jonathan before he ran a hand through
his hair. "Damme, Sykeston. I don't know what to say."

He wanted to roar, *Stay out.* However, the strategy to keep
these two men out of his life had proven an epic failure.

Randford stood. "Come and join us." He went to the table
and poured a glass for the marquess.

By then, Grayson was seated beside Jonathan. "I've come
to apologize. Under no circumstances would I have wished
to cause you both so much pain."

Jonathan stared into his glass. "It's my fault. North wrote
fantastical letters of me traveling for the Crown, thinking they'd help bring us together. I didn't find out until the
day Constance arrived, and she said that I'd asked her to
come live here. I should have told her the truth as soon as I
learned it."

"Why didn't you?" Grayson asked.

Jonathan exhaled, the breath painful as he laid the truth
bare. "I thought I didn't want her, but then I didn't want her
to leave either," he said quietly.

"You're driving her away," Randford said shaking his
head. He leaned forward and rested his elbows on his knees,
letting the half-empty glass dangle from his hand. "All the
while, even I believed you were on assignment."

"Randford, I'm in no mood for a lecture."

"Wallow in your own pity for all I care, but she doesn't
deserve what happened tonight." The duke finished his drink,
then set aside the glass. "You once told me that if you'd
known how my half brother had treated Constance, you'd
have called him out. What a misfortune that you can't call
yourself out."

"I wish I could, but then I'd have to care, wouldn't I?" he

asked matter-of-factly, hoping to hide the wounds the duke had unintentionally opened.

Randford laughed slightly. "You care, my friend, more than you'll admit to yourself." With a natural athletic ease, the duke stood. "We're granting your wish. All of us are departing in the morning for Brighton. Kat is inviting your wife to join us then return to London."

Jonathan laced his fingers behind his head and stared at those mocking little bastards with wings on their backs above him. Perhaps it was for the best if she left, but the idea squeezed his heart until it threatened to break. "I don't know what I'm doing."

It was a plea to himself, but Randford and Grayson heard it.

"You're like a whirligig spinning out of its orbit with no clear direction. I didn't risk my life saving yours on the battlefield that day only to see you throw everything away. It doesn't take a genius to see that you're distraught. What is it?"

Jonathan shook his head. "You wouldn't understand."

It was easier not to share the gut-wrenching pain tearing him apart about hurting Constance.

"Then find a way to accept your life and get on it." The duke lifted a brow in challenge. "Whether it's with Constance or not, that's her decision."

"What about my decision?"

"You lost it when you acted like a fool this evening. If I had a wife like Constance, I'd have protected her from this type of pain with my life." Grayson abruptly stood and set his half-empty glass on the table. "You can't convince us you don't care about her." Grayson's face hardened into an impenetrable wall.

"We all saw it on your face." The duke agreed, then nodded once. "Good night."

After they left, the silence in the room grew deafening.

He had no one to blame except himself. If she left, he'd be destroyed.

~

After a sleepless night, Jonathan forced himself to see their guests off to Brighton. It was awkward as hell, but he did it for Constance. They hadn't discussed the previous night's events as she'd locked her bedroom door. The first time she'd ever done that.

After kissing everyone goodbye, Constance stood in the drive and waved as the sleek black carriage with four impeccably matched grays drove away. A smile tugged at her lips shadowed with sadness. When their eyes met, she looked away but continued to walk toward him.

As she made her way to pass, he forced himself to speak. "Will you talk with me?"

"All right." Without sparing a glance, she preceded him into the house and made her way to his study, claiming a chair in front of his desk. Regina jumped down from the sofa and came to Constance's side. Without her usual smile, she greeted the dog with a few rubs behind the ear.

Jonathan crossed the room slowly, then lowered himself onto his customary desk chair. "Would you be more comfortable on the sofa? We wouldn't be so far away from each other."

"This is preferable for what I have to say." Constance sat on the edge of her seat, her back so straight that it could have been mistaken for a ramrod of perfectly forged steel.

He cleared his throat, all the while praying the right words would mend their differences. "Let me start. I'm sorry—"

She held up her hand to stop him. "There's no need to apologize. I think, for once, we should have an honest discussion of our marriage." She briefly glanced at her clasped hands in her lap, then raised her gaze to his. The blues of her eyes flashed with smoldering anger.

"Would you let me explain?" he asked. Slowly, he stood, then carefully made his way to stand before her.

"There's nothing to explain." She stared straight ahead without looking at him. "I've deduced that it was your butler who wrote those letters. In our first days together, North was usually present when we met. I thought it was sweet, but now I recognize it for what it was. He was trying to bring us together while making certain you behaved."

"Yes, it was North," he said warily. "I didn't know he'd written them. It came as much a shock to me as to you."

"He likely instructed the staff not to mention your presence here for the last year." Her lips pursed, then she swallowed.

The soulful sound of her exhale tore another part of his heart away. Really, there wasn't much remaining after he'd butchered it himself.

"That makes it even worse in a way," she said softly before shaking her head. "It's neither here nor there when you knew. What's important is that if I'd known the true circumstances, I wouldn't have come to Sykeston Gardens. Truth is, if I'd known your true feelings of not wanting me here, I wouldn't have married you."

He deserved that. It was because of his own selfishness that she was hurting right now. "That's not how I felt when I married you. It was only after I returned to Portsmouth that everything seemed to unravel around me. It was easier to stay hidden away and not face the world." He took the seat beside her, then reached for her hand.

"Don't," she said. "It merely confuses things."

"Touching you helps me think more clearly," he countered softly as he brought his hand back to his side. "Will you look at me?"

She looked up to the ceiling and took a deep breath, then

slowly turned his way. Tears welled in her eyes, but they didn't fall.

"Constance, I did want you. I just didn't know it at the time. I didn't know how to appreciate what you gave me." He didn't wince at her sharp intake of breath. "But that's not the case now, and it's frightening."

"Why?"

"I don't want to hurt you. I don't want to hurt Aurelia." He ran a hand down his face. "If I was any other man, a good, deserving man, I'd say I love you. But I can't see anything clearly until the court-martial is resolved."

She wrapped her arms around her waist. The protective stance a shield against the hurt he'd inflicted. "I've come to a decision about what will be best for Aurelia and me. I'm moving into my parents' house. Dahlia and Mary should have packed our things by now. You should know that I'm not doing it because of the court-martial."

He didn't move, praying time would stand still. If it did, then she wouldn't leave him. Even he knew this was for the best. The unbearable weight of grief threatened to rob him of his breath. No, it threatened to smother him. He couldn't fathom her being absent from his life. Then as if fate laughed at him, the *bloody* cupid clock chimed signaling the quarter hour, proving time didn't stand still for anyone.

"You don't have to do that." Jonathan's words sounded hollow to his own ears. "I will go to London until things are sorted out."

"There's nothing to sort out." She stood with her arms still wrapped around her.

Anger unfurled deep within Constance. For all her days, she'd never forget this moment. "There's no need for you to go to

London. For once in my life, I want to know what it feels like
to be the one to leave."

"I'm not leaving you." Jonathan shook his head. "I know
you need your distance from me."

Her lips cracked in a sad smile. She was no longer naive
enough to believe that he was doing it for her. The truth was
he did it to hide from himself. "I'm going to say some things
that will undoubtedly be hurtful, but you need to hear it. I
know life has been unkind to you, but I haven't." She shook
her head at the thought of him alone, but she had to continue
for both their sakes. "I wanted a life with you. I always have.
I believed the two of us could survive and conquer life's
challenges together. But my optimism can only take so much
battering. Just like you."

The stunned look on his face meant she'd shocked him.

"I won't allow my daughter to grow up like this. I won't
allow myself to live under these circumstances either."

"Believe me, I'm well aware of that. I'm detrimental to
your well-being." The curtness in his voice didn't cover the
pain in his eyes.

"Stop, Jonathan," she pleaded. "Please, stop." She fisted
her hands and stared at the carpet. It made little difference
at this point what she said. She'd never be able to change
his mind, but she could make her point with her head held
high. "I've never thought you a coward until now. At first, you
thought if you kept me at arm's distance, you'd protect me.
And Aurelia." Constance blew out a breath of exasperation.
"It was only to protect yourself. You believe if you keep
everyone at a distance, you won't be hurt. You're destined for
a life of emptiness. It's a self-fulfilling prophecy. But the truth
is, you cause your own suffering every day by denying yourself love. Don't you see?"

He stood then walked to the courtyard door. He was hurting, but so was she.

"You can't live in isolation. You're already avoiding friends and social situations. You should have taken this time and discussed the court-martial with Grayson and Randford. They would help you," she said softly. "I'm sorry. I love you, but I won't stand by and watch you continue down this path."

At the word *love*, he turned to face her. His grip on his walking cane was so tight that the silver handle creaked in protest.

"Yet, I have to thank you for one thing. After Meriwether, I finally understand what I need. I don't simply need a husband for myself or a father for Aurelia." As her tears fell, she brought her hand to her heart, trying to salvage the pieces that remained. "I need"—she pounded her fist gently against her chest—"no, I *deserve* a partner who will share with me everything that life has to offer, including all the good and the bad." Her voice cracked, but she continued, "I deserve to be loved."

Her words fell to silence as she studied him.

After a moment, he came toward her. Close enough that she could see the wounds she'd inflicted. The lines around his reddened eyes and the thinned lips were an attempt to hold in his pain.

"You do deserve that and so much more, Constance." He took a deep breath. "I wish I could be that man for you."

"I wish that too." Without a word of goodbye, Constance turned for the door.

"Wait," Jonathan called out.

She drew to a stop but didn't turn to face him.

"I don't want you to leave," he said softly.

It was on the tip of her tongue to answer that she didn't want to either. Instead, she said, "I have to."

Then, without another word, she left her husband to start a new life.

Chapter Twenty-Nine

J onathan squinted as some sapskull had the gall to open the curtains in his study. There was only one person who would dare interrupt his sleep. "Damn you, North. You've proven you've more hair than wit. Get the hell away before I shoot you."

With one eye barely open, Jonathan tracked his butler's movement until he stood before the sofa, Jonathan's new bed. For the past four nights, he'd not returned to his bedroom. It had once been his haven. Now there were too many excruciating and painful memories of all he'd lost.

Morning was the worst. No, that was a lie.

Every minute of the day was a lesson in excruciating torture. His wife, his Constance, had departed from his home and life, leaving his heart sickened and withering. The insufferable reality couldn't be denied. She'd been right about everything she had said. He was allowing his own darkness to define him. He'd forced her to leave, and he had no idea how to win her back or even if he should try.

"You have a visitor."

Jonathan popped up with such speed, he'd disturbed Regina, who was sleeping at the end of the sofa. "Is it Constance?"

"No." North sniffed the room. "It's Lieutenant Roth. I've taken the liberty of having Ralph prepare a shower and a shave for you this morning. I'll open the doors while you're upstairs dressing. By the time you come down, the room should be sufficiently aired out."

"Send him away," Jonathan growled.

"Pardon me for being blunt, but no." North grabbed his cane and pushed it into Jonathan's hand. "He says he has important information to share with you. Go. Make yourself presentable, then come back here."

"You talk to him," he grumbled.

"Lord Sykeston, may I remind you that your wife left you because of this very reason?" North muttered under his breath. "And because you're a dunderhead," he added curtly for good measure.

Jonathan answered with a grunt.

"You'll never win her back by hiding away," North challenged.

Without a word, Jonathan reluctantly made his way upstairs. His butler was beyond the pale. To make matters worse, he was right. When he entered his bedroom, Ralph waited with the shaving kit ready, the shower prepared, and a fresh change of clothes. It was doubtless the quickest morning ablutions he'd had since he was in the British army.

In fifteen minutes, he stood outside his study. He smoothed a hand down his waistcoat, then entered the room. It still reminded him of his wife, particularly when he looked out into the courtyard. North was obnoxiously correct as usual. He'd lost his wife because he was a dunderhead.

Lieutenant Roth stood at his entrance. "Captain Lord Sykeston."

"Good morning, Lieutenant." Jonathan made his way to his desk and sat without grimacing. "To what do I owe the pleasure of your company?"

"I need your advice on a delicate matter." Though

Lieutenant Roth wore his uniform, his bright red coat appeared out of place with the man's uncharacteristic look of defeat. "It's about Lord Faladen."

Jonathan cocked an eyebrow. Why in the devil was Roth coming to him? "I'm not on active duty with the military."

"I'm aware of that fact, but he's destroying the program I'm commanding." Still fidgeting, the lieutenant cleared his throat. "He's managed to drive out ten of the twenty recruits in the last month. It's his responsibility to secure the necessary firearms for the men to practice with, then take into active duty. Frankly, not only are the firearms of poor quality, but they're dangerous. Several have backfired, leaving one of the recruits injured. After that, several men asked to be reassigned. After Faladen denied their requests, they've purposely shot wild, missing everything in sight just to be relieved of duty." He lifted his gaze, the worry clear in his eyes.

"What do you think is happening?" Jonathan asked.

"I can't rightly say," Roth answered.

"But you have an idea?" Jonathan pressed.

The man bowed his head. "I believe he's receiving money from the supplier he chose."

"As in a bribe?" Jonathan asked incredulously.

Roth nodded.

"Why are you telling me this?" Jonathan leaned back in his chair watching every single move that Roth made.

"Simple, sir." Sweat covered the poor man's brow. "I can't go to Colonel Peterson or anyone else. My reputation would be ruined if it leaked that I'd broken command and had gone over Faladen's head to report my suspicions." He lowered his voice. "Even if they're true."

"Do you have proof?"

"Yes." Roth pulled papers out of his coat pocket. "These are the actual invoices that were supposed to have been sent to Lord Faladen. They were delivered to me instead."

As Jonathan read the papers, the urge to pound his desk into oblivion grew fierce. What Roth said was true. The supplier, Middleton Company, didn't have the God-given sense to hide the bribe. Faladen's share was plainly written on the invoice. "He's ordered enough to supply the entire British army for the next one hundred years."

It explained the real reason why Faladen wanted to supervise the training of recruits. He was earning a fortune and he knew that Jonathan would never have allowed such action.

"Indeed, sir." Roth leaned forward. "I'd hoped you'd go to Colonel Peterson on behalf of the unit."

Before the words were even out of the man's mouth, Jonathan was nodding. "Of course. I can't leave for London yet. Don't mention a word of our conversation to anyone."

The lieutenant quickly nodded. "I understand, sir." He stood, and Jonathan did the same. "I was confident you'd have a plan, sir. Colonel Peterson always sings your praises as an honorable man and one who was always one step ahead of the enemy. I may need your help with the recruits if you have the time."

"Of course. It'd be my pleasure." Jonathan shook the man's hand, then watched him leave.

He sat at his desk and reviewed the invoices a second time. The idea that Faladen would use the British army's faith in him to line his own coffers curdled Jonathan's already sour stomach. Indeed, the easiest action would be to stay cloistered in his study. Yet he wouldn't. The marquess was polluting more than Jonathan's life. He threatened the soldiers who were willing to defend their county. The court-martial be damned.

Before he could consider more, North strutted into the room practically beaming. "My, my, someone is Mr. Popular today. Another visitor to see you."

"My wife?" This time Jonathan didn't hide his hopefulness

as he took the invoices and locked them into his top desk drawer for safekeeping.

"It's not Lady Sykeston, but Miss Howell. She asked for you. Apparently, she knows Lady Sykeston isn't here."

"I'm still not receiving." Jonathan's voice deepened in warning.

The impertinent butler smiled slightly. "You miss your wife. The staff misses your wife. Even your dog misses your wife. You need to see Miss Howell. Think of it as taking your medicine when you're ill. You'll feel better afterward."

"Fine." It was easier to relent to the butler's demands than continue to argue with him. Frankly, Jonathan was curious why Beth would even come to see him, especially after their parting.

In minutes, North had escorted the woman into his study.

"Good morning, Beth," he called out as he carefully made his way to her side. The pinched looked on her face made him take notice. "Are Constance and Aurelia well?"

"They're fine," she murmured.

Jonathan's brow creased. "Pardon my bluntness, but why are you here?"

"May I?" She waved to a chair in front of his desk. After he nodded, she seated herself. "I'd forgotten to thank you."

Jonathan sat behind his desk. What the devil was this woman about? He wanted to ask about Constance, not delve into proper manners. "You have me at a loss."

"For killing a man." She smiled sweetly.

Completely stunned at such a subject, he sat motionless. "Whom are you referring to?"

"Your duel with the Earl of Aulton," she said stoically. "You see, after your sister passed and before anyone had known Aulton caused her death, my brother signed a marriage settlement with him. I was to wed him within the month. Once St. John discovered that the earl killed your sister, he couldn't rescind the contract." Finally, her icy veneer melted, and she gasped for breath. "I wouldn't be sitting here if it wasn't for you. Simply put, you saved my life. Aulton would have taken my dowry, spent it, then he'd have killed me too."

The room quieted as she composed herself.

"As you can imagine, it's a painful memory for me," Jonathan said quietly.

"You're an honorable man," she said softly. "My brother . . . had other concerns. His racehorses, for instance."

What she didn't say told another story. "I had no idea you were involved with Aulton."

She nodded. "Your action is something I'll never forget. I'm forever grateful. Now it's my turn to repay the favor." She arched a brow. "My brother has called me back to London. Normally, I'd ignore such a request, but he's threatening to announce my engagement if I don't return. Seems he's found a wealthy peer who will take me off his hands."

"You're of age, I assume?"

Beth nodded. "Twenty-five as of last month. My brother still tries to convince me that being a spinster isn't for the faint of heart. He says that being in trade is beneath me." She wrinkled her nose.

Jonathan leaned forward and rested his elbows on his desk to watch her closer. The slight nuances of her expression told more than she was sharing. The woman's life seemed to be careening out of control, everything at sixes and sevens.

"I enjoy being productive. Because of your wife's work on my behalf, I'll be able to continue if I can find my dowry."

"My wife has too much work as it is." A resigned sigh escaped. But that was Constance. She never refused those who needed her help, including him. That was until he pushed her away because he'd been too much of a coward to accept what life had dealt him. She had a true gift of bringing love and light into his world. She made him feel human. For some unbelievable reason, she'd chosen him to marry. He was the beneficiary of all her bountiful gifts—a family and love.

"She does enjoy her work. Sometimes to the extremes," Beth agreed. "But she took the time for me and organized the receipts Meriwether left the three of us. I'm going to find out what happened to our dowries and take them back. For once and for all, I'll be free of my brother's machinations."

"I wish you luck," he said. "But I still don't know why you're telling me this tale."

She smiled. "Because your wife took the time to take care of me. That's what she does. She takes care of the people she cares about. Me, Venetia, Katherine, Aurelia, and *you*."

He was well aware of that fact. He closed his eyes. His entire body ached from missing Constance. Having her near centered him. It always had. Letting her walk out of this room and his life had been the biggest mistake he'd ever made.

His guest tilted her head. "Did you know that your wife has been hounded by the Marquess of Faladen for close to three weeks now?"

Slowly, he leaned back in his chair, careful not to divulge his surprise. Yet his anger reignited all his feelings of loathing. He squeezed the arm of his chair until his knuckles turned white. "What do you mean, 'hounded'?"

Beth mimicked his movement but lightly thrummed her fingers on the arm of the chair. "His yacht capsized because he ran it ashore, but he's blaming Lysander & Sons. He's instructed his solicitor to hire a barrister." By the brief flare of her nostrils, she was livid. "Technically, he'll have to take her trust to court, but it makes little difference. It's Constance's property, and he wants it."

The idea that his wife was being badgered by a man such as Faladen raised his hackles. Immediately, Regina sensed his change in mood and came to his side. Idly, he ran his fingers through her soft fur.

Jonathan breathed heavily. That was why her employees had come to see her that day. Lord High and Mighty was the marquess, a perfect epithet for the scoundrel. Jonathan ground his teeth to refrain from roaring his fury. "Do you know more?"

"Constance plans on seeing him. She's desperate to convince him to see reason. In my opinion, facts don't seem to matter to Faladen." She leaned forward in her chair. "She didn't tell you because she thought it would be an extra burden on your marriage. She didn't want you to worry and go off half-cocked like one of your firearms." Beth sniffed her displeasure. "But you managed that yourself at our last dinner. You proved one thing that night. Your bark is worse than your bite."

Jonathan groaned at the mention of that dinner. "I apologize for my behavior."

Beth smiled. "It's Constance who deserves your apology." Her gaze became razor-sharp. "What she really needs is someone who cares deeply enough to stand beside her not only during this turmoil but for all her days including the ordinary ones. That person could be you."

Like a flash, the smoke cleared from Jonathan's thoughts. When Constance had first come to Portsmouth, he'd been lying to himself when he'd tried to keep his heart distant from hers. He'd loved her since that first kiss. He'd been a fool to leave her and go off to war. He'd squandered another opportunity when he hadn't sought her company when he'd returned home. It was a stroke of fortune—a gift—that Constance was his wife, and he'd be damned before he'd let anyone, including Faladen, take advantage of or harm her.

"No one will bully my wife or hurt her company." He would call on Faladen before joining his wife when she visited the marquess. That's what a good husband would do— lend support and protect his wife.

He should have visited the marquess much earlier. Now,

with the invoices, he planned to confront him over the court-martial.

He was late, but it was better than never.

Beth relaxed slightly. "You're the logical choice. Besides being her husband, you were the only one she trusted to help with Aurelia at night. She confided that you had nudged her about her worries about Faladen but she didn't share them. Hopefully, what I've imparted will bring you back together and you'll both learn to share more." She stood and gathered her things. "I know affection when I see it. Kat and Randford have it. Constance has it for you. I think you have the same for her. Don't prove me wrong."

Jonathan wouldn't comment on his deep affection for his wife. That conversation was for Constance only. He'd once believed that if he succeeded in creating a marksman's academy or a perfect cartridge he'd have a place in the world—for lack of a better term—a legacy showing that his life had meant something even if everything went awry. Such a belief was akin to another lie, one he'd used to protect himself from the hurt and anguish he'd experienced since he'd been home. Constance had said the same thing.

His real legacy would be creating a family with Constance, loving Aurelia, and living the best life he possibly could with them. Whatever he had to do to convince Constance he wanted a full life with her, he vowed to do—no matter how difficult it was.

He walked around the desk. "What about you and Grayson?"

Her smile slowly disappeared. "It was never meant to be," she said wistfully. "I always prided myself on my ability to move forward in life without regrets. Whatever ramifications resulted from my past, I accept them. I make the best of any situation." She grew silent for a moment before she spoke again. "I was forced to give Grayson up a long time ago. I can't go back, and it's in both of our interests that we don't revisit the past." Her voice wobbled slightly. "The marquess had wanted to court me when we were younger, but my brother had sent him on his way. In some ways our attachment mirrored yours with Constance, only we'll never marry. He needs an heiress. I need funds myself." She stared at the floor.

Jonathan stayed silent as she wrestled with her emotions. When she finally lifted her gaze to his, he spoke. "Thank you. You're a true friend to Constance. And me. Before you go, may I offer my assistance with your brother?"

With a sad smile, she shook her head. "My brother is as big a wastrel as Meriwether ever was. But my brother is family, and I love him. He has a hard time seeing that what he perceives as a solution to a nonexistent problem causes more harm than good."

Jonathan came to stand beside Beth. "I'm in your debt. If there's anything I can do for you in the future, don't hesitate to ask."

"There's one thing you can do." She reached up on her tiptoes and pressed a kiss against his cheek. "Give Constance a happy life."

Jonathan escorted Beth to the door, where North met her in the hallway. As their voices grew distant, Jonathan walked to the courtyard.

As always, his thoughts drifted to Constance. Through her hard work, the courtyard had been transformed. He'd never seen it so inviting. Lush greens and native flowers vied for attention. Constance had completely renovated the space with her own unique tastes. Everywhere he looked, he saw her.

An intolerable heaviness filled his heart. God, he missed her and Aurelia. Always before, he had accepted loneliness as his due. Since Constance had come back into his life, things had gone from dismal to bright. He vowed not to waste his life and the chance to love her. He would do his best to win

Constance back. He'd prove to her that her love meant the world to him, and he'd show her how much he loved her.

He may not be able to accomplish what he needed to do, but she deserved his best effort. She deserved his love. Before he asked her to come home to him, he was going to fix his life.

He only hoped he had enough time.

Chapter Thirty

❦

Constance stepped from the coach with the assistance of a Faladen footman who had been waiting for her arrival. She'd sent a note last week asking to visit, and the marquess had answered immediately with instructions to come today. Her stomach roiled at the prospect of seeing him again. What if he refused to listen to reason? She released a stilted breath and walked forward.

A modest neoclassical country home stood before her. Constance couldn't help but compare it to Sykeston Gardens. Faladen's home appeared bleak and drab whereas Sykeston Gardens majestically demanded one's attention.

She stopped for a moment and closed her eyes as the ache in her heart made it unbearable to walk. Sykeston Gardens wasn't her home anymore. She suppressed the compulsion to cry out, but it was becoming more and more difficult to ignore the urge. Jonathan was the root cause, and even thinking his name hurt.

Aurelia missed Jonathan. She cried for "Da" every night before falling asleep, another reminder that Jonathan was gone from both of their lives. Constance's aching heart was the worst at night, when she realized Jonathan wasn't beside her.

When she climbed the steps to the front door, the Faladen butler opened it without her knocking. Several liveried footmen stood at attention.

"Welcome, Lady Sykeston. His lordship is waiting," the butler announced. "If you'll follow me."

She nodded, all the while wondering if Daniel had felt the same as she did when he faced the lion's den. She stood tall and tilted her chin as she followed the butler to the marquess's study. She would not allow Lord Faladen to upset her anymore.

"My lord, Lady Sykeston is here." The butler bowed, then shut the door.

"Come in, my lady." Faladen stood from his desk and walked to her. He executed a deep bow, then slowly rose in an elaborate gesture normally reserved for formal ceremonies or when one met the royal family. "It's an honor."

Immediately, she became suspicious. "Thank you for seeing me."

"Let us chat over here." He waved his hand to a lovely sitting area in front of the fireplace. Though it wasn't chilly, a small fire blazed, giving the austere room a little warmth.

She sat in the chair he'd indicated and smoothed the skirts of her gown. It gave her hands something to do as she glanced around the room. Everything was cream or off-white and very impersonal. The gilded Louis XV furniture was overbearingly ostentatious yet beautiful at the same time. It was the type of room where children weren't welcome, and dogs couldn't enter. She shivered slightly. It was completely the opposite of Jonathan's study.

Enough. She had other business to attend to. She clasped her hands in her lap in a sign that she was ready to proceed.

The marquess sat on the edge of the cream settee directly across from her. "Lady Sykeston, since your last letter, I've taken the opportunity to contemplate—"

A gunshot rent the air.

"What the devil?" The marquess stood and called for his footmen. "If you'll pardon me, I need to see what's occurring outside. I've had reports of poachers on the estate."

Constance nodded.

The footmen entered. Without giving any further explanation, the marquess exited the room through the doors leading to the formal gardens, and his footmen followed.

Whoever the suspected poacher was, she hoped he fled. She wanted this confrontation over and done with. For an absurd moment, she considered whether it was Jonathan.

It couldn't be.

Jonathan retrieved one of the dueling pistols from its case. By rote, he loaded the shot and powder, then primed the firing mechanism. "Now what to shoot."

He glanced around the bountiful garden and discovered the perfect target, an apple core left standing on the edge of a fountain. It was approximately forty yards away. He hmphed silently. There was hardly any wind, making the shot extremely easy. He aimed, then decided to turn his head so that he didn't look directly at the target. Instead, he devoted his focus to the balcony exit of the marquess's study. He pulled the trigger. The blast rang in his ear. Smoke mixed with the pungent smell of sulfur floated through the air. When he turned to see the result, he smiled.

The remains of the apple were gone.

Exactly three seconds later, as planned, an agitated marquess stood outside his study overlooking the balcony. "What the devil are you doing?"

"Good," Jonathan murmured to himself. That was just a preview of the distress the marquess would soon experience if Jonathan had anything to do with it. With an ease acquired from performing the task routinely, he quickly cleaned the flintlock. "Faladen, I thought to take a little target practice."

The marquess stormed across the manicured lawn with two footmen following. "What is the meaning of this?"

Jonathan ignored their approach and prepared another shot.

By then, the marquess and his footmen had reached Jonathan's side.

"The Earl of Sykeston," one of the footmen mumbled.

"No need to announce me. The marquess knows me and my reputation well." Jonathan pointed the pistol toward the fountain. "Faladen, pick a target. The harder the better."

"Have you taken leave of every one of your senses?" the marquess exclaimed.

When the footmen took a step to remove Jonathan, he lifted a brow. "You don't want to do that."

Both halted at the menace in his words. Their gazes flew to the marquess.

With a resigned sigh, Faladen nodded to both. "You may resume your duties."

After bowing to Jonathan then Faladen, the pair left without another word.

"What is this about?" The marquess's cheeks were a brilliant red, as if he was either scared or thoroughly irritated.

"Humor me," Jonathan cajoled. "Pick a target and make it difficult."

"That apple tree." The marquess pointed to a small tree at least a hundred yards away. He smirked with an assuredness that meant he doubted Jonathan's ability to hit the bull's-eye. "There's a single green apple on the lowest branch."

The color of the small, unripened fruit blended into the background of the grass behind it. A difficult shot, but one that Jonathan would make.

"Excellent choice."

"You'll never make it," Faladen boasted.

"Now, why would you say that?" Jonathan's gaze bored straight through the marquess. "I'm not the same man you saw the last time I called upon you. And I've come to realize you're not the same man I thought you were," he added sardonically. "Shall we wager on the shot?"

Faladen brought his hand to his heart as if Jonathan had stabbed him. "I don't wager anymore. What . . . what do you want?"

Jonathan had hit another bull's-eye with that remark and grinned. "For you to grant my wish if I hit that target."

"And if I don't?" Faladen asked.

"There are other ways to receive satisfaction." Jonathan eyed the tree as he took notice of a sudden wind gust.

"You seem mighty sure of yourself." Faladen took a step back. Whether to escape the smoke that would result from the shot or fear made little difference.

"I've discovered that being married to my wonderful wife has turned my ugliest beastly manners into something productive."

"Are you . . . challenging me to a duel?" The marquess's red cheeks had paled significantly.

"Where did that thought come from? Surely you aren't fearful. Perhaps feeling guilty?" He shook his head slightly. "Come now, there's nothing to be scared about. You've seen how unsteady I am on my leg."

"Your dueling case is open on that bench." Faladen pointed to the burl-wood box. "We both know that a limp has little effect on the outcome of a duel. It's the shot that counts." Faladen's voice trembled ever so lightly. "Tell me what you want."

"Two things." Jonathan aimed the pistol and narrowed one eye, lining up the shot through the sight. "You've endangered men by your actions." Even with the weight of the pistol, his hand remained incredibly steady. "I know about the bribes you've received from the Middleton Company."

"What are you about?" the marquess sputtered. "Is this some hoax for revenge?"

"I have the invoices." Out of the corner of Jonathan's eye, he saw the marquess visibly deflate.

"I don't believe you," Faladen said.

Jonathan shrugged. "Believe what you want. You've been involved with this scheme for months. I'm taking them to Peterson myself. If he doesn't listen, I'll go to his superior. More important, whatever legal actions you're preparing against my wife and her business, I suggest you take a hard look at the facts again before you proceed." He slowly turned his gaze to Faladen. "She has my full support to stop you any way she can."

Faladen seemed to come out of his fog and jeered. "You can't make the shot."

Without turning his gaze from Faladen, Jonathan delivered his cockiest smile and pulled the trigger. The blast pierced the peacefulness of the courtyard, sending birds skyward to escape the noise. A plume of smoke surrounded Jonathan and Faladen.

When the marquess's face turned the exact shade of ash as the remaining wafts of smoke, Jonathan felt an absurd surge of satisfaction.

He didn't need to look to know that it had been a bull's-eye.

"You'd best pull yourself together." Jonathan wiped the flintlock with a cloth, allowing it to cool, then in his usual efficient manner reloaded it. "As soon as I saw the invoices with payment to you, everything clicked into place. You lied about the charging order to push me out of the way for your bribery scheme."

Faladen's cheeks turned beet red.

"But what I haven't deduced is why you started the rumors about me in the first place. I hadn't even come up with the idea for the recruit training." Jonathan placed the loaded pistol in the case, then picked up the second one and proceeded to load it. When he gazed at Faladen, the marquess's mouth opened and closed like a trout on shore unsure how to get its next breath.

"Please. No duel."

"We'll need seconds. Call your footmen back. Forget the surgeon." Jonathan looked down the barrel of the pistol, lining up a shot in the distance. "I aim to kill."

"All right." Faladen's voice quivered. "Put down the pistol, I beg of you. Any marksman that failed to complete a mission I took note of. If they came from a wealthy family, I told them a charging order was coming. For a price, I'd keep it in my desk."

Jonathan gritted his teeth. "How many?"

Faladen put up his hands as if surrendering. "Two. You were a special case. With no family to speak of . . . you were an island. Your wealth made me take notice. You were someone I wanted to keep in my pocket for future . . . opportunities. Then, when you presented your idea for a special training program, I realized I could make money on a steady basis." He stared at the ground.

Jonathan lowered his voice. "Why do you need money?"

"I'm practically insolvent due to gambling losses. I've lost everything," Faladen groveled.

"Yes, you've sunken to a new low," Jonathan said. "You're going to lose even more before I'm finished with you. We'll discuss the rest of it inside." Jonathan carefully put the pistols away. He leaned against his case, then turned his hardened gaze to the marquess. "If we don't come to an accord in your study, we're using these pistols."

Faladen's eyes widened. "You don't know who's here."

Jonathan lifted an eyebrow.

"Your wife."

Chapter Thirty-One

Unable to sit still after hearing a second shot, Constance started to pace. She rehearsed her speech again as she waited for the marquess to return.

"My lady, how fortuitous that we're calling on Lord Faladen at the same time."

At the familiar voice of her husband, Constance turned on her heel. Jonathan entered the room followed by the marquess and his footmen.

"That will be all," the marquess directed his servants. Immediately, he sat at his desk, dipped a quill into the inkpot, then started writing something.

With an undeniable swagger in his gait, Jonathan made his way to her side, then bowed. "Lady Sykeston." Dressed in a black morning coat, buckskin breeches, and boots, Jonathan looked like a typical country gentleman. Completely at ease and smiling as if nothing were amiss, he took her hand, then reverently brought it to his lips. "You are my pleasure." His voice almost a whisper. "You captivate me."

Her eyes had to be popping out of her head. Her husband, a self-described recluse, was handsomely dressed for a social call and stood before her in the Marquess of Faladen's study holding her hand and acting as if he was totally besotted with her.

"What are you doing here?" she murmured.

"I want to be a supportive husband and stand by your side." He looked to the seat next to hers. "Actually, I'll be sitting by your side in a minute. Why don't you sit first, then I'll take my seat."

She did as he suggested, but her gaze slid sideways. It was inconceivable that he was here . . . for her. The man who refused to see visitors or guests. Yet here Jonathan was in the room, giving her a nod of encouragement.

She forced her attention to the marquess, who had finished with whatever he was composing. Serious issues were afoot, and she couldn't be distracted by her husband—at least not until everything was settled. "Lord Faladen, I sent two of my best employees to the Isle of Wight to examine your yacht. Your ship capsized because you ran aground on a rocky shoal and twisted the hull out of true. It wasn't because of my company's workmanship or the quality of our products. If you don't drop your ridiculous and frivolous legal action, I'll have no recourse but to return the favor. Like you, my solicitor has hired a barrister on behalf of my trust. I have witnesses that will tell the truth of what happened. Once I win, then I plan to bring suit against you for slander and defamation."

Jonathan leaned in her direction with a secret smile.

Immediately, she wondered if he was taking care of himself. Though he was impeccably dressed, there were dark circles under his eyes, and his waistcoat hung a bit loose as if he'd not been eating.

"Brava, madam," he whispered for her ears only. "You have him right where you want him . . . under your heel."

"I owe you an apology for my past transgressions." Unaware of Jonathan's murmurs, Faladen cleared his throat and turned to Jonathan.

Jonathan shook his head. "There's no need to address me. This is my wife's business."

Faladen nodded, then turned to her. "This isn't easy for me, my lady." His smile appeared remorseful. "I must beg your forgiveness for spreading such rumors." He handed her the piece of foolscap that he'd written on. "I'll have this printed as a leaflet and posted throughout town."

She scanned the paper then slowly raised her gaze to his. "It's a full apology for casting rumors about Lysander & Sons' work. It's a complete admission that the rumors you spread weren't based in fact." She narrowed her eyes. "Why are you giving me this? Based upon what you've written here, I could bring a suit against you now and win."

"I'm aware of that," he said softly. "Whatever you see fit." His lips thinned. "I will call on the Hartfelds this morning and ask if they'd return their business to you. I'll also direct my solicitor and barrister to stop all work on the suit."

"What does the Hartfeld family have to do with this?" The coolness in Jonathan's voice made Faladen visibly tremble.

"They're longtime customers we lost because of Lord Faladen's accusations," Constance answered.

"Really?" Her husband's brow furrowed as his gaze met Faladen's.

Immediately, the marquess's knee started to bounce up and down.

Constance leaned back against the chair as she let the newfound sense of satisfaction sink in. Let Lord *High and Mighty* stew over his actions for a while longer. "Why did you start the rumors in the first place?"

He shook his head slightly. "Are you aware that your first husband liked to gamble?"

She didn't move a muscle, though the words were a direct punch in the stomach.

A muscle jumped in Jonathan's jaw, a tell of how irritated he was at the mention of Meri.

"He was many things," she answered. She didn't belabor the point that Meriwether had excelled at collecting wives and dowries. Not to mention, he'd been a consummate liar, gambler, spendthrift, and connoisseur of racehorses and erotic art.

"In a game of whist, he won a chalk mine from me. A very valuable piece of property. It provided a steady income. I shouldn't have risked it, but I was deep in my cups. My emotions got the best of me, Lady Sykeston. I thought if I put pressure on your business, perhaps you'd give it back to me. That's why I asked if Lord Meriwether had left you any other assets. I even directed my solicitor to contact yours for information. I offer you my most humble apology and beg your forgiveness."

"I wasn't aware my first husband had won such a thing from you." Suddenly dizzy, she closed her eyes for a moment until the sensation passed. Why should she be surprised at Meri's chicanery. She'd been through the receipts Meriwether had left all the wives. There were mine leases, but she never found any deeds to a chalk mine. "Perhaps you should check with his half brother, the Duke of Randford."

"I'll leave it be. It's a hard lesson to learn. I don't gamble anymore." He crossed and uncrossed his legs in obvious discomfort, then looked to Jonathan. "I've lost everything."

She hadn't noticed until this moment how wet his brow had become. He was actually nervous being in their company.

"Thank you for your time." Constance stood slowly.

Jonathan slowly stood after her. "Darling, if I could beg a few more moments with the marquess to finish my business, I'd appreciate it."

She returned to her seat, and Jonathan followed.

The marquess didn't look at either of them. "I'm truly sincere in my apology. If you'd accept it, I'd be forever in your debt."

She slid her glance to Jonathan. There was only one explanation for the marquess's nervousness and easy acquiescence. "Did my husband challenge you to a duel?"

"No." Faladen shook his head. His eyes grew red, and they glistened with tears.

"Of course I didn't." Jonathan smiled at her, then turned his attention to the marquess. "As a matter of fact, I never mentioned the word *duel*."

The marquess's wide-eyed gaze was glued to Jonathan. "Please don't worry about Middleton. I'll see that I repair what I've broken and repay the amounts."

Jonathan stood slowly. "It's too late. I'm taking the evidence to Colonel Peterson." Jonathan let out a breath. "You've gone too far. To trifle with a man's honor is despicable. To manipulate two brave men who served under you should be a capital offense." He turned to Constance. "Come, my dear." He offered his arm.

Soon they were outside. Jonathan's carriage had pulled directly behind hers. When her gaze landed on his, he greeted her with a warm smile. It reminded her of the one he'd bestowed when he left her all those years ago.

He took both of her hands in his and his gaze slid down the length of her body, then back up. "You are more beautiful than the last time I saw you."

Heat raced across her cheeks as her heart fluttered in her chest, desperate to reach him. Instead, she stepped away, keeping her voice steady. "What's going on?"

Jonathan reluctantly let go of her hands. "May we speak privately in your carriage?"

She nodded, then they made their way to the carriage without another word.

He opened the door, then held out his hand. Though she should refuse his touch, she still felt a little light-headed from meeting Faladen. Jonathan's warm hand was steady as she stepped into the carriage. After she settled into the forward-facing bench, Jonathan placed his cane in the carriage, then grabbed the sides of the coach and made his way beside her, closing the door behind him.

"Faladen?" Everything seemed to be crashing together like two rushing rivers colliding. Constance's life had taken such drastic turns over the last few days. The meeting with the marquess was successful, but leaving her husband had left her life in shambles. Yet here he sat beside her.

Jonathan didn't wait for her to complete her thought. He cupped her cheeks and stared at her face, his earlier humor replaced with alarm. "Are you unwell? Your cheeks are red."

She placed her hand on his wrist, the feel of his strength so familiar. She meant to push him away. Instead, she held him as if he were keeping her above water. "I'm a little overwhelmed. I was prepared for a fight. I vowed not to let him take advantage."

"You didn't."

"None of this is what I expected today." From nowhere, her body started to tremble, and she clenched her teeth so tightly, her jaw hurt.

"Constance," Jonathan said softly, the sound of her name an endearment on his lips. He scooted closer, and she suddenly found herself in his embrace. "It's all right," he crooned softly. "You were magnificent in how you handled him. You did it." His voice was smooth and steady while his hand slowly skated up and down her back.

She didn't know what to do. Meriwether had made her distrustful. Jonathan's lies about the letters had made her doubt even more, but now he was breaking through her defenses. He was here supporting her as a partner, sitting beside her giving her strength. Yet things that had been so simple between them before were now complicated. She half expected him to kiss her. In response, she stiffened. Instead of such intimacy, he just held her, not tightly but tenderly. She buried her nose in his morning coat and breathed deeply. His familiar scent made her homesick, and she gasped slightly.

He continued to hold her and lightly rested his chin on top of her head. "It's all right," he repeated. His nose nestled against her hair. His fingers ran down the length of her spine then back up. He repeated the comforting gesture until she relaxed.

She couldn't pull away, not when she'd craved his touch. How she'd longed to be held by him. Comforted by him. It was as if by holding her, Jonathan acknowledged his troth to her.

After a while, he leaned back. She wanted to protest, but then he cupped her cheeks again. "Better?"

She forced herself to create more distance between them. "I can't believe you're here. How did you know he was threatening my company?"

"Beth. She came to see me."

"My Beth?" Constance asked incredulously.

He nodded. "She explained how difficult it was for you." Back and forth, his thumb caressed her cheek gently, the touch soothing. "Faladen was the one who stole my idea for an elite training school for marksmen. I found out that he took bribes from some of the suppliers. He used soldiers and officers like me for financial gain. I happened to be at the wrong place at the wrong time. There was no charging order about to be filed. What makes me so angry?" He shook his head slightly. "I let him define me when he said I was weak and wretched. I regret all those wasted days. I should have pressed to have the accusations aired." He gazed deep into her eyes, the emotions swirling in their brown depths. "But when Beth told me what he'd done to you, I was so livid I had to see him."

Constance pulled back even more. "Did you intimidate him on my account?"

He shrugged with a devil-may-care smile. "I may have loaded my dueling pistols in front of him." He lowered his voice. "Knowing he was threatening you drove me to act. It's what I had to do for you."

She closed her eyes and concentrated on his touch.

"I want to be the man you trust. A man who deserves your love," he whispered.

God, how she missed him. If only it was true what he said. She stood frozen except for a tear that fell and collided with his thumb. Neither acknowledged it. He continued to stroke her skin.

"For a man who prefers to grunt, you're certainly having little trouble being eloquent," she murmured.

He laughed softly. "I've had a lot of time on my hands to think about what I wanted to say. Are you angry I joined you today?"

His deep voice swept through her, tangling her thoughts. "No." She opened her eyes. "Thank you."

"My pleasure." A corner of his mouth tipped into a grin. "I enjoyed seeing Faladen capitulate to your demands. This was all your doing today. It had nothing to do with me, or with people thinking I have an itchy trigger finger."

But he still possessed the uncanny ability to hit the bull's-eye of her heart at fifty paces.

His face didn't betray his thoughts, but a muscle ticked in his jaw. He took a deep breath and exhaled. "The bloody bastard," he said softly. "His foolishness has hurt a lot more people than you and I. He must pay."

She glanced outside briefly. She ached knowing that all the worry and angst Jonathan had suffered was a result of the marquess. "I'm sorry, Jonathan."

Jonathan placed his hand over hers. "What for?"

"Faladen." She cleared her throat and returned her attention to her husband. Another tear fell. "He made your life miserable."

"But you brought me joy." Jonathan squeezed her hand. "If we discover there are any more Meriwethers or Faladens in our future, we'll deal with them together."

"Jonathan"—she glanced at their hands—"I'm unsure if I'm ready to come home." She swiped another tear from her face.

"May I ask for another chance? I miss you. I miss our daughter."

Her heart skipped a beat at the words. "That's the first time you've called her 'our daughter.'"

"No, it isn't. Since the first time I held her, I've considered her my daughter . . . if you'll allow it." Before she said another word, he tangled his fingers with hers and rested their hands in his lap. He leaned close and rested his brow against hers. "Constance, I need to tell you something."

"What is it?" Her insides tightened in preparation.

"North considers himself a cupid of sorts. He must have received divine inspiration from those damnable cherubs in my study. I'm not trying to make excuses for his actions, but I beg of you not to be angry with him." He pulled away, cupping her cheeks with his hands. "He loves me, Constance." He closed his eyes as his face betrayed his pain. "Besides you . . . he's the only one."

"Oh, Jonathan," Her voice broke at his words. He'd endured so much loneliness in his life.

He leaned back and took her hands in his. His eyes were red. "That year we were apart was my self-imposed hell. I read every one of your letters at least fifty times. Each gave me strength during my darkest hours. Sometimes, I stayed up all night just reading them over and over. It was as if I held a piece of your heart in my hands. I never told you the truth about the letters because I was afraid . . . you'd leave me." He studied their clasped hands. "I never, ever wanted to hurt you or Aurelia. I want Aurelia as my daughter."

A tear fell down his cheek.

It ripped her own heart apart.

"I want *you* as my wife. More than anything." He squeezed her hands. "Give me a chance to repair your broken heart."

She cupped his cheek with one hand. "It's all right. I forgive you."

"I never thought I'd have this . . . you as my wife, a woman who loved me unconditionally. I know I betrayed your trust, and I'm profoundly sorry. The monumental strength you possess to forgive me leaves me in awe." He shook his head slowly, as if grappling with his emotions. After a moment, he continued, "You"—he pressed a kiss to her temple—"are my inspiration. I've learned so much from you."

By now, her own tears fell. The pain that flashed across his face was raw and jagged.

"There's something else." He squeezed his eyes shut. Slowly, he opened them. His eyes searched her face as if cataloging her every feature. "I must go to London," he said softly.

"For Colonel Peterson?" she asked.

"Yes. Faladen has ruined lives. He almost ruined me. But luckily, I had you to help guide me. I want to return to the man I once was." He dipped his head and held her gaze. "*I'm not leaving you.*" His eyes uncertain she'd believe him. "That is . . . if you'll have me, Constance Lysander." He said her name as if a prayer.

"It's Sykeston now," she said through her tears.

Jonathan smiled. "Your husband is a lucky man." He brought their clasped hands to his mouth and pressed a kiss. "You said I was hiding. I don't want to hide anymore. I want to be out in the world with you, living a full life. I want to be by your side experiencing everything, all the joys and heartache, with you."

She sobbed silently and grabbed his lapels, determined not to let him go.

"I don't know when I'll return, but I have to see that

Faladen receives justice. So I need a few things from you." He cupped her cheeks with his hands, his eyes never leaving hers. "Will you take care of Regina while I'm gone?"

She nodded.

"Will you take care of our daughter . . . and yourself?"

"Yes." She bit her lip hoping she wouldn't sob.

"Here's the last thing, darling. I *need* you to believe that I will never leave you. I can't leave for London otherwise."

She closed her eyes, and another tear escaped. Eventually, she could speak again. "I believe you."

He pressed his forehead to hers. "I'm going to try my damnedest to come home quickly, and I hope you'll wait for me." A tear fell down his face, and remarkably, he didn't brush it aside. It was a testament to how deeply he felt about her and their future together. "You told me I can't change if I don't try. I'm ready to try now."

Before she could say a word, he pressed a reverent kiss to her forehead, one to the tip of her nose, and finally, his lips settled gently against hers. She could taste the salt from his tears, and she knew he was ready to depart Portsmouth.

"You were the one that kept me alive in that field hospital when I wanted to die. Your voice, your words, your kindness, they stayed with me, comforting me. When death came to take me, you pulled me back." He brushed his nose against hers, the act endearingly intimate. "You should know that North didn't send the perambulator and the note. That was from me," he whispered against her lips. "All me to you."

Without another word, he carefully climbed down the carriage. She watched every step he took, memorizing his movements and the way his black locks shone in the sunlight. Her chest and heart seized when he disappeared from sight.

He never told her he loved her.

She didn't need those three words. Because his other words kindled hope and reassurance that he'd come back to her. Constance pressed her hand against her stomach in a desperate attempt to keep from fainting and took the deepest breath she could manage. She closed her eyes when his carriage drove away.

Strangely, when Meri had left her, she'd suffered something completely different, a sterile nothingness. She'd known deep in her heart that her first husband wasn't coming back—ever. There was only one reason why this time felt completely unlike last time.

This was Jonathan, and he'd told her his plans. Another tear fell, and she brushed it away. She loved him and would keep her faith in his words.

He said he wasn't leaving her. It was enough.

Chapter Thirty-Two

⌬

Jonathan's confidence was getting stronger by the day, but he still had work to do. That's why he was at Randford's home, and why he'd been there visiting weekly for the last month.

The butler greeted him at the door, then escorted Jonathan to Randford, who'd been waiting for him.

"Sykeston, come in." Randford stood from his desk and made his way to Jonathan's side. Before Jonathan could stick out his hand, his old friend had wrapped him in a bear hug and patted his back. "It's good to see you."

By then Grayson had come to his side. "Sykeston."

Jonathan held out his hand and the marquess took it, but a troubled look dulled his gray eyes. "Grayson. Actually, it's good to see you both." He turned to Randford. "It's finally over."

"Let's sit down." Randford preceded them to a sitting area that looked over the Rand House courtyard. It was a riot of color from the duke's roses. He was an excellent gardener and found comfort in working with his roses.

Then and there, Jonathan decided he'd try his hand at something similar. Perhaps he and Constance could renovate another part of the lawn surrounding his house with his mother's wildflowers. It would be a safer place for Aurelia to play. He released a deep breath. He hadn't seen his wife in two months. If there was one infirmity that he'd suffered without relief while in London, it was missing his wife. It seemed an eternity.

"Tell us everything," Randford said. "The story was in the papers daily."

"Faladen was relieved of duty. The Prince Regent was informed, and Faladen will face a court-martial for behavior unbecoming of a gentleman." Jonathan smiled when Grayson's eyes widened. "For the first time in ages, I feel empowered. Coincidentally, I finally received a letter from Jean Davout. He declared that Faladen was a liar and that I never ran from him. He signed it *Until we meet again*."

"Good for you," Randford said softly. He reached over and grabbed Jonathan's shoulder, then squeezed. "What does your lovely wife think about this? Will she come to London?"

He paused for a moment before answering. He'd been horrid to the two men in this room, his best friends, but they still treated him with concern and affection. He was lucky to have them in his life.

"Constance is in Portsmouth. I told her I had to see this through before I could return to her." Jonathan held up his hand at his friends' shocked faces. "She moved back to her parents' home the day that you left for Brighton. It shook me to the core. However, I vow to win her back."

There was something cathartic telling something so intimate to his friends. Constance had taught him that. How to give more of himself to others.

Randford nodded, but Grayson seemed preoccupied with other matters.

"I meant to mention this earlier. You'll both be surprised to hear who came to see me after you left."

"Who?" Randford asked.

"Beth Howell."

Grayson whipped his head around. His gazed honed to Jonathan's face. "When was this?"

Jonathan furrowed his brow. "About four days after you left Sykeston Gardens. Why?"

"Tell him," Randford coaxed.

Grayson let out a pained breath. "Beth's brother has become unbearable to her."

From the first time Jonathan had seen her, Beth Howell seemed confident with a good head on her shoulders. "She's of age, and she's the partner in a successful business with the Duchess of Randford. I can't imagine her ever being obsequious to her brother. Why doesn't she move away from him?"

"Her brother claims he hasn't been well and needs her to stay at home with him. I wager he needs money again." Grayson possessed the look of a defeated man.

"Is there anything I can do?" Jonathan leaned forward in his chair.

Grayson cracked a smile. "No, my friend. But I appreciate the offer."

"Sykeston," Randford said softly. "When are you going home?"

Jonathan turned his gaze to the duke. "Soon, but I need to talk to your valet, if possible." Randford's valet, Jacob Morgan, had lost an eye during a battle. He met with Jonathan several times a week to discuss their time in the military.

"Jacob?" Randford's scowl turned into curiosity. "If you're looking to hire him away, he won't leave. He's loyal not only to me, but to Kat and her companion as well."

Jonathan shook his head. "It's nothing like that. I still have my same valet. Though sometimes I wonder how he ever stayed with me through all those years." He grew solemn. "Jacob and I have been meeting several times a week. For the first time since I left the war, I'm talking about my experiences. It's cathartic to discuss it with someone who's been through what I have. I hope to do the same with you, Rand-ford. I'll soon be ready to go home to Constance."

"War left its mark on all of us." The duke smiled, but understanding shone in his eyes. "Jacob's upstairs with Willa. Shall I call him? You can meet in the formal salon."

Jonathan smiled. "That would be kind of you. I hope you can join us."

Randford nodded and smiled. "It would be my honor."

Jonathan felt a rush of affection for the duke. He turned to his other friend. "Grayson, will you come too?"

The marquess smiled. "I thought you'd never ask."

~

"Ma'am?" Dahlia knocked on the sitting room door balancing a chipper Aurelia on her hip. "If you don't mind me asking, what did the midwife say?"

"Mrs. Albertson confirmed it. She said everything was normal. My tiredness was to be expected." Constance had suspected she was carrying when she'd lost her usual energy and required daily naps. Some days, she even slept longer than Aurelia. "She'll come by again next week."

"Are you going to write Lord Sykeston?" Dahlia put a squirming Aurelia on the floor, and the baby made a beeline to Regina who was curled at Constance's feet.

"After the party." She smiled, then let out a silent sigh. She didn't want her condition to be the reason he came home. He wouldn't stay away if he thought she needed him. Not seeing him these past two months had been harder than she'd thought. But he'd written to her regularly asking after her and Aurelia. When she'd answered in return asking how he was faring, he'd always shared that being away from her and their family was one of the toughest things he'd ever done, his words heartfelt and real.

She only prayed that his work in London would be successful. She was anxious for them to start their life again.

A faint knock sounded on the front door.

"I'll go see who it is," Dahlia announced.

Constance nodded. When her gaze fell to Aurelia, the baby was curled up around the mastiff petting her as best she could. It was more like hard pats, but the dog wagged her tail, enjoying the attention.

Soon Dahlia reappeared. "Mr. North is here to see you." She picked up Aurelia, then kissed the baby's cheek. Aurelia returned the favor by smacking her lips against her nursemaid's ear.

As Constance looked at Aurelia with Dahlia, an overwhelming sense of gratitude swept over her. She would be forever in Dahlia's debt for the kindness, love, and patience she'd shown with Aurelia. These past few weeks, it had been impossible for Constance to do her fair share of taking care of her own baby. This pregnancy seemed to be taking a toll on her, but at least she was healthy. "Will you show him in?"

Dahlia nodded. "I'll take Miss Aurelia." The nursemaid left the room.

Constance turned her gaze to the view outside. It wasn't simply Dahlia whom she cherished. Kat and Beth had been there for her when she was troubled. Beth had even gone to Jonathan to ensure that he knew what was happening in Constance's life. Her love, her Jonathan, was a blessing in so many ways. He'd been beside her when she'd stood up to Faladen. How could she ever forget how wonderful he'd been with Aurelia. She had little doubt he'd be involved in the new baby's care too.

Life was so much easier when she allowed herself to rely on others. She didn't have to do everything on her own.

The English Channel was beautiful this afternoon with the

sun reflecting off the waves. Before she could become lost in the tranquility, a knock sounded on the door.

"Lady Sykeston, am I interrupting?" North's demeanor was still the suave and elegant butler, but a slight apprehension colored his expression.

Constance waved a hand. "No. Please join me and Regina. Dahlia has taken Aurelia for her afternoon nap." A nap sounded like heaven right now, but she stifled the yawn that threatened.

Mr. North nodded and took a seat beside her. "Everything is ready for tomorrow evening's party. Mrs. Walmer and the entire staff are abuzz with excitement for the event." He leaned as if divulging a secret. "I hope you'll save a dance for me."

Constance laughed. "I'd like that. I have high hopes the event will be a resounding success with all the staff at Sykeston Gardens helping me plan it. I know everyone at Lysander & Sons is looking forward to attending."

"Every tenant is attending, and the staff can talk of nothing else." Mr. North nodded once with a satisfied look on his face. "You're generous to host it, my lady. In years past, the harvest party was an expression of the Sykeston family's appreciation for their staff and tenants. You're continuing the tradition." Before Constance could reply, he continued, "I only wish Lord Sykeston were attending."

There was nothing she wanted more than for Jonathan to return to her, but he'd been correct. He had to finish his work. In his last letter he told her that Faladen had been relieved of all duties. But he hadn't mentioned anything about how the army was training the new recruits.

"My lady?" North's question broke through her reverie. "I've also come to apologize."

"Apologize? For what?"

The worry on the butler's face had reappeared. "We've never discussed it, but I wanted to apologize for writing as his lordship. I know that it's been an issue of contention between you and Lord Sykeston." He clasped his hands in his lap and stared at them as he twiddled his thumbs.

"Why did you do it?" she asked softly.

He had the good manners to look contrite. "He needed you. He was getting worse. I could see him retreating more and more from the world that he found unwelcoming. Please don't think he didn't want you. He was simply afraid." His quiet voice was laced with empathy. "Your husband believed that if he could stay in that study, he'd keep the world away. If it came too close, he'd attack like a wild animal, as you saw that night. Normally, he never cares about the carnage that he reaps. For the first time ever, he saw the costs when he saw your face."

She couldn't find fault with North. He'd done it to help Jonathan, a man the butler had lovingly watched over for so many years. Her eyes burned with unshed tears, and she blinked to keep them from falling.

"When you left, he discovered how far he'd fallen." He bowed deeply before her. "You're everything he wants. I beg of you to be patient with him."

After a moment, she could speak again. "Thank you, Mr. North."

"If there is anything I can do, please don't hesitate to ask. Again, I'm sorry."

His kindness wove a thread that helped mend a part of her broken heart. The only way for it to heal completely was if Jonathan came home to her reconciled with his past—and his future.

"Mr. North, we are in rare company." Her smile didn't hide her sadness. "We're the only ones whom he trusts, because we see his worth and his sorrow."

"Indeed." North stood, then pulled an envelope from a satchel he carried. "You received this from the Duke of Randford's solicitor. Until tomorrow, my lady. I'll see myself out."

Constance waited until she heard the faint click of the front door. She turned the letter over in her hand and broke the seal. Whatever it said, it wouldn't surprise her. It probably had something to do with a trust that the Duke of Randford wanted to establish for Aurelia. She scanned the letter, then reread it. She slowly lifted her hand to her chest and forced herself to take a deep breath. It was inconceivable.

Meriwether had assigned his interests in an iron ore mine to her. It had been forwarded to Mr. Hanes from a solicitor in Cumberland. She grappled with the words. "Ten thousand pounds has been deposited in your name at the London bank E. Cavensham Commerce. More to be forthcoming."

Chapter Thirty-Three

Instead of having the annual party at her parents' home, Constance had decided to host it at Sykeston Gardens. It was easier for the tenants and staff to attend. Lysander & Sons' employees were more than happy to come to the Earl of Sykeston's home, as the majority of them had never had the occasion to see the beautiful courtyards and gardens that surrounded the house. Even her best friends had arrived from London to help her celebrate. Kat, Randford, Beth, and Grayson were making merry with their full entourage and were staying with Constance at her parents' home. Mrs. Butler had been kind enough to send a few maids to help with the extra work.

The last notes of the country dance drew to a slow close, and with an exaggerated bow, James Selwyn released her hand. "Constance Lysander, you can be my dance partner any day." He winked her way as he led her back to the side of the dance floor.

"Thank you, James." Constance waved toward the refreshment table. "I believe Lucy brought out mulled wine as a treat for this evening." It was James's favorite drink, and Constance had asked Mrs. Walmer to prepare it.

James nodded, then headed toward the table.

After he left, Constance took a deep breath. The early-autumn flowers were in full bloom, and tiny lanterns hung from every available tree branch. It looked like a magical realm, a perfect wonderland where all sorts of mythical creatures would cavort through the night. Music wove its enchantment through the air, making Constance's foot tap in time with the delightful rhythms. Before the guests had arrived, Mrs. Butler had several footmen move the pianoforte outside, and the Sykeston housekeeper was beaming while sitting behind the instrument playing various dancing medleys. Mr. Bridges had brought his fiddle to play in accompaniment.

Mary Butler and Dahlia sidled up next to Constance. Both were out of breath, as they'd recently danced. Mary had partnered with a successful young farmer who appeared quite taken with her. Dahlia had danced with Thomas Winstead. It had been their second set of the evening.

"Ma'am, this night is . . ." Mary sighed her pleasure. Her eyes twinkled with an excitement that reminded Constance of her first dance in Portsmouth.

"Wonderful," Dahlia said. She waved a fan Constance had let her borrow in front of her face. "Neither of us has stopped dancing."

"That's what this party is for." Constance laughed and looked around. "A little celebration before the long winter settles in."

Earlier, Constance had danced with Randford, North, Alin, then James. Now she stood on the sidelines, clapping her hands. North had never left her side when she wasn't dancing.

It was a perfect evening except Jonathan wasn't there. Yet the good people before her deserved a night of celebration, and she planned to do her part and play the happy hostess.

She smiled as Randford held Aurelia in his arms, twirling

her around the makeshift dance floor of wooden planks. Kat stood on the other side of Constance and smiled while she held Arthur, bouncing him gently to the music.

Constance frowned slightly when her gaze caught a stoic Beth and Grayson, who were in the center of the dance floor. Suddenly smiling, Grayson said something, and Beth laughed aloud.

Kat leaned close. "Will they ever see how right they are for each other?"

Constance studied the two. "If only it were easy for them. The issue of money seems like a constant struggle for Beth. I offered her funds from the iron mine, but she refused."

Kat furrowed her brow. "Christian and I offered her money too. She said this time, she'd be the one to help herself."

By then, the song had come to an end, and Randford came to his wife's side still holding Aurelia. Mr. Bridges and Mrs. Butler stopped playing for a brief rest. At the same time, Regina, who'd been exiled from the refreshment table for stealing a meat pie, started barking as Aurelia screamed at the top of her lungs. When Regina dashed across the dance floor and up the terrace steps that lead to Jonathan's study, every guest turned their attention to follow her. Instantly, the entire courtyard grew quiet except for the occasional song of crickets.

Constance did the same. An uncontrollable gasp escaped as her hand flew to the middle of her chest. For a moment, she couldn't believe the sight before her. Her husband had finally arrived home, safe and sound.

At the top of the steps, Jonathan stood in formal evening wear with his gaze glued to hers. Only for a moment did he look away, when he greeted the whimpering Regina by his side. He wore that familiar sweet smile from their youth.

Constance's tears sprang from nowhere as the cheers of welcome rang out from their guests. Jonathan waved in greeting, but his tender gaze returned to hers.

Randford chuckled beside his wife. "We're going to see a bit of romance tonight, I wager."

"He looks determined," Kat said, then leaned close. "Go to him."

Constance shook her head slightly as if coming out of a trance. "I will." She hurried across the dance floor, then picked up her skirt when she reached the stairs. Slowly, she made her way to the top of the steps where he waited for her. He held out his hand, and she placed hers in his.

"Constance," he murmured, then brought her hand to his lips. "My darling wife." He squeezed her hand but didn't let go as he addressed the crowd. "I have a few things I'd like to share with all of you, if you'd be so kind."

~

Jonathan stood on the top step, unable to look away from Constance. The undeniable urge to sweep her in his arms and kiss her in front of the crowd filled him with nervous energy. More than anything, he wanted to claim her as his forever.

Two months away from Constance's side turned as painful as their earlier ten years apart. Frankly, a day without Constance would be as dark as the longest winter night.

"Jonathan," she whispered. "You're home."

"I am." He couldn't keep from touching her. He brought her hand back up to his mouth and held it there. The sweet softness of her skin, a beacon that he would always yearn to come home to.

"Tonight's the party. If I'd known you were arriving this evening, I'd have postponed it." Her eyes searched his. "Everyone is here, including Kat, Beth, Randford, and Grayson. Does that displease you?"

"No, darling. The more, the merrier." He glanced at the crowd and smiled. He lifted a hand in greeting. His perfect wife had created this festive atmosphere for the tenants and staff who had served their families for generations. Through their marriage, all of these people had come together. He stepped closer to her side. The questioning look in her eye humbled him. "What you've done here tonight is a beautiful sight, but it's nothing in comparison with you."

As he studied her face, he noticed several things. Her cheeks were reddened, the cause most likely dancing. Her lips were still as pink as he remembered. Perfect and perfectly kissable. Lastly, her familiar scent wove itself around him, locking him in place. There was no need. He'd never leave her side again if he could help it.

Still holding her hand, he announced to their guests, "I'm so happy you're here. If you'll indulge me, please?"

Murmurs spread through the crowd and rustling hummed in the air, but within seconds they all quieted. Everyone had moved closer to hear his words.

Jonathan took her other hand and faced Constance. From the corner of his eye, he could see North, who was practically floating in happiness. The butler nodded in support.

With a smile, Jonathan squeezed Constance's hands. In a loud, clear voice that their guests could hear, he spoke to the woman he cherished. "I love you for who you are, the kindest, gentlest, and most patient woman in the world. You're hardworking and generous to a fault. I'm the perfect example of your giving spirit. When I was at my worst, you stood by me, encouraging me while telling me when I was wrong."

Her eyes widened, and her breath hitched.

Tears clouded his eyes, but he didn't care if the whole world saw how much he valued and loved the woman who stood before him.

"I love who I become when I'm with you. I would never change you. You're my North Star. You've brought me home and given me back my life, Lady Sykeston."

She squeezed his hand. "I love you with all my heart."

"I want to be the man worthy to call myself your husband. I hope you'll give me that chance once again."

As cheers rang through the courtyard, tears fell down his wife's cheeks. Her hand flew to her mouth in utter disbelief. "All of that was from your list of how to pick an acceptable gentleman."

"I'm determined to be that man." Jonathan nodded to Mrs. Butler and Mr. Bridges. "Would you play a little something for me and my wife?" He turned to Constance. "May I have this dance?"

⁓

"Here? Are you sure?" Constance rested her hand on her chest, amazed that her husband had actually suggested such a thing.

"More than anything. I'll still use my cane," he whispered conspiratorially. "You did save a dance for me, didn't you?" He winked with a grin as he wrapped his arm around her waist. "You always said you'd save me a dance."

"I'd be honored," Constance said softly as her heart pounded to break out of her chest and reach him.

On cue, the music for a waltz started. Without taking his eyes from hers, Jonathan simply held her in one arm, supporting himself with his cane in the other. He swayed slightly in time with the music. They were the center of attention with everyone watching, and she'd never been more thrilled. "This is everything I've ever wanted, Jonathan."

He lifted a brow. "To dance with me in front of a crowd?"

"Stop teasing me."

He bent his head and whispered, "That's no fun, dearest. I'd never get to see that blush, the one you're wearing now."

By then, the rest of the crowd was on the makeshift dance floor and had joined in the fun.

"Let's stop," Constance said.

Jonathan did as she asked, but his brow furrowed. "Is something amiss?"

"No." Her tears of happiness flowed freely. "Everything I ever wanted was you. Us, to be a family." Without hesitating, she took his hand and pulled him into his study where they could be alone. Once inside, she closed the door. The music, now softer, drifted in through the windows. A single candle was lit inside, casting the room in a dreamy light. Jonathan took charge then and pulled her into a corner hidden away from prying eyes.

Resting his cane beside him, he leaned against the wall, then took her into his arms and simply gazed, drinking in her features. She did the same, stroking his cheek with her hand. It was hard to believe that she was in his embrace once again. Nothing had felt this right in a long while. He gently took her wrist and pressed a kiss to her pulse, the touch of his lips waking every sense. In answer, she stood on her tiptoes, then pressed her lips to his in a gentle kiss designed to reacquaint themselves with each other. A promise of their future together. Yet when his tongue swept across her lips, the burn that always ignited when they were alone threatened to blaze out of control.

He pulled away, keeping her in his embrace. "You can't conceive how much I want to take you upstairs. We wouldn't come down for a week." A naughty grin tugged at his mouth. "We'd break for sustenance, a bath or two, and of course playtime with Aurelia."

"I'd like that." Constance's cheeks heated at the smoldering look in his eyes. He made her feel as if she were a new bride becoming acquainted with her husband on their first night of marriage. She pulled the lapels of his coat down so she could press a kiss to his lips. "I'm so proud of you for seeing everything through with Faladen."

He kissed her again. "There's more." Jonathan smiled

gently. "Jacob Morgan has helped me so much . . . with how to share myself with people. We met several times when I was in London. I don't have to be an island anymore."

Her heart ached for all he had suffered. "You are amazingly brave, and I'm incredibly proud to be your wife."

"I'm simply a husband and father who wants to be the very best he can be for his wife and family." He brushed his nose against hers.

It was wicked on her part, but it was a perfect opportunity to tell him they were expecting a child. "Speaking of family, how would you feel about adding to that family?"

A grin tugged at his lips. "Is that an invitation to go upstairs?"

"Be serious." She shook her head and laughed.

"A man can only hope." He joined in her laughter, then bent his head until his gaze met hers. "I'd want that. I'd be thrilled to have more children with you."

"I'm carrying."

He pulled back, the shock on his face evident. Then a huge smile broke, and he looked like he did when they were younger and carefree with their whole future in front of them. "A child." The awe in his voice clear. "Another baby."

She drank in the joy on his face and couldn't help but smile. "I'm moving home tomorrow. You're pleased?"

"I'm ecstatic on both counts." His eyes watered as he gently brought her close. He was as emotional as she was in the moment. "I love you. I love Aurelia, and I'll love this baby with everything I possess."

Constance wrapped her hands around his neck. "We shouldn't leave our guests too long."

"First, let's go find our daughter." He brushed her cheek with the back of his hand. "I can't help but want to stay here with you a little longer. I'll remember this moment for the rest of my life. You and Aurelia are the most precious gifts I could ever receive." Wiping away her tears, he stroked her cheek again, his gaze never leaving hers. "Thank you for . . . wanting me." He bent down and pressed a kiss beneath her ear. He stole another kiss. "I meant what I said out there. I love you with my entire being. I've been in love with you since we were best friends."

"And I you," she said softly. Tears threatened again. "I realized something about myself while you were gone. You helped me learn to trust again. You're my best friend, and the love of my life."

Jonathan took her in another kiss, one that stoked the fire between them. "I want you to know one more thing." He clasped her head in his hands, then pressed a kiss to her cheek. "I could never leave you. Your love brought me home. You're the moon to my sea. You bring me into the light, just like the moon brings the tide. Love me forever?"

She cherished this man with her entire being. "I'll love you forever and a day."

Epilogue

Six Months Later
Sykeston Gardens

At the knock on the door, Constance looked up from the list she was compiling of all the things she and Jonathan had to do before the baby was born. At the sight of her husband and their daughter, she immediately put down her quill. "My two favorite people in the whole world have come to see me."

"Don't get up. We'll come to you." Jonathan stayed her with a hand.

She loved that man for his thoughtfulness. It was becoming more and more difficult for her to maneuver out of a chair. It would only be a month or less before their baby was born.

Aurelia practically hopped to her side with Regina in tow. "Mama."

"Hello, love." She couldn't pick Aurelia up anymore when she was sitting, but their intrepid daughter pulled herself onto the sofa next to Constance. She leaned over and gave her a kiss. Always the loving girl, Aurelia returned the favor.

"Damnation." Aurelia pointed to Jonathan.

Constance's gaze flew to his. "What did she say?"

Jonathan bit his lips trying not to laugh. "You heard her. I think it was very clear."

"She can't curse." Constance let out a restrained sigh. "Did you teach her that word?

"Da, damnation," she repeated while looking at her father.

"All right, princess. You're ready to give your mother her *commendation*." He winked at Constance, then carefully lowered himself to sit next to Aurelia.

A wicked smile tilted her lips upward. Up until a few months ago, she still gave nightly massages to her husband. They'd always made love afterward. Now, due to the size of Constance's middle and the fact she had a hard time standing if she'd been kneeling, they'd moved the massages from their dressing room into their bed. Jonathan adored it as he always returned the favor and gave her a massage.

He whipped out a piece of parchment from the inside of his morning coat.

Aurelia squealed, and Regina barked.

With a flourish of his hand, Jonathan presented her with the paper. "It's a royal commendation for the princess's mother." He leaned close and pressed a kiss below her ear before he whispered, "And the king of the castle's most beautiful and kind queen."

Her hand flew to the middle of her chest in playful surprise. "For me?"

By then, Aurelia had moved to Jonathan's lap, gleefully waiting for her to open it.

"How wonderful," she exclaimed.

Jonathan nodded with a feigned seriousness. "North was the one who came up with the idea. He said anyone who could put up with me deserved one." Jonathan winked. "He's getting one tomorrow from Aurelia and me with a gooseberry pie."

"I'm honored to receive the first one." Constance winked at him, then kissed Aurelia. "Thank you, darling girl." She opened the letter, and tears welled in her eyes over the sweet words her husband had written. *To the mother of my beautiful Aurelia and her soon-to-be-announced brother or sister, you are hereby declared the most magnificent mother—and wondrous wife—in all the land.*

Another knock sounded, and Dahlia peeked in. "Begging your pardon, my lord, my lady, it's time for Aurelia's nap."

After she and Jonathan kissed Aurelia and wished her sweet dreams, their daughter went with her nursemaid without a whimper.

Jonathan scooted closer and placed his arm around her shoulders. "With every royal commendation, there's a token of esteem awarded." His gaze captured hers.

She curled into his shoulder, and immediately he wrapped his arms around her.

"I love you." Her words were a little breathless. "Some days I wake up and can't believe how happy I am."

"I feel the same." He pressed a kiss to her brow. "I owe it all to you." He snapped his fingers, and Regina bounded onto the sofa next to him.

"Mrs. Butler will not be pleased if she finds out Regina has been on the furniture again."

Jonathan lifted one brow. "I won't tell. Will you?"

She pressed her nose into his chest and laughed. "Of course not."

Still keeping one arm around her, he took something from Regina's collar. Facing Constance, he hid his arm behind his back. "Lift your head and close your eyes, madam."

When she did as asked, he placed something heavy and cold around her neck.

He pressed his lips against hers. "You can open now."

When she did, he held a hand mirror in front of her face. She gasped at the necklace around her neck. There were the most stunning sapphires she'd ever seen. Perfectly matched, each one had to be the size of a robin's egg. "What in the world?"

"The Sykeston sapphires," he declared with a smile.

"They're beautiful."

"For the woman who rules my heart forever." He released a deep breath. "They're not as beautiful as you, but I've wanted you to wear them ever since that night I returned home from London. When Aurelia demanded you receive a 'damnation' today, I knew this would be perfect." He took her hands in his and pressed a kiss upon each. "I have another gift." He reached into his pocket, pulled out something gold, and placed it in her hand.

"Oh." Her voice cracked with emotion. "It's a brace." Her initials were engraved on the inside. "What is this?"

He bent over until they heads were almost touching. "I was telling Lieutenant Cowden about the braces being twisted when Faladen's yacht capsized. Seems he's something of a metalsmith. I had him make it for you and Mr. Zephyr. It's steel coated in brass. He thought it might be stronger than what you're currently using at Lysander & Sons."

"You are incredibly thoughtful. I love it." She pressed a kiss against his lips. "Alin and I were talking about replacing our current stock with something stronger." She scooted a little closer, and he hugged her tighter. "You know what I love . . . braces, spades, feather dusters, and you. Now tell me how your day was?"

"Busy. I sent all my cartridge designs to Manton. If anyone can figure it out, he can."

"Are the new class of recruits ready for your marksmanship class?"

He shrugged. "They're a little rough around the edges, but Colonel Peterson came by yesterday. He made a point of telling me how pleased he was with how I handled the whole class after Faladen almost ruined the entire concept."

"As he should be. He's lucky to have you training the men." Constance tilted her head. "Did he have news about Faladen?"

One of his half smiles appeared. "He sold off all of his

possessions to reimburse the army all the money that he'd received from Middleton. He also repaid the other two officers he blackmailed, then retired to the country. He was found guilty in his court-martial. He was sentenced to death, but as is sometimes customary, they commuted it to a stiff fine. I've heard there's talk of the Crown taking his lands."

"It proves that there is justice in the world," Constance said with a smile.

"Indeed." Jonathan had his hand lightly resting on her belly. The baby must have taken exception, because it kicked hard enough to make his arm move. "Did you see that?"

"See it? I felt it."

He pressed another kiss to her lips. "Let's have a dozen more."

She lifted a brow. "Now is probably not the best time to be asking me that."

He laughed, the rich sound filling the sitting room. "Point taken, wife." Jonathan pressed his lips to hers, then wrapped her in his arms. At his tender touch, the world fell away as it always did when they embraced. Their kiss, gentle at first, turned into a testament to their enduring friendship, their commitment to their marriage, and their forever love.

Eventually they broke apart, but the magic they created still hummed in the air. Jonathan trailed his finger slowly across her cheek. His eyes glimmered with a brilliance that warmed every inch of her.

He leaned close and rubbed his lips against her ear. "Who knew that bending a few rules would lead to such an unbreakable bond?"

Author's Note

Jonathan, the Earl of Sykeston, exhibits extraordinary honor on the battlefield, a keen eye, and the ability to accurately shoot across great distances. My inspiration for his character came from a British army marksman who fought in the Revolutionary War.

The Scotsman Captain Patrick Ferguson famously claimed to have spared General George Washington's life. In 1777 when Ferguson was hidden in the Pennsylvania woods along Brandywine Creek, he had a chance to change history by shooting General Washington. However, the captain's honor prevailed that day when he refused to shoot the general in the back and allowed Washington to pass unharmed. Ferguson was famous for his ability to shoot accurately at distances of up to three hundred yards, a feat in those days of unreliable guns. He's best known for developing the Ferguson rifle.

Read on for an excerpt from

HOW TO
BEST A
MARQUESS

BY JANNA MACGREGOR

Coming soon from St. Martin's Paperbacks

Chapter One

❧

London 1816
The Mayfair home of Viscount St. John Howell

The turtle soup tasted off in Miss Blythe Elizabeth Howell's opinion. How could it not when her brother sat next to her laughing like a deranged hyena after their dinner guest had just lost his false teeth in the soup with a splash?

Her brother, Lord St. John Howell, motioned a footman over carrying several fresh serviettes as the Marquess of Siddleton fished his teeth from the soup.

"Lord Siddleton, you can dry them off with one of these," St. John offered. He slid a side-eyed glance her way and lowered his voice. "Blythe, pardon my outburst of laughter."

"Don't offer your apologies to me. It's the marquess who deserves them," she answered quietly, but politely. She didn't want to look at what was happening directly across the table from her. But like a carriage wreck, she couldn't turn away from the scene playing out before her. The seventy-eight-year-old marquess couldn't capture the teeth with a spoon, so the poor man dipped his fingers into his soup to retrieve them.

"Porcelain." Sporting a gleeful toothless grin, the marquess offered up his teeth dripping with the creamy soup. "The finest made in all of England."

She vowed then and there never to eat turtle soup again.

As her stomach roiled, Beth, who detested her given name of Blythe, smiled weakly.

St. John's delirious grin melted from his face. "Only the best for you, my friend."

"Eh?" The marquess cupped one palm to his ear signaling he needed St. John to repeat his statement.

"Friend," St. John's booming voice ricocheted around the room. "You're my friend."

Beth wanted to roll her eyes at the exchange. *Friend* was a misnomer if she ever heard one. Her one and only sibling called the marquess that affectionate term because he wanted something from him.

Probably for the elderly lord to ask for Beth's hand in marriage this evening.

The marquess pointed one bony finger in her direction and chuckled. "I'll be more than a friend if we can convince the little filly to accept my suit. We'll be brothers."

"Indeed," St. John retorted. "A joyous day for all." He grabbed her hand with his and squeezed. "Isn't that right, sister?"

She slipped her hand from his and neatly folded it in her lap with the other. There it was. The verification that she didn't want. Her brother had invited the marquess tonight to propose marriage.

Which provided a good reason why the soup was off along with everything else in her life.

There was only one decision to make. Take control of her future once and for all.

Starting now.

She should have started weeks ago when she heard two upstairs maids giggling about her soon-to-come proposal this evening. Beth had thought one of them had a beau. As soon as they saw her, they'd rushed into another bedroom. Now she realized they were talking about her.

An undeniable feeling of isolation had immediately encased her, and she'd stopped in the middle of the hallway. Not a single member of the new staff possessed any allegiance to her. For God's sake, even her lady's maid had more loyalty to St. John than her.

Of course, a small monthly bonus in the servants' wages did wonders when St. John had decreed that he needed to know whom Beth associated with.

He could have saved his coin and simply asked her. She had nothing to hide.

She stole a discreet glance at the marquess again. With a full head of white hair, bushy eyebrows, and a stooped back, the marquess seemed relatively harmless until she'd learned that he was desperate for an heir. She was more certain there was money involved in the proposal than she was of the day of her birth. Specifically, the marquess was willing to pay St. John a fortune if he could marry her.

She'd not participate in this farce any longer. With her serviette, she tapped the sides of her mouth, then stood. Immediately, her brother followed while the poor marquess struggled to do the same.

"Please don't stand on my account, my lord." Beth held out her hand to keep the marquess seated. With a relieved sigh, the marquess nodded then collapsed into the chair. She turned to her brother. "If you'll excuse me for a moment?"

"Of course," he nodded.

She turned to leave the room. At the door, she lowered her voice and addressed the head footman. "Please serve the next course."

Without a look back, Beth continued her way. She climbed the steps to the wing where her bedroom was located. Once outside her door, she glanced up and down the hallway to ensure there were no servants scurrying about. Satisfied she was alone, she didn't enter her bedchamber. Instead, Beth

walked down the hallway with a poise and posture that proclaimed her confidence and excellent deportment skills.

Eight years ago, at the age of seventeen during her first
Season, she'd been declared the young woman most sought
after for marriage. The dream of every society miss during
their introduction to society. She'd been courted and proposed
to. Her dowry and features—in that order—were declared in-
comparable.

It stood to reason that she expected her life to be exactly
as her devoted father had promised. She would have a marriage just like her beloved parents. He'd even promised her
that he would help her pick the right young man to make
her happy.

Then her father died before her introduction to society.
Thus, leaving that promise unfulfilled.

Dare she say broken?

Her brother had promised her that her arranged marriage
to Lord Meriwether Vareck was the best match, the kind her
father would have chosen for her.

Even Meriwether, who preferred to be called Meri, made
a vow that he'd broken as soon as he'd uttered it. He married
her and promised to keep her in sickness and in health. But
her *dearly departed* husband had failed to share his peculiar hobby.

He'd collected wives, and Beth was his third and last wife.

To say she was shocked that her supposed husband had
more than one wife was akin to believing that the North Sea
was a balmy swimming pond.

But what hurt as much—if not more—than the previous
broken promises Beth had endured was the one that society
had so callously broken.

Society had promised her that if she followed the rules,
she'd make a brilliant match. All she had to do was marry a
man chosen by her family and approved by society. He'd be
worthy of her, and she'd be worthy of him. She'd saved her

virginity for her wedding night. Society and all its machinations had promised that if Beth kept her part of the bargain,
all her hopes and dreams for a brilliant future would come
to fruition.

Ever since she was a young girl, she'd believed in those
fairy-tale promises.

But society had lied to her. She'd done everything right.
She'd listened to her family, married the man they'd chosen, and religiously followed society's dictates of proper and
moral behavior.

After Meriwether had died, the whole sordid story came
to light.

When her world fell apart through no fault of her own, society did what it always does best. It turned its back on her as
though all of it was her failure.

Because of that, her life was now completely different. She
would never marry again.

It sickened Beth that her brother ignored her wishes and
was now trying to sell her to the highest bidder much like
an aging broodmare. She didn't fault Lord Siddleton. He
seemed a pleasant man, but for God's sake, he could be her
grandfather.

It was St. John's latest attempt to recover his lost fortune.
Her brother had gladly handed over Beth's dowry along with
most of his fortune to her husband, Meri, the second son to
the seventh Duke of Randford, when he'd promised to invest it wisely. Her brother was certain that Meri had gambled
every single pound at the game tables and horse races he'd
liked to frequent. Unfortunately, he'd passed shortly after
their marriage.

Her husband didn't leave Beth anything except a ruined
reputation. There was no money. He'd not even left her his
name as her marriage was declared void as the third wife.

But one good thing had come from the whole debacle.
She'd forged friendships with Meri's other two wives.

Without those women, Beth would have been destitute . . . in more ways than one. Their friendships also gave her a new purpose in life. The former Katherine Greer, now the eighth Duchess of Randford, and the former Constance Lysander, now the Countess of Sykeston, had become her sisters. Though they didn't share a drop of blood, they were family.

Yet she couldn't ask for her friends' help tonight. They were busy with their own lives. Both Katherine and Constance had been blessed with children and husbands who adored them.

She couldn't ask for her lady's maid. The woman would run straight to St. John.

Without wasting a second, Beth silently descended the servants' staircase. She paused on the last step ready to retreat into the darkness if she heard any movement or bustling from the staff.

Thankfully, the only sound that drifted through the kitchen and the attached hallway was the scolding voice of her brother's cook. Mrs. Ainsley's instructions were as sharp as her butcher knives. She wanted the sauce for the baked salmon poured when the footmen entered the dining room and not before.

As the cook droned on about the blasted dish, Beth tiptoed through the kitchen and past the scullery maid who was washing dishes. It took a little maneuvering, but she slipped out the door and shut it without making a peep. Luck was with her as the normal creak of the door was absent tonight.

She waited to see if anyone had noticed she'd left or heaven forbid, followed her.

Nothing.

The still of the night surrounded her. The soft echoes of insects were a faint buzz in the courtyard while a single nightingale serenaded its mate. Though it was a normal night outside of Howell House, inside would soon erupt into chaos.

She'd have hell to pay when her brother discovered her determined insurgence. But she'd worry about that tomorrow. No matter how he blustered or cajoled, she would not marry again. It was a promise she'd keep for herself, and it would not be broken.

Ever.

Beth started to walk behind the mews. The two groomsmen her brother kept on staff were too busy with a game of dice to take much notice.

Out of sight, Beth finally took a deep breath. The sweet scent of a summer's night swooshing into her chest felt as marvelous as when she was finally free of her stays after a long day at the linen workshop where she worked. After losing her husband, she'd come to London hoping for the return of her dowry. When she'd discovered her money lost, she'd started working at her friend Katherine's linen shop. In no time, Kat had made her a full partner.

Beth had never regretted working for a moment.

But truthfully, she was caught between two worlds much like a governess. Invitations and social calls ceased when word escaped that she, the former belle of the ball, was the third wife. The family servants, tradespeople, and even her "closest friends" from finishing school didn't want anything to do with her.

Which was fine with her. She'd decided to create her own destiny. Maybe she'd take a lover. Maybe she'd write a book disparaging the world that society had created for women like her.

Her traitorous gaze ventured to the lovely Palladian manse just down the alleyway on Burlington Street. The gray brick home was as intimidating as its owner, Julian Raleah, the Marquess of Grayson.

He'd been the first man who'd asked her to marry him. She'd fancied herself quite in love with the marquess. Beth found him honest, polite, with a hint of devilment in his eyes.

When her brother had refused the marriage, Grayson hadn't tried to convince him. He'd simply left without saying goodbye.

She'd been devastated by his actions. Obviously, the blasted man hadn't cared for her the way she'd cared for him.

But this was business.

He'd be the one she'd ask for assistance since he was in the same position as she. He needed a fortune and so did Beth.

Yet, the heartache still lingered. After Grayson had walked away without even fighting for her, she'd never given any other man the same regard. It was as if she'd become an empty shell of who she once was.

In a matter of minutes, she stood outside Grayson's home. At the black iron gates, she straightened her shoulders.

If there was one thing Beth was certain of tonight, it was that she'd finally take her own future into her own hands. Whether Grayson helped her attain it was not a certain outcome. But he was the only person she could turn to.

As Beth pulled the handle of the door knocker, the sight of the man ready to clang his lips against the woman on the door made her smile. She'd never seen such a whimsical door knocker in her life. While most saw Grayson as an aloof marquess, there appeared to be a lightheartedness to him, if the door knocker was any indication.

Beth had seen such frivolity before when she'd thought he was going to court her. He'd once taken her for a walk in the park where they'd happened upon a young burrow of rabbits. Grayson had named each bunny, only after asking for her advice. Every day after, when he'd call upon her, he'd share some charming story about the bunnies. The affection in his voice made him sound like a proud papa, and she'd fallen head over heels for him.

She let the knocker fall. The whimsical man kissed his mate sending the sound of brass hitting brass echoing around her. Instantly, one of the massive oak doors swung open.

"Good evening," a butler in his early thirties with black hair and green eyes answered the door and waved her inside. He was dressed in the Grayson livery.

"Is the marquess at home?" Beth nodded as she stepped across the threshold.

"Your name?"

"Beth Howell."

He tugged at the waistcoat of his formal livery. "This way, my lady."

"I'm a miss not a lady," Beth corrected him.

The butler's eyebrows rose a fraction. "Come with me."

Right before they reached Grayson's study, an unholy roar erupted from the direction of the room. "*Cillian, another cravat.*"

The butler glanced at Beth with a raised brow. "His father should have named him Fumble Fingers Raleah." An exaggerated sigh of unerring patience escaped. "That makes the fifth neckcloth he's ruined in a half-hour."

"Is he going out this evening?"

"*Cillian.*"

At the epic bellow of frustration from the marquess, the butler rushed into the room. Beth followed a discreet two steps back.

The Marquess of Grayson stood in front of a floor-to-ceiling mirror desperately trying to untangle a neckcloth. Instead of his usual courteous and refined visage, he appeared to be in a high temper. He and his cravat were in a fight to the death. At this point, the neckcloth was clearly winning.

With his great height and massive shoulders, most people were wary of approaching such a man. The color of his perfectly angular cheekbones resembled a blazing fire. Flames of fury shot straight from his gray orbs in sharp contrast to his black formalwear. In all the times she'd ever seen him, it was the only color he wore.

Odd. He must like to appear imposing wearing all black except his shirt. It certainly lent him an air of formality.

As soon as he saw her in the mirror he whipped around.

"Miss Howell." The low rumble of her name on his lips sent goose bumps across her flesh. He dropped his hands to his side and bowed slightly. "What are you doing here?"

"I was wondering if I might have a moment of your time?"

A scowl appeared as he pulled at the tight knot until it finally loosened. In seconds, he had the cloth dangling from his neck. A glimpse of his bare chest appeared as he pulled the material from his body. She forced herself to look away. It was unseemly that she noticed such a sight. Instantly, her body became overheated. The temperature in the room had risen by twenty degrees.

Hadn't it?

Such an inconvenient thought didn't even deserve consideration. Yet, there was no denying how handsome he was dressed in his formal eveningwear. There was a time long ago she would have looked forward to dancing in his arms and relishing the feel of his embrace.

But not now.

The earlier fire in his gray eyes had now transformed into smoldering embers. "Won't you sit down?" He lowered his voice. "Your lady's maid is free to join us."

"No need. She's with my brother," Beth said.

His eyes widened at the pronouncement. "Your brother requires your maid's assistance?"

She could not allow him to unnerve her. This was a business transaction. "No, of course not. She's still at the house. I didn't ask for her to accompany me."

"If anyone saw you come to an unmarried man's house, they'll come to the wrong conclusion."

"And what conclusion would that be?" She baited the bear when he pursed his lips into a thin line, but she didn't care a whit for what he or what anyone else thought. She needed to recover her dowry and get on with the rest of her life. If society thought her a woman of loose morals, that was their misjudgment and not hers. "Thank you for your concern, but there's no need." She blinked, an outward appearance of calm as a storm of nervousness raged within her. "Since you're engaged this evening, I'll only take a moment of your time. I have a proposal I'd like to discuss." She straightened her shoulders to embolden her self-confidence.

Grayson's bergamot orange scent followed her. She inhaled the fragrance and held her breath. Hopefully, he could be late to his event. She needed him.

For her sake, she had to convince him to run away with her.